# THE BIRD
## of
# ENDURANCE

BILL COOKE

Order this book online at www.trafford.com/07-1081
or email orders@trafford.com

Most Trafford titles are also available at major online book retailers.

© Copyright 2007 Bill Cooke.

All rights reserved. No part of this publication may be reproduced, stored in a retrieval system, or transmitted, in any form or by any means, electronic, mechanical, photocopying, recording, or otherwise, without the written prior permission of the author.

Note for Librarians: A cataloguing record for this book is available from Library and Archives Canada at www.collectionscanada.ca/amicus/index-e.html

Printed in Victoria, BC, Canada.

ISBN: 978-1-4251-3007-7

We at Trafford believe that it is the responsibility of us all, as both individuals and corporations, to make choices that are environmentally and socially sound. You, in turn, are supporting this responsible conduct each time you purchase a Trafford book, or make use of our publishing services. To find out how you are helping, please visit www.trafford.com/responsiblepublishing.html

Our mission is to efficiently provide the world's finest, most comprehensive book publishing service, enabling every author to experience success. To find out how to publish your book, your way, and have it available worldwide, visit us online at www.trafford.com/10510

 www.trafford.com

**North America & international**
toll-free: 1 888 232 4444 (USA & Canada)
phone: 250 383 6864 ♦ fax: 250 383 6804 ♦ email: info@trafford.com

**The United Kingdom & Europe**
phone: +44 (0)1865 722 113 ♦ local rate: 0845 230 9601
facsimile: +44 (0)1865 722 868 ♦ email: info.uk@trafford.com

10 9 8 7 6 5 4 3

# PREVIEW

After a life filled with destruction and loss during WWII in France, Anne La Fleur and son Matthew go the America. In northern Michigan, Anne endures the pain brought on by the cruelty of her second husband, and Matthew deals with his emotional problems before going on to become a classical musician.

In BOOK ONE, Matthew has a difficult time adjusting. He hates his mother's husband and feels lost. However, he manages to graduate from college with honors and fall in love with another talented musician. Unfortunately, the young woman dies, and once again he's left feeling alone and lost. He goes to Salzburg and studies at the Mozarteum. During this time he falls in love with the daughter of the man who killed his father during the war.

In BOOK TWO, Anne talks about her first husband, who was killed fighting with the French Resistance. After his death, Anne, in an effort to survive and care for her son, takes a thief for a lover. Then, after meeting an American army major, she sees a way out of her sorry relationship with the French thief. After lying that he is a wealthy man, the major asks her to marry him. For her son's future, she agrees to marry. After pressure from the major, who is with Criminal Investigation, she tells him that the thief's ill-begotten money is hidden in her house. Jealous and drunk, the thief threatens her with a knife, but the major comes in and kills the thief—and then tells the authorities that Anne killed him in self-defense. Taking the money and marrying Anne, the major takes her and Matthew to northern Michigan, where he invests the stolen money, becomes a millionaire, the mayor of Point Stevens, and a womanizer. After he dies of a heart attack, Anne moves to Paris, where she gets involved in saving her niece's life, with the help of a friend who is a CIA agent. After saving the kidnapped young woman, she goes on to save other young women, having decided by now to devote her life to the prevention of international kidnappings.

… … … … … … … … … … … … … … … … … … … … … … … … … … …

BOOK ONE **MATTHEW**
• • • • • • • • • • • • • • • • • • • • •

## chapter 1

Sunday midday, while church bells and a glockenspiel sounded, I weaved my way through the summer crowd in Mozartplatz and Getreidegasse and thought about the conversation I'd had with Old Man last night. He'd called and said, "I can't believe it's been almost three years since you left our noble nuthouse and went to Salzburg. What did the nutcracker have to say? You never did tell me."

"Dr. Ames? He said I have acute anxiety and profound insecurity, and then he discharged me."

There was a pause, before he said, "I told you that all you had to do was to talk to somebody."

"Old Man, you were right about a lot of things." Then, after he'd finished chuckling, I asked, "How're you getting along with your daughter and her family?"

"Her husband and two kids are a pain in the ass, but I'll stick it out until I can afford a place of my own."

"Are you still doing ceramic painting?"

"Nope. Gave it up. I'm now a doorman at a swanky restaurant here in Jersey City."

"I didn't know there were any swanky restaurants in Jersey City."

Chuckling again, he said, "No bull, I dress up in a fancy uniform, talk to people, and get a lot of tips."

"And open the door."

"Sometimes, I get to talking and forget to open the damn door for them."

Laughing, I said, "You like being a doorman, I gather."

"I like it all right. Not much isolation. Know what I mean?"

"I hope you haven't given up on your painting. I liked the last Christmas card you sent, done in watercolors."

Chuckling, he said, "That must be the one showing you as a jackass, standing by the manger. I'd thought you'd enjoy it."

"It was great, Old Man."

"What have you been up to lately, Matthew?"

"Same-- studying and writing music, teaching a little, doing local concerts. I paint—mostly landscapes."

"Still at the Mozarteum?"

"Yes."

"Destiny's running over you, Matthew. It'll do it every time. You can't stop the load, and you can't get out of the road. Who'd ever think you'd be doing all you're doing when you were in the nuthouse!"

"Destiny..."

"Soon the closing bell with ring for me, and you know what my destiny has been."

"Don't talk like that, my friend."

"Reality," he said softly. Then, after a pause, he asked, "How are you feeling, Matthew—really feeling?"

"I'm getting better, thanks to you. I've reached the point where I can let the past in, look at it, and move on."

"Just don't sell yourself short again in the world of imagination. Open the door to get some more. Don't become insolvent again. Keep letting out self-doubt, or it'll destroy you. You know all this, but I'll remind you. Open the door and keep it open, even to harsh realities. Harsh realities will slap your face and revitalize your spirit, if you let them. Be vulnerable—open to pain, for pain is a valuable symptom of something wrong. Don't ever let an oversized ego or false pride tell you that you're too good or too talented to be hurt by life. Keep letting it out and taking it in. Don't close the door."

"I'm trying."

"You're not trying, Matthew. You're in a goddamn rut. Change is what life demands. I found that out. Change is the living in life. Transition. We've gotta go with the flow, or we'll never know. Knowledge is power."

"What changed your mind about leaving the hospital and going to live with your sister?"

"You, Matthew. I saw me in you. When I saw you drowning in the waters of your mind, I saw myself. And that was when I quit deceiving myself by saying I could remain in the nuthouse and fly to all things through my imagination. After seeing you, the reality in my heart became stronger. I knew that sooner or later I'd drown in the stagnant waters of my mind. I awoke to the limitations of space and time. I awoke to my limitations—where I was, how old I was, and what I had become. At that moment, I no longer wanted to play a cruel joke on myself, and I realized the almost-forgotten categorical imperative, which told me I wouldn't want my behavior to be the standard for all humanity—especially not for you, Matthew. So now, I'll do my best to work, and love, and laugh—to be free, in all ways. I'd used up my feelings of freedom in the nuthouse, and so I had to find new feelings of freedom on the outside. I, too, must open the door and let my spirit breathe—to live. Now, I must hang up. This call is costing me a fortune. Happy thirtieth birthday, my friend."

"Thank you, Old Man. I'm grateful."

"Stay loose, and remember to at least change your socks."

"Transition!"

"Transition!"

Leaving the Winkler Haus, I walked over to Mirabell Gardens and listened to a brass band play Austrian folk music and marches. After maybe twenty minutes, I returned to my small apartment across from the Mozarteum just in time to receive a telephone call from Herta Müller, the daughter of the man who killed my father during WWII. Nervous, I asked, "What do you want?"

"Your mother said you were here for some time now. You have not contacted us. I have been trying to reach you today, but you were not at home."

"I was at Mirabell listening to the band music."

"My brother plays trumpet in the band. He is an engineer for the railroad. I was there but didn't see you."

"And I didn't see you."

"Perhaps we didn't recognize each other. I have short hair now."

"And mine is much longer."

"I waited for you to contact us. I have a gift for you from my father."

"I didn't contact you, because I felt I would be intruding. It was the same feeling I had when I went to visit your father."

"He died three years ago, soon after you visited him."

"I'm sorry," I said, trying to keep my voice steady. "Well, thanks for calling."

"Please listen, Matthew. He left you a gift. Should I bring it to you?"

"Where are you?"

"At the train station. I must return to Vienna shortly. I have little time before the train leaves. I have a gift for you from my father."

"Why are you going to Vienna?"

"I work there. I am a doctor at Unfall Krankenhaus."

"Are you a psychiatrist?"

"No, I'm an intern, then orthopedics. Matthew, should I mail the gift from my father, or shall we see each other?"

"Where are you?"

"I said I was at the train station—Bahnhof."

"Can you take a later train?" I asked, curious now about the gift.

"Yes, of course. One will leave every hour. If you wish it, I will wait in the restaurant for you."

"What's the gift?"

"You will see when you come."

I hung up the phone, wishing I hadn't said I'd meet her. Seeing her would bring on the memory of the unpleasant visit with her father. However, now thinking of what Old Man said last night about keeping the door open, I got ready. I didn't want to shave, but I did. I didn't want to put on a clean white shirt and khakis that were too small and short, but I did. I didn't want to run water on my hands and plaster down my hair, but I did. I didn't want to laugh at myself in the mirror for acting as if this were my first date, but I did. I didn't want to wish that I had some kind of medication, but I did. I felt I was getting out of control again, but I wasn't. Looking at Elsie's portrait without thinking, I left for the Bahnhof.

Drinking espresso, we sat across from each other by the front window. She smiled and said, "Tonight I must work, and tomorrow I will return to spend the rest of the week here at home."

"What do you do at the hospital?"

"I'm in orthopedics much of the time, with Dr. Beohler, the famous surgeon."

"Never heard of him."

Smiling, she said, "He is very good." Then, after smoothing the front of her blue dirndl, she asked, "Should I give you the gift now?"

Practicing restraint, I said, "Later. Maybe when you return from Vienna."

With surprise on her face, she said, "You seem to not want the gift. It's from my father, and he wanted so much that you take it."

Trying now not to show too much restraint, I said, "Yes, of course I want it. You can give it to me after we finish our espresso."

"Yes, that would be good."

We smiled at each other and drank our espresso. Then, for the first time, I began to look at her closely—her short, dark hair, dark eyes, and the blush lighting up her lovely face. I looked then and imagined what was inside of her. It seemed obvious that she was a young woman meeting the world on its own terms and thriving, and that she knew her purpose in life and gained strength and beauty in developing herself to that purpose. She seemed simple and direct, yet warm and polite, and I got the impression that she never concerned herself with philosophical absurdities, such as, whether or not it is better to be or not to be. She was probably too busy for that, I told myself. She just did her best at all times, and feelings of failure, guilt and worry and self-pity, had little chance to keep her down for long. Further, putrid theo-philosophical arguments were a waste of time for this kid, and if she made a mistake, she wouldn't walk the floors all night pleading her case in front of an imaginary jury of peers. She was pragmatic by nature, not design, and the slight irony in her eyes said that she knew all the theo-philosophical arguments, and was open to more, but she'd rather spend her time helping others through medicine. And I thought I saw even more in her eyes—that she'd known great pain in her emotional life, but had also known great laughter and love.

She was saying, "I told you my father died soon after your visit. Your mother didn't tell you?"

"She doesn't tell me much, since we've been living apart."

"She has called a few times to see how we are. She told us you were here. We agreed you were too busy to call us. I know from experience that one can become very busy."

"I was busy, and as I said, I didn't want to intrude."

"You never would intrude us. Never."

"Thank you for that."

Taking a gold ring with a small ruby from her large leather bag, she gave it to me, saying, "This is the gift my father wished for you to have. I'm happy I can give it to you, and not put it in the post. My father liked you very much. When he spoke of you, he would always smile. Because you and your mother came, he was able to die happy." Then, taking out a card, she said, "I also wish to give this to you. It's a Toten Billette—how do you call it?"

"Taking the card, I said, "Remembrance card, I guess."

"As I looked at the picture inside the cover, I said, "So, this is how he looked as a young man."

"That is how he looked, before the German army, " she said, losing her smile. "They destroyed him."

I read the verse across from his picture. I read aloud:

"Nach langen, schwerem Leid gingst du zur Ruhe ein. Nun wird in Ewigkeit um dich nur Friede sein."

After a moment, she asked, "Do you understand?"

"I think so," I said. Then I read aloud in English: "'After long, heavy suffering, you went to rest. Now there will be eternal peace around you.'"

Smiling, she said, "You speak German now, no?"

Putting the card in my wallet, I said, "Not well. I read German better than I speak it."

Touching my arm, she said, "We must speak English very much. I will be happy for the chance to brush on it."

"Brush up on it."

"Of course—brush up on it. Brush up!"

Putting the ring on the little finger of my right hand, I said, "Thank you for the ring."

"I'm happy you wear it," she said. Then, looking at her watch, she said, "I must go soon, but before I go, I wish to ask you if you have someone."

"You mean, like a girlfriend?"

"Yes."

"No," I said, intending to change the subject as soon as possible. Then, not wanting to chop it off too fast, I asked, "Do you have a boyfriend?"

"I have been too busy, and I have never seen someone I would like very much."

"Never?"

Blushing, she said, "Well, I thought I did, when I was only a young girl. I met an older boy at a swim place. He was a lifeboat."

"You mean a lifeguard?"

"Yes of course. You see, I need very much to train in English."

"You're doing all right," I said, smiling. "Well, what about the lifeboat?"

Laughing, she said, "Well, I went to the swim place almost every day with my girlfriends. I was crazy for him, along with all the others. Then, finally we spoke, and that's when I changed my mind about him. You will not believe it, but I'll tell you, anyway. He said he had great passion for me, and that for a long time he was looking at me. Then he said, 'You always look like a nice biscuit, with butter all over you.' Then he laughed with very bad teeth and said, 'Should I eat you now, or later?' Well, I had so much fear that I never went there again. And that is not the end of it. That night I had a bad dream that I was in my swimsuit and under some wet sand that I couldn't get up from, and I was shouting for help. And then he came to save me, and when I saw his hand trying to catch me, I screamed... and then I was awake. It was a very bad experience."

Looking at my watch, I said, "I don't want to hurry you, but you said you have a train to catch."

"Yes," she said, looking at her watch. "I must go. The train leaves in five minutes. But before I leave, I wish to ask you something. Franz Lehar's *Merry Widow* is playing this week. Would you like to go to the Festspielhaus and see it?"

"Maybe."

"We will see. When I return, I will call you. Is that all right with you?"

"Okay."

Taking my hand, she hurried us out to the platform and got on the train. Then she was gone, waving from an open window, and looking more beautiful and excited than when we met.

Leaving the train station and walking to my apartment, I remarked to myself that her father must have been a good man to have raised such a fine daughter. And then I realized that her father, Hans Müller , had been a valuable catalyst in my life. Through him I had learned that I didn't hate anyone, including Major Danny, and what I thought was hate turned out to be nothing but psychological gas, which was easily dispersed by a little perspective and compassion.

Meeting Hans Müller...ex-colonel in the German army, was my mother's idea. She said that a one-on-one meeting with the man who killed my father would get rid of the hate in my heart and stop me from having nightmares. So, there we were at his house on the outskirts of Salzburg meeting his wife, Alysia, and his daughter, Herta, and finally, Hans, who was in his bedroom dying of cancer. And suddenly I was alone with the man I believed had cheated me out of the love a father can give—who had cheated me out of showing love and respect for my father-- who had cheated me out of being able to hold his hand, listen to, and talk to—who was the demon of my yesterday's nightmares. And that man was there in front of me now, body and soul, stinking and dying. And then, as I looked at the man, with his face and hands wasted and jaundiced, and with death setting a stare in his blue eyes, I saw the hard truth in my heart, that in all those years since my father was killed, it had been my wish to be able to hate that was the demon, and not this man.

With a weak, hoarse and almost inaudible voice, he said, "Greetings." Then, after removing a small pistol from underneath a blue blanket, he asked, "Did you come to kill me?"

I just stood there beside his bed, paralyzed with fear now and staring at the gun.

"Here," he said. "Take this and put a bullet in my head, if you wish. My family has promised not to involve you with the authorities."

I ran for the door.

"Halt!" he yelled, his voice breaking hoarse and high. Then, after I'd stopped, he said, "Please, sit. Listen to what I have to say."

I sat and said, "I'm listening."

After clearing his throat and spitting into a piece of gauze, he said, "As I told your mother, I had great respect for your father. What happened was worse than war. An informer who would not give his name called to say your father and others were loading guns and ammunition on a truck in Landes de Bussac, just outside of Bordeaux. We hurried there to capture the Resistance Fighters. I was very nervous. Suddenly there appeared a man in the light coming from our vehicles. I could not see who it was, but he was coming at me. I reacted and shot him. I feel sure one of his men pushed him. I told this to your mother, and she believes she knows who it was. I'm very sorry. Now, if you wish, kill me."

Staring at the man's stoic expression of acceptance, I could feel nothing but compassion. I believed his story—that someone had pushed my father into the light, and I knew who that someone was—Maurice Martineau, who later became my mother's lover. "Does my mother know what took place that night?" I asked.

"Yes. She came from Paris to see me. She said she would not tell you. She said she wanted me to tell you."

It was then something strange happened inside me. As I stared at the gun, Elsie Quinn, of all people, entered my mind, and I found myself thinking of something she might say in a moment such as this. "Sir," I said calmly, "with your ass all chewed-up the way it is, you've got a helluva nerve asking me to blow your brains out and ruin my life!"

A long, steady moment of calm and silence came, before he chuckled, put the gun back beneath the blanket, and said, "I see that you don't think my ass is worth the trouble. Thank you for your good humor, young man. It will make what life I have left much easier."

"Goodbye," I said, shaking the dying man's hand. Then, as I walked away with the feeling I'd never see the man again, I told myself I'd done the right thing.

His daughter, Herta, was waiting outside the door. With her eyes filled with tears, she took my hand and kissed it. "Thank you," she said. "And forgive me for listening at the door."

My mother and I said our goodbyes and returned to our hotel. In the afternoon, I went to the Mozarteum and asked about study programs, just out of curiosity and with no intention of attending. That evening, after deciding to go to Bordeaux in the morning, and then to Paris, we went to eat at Winkler Haus, far above the city, and as the full moon danced a waltz on the River Salzach, we listened to a small orchestra play selections from Johann Strauss's *Gypsy Baron*.

Early the next morning, we caught a flight to Bordeaux, and in the afternoon, as we stood at my father's grave, I listened to the bittersweet medley of change playing in my heart. I recalled the past, with its moments of love and peace and laughter, and of death and destruction.... And I recalled a day just like today, a day of sunshine, when I'd helped my father with the rose bushes, and my mother had come and with her eyes like two bluebirds fluttering in the sun, she said, "I see my strong men are making it beautiful. I am so lucky."

After that moment we went to Paris, where my mother had an apartment on Rue de Ponthieu. The next morning, placing my life in jeopardy, I crossed the traffic circle at the Arc de Triomphe and walked the Avenue de la Grande Armee until I came to Café Le Presbourg. After I'd read a newspaper and was on my second cup of coffee, and after I'd listened to some other patrons for awhile, I realized my roots were no longer in France—that I was an American and my roots had been transplanted. I now felt like any tourist might feel, and I'd felt that way as soon as I had arrived in Europe almost a month ago.

It was a moment of loneliness now. I missed Point Stevens, Michigan. I missed the leaky, green rowboat and the delicate solitude of fishing alone at dawn. I missed the Dark River I'd once been so afraid of. I missed playing the grand piano and letting my eyes wander to my paintings. I missed the sound of foghorns coming off Lake Huron. I missed the forest and the animals and birds. I missed Chief Morely Horton and his bragging fat. I missed Major Danny and his statue standing by the lake. I missed the Indians, especially Charlie Baxter, who once said, "People around here look at me like I'm an undesirable alien. They don't want to have anything to do with me, and that suits me just fine." I missed it all, and everyone, especially Elsie Quinn.

Returning to my mother's apartment, I decided that regardless of where I might travel, America would always be home for me. I would help my mother get things in order, so she could return to Paris to live, and then I would make a home for myself, maybe even in Point Stevens.

In the apartment, I found my mother sitting on her new sofa listening to Edvard Grieg and crying. I sat down next to her and asked, "Mama, what is it?"

Managing a smile, she said, "I'm remembering when we were at your father's resting place. The sun was going down and the birds were just about finished singing for the day. And I was thinking about life. A graveyard is a perfect place to think about life. It was a moment of peace for me, and a moment of deep gratitude to God for His allowing me another day and for giving me you, Matthew. My soul no longer cried out for anything, in the moment. Oh, Matthew, I have so much to do."

"Like getting married to Mr. Fowler?"

"How could you ask that?"

"For one thing, the music of Norway that you're playing."

"No, no, just the opposite. I'm saying farewell to Norway and to Mr. Fowler."

"You're no longer friends?"

"Just friends. That's all it has been, and will ever be, for you see, Mr. Fowler is still married to his dead wife. He isn't able to move on with life. And that suits me just fine. Oh, Matthew, I have so much to <u>do</u>. I'm free. I'm out of the shadows of the world. No longer do I play hide-and-seek with life. No longer do I close my heart to the Will of God. I'm aware of my nature and I'm going to live in accordance with it. The fire in my blood cries out for the good, the true, the beautiful. I'm a new woman. I'm no longer just flyash!"

"Good for you" I said, yawning and going to my bedroom to pack my suitcase.

At my apartment across from the Mozarteum, I poured myself a glass of apple juice, sat in an old armchair by the piano and read the Remembrance Card again:

"After long, heavy suffering you went to rest. Now there will be eternal peace around you."

Then, after looking at the two portraits across from me, my father's and Elsie's, I went to my father's and sticking the card in the lower left corner of the frame, I whispered, "Now you two victims of war can rest together."

Sitting at the piano, I played Robert Schumann's *Leichenfantasie* and emphasized *Kuriose Gesellschaft*, or Strange Company. And, as Schumann said about his dead brother—that he could hear his brother sighing in his heart—so, I too, could now hear my father and Müller sighing in my heart.

*Leichenfantastie* completed, I played Franz Schubert's *Moments Musicaux* and thought of what Schubert once said, that his fingers "transformed the keys into singing voices." And now, as I played, the keys sang for me, as I went into downward motions and dotted rhythms of the opening piece, *Poco lento e sposso ritenere*. And with this opening piece pervading most of the contrasting episodes, the keys sang of love and how it had held, regardless of suffering, regardless of abandon—how it had held on, regardless, and I said to myself, Oh, heart, don't lie to me now, after I've followed you through so many impossibilities.

And the days of my past came along to be filled with love, not regret, and the keys sang of how I helped my father with the rose bushes, and how the roses grew, of warm days and picnics, of laughter and kisses, of lawn parties and how lovely my mother looked in blue. And as I played through another downward melodic motion, they sang of war and fire, and how my father's world tracked him down and threw the ashes of death in his face. And I asked: Is my world any better? Then, passing through two scherzos and a delicate arabesque, the keys sang of my mother's courage through heartbreak and tears, and now she called out to me, *My dear, dear son, do not run away. It's going to rain or snow. Come. Your supper is getting cold. Where are you, my dear, dear boy?*

And now the keys sang of Wanda Ross's ambition, and how I thought I loved her, and of Elsie's saving grace, still flowing to me, like a warm and eternal spring. Then, with reflective modes and rolled chords, the memories of my nightmares came—the sick fictions—the sucking vortexes of fear—and of how I fell into the World of Lows, where I couldn't speak of yesterdays, and my heart wanted no tomorrows. And finally the keys sang of Herta, and after the final note of the Allegretto in

A-flat Major, Old Man, in my mind's ear, asked, *What's it all about with Herta, sonny?*

"Change," I whispered, closing the cover for the keyboard. "Never-ending change."

Sitting again with my apple juice, I took a new inventory of myself. For so long, music was gone from what I did, and my soul was littered like the streets I walked. I dwelled on the idea that I was a victim of life's wrecking ball, but now, as I prepared for world competition, I had new and better perspectives and values. Never, I told myself, would I ever again allow destructive, political power to trespass on my soul and spread its poisonous gas. I prayed then, that I would be able to give freely of the baroque medley of my life, as expressed in my music.

Then, once again, I reviewed my past, in order to learn from it.

## chapter 2

Five years ago, just after finishing my studies at University of Michigan, I was on my way to Wanda Ross's. It was early morning. The blue sky looked sick and pale. The trees and flowers looked sick and pale. The whole world looked sick and pale, because I was sick and pale inside. I was messing with love and hate and couldn't tell which was which. Love and hate were like two big mushrooms inside me. I knew one was poison, but I kept nibbling away at both of them. It had been like this since I'd been forced to come to America—nibbling away inside myself and blocking out painful memories.

As far as hate was concerned, I knew I hated Major Danny because he'd married my mother and brought us to Point Stevens in northern Michigan. And I hated him because he was a tyrant and a womanizer who hurt my mother all the time. And there were others I thought I hated, such as the man who killed my father, whoever that man was, and a few people in Point Stevens, including myself for being such a greenhorn about life. But hating wasn't the main thing on my mind right now as I walked in the morning sunshine, thinking I loved Wanda Ross and that it was definitely true love, because just thinking of her hurt so much, as if she were a snake inside me, twisting and crawling and devouring my guts, and making me love every painful second of it.

You see, Wanda was the closest thing to a friend I had. She was also crazy, but very beautiful. Crazy, beautiful and independent as hell. She'd come up from Bad Axe, because she couldn't get along with her mother and then in Point Stevens she couldn't get along with her aunt Mabel

Grimes, so now she was renting an old, clapboard house with Nancy Hunter, who worked as a waitress at The Devil's Den, a bar better known as The Devil's Outhouse.

Coming to a small park across the highway from the house, I sat on a bench and collected my thoughts before surprising Wanda with my visit. How I'd gotten involved with her began playing in my mind. As soon as she arrived in Point Stevens, she got a job at a drugstore and, as everybody but the owner knew, she began stealing money and loaning it out to people she called "poor and needy." Obviously, she considered me to be one of those unfortunates, because she came up to me one day in front of the library and shoved a paper bag of money into my hand saying, "Take this money, La Fleur, and put some food inside you and some new clothes on your skinny ass. It's only ten percent interest." Then thinking she was a real flake, I took the money and immediately fell in love with her.

Of course I wasn't poor and needy. I just looked it probably, being tall and thin and pale and with my eyes dark and sunken-in from reading too much, and of course, from having some kind of dementia fall upon me, especially in the last year when for some reason I changed from being clean and neat to being a stinking slob who didn't please my mother as I once did by writing poetry, painting pictures and playing the piano. And now, taking what I knew was stolen money—a paper bag of it in small bills and change—plenty of change—I was changing from doing good and avoiding evil, to doing evil and avoiding good.

However, aside from the fact that she'd forced it on me, I took the money so I could get close to her, thinking with confidence that if I owed her money, we would have something in common that would bind us together. It didn't matter that maybe she'd think she owned me—in fact, when the thought did cross my mind, the idea of being owned by Wanda Ross put a lump of joy in my throat and quickened my heart with possibilities. She was that attractive, and I found myself wanting to be around her all the time. I even started hanging around the drugstore, in order to feast my eyes on her and, without treachery, try to catch her stealing from the cash register, in sort of a unilateral shell-and-nut game. Wanda Ross's stealing was common knowledge, excluding the store owner, and it was common knowledge mostly because of Nancy Hunter, her housemate, who had the biggest mouth in the world and had passed on this information as trashy scuttlebutt. Anyway, in the drugstore I'd not once been able to catch Wanda knocking-down at the cash register. She'd been too slick and quick. But then I didn't watch her hands all that much. It was her little fanny that stole my interest, and the cute way she perked it up all the time—and then there were those long eyelashes of hers, which I imagined were always fluttering bright, blue friendliness at me, and made me dream of us being married and going fishing all the time. And, as a matter of fact, that was exactly what I wanted to do this morning—marry her and take her fishing, or at least take her fishing.

Leaving the park bench, I went to the house and rang the doorbell. When I received no response, I knocked on the door, hard, and when I again received no response, I took a deep breath and walked in the unlocked door. I didn't see Nancy, but I did see Wanda. She was in her bedroom sleeping, with her fanny perked up in the air and her feet all tangled in a bed sheet. In my world of fantasy, then, I whispered the words from some opera, 'Her soul went down with cruel fate… there were chains around her feet.' You see, I was getting sicker by the second.

Taking a seat at the metal table in the kitchen, I looked through her bedroom doorway, as if I were hypnotized, seeing now that her fanny was stretching out an old sweatshirt. I felt glad she had a sweatshirt on, because it saved me from feeling like a peeper. I wasn't completely sick and evil yet, although I was getting there fast. I began to speculate now, as to why she stuck her fanny in the air. I told myself it was up there for all the world to kiss, or maybe just the world of hypocrisy, greed, cruelty and violence she always talked about—even violently sometimes, being as flaky as she was.

Suddenly she awoke, saw me and yelled, "What the hell you doing here, La Fleur?"

Her voice was sharp and cut deep into what sanity I had left, and I began to babble. Looking at the floor, I said, "You know, Wanda, for the first time, I realize that if you stare at a sleeping woman, she'll wake up. I'll bet that if someone stared at a woman from a million miles away, she'd still wake up. Probably, if someone just dreamt of staring at a woman, she'd wake up and look around to see who's staring at her. That's the way women are, I guess. They have instincts and reflexes that even they don't know about yet."

She slammed the bedroom door and I began to tremble and sweat. That's what being deranged was doing for me. I waited, and finally she came to stand in front of me. She was in a dark, blue robe that matched her eyes, and she had a green ledger in her hands. Opening the ledger, she put her finger on a page and said, "See this? Well, just in case you can't read, I'll read it for you. It says you owe me two hundred bucks, and I want it back, now!"

Seeing she was very angry and spoke through her teeth, I said, "Don't worry about it. I'll return every cent of it."

"La Fleur, I loaned you the money in good faith. Then I finds out from Nancy that you've got millions. You rotten thief. I want it back now!" Then, after banging on the top of the metal table, she asked, "Why didn't you tell me that you're the son of a millionaire—the mayor?"

"I'm not his son!" I said defensively. "And if you think I'm a millionaire, just look at this old army jacket I've got on."

"What about it?"

"Well, where do you think I got it?" I asked, keeping my eyes lowered, in case she might read something misleading in them. I was fully aware that she could read eyes, and she could read them as easily as she could read a comic book. She had it all, that Wanda. She was something else!

"I couldn't care less where you got that stinking, old jacket. I want my money."

"Well," I said, my eyes still lowered, "for your information, I had to buy the damn thing from the millionaire mayor for twenty dollars—and I had to work for the money."

"Where in hell did you ever work?"

"Over at the country club, caddying."

"Where's the two hundred bucks?"

Knowing the money was under a pile of underwear in my dresser, I said, "It's in the bank."

"You're a damn liar!"

"I don't lie."

"If it's in the bank, then get your skinny ass over there and get it!"

"The bank's not open yet."

"I don't believe it," she said, getting up and putting a pot of coffee on the stove. "Nancy said that you were over at Belda Bird's Bar buying everybody drinks. Is that right?"

I looked at her, saying, "Nancy doesn't know what the hell she's talking about. It isn't true."

"Well, I heard it from another reliable source too."

Suspecting the fishing she was doing now was the only fishing she'd be doing today, I said, "You're wrong if you believe that. I haven't been in Belda's since, well, I can't remember."

"Is that so?" she said, turning the stove off and lifting the coffee pot with a dishrag.

I kept my eyes fixed on her and the coffee pot. I knew that was the thing to do when she was in a squirrely mood. She was known for throwing things. Over at the drugstore, for example, she threw things all the time and once she threw a box of Epson salts at Widow Stevens when the widow argued about the price. Still watching her even as she sat next to me, I asked, "Why are you so mad at me?"

"You let me believe you were poor and needy. You made a damn fool out of me."

Watching her cross her legs and seeing her robe slip from her naked thighs, I told myself that there was nothing deranged about her legs. Then I said to her, "I only took the money so I could get to know you better."

With a smile on her full lips, she said, "Now I've heard every line there is—another goddamn lie!"

"It's not a lie."

"It is a lie. Don't you think I know a lie when I hear it?"

Seeing she poured coffee for herself but none for me, I said, "You sure have a lot of money to give away."

"I don't *give* anything. I loan, at ten percent."

"Why only to the poor and needy?"

"Well stupid, because they're the ones that need it."

"That makes sense," I said, not about to ask where she gets the money. Staring at her coffee now, I asked, "How about some of that coffee?"

Wrapping her long, delicate fingers around her cup, she said, "You can't have any coffee, not until you get the money." Then, in a softer tone, she asked, "Why don't you have the same last name as Mayor Horton—

did he disown you?"

"Because he's not my father, that's why. And I wouldn't let him adopt me."

"Where is your father, Matthew?"

Appreciating her show of interest, I said, "My father's dead. He was killed fighting in the French Resistance during World War Two."

Suddenly she was on her feet, screaming: "Don't you dare tell me any war stories!" Then, turning away, as if to hide her tears, she said, "I know all about it. My daddy was killed in the same goddamn war. Now get the hell out of here and get my money!"

This was the moment I'd been waiting for—the moment of closeness. "Wanda, I love you," I said softly.

Turning, with tears on her cheeks, she said, "Please don't say that."

"But I already said it."

"Then don't ever say it again." Then, as hardbitten as a drill sergeant, she yelled: "This place's off limits to you until you get the money—and while you're at it, bring some whiskey back! I only have a little left."

I went but didn't go far. I returned to the small park across the highway and examined my first real closeness with Wanda. For one thing, she'd used my first name, for the first time. Before today, she'd only used my last name, when at the drugstore, for instance, she said, "Go on home, La Fleur, your mother's calling you." And then, of course, there was the time she said, "La Fleur, take this two hundred and put some food inside you and some new clothes on your skinny ass." And all the other times, right up until today, when she'd used just my first name, and beautifully, with plenty of lips.

Tears were in my eyes now, but not because of her using my first name. They were there because of the tears she'd shed, after saying her daddy had been killed in the same war as my father. I felt certain now that she and I belonged together.

Returning to the house, I sat on the front porch and it wasn't long before she came out and told me to come inside, before the neighbors accused her of leaving garbage on the doorsteps. And I laughed, realizing that was another thing I loved about her—her great sense of humor—and so I went in, sat at the metal table again and stared at the coffee pot until she broke down and gave me a cold cup and a stale doughnut, while she held out her hand, asking, "Where's the money?"

"Sorry, the bank's still not open," I said, being extra careful not to spill anything, rattle the table and get on her nerves. And I was careful not to say the wrong thing, such as telling her about the white frosting, the size and shape of a horseshoe, that was on the seat of her dark skirt. I wanted to tell her, but I was afraid she'd blame it on me and kick me out again, before I finished the coffee and doughnut.

She was in the bedroom again, primping in a full-length mirror. Her hair was long and dark and shining. I'd always liked long hair on a young woman, if it wasn't matted too much. Continuing to observe her, I got the pleasant impression that she'd left the door open on purpose so I could watch her moves, as if we were married. She finished and returned to the kitchen, asking, "Did you know I was going to split from this one-horse town as soon as you gave me the money?"

"No, I didn't," I said, choking a little on the doughnut. "But what about all the money you loaned out?"

She was quick, saying, "I've got everybody's address. I'll send invoices."

"What about me? You could send me an invoice."

"No invoices for you, La Fleur. I don't trust you. I want the money from you today—now!"

With my heart pounding and rushing the blood to my head, I asked, "Why are you leaving?"

"Because I want to live where people aren't hypocritical, violent, cruel, greedy and phony—like around here."

"Where you going to find that place—heaven?"

"Heaven, hell! There's plenty of greener pastures out there. I just might head for California, or Hawaii, or I might even go to Europe, where I won't have to listen to a lot of bullshit because I won't be able to understand the language."

I could see the big smile, and I could see her not being able to get rid of it. It was a beautiful, spontaneous smile, showing all of her beauty, strength, independence and high intelligence. And then I saw that the smile was not only on her face, but it was on her hair and skin and red sweater and dirty, blue skirt. And now it was on the walls and metal table and coffee pot and cups—and then I saw it inside the cups, dancing on the coffee and having a ball. It was then that I told myself that the whole damn world was being fulfilled by her smile, after waiting five billion years, more or less. It was in that moment that, with all the emotion that had built up inside me, and with all the tears that were collecting in my throat and behind my eyes, I whispered, "I love you, Wanda."

She quit smiling and in a small, childlike voice asked, "Do you really love me, like you say?"

Seeing her blue eyes soften, I said, "Yes, I really love you and I want to marry you, okay?" Keeping my eyes on her, I waited for maybe two minutes for her to say something, but she said nothing. She just sat there, looking like a stone statue of a Greek goddess, staring at me, and unnerving me so much that I said the wrong thing, asking, "Could I please have some of that whiskey you said you have left?"

Grabbing her long, slender throat, as if I'd just forced a cyanide pill down there, she screamed: "I knew it!"

Alarmed and high on paranoia, I asked, "What?"

"You only told me that you love me and want to marry me so you can get something from me."

"But I only wanted the whiskey—you know, to celebrate."

"La Fleur, you're a liar and a con man."

"But…"

"The bank's open now—go!"

Getting up, I accidentally stepped on her toe, which was like stepping on a land mine.

"Yee-ouch!" she exploded. "Get out! Go!"

I hurried over to the park bench. I was determined now not to return the money yet. I felt that I was making progress. For one thing, we'd had a little spat, just like married people and then there was her lack of indifference—a very positive sign. Relaxing, I stretched out on the bench and as I listened to the stream running fast behind me, I looked at the blue sky and imagined that I was a skywriter, writing I LOVE YOU, WANDA. Then, just below my declaration of love, I saw her write: I LOVE YOU TOO, MATTHEW. And then, as the sun warmed me, I dozed off, but not for long.

Major Danny came by in his red Cadillac and blew his horn. When he stopped, I saw Nancy Hunter hanging out of a window. She was laughing at me with all she had, including her green eyes, bleached-blonde hair, crooked mouth and the wide gutter of her breasts, disappearing now as she leaned out the window with just her head and yelled, "Hey, La Fleur—what you doin'?"

"Get in—let us take you home!" Major Danny said, as if he were still in the army giving orders.

I didn't want to get in but did—but only so I could tell them that they were a couple of rotten, adulterous weirdoes. But then, once I was inside sitting in the front next to Nancy, I couldn't find the guts to say a word. And even after we stopped at the house and Nancy told me I smelled bad and Major Danny told me to take a bath, I couldn't tell them what I thought of them. Watching them speed away now, with tears of anger and humiliation threatening to spill out, I felt like a greenhorn without guts—the same way I'd felt the night Maurice Martineau, my mother's lover, had been killed.

Although I tried desperately to get rid of the memory, I didn't have strength enough. I saw again the violent spring storm that had hit Bordeaux. I was afraid of the storm outside, but I was more afraid of the storm going on inside the house. I was in my bedroom, but I could hear my mother and Maurice arguing in the living room. She was calling him a murderer. He was calling her a slut and a whore. Forcing myself to the door, I peeked out and saw my mother crying with her hands on her face. I wanted to go to her but didn't. I couldn't find the courage. I wanted to scream but couldn't. I saw the big knife in Maurice's hand and heard my mother tell him to stay far away from her. When she ran out into the storm, Maurice ran after her. I wanted to do something to stop Maurice, but even then, with my mother's life on the line, I didn't have the guts. The only thing I did was to crawl to the window and look out. In a flash of lightning, I saw Maurice on the ground, with his face in the mud. Then I could see Major Danny. He was standing next to my mother, with his arms around her shoulders. When they came in, Major Danny called his office and told someone to come and pick up the dead body of a dope dealer. I knew what he said, because I'd studied English. I also knew he was an investigator for the CID. Then, while he was still on the phone, I put my arm around my mother and got Maurice's blood all over me. I was terror-stricken, but somehow I was able to walk my mother to her bed and give her water. Soon an ambulance came and took Maurice's body away, but not before a soldier stuck needles in me and my mother. I fell asleep soon after that, thinking my father had given me too much wine at dinner. I didn't realize he was dead.

No one was home, not my mother, the maid, the cook, our dog Gussie, or Major Danny, of course. I made myself a chicken sandwich but didn't eat it. I was too angry at Major Danny, the barbarian. I wanted to get a knife as big as Florida and stick him. He'd fooled around on my mother once too often. Now I wanted to get one of the barbarian's shotguns and blow him to hell, where he belonged. Next, I thought of getting some arsenic and poisoning his chocolate éclairs, and I maybe would have, if the phone didn't ring.

It was Wanda on the phone demanding her money. I said I'd just returned from the bank and had the money. It felt good to lie. I could hear Nancy in the background, yelling that I was just like Major Danny, a cheapskate and a credit risk. "Why is Nancy saying that?" I asked.

"Because she's just had a bad day with the mayor," Wanda said. "And as soon as you bring the money, we're both going to split from Fartsville!"

By the way she slurred her words, I knew she'd been drinking. Steady, and as cold as purple, I said, "Well, when you get to where you're going, send me a postcard."

"Bring me the money—all two hundred—or is it three hundred?"

Listening to her chuckle, dirty-like, I decided to take control and beat her at her own game. "It's four hundred—or is it five?"

Chuckling again, she asked, "What's the matter, La Fleur, can't you take a little joke?" Then, slurring her words even more, she asked, "Do you really have the money?"

"Yes."

"Well, if you don't have all of it, I'll take fifty on account."

I understood. She was drunk and writing numbers in outer space. Lying big, I said, "I've got the two hundred, and more—much more."

"You're lying through your teeth, but even if you don't have the money, come on over anyway. Nancy and I have a surprise for you." She hung up then.

Wondering what the surprise was, I hung up and stole a chocolate éclair from Major Danny. Then, as if the éclair had already been tampered with, I began to feel strange.

As I watched the sun catch tiny particles of dust flying around the kitchen, the demented moment came in which I imagined the dust now was penetrating my skull and forming into little dirt balls in my brain.

The phone was ringing again. It was Wanda saying, "I want you to know I wasn't serious about taking fifty bucks on account. I want all two hundred. I'm not playing around, La Fleur!"

"I told you I have the money, and more." I said, lying more easily. "Major Danny just died and left me a bundle. However, I can't get it until after the funeral. Can I still come over for the surprise?"

Wanda shouted to Nancy that she'd screwed the mayor to death. Hearing their vulgar laughter, I felt good. I knew they weren't laughing at me, for a change, and that knowledge gave me a sense of freedom—thus proving that a lie can set you free, just as much as the truth can, if not more.

Wanda was asking, "So, what did he die of?"

"A heart attack."

Chuckling again, she said, "That's funny, because Nancy said he didn't have a heart."

"What's the surprise you got for me?"

She hung up.

I hurried over but found no one at home. Hot and angry, I didn't want to wait but did. Returning to the park, I sat on my bench and told myself I was crazier than I'd thought. The afternoon sun made it worse. Instead of singing sweetly, the birds screamed at me, and the stream behind me began making sucking and swallowing sounds at me. Boiling in my own oil, I moved to a shady spot near the water and removed everything but my Jockey shorts. Stretched out on cool grass, I eventually felt better and thought of Wanda without anger. She had a right not to be home, I told myself. Then, closing my eyes, a moment of ecstasy invaded my premises. I imagined we were kissing and nibbling and holding each other for dear life, and there was no more loneliness, guilt or shame as love lifted us over the prison walls of sin, built by people of hypocrisy, greed, cruelty and violence. And now on the other side of those walls, the air was sweet, the birds were singing and the stream ran quietly.

Suddenly, the moment was over. Reality stormed in, and I knew I was alone. The birds began to scream at me again and the stream ran loud and hollow. Opening my eyes, I stared at the sun and prayed it would burn me out of existence; however, as luck would have it, the sun disappeared behind some trees. Cold and angry again, I dressed and went home.

No one was there. I stole another éclair and just as I finished it, the phone rang. It was Wanda, chuckling and saying, "Thought you were coming over."

"Over where—your ass with a scrub brush?"

"Over here, Matthew—you coming or not?"

I wanted to hang up but didn't, feeling that there was too much at stake. I was closing in on her, taking complete control. "I was there, but you weren't," I said calmly and firmly. "What you trying to pull?"

She actually whined, saying, "Nothing. I'm not trying to pull anything. We weren't home, because we went for some whiskey. You could have waited."

"I've got boils on my ass from waiting!" I said, startled at my verbal swagger.

"What about the money? You don't have to have it, but it would be nice if you did."

Like a poisoned arrow, an idea ripped into my head. "Hey," I said with enthusiasm. "I promise to give you all the money, if you meet me at Major Danny's statue at eight tonight—okay?"

"Why can't you come here?"

"I've got to make arrangements for the funeral. You understand, don't you?"

"Well, you better be there at eight."

I hung up, and immediately afterwards the phone rang again. It was my mother, telling me Major Danny was in the hospital after suffering a mild heart attack. "We'll all be home soon from the hospital. Fix yourself something to eat, if you can't wait," she said, before hanging up.

Feeling like a warlock and that I'd cast a spell on Major Danny, I went to the kitchen and ate the last of the chocolate éclairs.

## chapter 3

Suzette, our maid for many years now, came to my room and told me my mother wanted to talk to me in the Music Room, which was downstairs next to the library of the mansion Major Danny's father built and left to Major Danny over the objections of his younger son, Morely, who was now Chief of Police and the biggest pain in the ass in the world.

My mother, Anne, was seated next to the grand piano looking at the large portrait I'd done of her several years ago, when it seemed I was on the road to heaven, not hell. It was a delicate moment then, when she let tears fall down her cheeks and looked down now at the book of poems on her lap—my poems, published in France with the help of her friend, Jean Paul Sartre. Taking a laced handkerchief from the sleeve of her white robe, she dried her eyes and gestured for me to sit across from her at a small table. When I'd done so, she looked at the portrait again, saying in French, "It's a fine portrait, worthy of high praise." Then looking down at the book and then at me, she said, "You surely knew how to spend your time when you were younger. You created beautiful things, when most of the boys were out not striving for perfection and getting girls in trouble."

Suzette came in and placed milk and cookies in front of me and while she fussed and apologized in Canadian French for the interruption, my mother read from the book and I read my mother, noting what I'd found perfect about her and had highlighted in the portrait—her dark hair, deep-set blue eyes, her finely textured skin. Focusing on the elegant robe, the same I'd painted her in, I saw that I'd gotten it just right, just as I had her swanlike neck, slender body, long, delicate fingers. Returning to her skin, I saw that I'd painted it darker in the portrait, darker, so that it would bring out the evasive quality, which was so much a part of her.

After Suzette left, my mother looked at me and said, "You've changed, drastically." Then, with tears in her eyes and her lips quivering, she went on, saying, "I don't want to continue with this, but I feel I must." Dabbing her eyes with her handkerchief again, she said, "Look at yourself. Is that the way a college graduate should look—a *cum laude*? You look like a sloppy ragamuffin. You break my heart. What happened to you?"

Looking at the cookies, I forced myself not to take one. I knew she wouldn't appreciate my eating one right now.

She was saying, "So, you have nothing to say for yourself. Just as I thought."

"I'm sorry, Mama," I said, seeing more tears flooding her eyes.

"You don't talk to me, Matthew. Why don't we speak of the good times we shared in France, when your father was alive?"

"It's all my fault, Mama."

Suzette looked in but closed the door again, as if she didn't want to get bitten by the insects of guilt flying around the room.

Looking at the door, my mother said, "Dear Suzette, she's been a salvation to me. It's been so good to be able to speak French with another woman. Aren't you happy she answered the ad we put in the Montreal newspaper?"

"Yes, Mama," I said, taking an oatmeal cookie.

Smiling now, she said, "I wish your father could see how tall and handsome you are."

"Maybe he can," I said, smiling.

"Yes," she said. "Maybe he can see us from his place in heaven. Yes, we must believe he can."

Looking at her sitting erect, with her head held high, I said, "You're beautiful, Mama."

"Thank you, dear. But we were speaking of your father, weren't we?"

"Yes," I said, taking another cookie and making sure I chewed with my mouth closed. Then, after taking a drink of milk, I asked, "Would you speak of the brave things he did, Mama?"

She spoke then of my father, Henri La Fleur, who worked for Post, Telegraph and Telephone and over the objections of my mother, joined the

Resistance and helped set up a warning system, through which German messages were intercepted and passed on to friends. And she said that he was a key figure in the Underground and worked with Richard Fowler, an Englishman who was also an electrical engineer and had come to France by parachute after fighting with the Norwegian Resistance. Together, they had helped break the code used by Joseph Darman, head of the French Forces and Milice, and after the code was broken, four V-1 launching sites were found in just one month, and the V-2 underground fuel tanks were found in Chartres. "And," she went on to say, "your father and Mr. Fowler were very instrumental in planning Plan Violet, the Master Plan for sabotaging all the underground cables on D-Day. Oh, my dear son, your father was so brave, and I was so proud."

It just came out. If I'd thought about it, I wouldn't have asked the question. I would have blocked it out, as I'd done so many times before. "Who killed my father?" I asked.

With her skin and eyes darkened with what I took to be evasiveness, she said, "I'm too sad and too tired to talk about it. Why haven't you asked about this before?"

Looking down at the floor, I said, "I was afraid of hurting you."

"Oh, dear heart, don't be sorry. You have a right to know everything about your father's death and the rest of it."

"What do you mean by *the rest of it*?"

There was a long pause, before she said, "I'll tell you what I know about your father's death and then we'll see. I don't know everything, but someday I hope I will. On D-Day, your father was near Bussac secretly loading a farm truck with guns and ammunition. He and his friends wanted to go all the way to St. Nizier to help the mountain troops. There were only two hundred maquis there and over five hundred Germans. Suddenly, the Germans came to the truck and your father was shot. Only your father was killed, no one else. I've always wondered about it. Someday, I hope to find out all of the details." Then, after resting her head on the back of her chair, she said, "At first, Maurice Martineau said the officer in charge shot him, for no reason. Later, he told me that he was the one who shot him—but we were arguing that night, and he was drunk."

She was sobbing. I went to her and placing my hand on her shoulder, said, "Some other time, Mama. We'll talk again, some other time."

Dabbing her eyes again, she said, "Yes, we'll talk again and I must speak then of something else. I must tell you all and then do penance, so I will be beautiful again. I'm forty-three, but I feel so old and ugly."

"You're forty-eight, Mama," I said, wishing then that I could suck those words back into my mouth.

"Don't tell me what I am!" she snapped. Then, smiling a bit, she said, "I suppose it matters little how many years I've got. I'm old, because of what I've done. Sin makes one totally old."

"What've you done, Mama?"

"I will tell you soon, but not tonight. Be patient. I'm going to bed; but first, I want to tell you that I'm going to quit interfering in your life. If you want to dress like a bum all of your life, that's your business. You see, after what I did, I have no right to condemn you, in any way. Now I must go to bed." Then, after I walked with her to the stairs, she kissed me and said, "Goodnight, Matthew."

Thinking that you better be careful if your mother tells you she's going to quit interfering in your life, I said, "Goodnight, Mama. Have a good rest."

It was almost eight when I left to meet Wanda at the statue. Darkness was coming on and there was a full moon. When I arrived at the small park on the shore of Lake Huron, I sat on a bench and looked at the large, bronze statue of Major Danny, the statue people donated money for after he said he deserved it because he was the best mayor the town ever had, and a war hero. I heard one of his speeches, and it was running through my head now. "Good people and fellow townspeople," he'd said, standing on a flag-decorated platform on the Fourth of July. "I'm not one to brag, but I've done a helluva lot more for this town than any goddamn mayor before me, and probably after me. You know I've worked like hell, and you know I'm not bullshittin' you. I've sacrificed and worked my ass to the bone (he weighed about three hundred pounds) to make this town the best and cleanest in America. Well, fellow Americans, a reliable source tells me that you want to give me somethin' in return for being an excellent mayor, and for servin' my country and becomin' a hero. So, let me tell you a little secret—I wouldn't mind, at all, if you donated a few bucks, or more, for a token of appreciation. In fact, I'd be proud, if you put up a statue of me, right here where I'm standin'. It would do your heart good, my friends, and it would bring us even closer together—you know, sort of bind us up for all eternity. Now, I'm not gonna be an asshole and dictate what you should give, I'll leave that up to you, my friends. Just think about it, and when you see those people on the street with their cans, then put a little somethin' in it—for your statue. God bless you and God bless America!"

I was still staring at the statue. It had birdshit all over it, but not enough birdshit to suit me. I was surprised Major Danny didn't make some lackey shine it every day, so the birdshit wouldn't conceal any of the image of the barbarian standing at attention and saluting the town with his fat hand held up to his fat head. I wished I'd brought some dynamite. Turning now and looking at the moon over the lake, I wanted to howl at it in anger and frustration. Life was getting to be too much for me. I wasn't succeeding in blocking out the destruction, confusion and loss of my miserable and lonely childhood. Tears were drowning me now, as I looked at the statue and wished I could paint all of the bad experiences of my youth on one big canvas, with Major Danny right in the middle. It was no wonder, I told myself, that I'd wanted to meet Wanda at the statue. It had become the centerpiece of my life, and I'd always been drawn to its ugliness as I'd been drawn to sin. I thought of it now as some kind of demonic magnet that was pulling and tormenting me, and now making me remember the day in Frankfurt, Germany when Major Danny had held my hand and had held it almost all the way to Point Stevens, as if I were a prized French poodle. And the major's hand had felt like cold bronze, like that of the statue's, and after we'd reached Point Stevens, I'd never let him hold my hand again or even touch me.

Sharp, dark things of the past fell from a shelf inside me and cut me. I saw myself as a young boy, dressed in a blue suit with short pants and clutching the soldier doll my mother had given me. The doll looked like General Charles de Gaulle. My mother and I, and my mother's new husband, Major Danny, had arrived in Frankfurt, after flying from Bordeaux that morning. Major Danny held my hand and led us to an army staff car. The driver saluted and opened the doors for us. I sat in the middle in the back, clutched my soldier doll and thought of General de Gaulle, who was brave, held his head high, and pointed his nose like a bird dog. I also thought of my father, who'd been brave and held his head high. I wished I knew who'd killed my father, so I could find him and strangle him with my bare hands. Holding my head high, I tried to be brave but couldn't. My throat was sore, and I was too heartsick because of leaving home. Looking out the window, I could see the greening of spring coming up through the ruins of the city, but the fresh green did nothing to make me feel better. And now, I heard the major talking about the ruins of war.

Pointing out piles of rubble and shell holes in buildings, he said, "Look at all the destruction and waste. It's been years since the war's been over and they still ain't fixed things up. Lazy bastards!" Then, after taking my hand again, he laughed, saying, "See what they get for startin' a war!"

I couldn't think about the ruins. I could only think about the man with greying hair who was holding my hand. I didn't trust him. He'd shown kindness to me, but when I was around him, I always got the feeling that he wanted to hit me and steal something from me. He had pasty blue eyes that were shifty and squinty. Sometimes, when he looked at me, I got the feeling he was trying to figure out how to get rid of me, with an axe, a gun, or bomb. And then there was the cruel way he laughed, as he was doing now, talking about the waste of war, as if it were a treasure he'd just found. Pointing out a pile of small desks, sinks and toilet bowls, he said, "Yep, there's plenty of waste here, but it'd be a waste of time thinkin' about it, wouldn't it?" And wondering now why it would be a waste of time thinking about it, I freed my hand and looked at my mother. She had her face to the window and was weeping. Turning then to the rear window, I saw delicate rays of sunshine streaming through the shell holes in the roof of the train station and settling in its waste-filled bowels. I began to cry, but I hid my tears by putting my face on my mother's shoulder and pretending I was sleeping.

Just before the Army Replacement Depot, we were forced to stop. Some soldiers were marching on the road and holding up traffic. Seeing the impatience of some German civilians, who were waiting to cross the road, the major opened his window and yelled: "You goddamn krauts got one helluva nerve bein' impatient. You're just lucky our boys don't stomp all over your ass!"

When we were able to pass through the gate, we went up to the second floor of a stone building and were met by Dr. Trudi Becker, a heavy-set woman with a weak smile and a weaker handshake. Right away, she took me into a room and examined me, and then she told me with a thick

German accent to wait in the hall. Then, after examining my mother, Major Danny went into the room and stayed there a long time. Finally, when they came out, they were both breathing hard and straightening their clothes, as if they had been working hard at examining each other.

We all went into a dining room for lunch and sat at a round table with a white tablecloth and two unlit candles. With a sour smile, the doctor yanked the soldier doll from my arms and threw it on an empty chair, saying, "For sure, the General will be better there!" And now, without my doll, I was sad and afraid, thinking that the only friend I had left had just been taken from me. I wanted to reach for the doll and take it back, but I was afraid the woman would cut off my arm. I looked at my mother but found no help in her eyes, as she looked down at her folded hands. I looked at the soldier doll for help, but it could only stare at the woman, with a look that said: "I'm glad you lost the war, you cruel, evil, ugly woman!"

Moving his eyebrows up and down, Major Danny was saying, "My, my, we got ourselves a table fit for a king!" Then, turning to my mother, he said, "Anne, will you just look at them candles. They're beautiful. Guess I'll light 'em up, before I eat 'em. I'm hungrier'n a hundred pigs!"

My mother kept her hands folded on her lap. Her dark hair and coat gave her rougeless face a ghostly look. When the major lit the candles, I stared at the flames and recalled how my father would allow me to light the candles, even if I scraped my plate with my knife and fork. I recalled the last time I'd scraped my plate, and how my father had wriggled his mustache, saying, "Don't scrape your plate. The plate is not for you to cut into little pieces. If you scrape again, I won't let you light the candles tomorrow." And then I'd scraped again soon after that, but as usual, the next evening I'd been allowed to light the candles.

I began to cry, but before anyone could see my tears, I left the table and found a toilet. Washing my face with cold water, I felt my tears had defiled me in some way, making me so weak that I thought I'd never be able to be as brave as my father and General de Gaulle. It was at that moment, that I vowed to never remember things that would make me cry, and it was then that I began to block such memories from my mind....

Wanda showed up, finally. Out of breath, she asked, "You got the money?"

By the light of the silvery moon, I could see she was in a good mood.

I was glad she was in a good mood. If she were already in a bad mood, I believed it would diminish the effect of my next move on her. "Hello, Wanda," I said, falling into a bad mood.

"Well, where's the money?" she asked, holding out her hand.

Looking at her and becoming aware she smelled of whiskey, I frowned and said, "I don't know what the hell you're talking about. I don't have any money."

Her eyes disappeared behind thick walls of blue mascara. When I saw her eyes again, they were filled with violence. "You lousy bastard!" she yelled, wiping the smile from my face with a roundhouse right to the side of my head. "You lousy, rotten bastard!" she yelled, hurrying down the road, scraping and wobbling in her high heels.

Rubbing the side of my head, I watched her stumble towards Belda's Bar. Finding myself in a good mood now and laughing, I imagined the man in the moon was laughing along with me. I headed for the drugstore to get a Coke, but I didn't get very far, before I saw Elsie Quinn coming at me with a silly-ass grin. In no mood to talk to Elsie, I hurried across the street to Bob's Gas Station and, putting my head underneath the hood of a car someone was working on, I was thankful that Elsie hadn't followed. It wasn't that I didn't like Elsie, I just thought she was too aggressive to be around, especially now.

While still under the hood of the car, I thought of two weeks ago, when I'd been on my way home from working at the country club and saw Elsie waiting for me in a sandtrap on the fourth hole. I'd always gone home that way and obviously she knew it. There she was, all naked and blonde and beautiful, with her body glistening in suntan oil and sand and with the sun shining on sand crystals and making them sparkle like little sequins. Then, watching her bellybutton twitch a lot, as if ants were in there biting her, I yelled, "Hey, Elsie, what you doing in there, waiting for a bus?"

Giggling, she said, "Hi, Matty. I've been waiting for you."

I couldn't take my eyes off of her. Smiling, I said, "You sure look nice with all that sand sparkling on your body."

Closing her eyes, as if the sun would fade the blue, she said, "It might look nice, but all this sand is making me itch. What say you come in here and brush it off for me?"

There was no one around. I wanted to jump in and join her but I didn't because I thought I was being true to Wanda, even though I hadn't got to first base with her yet. "Sorry, Elsie," I said, "I have to go home and practice my piano and guitar."

Opening her eyes, she said, "Damn! I knew you wouldn't want me, and it's because of Wanda Ross, isn't it?"

"No comment."

"You don't have to comment. I see you at the drugstore, looking at her with your tongue hanging out. Damn, and after I waited here all afternoon, and almost got myself killed by some golf balls. And I had to get dressed about ten times because people were coming. Damn it all!"

"I was caddying, but I didn't see you."

"Well, I didn't see you either. I guess we missed each other."

Watching her slip into a long, print dress, I said, "Sorry, Elsie."

Smiling now and holding her hand out for me to help her out of the trap, she said, "Hey, Matty, what say you get your guitar and come over to my house, so we can play our guitars together? I've got a piano, too."

"I didn't know you play those instruments."

"Sure do. I graduated in music from Michigan State. I got a scholarship, and I got all A's all the way through."

"I didn't know that."

"Well, you haven't paid enough attention to me, Matty, or I would've told you."

Feeling guilty about not jumping into the sandtrap, and feeling I owed her, I said I'd go. Then, after picking up my guitar, we went to her house and jammed on our guitars, until she went to the piano and played so much classical music, you'd think it was going out of style. I was surprised. Before, I'd thought of her as a party chick, who did nothing but live it up and chase men. But then, I hadn't known her all that well. She had gone to school at St. Joseph's also, but she'd graduated a few years before me—meaning of course, she was maybe a couple years older than me. Anyway, I knew her better now and I had a lot more respect for her, even though she talked funny sometimes, and was always chasing me. And I felt that respect now, hiding from her underneath the hood of a car, at a gas station where I wouldn't take a tricycle to be repaired.

Peeking out, I didn't see Elsie, so I headed for home but didn't get very far, before Wanda came out of nowhere, smiling and saying, "Matthew, I just heard you were telling the truth about the mayor having a heart attack, but did you know he's still alive?"

"Well," I said, walking beside her, "no doubt they brought him back to life with those jumper cables they have over at the hospital."

Stopping me and tugging at the sleeve of my army jacket, she looked up and said, "Look at me, Matthew."

"What?" I asked, looking at her.

"I'm sorry I hit you. How can I make it up to you?"

"Are you working tomorrow?"

"No, I got fired," she said matter-of-factly, as if she'd gotten fired from every job she'd ever had and was used to it.

"Well, would you like to go fishing with me?" I asked, walking on.

Catching up, she said, "Okay, I'll do it."

With Wanda on my arm for the first time, we walked in silence, until we were in front of her house, and I asked, "What was that surprise?"

Chuckling nicely, she said, "Okay, come on in and we'll give it to you."

We went inside. I wanted to give Nancy a dirty look but didn't. She acted too warm and friendly, saying, "That's a great jacket you got on, Matthew. I had one like it once, but somebody stole it."

"Where'd you get it?" I asked, trying to be nice and not ruin anything.

"My father gave it to me. I guess he stole it from somebody, because he wasn't in the army."

"Where is he now?" I asked, interested.

"My father?" she asked, obviously whiskeyed-up.

Impatient with her but not showing it, I said, "Yes, your father."

With a faraway look, as if her green eyes had died, she said, "Oh, he's around, here and there. I haven't seen him in years. The last I heard from my mother, he's bumming around Canada."

"Where's your mother?"

"My mother?"

"That's what I said—your mother."

After pouring us whiskey, she said, "My mother's in Detroit, living with some asshole-lawyer who handled the divorce for my mother. She got a discount."

We all laughed, and I asked, "Nancy, how come you live up here?"

Sitting up, seeming more alert, she said, "I like to ski. Good skiing up here." Then, after downing her drink, she turned to Wanda and asked, "When we going to show him the surprise?"

"Right now!" Wanda said, pulling me into her bedroom and pushing me onto her bed. "Stay!" she said then, before leaving the room and returning shortly with Nancy. Then as I lay there smiling like pudding, they stood at the foot of the bed, yelling, "Surprise, surprise, surprise!" And now I could see that they were naked, except for garlands of flowers around their heads. Then, as I stared in disbelief, they began to throw themselves around in a kind of a ritual dance, giggling all the while and chanting": "Sur-prise, sur-prise…." And now I could see Wanda's smile all over everything again, and I could smell the sweetness of the flowers mixing with the smells of whiskey, cologne and sweat. And then, just as quickly as they'd come in the room, they left, but only for a quick moment, until they returned with their clothes on. Wanda came to lie on the bed with me, and Nancy went to sit and sweat on a loveseat, before she seemed to get sick and left the room. Drunk and laughing almost hysterically, Wanda sat me on the edge of the bed, took off her clothes again, and climbed up onto my shoulders, yelling, "Yay, yay, yay, Matthew is our man, if he can't do it, nobody can!" And that was when I got to my feet and began jumping around the room like a jack rabbit, until she got down and dressed and pulled me back into the living room. Sitting on the couch now by ourselves, Wanda, with a smile and fluttering eyelashes, asked, "Matthew, do you really and truly love me?"

"Yes," I said, seeing her eyes beginning to lag behind. "I really and truly love you."

"What time are we going fishing?"

"About six."

"Oh, God," she groaned, putting her fanny in the air and falling asleep.

So, not wanting to stare at her and wake her up, I went home.

## chapter 4

Major Danny's cabin was on the Au Sable River, which I called the Dark River. The river was dark and its currents were strong and treacherous at times, but that was not the reason I called it the Dark River. I was afraid of it, for some dark, unknown reason, and I'd always been afraid of it.

The cabin wasn't far from town, so we walked. I carried a bag of groceries, and Wanda carried two quarts of beer. After we put the food and beer in the cabin, we went down to the water's edge and bailed out the rowboat. The boat was green and it leaked. It didn't leak much, so I didn't fix it or pull it out of the water in the summer. Besides, it belonged to Major Danny, and I wasn't about to ingratiate myself on him. He never used the boat now, because he had a new yacht on Lake Huron.

It wasn't long before she began to get on my nerves. When I caught a fish, she'd make me throw it back into the water, saying, "Throw the little fishie back or I'll go home!"

I sat in the back of the boat, wearing my army jacket and blue jeans. She sat between the oars, wearing a long, white dress with a blue ribbon around the waist, and the ends of the ribbon kept falling into the water that had returned. When I caught my sixth perch and was told to throw it back, I got so mad I could feel the veins in my neck pop out. "I'm going to keep the next one, Wanda—no matter what!" I said, not hiding my anger well.

"Do you really love me?" she asked, smiling.

"Yes," I mumbled , watching her trail an end of the ribbon on the water and sand at the bottom of the boat. Realizing she was writing my first name, my heart began to smile a little. I continued to fish and caught the biggest walleyed pike I'd even seen—a real beauty. "Look, Wanda, look at it!" I yelled.

She looked, frowned and said, "Throw the little fishie back, Matthew."

"Little? For God's sake, Wanda—it's a monster!"

"Let the little fishie go home again or take me home!"

With the gaskets of my brain blowing, and with my veins popping, I threw it back and watched as the fish hurried home. That was when I withdrew into myself and sent my eyes diving into the water.

Chuckling, she said, "Look at me, Matthew, and let me see those big, beautiful, brown eyes of yours. Look at me."

I didn't want to look but did.

"My," she said, smiling. "Your eyes aren't brown. They're the same color as the little fishies' eyes."

I cast into the water again, definitely determined to keep the next one, regardless of whether she went home or not. I was angry, but soon the anger was gone, when I realized she'd let me see something of herself. I didn't know exactly what it was, but I knew it had something to do with her saving those "little fishies" and her determination in doing so. Then, as I thought about it, I began to feel guilty for wanting to keep the fish. Funny, I said to myself, how the hot sun can blister your brain and make you feel guilty over catching a few fish!

Shrugging off the guilt, I asked her to row the boat to where the water was rolling over some weeds. I pulled up anchor and she began to row. As we moved along slowly, I let my line and spinner out in order to troll. Then suddenly, it happened. The boat began turning in circles and the line got tangled on an oar and broke. "Damnit to hell!" I yelled. "You're supposed to use both oars when you row. Good God, I don't have any more spinners or even a hook." I stood up and wanted to dive in after it all but I didn't. I was too afraid. Fear, like a flash flood, had risen inside me. Then, after I sat down again, shame, like a poisonous eel, bit me.

"Well, hothead," she was saying, "are you going to jump in or are you going to throw me in after that cruel, goddamn hook?"

I didn't know what it was, but when I looked at her, something in her eyes got rid of all my fear, anger, and shame, and I was able to laugh, saying, "Let's have some lunch." And then I watched as she pulled the long dress up over her knees and started to row ashore with all she had, and that was when I saw it, for the first time—a distant, tight, enigmatic smile.

Once in the cabin, the smile had been replaced by her usual smile, filled with, so I thought, the joy of living and being with me. After eating a hamburger and drinking beer, she suggested we stay the night and I was all for it, of course. I called my mother and told her I'd be staying at the cabin and she told me to have a good time with my fishing. Then, after Wanda and I built a fire, we stretched out in front of it and made love, and we went at it again and again, far into the night. It was the first time for both of us. "Funny, how things can fall into place, even if you've never done it before," she said, before putting her fanny in the air and falling asleep.

Not long after, I fell asleep, had a nightmare and woke myself up, screaming: "I'll kill you! I'll kill you!"

Waking up and turning on a bedside lamp, Wanda asked, "What is it?"

Sweating and out of breath, I said, "I'm sorry I woke you up. I had a nightmare."

"Poor baby," she said, wiping sleep from her eyes. "What was it about?"

I told her about the man in the black uniform with swastikas all over it, who'd threatened me down by the river. "He had a hateful smile and a wart on the end of his nose," I said. "And it looked like he was using the wart as a gunsight, in order to zero in on me. Then he told me that he'd killed my father and that he was going to kill me. When he started towards me, slow but sure, I felt trapped. I had only the Dark River behind me, and I was afraid of the river. I was too afraid to turn around and swim for it. Then, I realized I was more afraid of the Dark River than the man, so I took my chances, looked the man straight in the eyes and told him that I was going to kill him, because he'd killed my father. That's when I woke up."

"Poor baby," she said again, kissing my bare shoulder and then holding me tight until I feel asleep.

And a bright new morning came, and we ran naked down to the riverside and bathed in the generous sun on a quilt of many colors. And I said, "We need this."

"We need each other," she said, with that tight, distant and enigmatic smile, heavy around the eyes now.

"Yes," I said. "We need each other, but we also need the smell of pine, the feel of sun and sand, the green grass over there, the grey stones and blue sky and..."

"We need only each other!" she said, climbing on top of me and staring into my eyes.

I saw it in her eyes, something, I believed, of an evil, ulterior motive. And now I could feel her body run cold and stiff, as if she'd turned into a corpse. I fought against the terror building inside me and tried to lighten things up. "You're absolutely right," I said, smiling. "However, my nymph of the wilderness, don't you think we could also use other things, such as the songs of birds and the clouds up there, casting soft shadows?"

Pinning my shoulders down with her knees, she put her face close to mine and said, "Tell me you need only me—only me!"

Warning bells went off in my head, telling me that this was all wrong and that she was even more deranged than I. But to please her, I said, "Yes, I need only you, Wanda."

"Now tell me you can't live without me—tell me!"

Closing my eyes, I said, "Okay, I can't live without you."

"Open your eyes and say it again!"

"Why are you making me say these things?"

"I shouldn't have to make you say them. You should be saying them on your own. After all, you told me you love me. Now say it again, that you can't live without me."

Confused and sick at heart, I said, "I can't live without you. There, are you satisfied?"

"Now don't forget it!" she said, rolling onto her back and closing her eyes.

The warning bells sounded again, telling me now that what she'd shared with me last night had been a lie, and that she'd just planted some kind of poisonous seed inside me, and that I, once a beautiful figment of God's imagination, was surely doomed, because I had denied my soul in the most destructive way by telling her that I couldn't live without her. And now, as panic rose in me like another flash flood, I told myself I'd never know the difference between love and hate and would soon be consumed by flames of ignorance, emotional pain, and self-pity—the flames of hell. Then, as I concluded I would be eternally cursed by obsessive thoughts of love, hate, peace, happiness and self, an experience of the past seeped into my memory, and I was too weak to block its way.

As a young boy, I was camping with my father in the woods near the Garonne River in France. We had fished all day and we were sitting by the campfire. My father spoke of a Bird of Endurance, and he said it was out there in the wilderness. When I asked what it looked like, he said I'd know when I found it. Then, when he was on his cot asleep, I went to look for it. It was dark, and I knew I might get lost and have to remain in the wilderness forever, but I continued on, looking for it, stumbling and falling, sweating and fighting off bugs, and not finding it. Finally, I found some sticks and leaves and built a little house—God, how I loved that house! All night I was awake, thinking about how I could find the Bird of Endurance. It began to storm, and there were lightning strikes nearby, but although I was afraid, I didn't cry. In the morning at dawn, as the storm continued, my father came to me and told me that I'd found it—the Bird of Endurance. Then, after I told him I didn't even see it, he said, "You don't have to see it to find it." That was when I cried, when I saw what it all meant. And that was when Papa smiled and held my hand, nodding and wriggling his mustache. After that day, we said no more about it....

I looked at Wanda, the cold stiff. I now guessed she'd gotten so angry because I'd made her row the boat all the time. Then, after she opened her eyes, I crossed my eyes and touched my nose with my tongue. Things got better after that. Laughing, we returned to the cabin, found ourselves boiling again, so we made love again. But afterwards, while we dressed, she put that strange look on her face again, saying, "It'll be even better in the sack, after we're married. You can count on it, Matthew."

On our return, we walked in silence, until we were in front of her house when she said, "Major Danny will probably be out of the hospital one of these days. That's when I'll be over to your house for dinner." Then, after kissing me on the cheek, she rushed into the house.

Walking home, I refused to think about her coming to dinner with Major Danny there. It was too painful.

When I got home, my mother and Major Danny's brother, Morely Horton, were sitting on the long, shaded veranda. I said hello, kissed my mother, shook hands with Morely and sat down with them. I could tell my mother was anxious for him to leave, because she kept squirming around in her wicker chair and stifling yawns. Police Chief Morely "Bulldog" Horton, fat and in uniform, held up a paperback copy of the The Prince, by Machiavelli, put it in front of my mother's face and asked, "You read this?"

"No," she said, smiling.

"How 'bout you, Matt?"

Thinking he looked more like an elephant than a bulldog, I said, "Not yet, Morely."

Chuckling, he said, "I thought all you power-and-money people read this book, as soon as you were able to read."

"What do you want, Morely?" my mother asked, surprising me with her abruptness.

With a lot of effort, he put his feet up on the railing and said, "Bein' the younger brother of a rich man ain't good, 'especially if the younger one's poor as a church mouse."

"What are you trying to say, Morely?" I asked.

"Well, seein' you asked, I'll tell you." Then, turning to my mother, he said, "Anne, you'll be needin' a good man to handle all that money Danny's gonna leave you, when he dies of heart trouble."

"Why are you talking like this, Morely?" my mother asked. "I'm surprised at you."

"Well, seein' you asked, I'll tell you. I'm talkin' this way 'cause of this book here. It says you gotta watch out for yourself."

"It's sinful," my mother said. "Why, you practically wished your brother dead. You should confess that to Father O'Grady."

Squinting at her, he said, "I don't confess to a priest. I don't believe in confession, and I ain't a Catholic—not any more. If I ever did get a sin on me, I'd go straight to God with it, like a Lutheran does."

"Is that what you are now—a Lutheran?" I asked.

"Hell no, I ain't no Lutheran, 'cause I hate Martin Luther, that's why.

In fact, I hate all excommunicated people. They're criminals and you know how much I hate criminals. It's just natural of me, bein' Chief of Police, and all."

"Lot of criminals out there, Morely," my mother said. "Why don't you go and catch them?"

Winking at me, he said, "Now that's gratitude for you, ain't it?" Then, looking at my mother, he said, "I comes all the way over here to ask you to marry me when my brother dies and you're tryna get rid of me."

"I'm going in the house," she said, getting up.

Reaching out and putting his hand on her arm and getting dirt on her white dress, he laughed, saying, "Aw, come on Annie, don't get all upset and run off on me. I got some more important things to tell you."

Sitting again, she said, "Tell me then and hurry!"

"Well, seein' you asked. I'll tell you. First off, I gotta tell you I'm gonna strike it rich one of these days. Mark my words. I'm gonna be as rich and powerful as they come, like a prince, you might say. And I'm gonna do it on my own, without money from my brother's death. Then you'll come aroun' Annie."

"Good luck, Morely," she said. "And please don't call me Annie. My name is Anne. Now, if you'll excuse me, I have some things to do in the house."

Holding up his hand, the size and shape of lower Michigan, he said, "Wait, there's more!"

"Well," she said, "If it's about your brother Danny dying, then forget it."

"Aw, Anne, I was kiddin' about that and about that you should marry me. I know I don't stand a chance. Why, you wouldn't even look at me, if I weren't my brother's brother."

I asked, "Why don't you and your brother get along, Morely? There seems to be a lot of animosity between you."

Letting his mammoth legs fall from the railing and with his eyes filled with tears now, he said, "We weren't always animostin' each other. It just got like that, ever since we were kids and I beat him up over at the ice house."

Seeing him turn away and wipe away tears with a red-checkered handkerchief, I said, "You don't have to talk about it, if you don't want to, Morely. Does he, Mama?"

"No, he doesn't—of course not."

Looking at her again, he said, "I'll tell you, so you can hear the truth, before Danny tells you the lie he's been tellin' ever since that day. He says he beat the livin' hell out of me, because I insulted my ma's cookin'—pannycakes, to be exact. He told everybody that I said they tasted like rubber—but it was the other way aroun'. He's the one who said that insult."

Seeing that he was retrogressing into a childlike state and talking like a child, I asked, "What about the icehouse?"

With a voice that hadn't changed yet, he said, "We were at the icehouse gettin' free splinters of ice. When it was hot out, we always went there to get free splinters of ice. Well, this day the splinters tasted like they'd been rubberized. And then Danny pipes up and says they taste just like my ma's pannycakes—like rubber. Then I says take it back, Danny, and he didn't take it back, so I hauled off and split his lip. And then his red blood starts comin' out of his lip—the top one—and I could feel his pain and surprise come at me from his eyes when he looked at me. Then he pulls his shirt out of his pants and wipes his mouth. I just stood there with a scowl on my face watchin' him bleed to death and pretty soon he started spittin' these long, red strings of..."

"Morely, please," my mother said, covering her ears with her hands.

"... and so I says to Danny, bein' the good-natured boy I was, 'Why not go back over to the icehouse and put some cold on your mouth?' And so we both of us went over to the icehouse and Danny asks the man, 'Can I please have a piece of ice? My mouth got hurt in an accident.' And I was consideratin' enough not to tell the man that it wasn't an accident—that I'd punched him in the mouth. Then, after Danny got the ice, we went home and became nasty to each other ever since then."

When Morely stopped, my mother took her hands from her ears and said, "I've got things to do in the house."

"One more minute, Anne please," Morely said, his voice sounding gutteral once again.

"One more minute, Morely," my mother said. "Not a second more."

"I just wanna tell you why I wanna get powerful and rich," he said, looking at her as if he were a loving, oversized puppy. "But first of all, I wanna confess that I got the idea of gettin' rich from the Stevens Family—from old Egwon, before he died, and from young Egwon, before he got killed in Korea, and from Clarissa, old shitface—if you'll excuse the expression—who ain't dead yet, of course. Anyways, I used to hang aroun' with young Egwon, and I was surprised when he got his balls shot off in Korea, if you'll excuse the expression."

"Why were you surprised?" I asked.

"I was surprised when he went in, in the first place. He got drafted, but he could've got out of it 'cause he had so much money. Know what I mean? He could've bribed somebody not to take him, like a lot of 'em did."

I watched as he removed his service hat and wipe sweat from his brow with his red-checkered handkerchief. Then, as I looked in his eyes, I could see something boiling and bubbling inside him, like lava in a volcano. "I think I know what you mean," I said. "You thought he would dodge the draft."

" I thought that, but he didn't," he said, putting his handkerchief on his lap. Then, turning to my mother, he said, "Anne, I confess I love money and power, 'cause I want to be one of the chosen ones, like all the rich people are, 'cause they're rich and powerful."

"Chosen for what?" she asked.

"Chosen for heaven, that's what! And only the rich and powerful get to go there—to the Kingdom of Heaven. That's what old Egwon said, and I believe it.".

"I can't argue with that, if it's what you believe," she said.

"You damn right you can't argue with it, 'cause it's pure and simple logic, that's why. I rest my case."

"May I go in now, Morely?" she asked.

Raising his hand again, he said, "Let me tell you 'bout the Stevens family first. They owned all the land 'round here once. I bet you knew that, right Anne?"

"I think everybody knows that," she said, smiling in sort of a patronizing way.

Erupting, pointing his fat finger at her, he said, "That's it! That's the power-and-money smile that rich people smile at crowbait like me all the time."

"But I didn't smile at you," my mother was quick to say.

"Don't lie to me, Anne!"

"First of all," she said, fighting back, "I'm not rich, so how could I smile like you say. Your brother is, but I'm not."

"But you will be when he dies—see what I mean?"

"What do you mean, Morely? What's this all about?" she asked, her eyes igniting.

"It's first about that smile of contemption that rich ones like you and Danny smile at poor bastards like me." Then, after wiping his brow again, he grew more calm, saying, "I have to confess I'd like to be a Chosen, and be able to smile like that. And just between me and you and the bedpost, I confess my father wasn't chosen to go to heaven, even if he was a doctor. And you know why he ain't in heaven?"

Seeing he was doing a lot of confessing for someone who didn't believe in confession, I asked, "Why isn't your father in heaven?"

"Matt, seein' you asked, I'll tell you. He ain't in heaven, 'cause he was too damn lazy to collect from all the deadbeats aroun' here. They owed him at least a million, I figure. And I'll confess somethin' else while I'm at it. I'm gonna get my legal share of Danny's money when he dies. It's not gonna be like after my father died, when all he left me was an old shotgun and a note tellin' me to blow out my brains. Can you 'magine a father doin' that to his own flesh-and-blood son?"

"Your father didn't love you?" she asked, looking sympathetic.

"No, Anne, and seein' you asked, I'll tell you why. Forever after that day at the icehouse, Danny kept puttin' big lies in my father's head."

"How about your mother—she loved you, didn't she?" my mother asked.

"You damn right she loved me, a lot. But she died when I was just a little boy."

"Did she go to heaven?" I asked.

He didn't answer. He just stared at me and wiped more tears from his eyes.

My mother was saying, "I'm sorry, Morely. I didn't know she died when you were just a boy. Your brother has never talked about her."

Putting his handkerchief back on his lap, he said, "My mother died of heartbreak 'cause of him and my father—that's why he never talked 'bout her. When I went to visit my mother's sister over in Glennie, she told me the whole story. She said they treated her like a slave and worked her to death and that's how she died—overwork and 'cause my father wouldn't get rich and powerful. And you know somethin' else? After she was dead and in the ground, my father and Danny had the gall to tell me that I killed her—that I'd been too heavy a baby and she had to carry me all the time. Now I ask you: How could a poor, little baby kill his mother—the only one in the whole world who loved him? You see how stupid they were, and Danny still is—and that's what's killin' him—stupidness!"

I knew now why people called him Bulldog. He had bulldog eyes and bulldog jowls and he breathed like a bulldog, as he was doing now. But, I told myself, that's no reason to think of him as a bulldog, just because he looks like one and because others call him Bulldog.

My mother was saying, "I guess I'll go in now."

"One more thing!" Morely said sharply. "You know, Anne, I'd bet my last pair of socks that there's somethin' very criminal 'bout how my brother came to get all that money. And if I discovers just one clue that he's not gonna leave me anythin' in his will, then you can bet your sweet ass I'm gonna investigate all his financial doin's, if you'll excuse the expression."

Seeing he was sweating a lot, I suggested, "Why don't you go on over to Belda's Bar and have a cool one. It'll do you good."

"Don't tell me what to do!" he snapped. "You see how you rich asses are? You got drinks there in your goddamn house and you wouldn't offer me one, if my goddamn tongue was on fire!" Then, getting up and lumbering off the porch, he yelled: "You'll be sorry, Annie, when I'm through with you and Danny. You won't have a pot to piss in!" Then, after squeezing into his police car, he thumbed his nose at us and drove off.

"Oh dear, oh dear," my mother said. "Now look what I've done. I should have offered him something to drink."

"It's my fault," I said. "I wanted to, but didn't."

## chapter 5

SITTING with me on her porch one evening, Wanda said, "The mayor's home from the hospital now, so I'm coming over for dinner. Make arrangements. Seeing we're getting married, and I'll be moving in, I think it'd be a good idea if I got to know the mayor and your mother better, don't you?"

Looking up at the darkening sky and thinking that Major Danny would make trouble, I said, "Yes, good idea. But maybe we better not mention us getting married, not until I get a good job—understand?"

"I understand. They'd probably only make a big deal out of it, and that'd foul things up right off the bat. And, believe me—I don't want anything, or anyone, fouling things up and wrecking it for me."

"I understand perfectly."

"Good. Now go on home and fix it for tomorrow night, Friday, at seven o'clock."

"That's sort of short notice, isn't it?"

"Well, try for it," she said sharply. "If tomorrow is out, then the next night will have to do."

"Okay," I said. Then, after a goodnight kiss, I went home and asked Mama if I could bring a lady-friend home for dinner tomorrow night. "Do you think Major Danny will mind?" I asked softly.

"Tomorrow evening will be fine," she said calmly, as if it were a common occurrence. However, let's not tell Daniel until the last minute, so as not to make him too anxious beforehand. You know what happened a year ago, when you brought a friend home for dinner."

"I remember very well," I said, thinking of Hiram Ludwig, the one and only person I'd invited for dinner. Major Danny, drunk as a skunk, had called Hiram's father a bum and had pushed Hiram's face down into his casserole, saying, "Okay, little guy, now go tell your pop to vote for me next time!" Humiliated and wiping tuna from his face and clothes, Hiram had hurried out the door, crying. After that, of course, I didn't invite anyone over for dinner, or anything, not until now, after Wanda invited herself.

The following evening Wanda called and insisted I come to her house and ride back with her in Nancy's car, which she'd borrowed for the occasion. "I want for us to arrive like any other engaged couple," she'd said. "Besides, if things get fouled-up, I don't want to have to depend on anybody to take me home. Understand?"

"I understand."

And so now we were on our way moving right along in Nancy's old jalopy, with Wanda gripping the steering wheel hard because it had rained earlier and the roads were still slippery. I'd offered to drive, but she wouldn't let me, saying I didn't know how very well, which was true. "Now remember," she said, staring at the road. "Don't mess things up for me." Then, after stopping in front of the house, she said, "I'm too nervous to go in."

"Don't be nervous," I said nervously, worried that she might leak it that we were getting married. "I guess I'm a little nervous, too."

"What the hell you got to be nervous about?"

"I guess I'm nervous because you're nervous."

"That's stupid. Now get hold of yourself!"

Studying her now, as she primped in the mirror, I said, "You look beautiful, Wanda."

"I do? Well, I think we better go in. I see they just turned the porch light on," she said calmly.

Seeing her calm now, made me more nervous. Since yesterday, after the dinner had been decided, I'd been hyperderanged and it had shown. For example, I didn't sleep last night. All night long, I thought of things that had happened, such as what happened to Hiram Ludwig, the evil look on Wanda's face that moment during the one-day fishing trip and other bad things. And I would think of other things, not especially good, but not bad, such as when I acted like a high-school jerk, when Wanda and I had celebrated our birthdays together last week at a motel, even though hers had been in July and mine wouldn't come until October. We'd chipped in for a chocolate cake, bought each other gifts and put fifty candles on the cake—twenty-five for her and twenty-five for me. Then, after I gave her a rhinestone barrette, and she gave me a bottle of champagne, we sang the birthday song, kissed, ate a piece of cake, and drank champagne. And that's when I got all excited and jerky and had eaten the rest of the cake by myself, including the fifty candles.

My mother and Major Danny were waiting at the door. Inside, my mother greeted Wanda warmly, saying, "How nice it is to meet one of Matthew's friends."

Wanda actually curtsied, saying, "The pleasure is all mine. Matthew has said a lot of nice things about you," she said, lying, because I'd never said any nice things about my mother, at least not to her.

After the introductions, I just stood there like a giraffe, looking down on them and seeing now that Major Danny, after taking Wanda's black chesterfield coat, was rubbing her bare shoulders with his horny hands, saying, "My, my, what a beautiful dress—same as yours, right Anne?"

Smiling at Wanda, my mother said, "Not at all, Wanda's is much nicer."

Clothes-conscious now, I adjusted my dark blue tie and blue blazer; then, after chastising myself for wearing brown shoes, I looked at Major Danny's green pants and yellow shirt, both dirty. Looking at the dresses, I saw they were alike only in that they were dark blue and lowcut in front. That was where the likeness ended, for my mother's was simple, petite and elegant and Wanda's was too short and had colored rhinestones all over. Comparing their physical attributes, however, I saw striking similarities. Easily, they could have been sisters, or even mother and daughter. They both had blue eyes, pale, flawless skin, high cheekbones, dark hair, and tall, slender bodies. They were lovely, especially tonight, even in the glitter of Wanda's rhinestones.

Major Danny was asking, "Wanda, are those real diamonds in that thing in your hair?"

"Yes," Wanda said, smiling. "Matthew gave me the barrette for my birthday."

Turning to me, he asked, "Where did you get the money?"

Quickly, my mother said, "I think we should go in the library and have cocktails."

"Good idea," he said, taking Wanda's hand. Then, after we were seated, he asked, "Anne, did you give him the money for that diamond thing Wanda's got on?"

She just smiled at him, then at Wanda and me.

"So," he said, smiling like a canary that had just eaten a cat. "You did give him the money."

Suzette came in and asked what we'd like to drink.

"Bring us a batch of martinis," Major Danny said. "And make 'em dry." Then, turning to Wanda and me on the couch, he said, "You like martinis, right?"

"That would be fine," Wanda said. "How about you, Matthew?"

"Okay," I said, thinking that I could use a whole pitcher right about now.

Looking at Wanda, my mother said, "I suppose Matthew has told you that his birthday is coming soon."

Guffawing, Major Danny said, "And we all know what you're gonna give him—right, Wanda?"

Just as I was thinking I'd like to wipe the slimy smile off his face with my fist, Suzette came in and told us dinner was ready.

"Dinner?" Major Danny yelled. "For Christ sake, I haven't even finished one martini." Then, after gulping down what was in his glass, he said, "Goddamnit, I'm gonna have another one."

Putting her fingers to her throat and wincing, my mother said, "Please, Daniel—your language."

"Shit on my language!" he yelled. Then, after grabbing his chest, doubling up and straightening up again, he said meekly, "Well, maybe we should have a bite to eat."

We proceeded to the dining room and sat at the large, ornate table loaded with fine porcelain, silver and seductive food. He ate like a pig, as did Wanda. My mother ate little, as always, and so did I, being anxious that Wanda might say something about us getting married. After the meal, we returned to the library for coffee and Wanda, even before the coffee was served, fell asleep in one of the big armchairs. She seemed to be asleep, that is, but knowing that she always puts her fanny up before sleeping, I was suspicious. In any event, she was slumped in the big chair, sucking in air and blowing it out, and making whistling, snoring sounds. I was pretty sure now she was faking, but I could only guess as to why she was doing all that sleep-faking. I thought maybe she wanted to know what my mother and Major Danny would say about her, if they thought she was sleeping.

With surprising warmth, Major Danny was saying, "Look at Wanda—sleepin' her ass off. Nice lookin' young woman. If I had a daughter, I'd want her to look just like her. Too bad we never had a daughter or any kind of a child, Anne—not that Matthew here ain't like my own flesh and blood—you know what I mean."

"God's will," my mother said softly.

"I guess you're right, Anne."

Looking at Wanda, my mother said, "Poor dear is exhausted."

"I know how she feels," he said. "I get like that a lot doin' my duty for this town. And I know you must be exhausted, Anne, 'cause you attend all those functions with me. Maybe we should take a little vacation and go to Florida this winter."

Witnessing the warmth between them, and forgetting for a moment Major Danny's dark side, and forgetting that Wanda was sleep-faking, I got really nuts and said, "I love Wanda and I want to marry her."

My mother left the room in tears.

Major Danny, returning to his rotten self, said, "So, you're gonna marry that sleepin' beauty. You can't be serious. You'd mess up your whole life. I know who this one is—she's a thief and a tramp."

Angry and confused, I said, "You just said that you'd like to have a daughter like her and now you're condemning her."

"I said, I'd like to have a daughter who looks like her. Christ, you're messin' up the whole goddamn works by bringin' her here. Next, you'll be tellin' your mother about Nancy and me."

"You rotten barbarian!"

"Tell me you're not gonna marry that weirdo slut!"

"She's a beautiful person and we're getting married as soon as possible."

"Person?" he yelled, coughing. "She's no person. She's a goddamn gold-digging machine, just like Nancy."

Returning, my mother said, "The weather is very bad. I do not want Wanda driving in such weather. She'll stay here tonight in a guest room."

"Over my dead body!" he said, getting up. "I won't have it."

"Oh, yes, you will have it!" my mother said. Then, after he'd left the room, she turned to me and said, "When she awakes, show her to the room at the top of the stairs and don't take no for an answer."

When she left the room, I saw Wanda's eyes open. "Were you sleeping or what?" I asked, in a bad mood.

"You jerk!" she said, snarling the words out of her mouth.

"Why do you call me a jerk?" I asked, smiling inappropriately, seeing she was also in a bad mood. And in that moment, I somehow realized that smiling that way was becoming the worst part of my mental dysfunction. Perhaps it was some kind of involuntary, defensive reaction that made me smile inappropriately, but I did it often now, especially when someone was in the same mood I was in. I felt threatened in a paranoiac way when someone was in the same mood I was in. It had first happened, I knew, that evening at the statue, when Wanda had asked for the money and I had smiled inappropriately and said I didn't know what she was talking about. She'd been in a good mood before that, and I'd been in a bad one. Then, after her mood changed for the worse, I felt threatened and the involuntary, defensive reaction changed my mood to good, making me laugh along with the man in the moon and think that it would be one crazy world if everybody was in a good mood and laughing all the time.

"What're you thinking about now?" she was asking. "Some more ways that I can be humiliated in? I knew you'd wreck it for me. You told them about us getting married."

"Isn't that what you wanted, for us to get married?"

"We agreed not to tell them tonight. Goddamn you!"

"I'm sorry. By the way, my mother wants you to stay here tonight. The weather's bad."

"I heard her. In fact, I heard everything—every stupid, goddamn thing!"

The next morning I looked in on her and saw her staring at the ceiling with a bitter look on her face. When I asked her if she was going down to breakfast, she didn't answer. I went down to the kitchen, where we took breakfast when the cook was off and my mother did the cooking. Seeing Major Danny there, I wished I'd left the house and took Wanda with me. And I still would have, if I didn't want to know how my mother felt about us getting married. And I soon found out.

Without saying good morning, she shoved a cup of coffee in front of me and busied herself at the stove. Then, apparently having a change of heart, she said good morning, but toned it with something that told me of her disappointment and pain. Then, turning to Major Danny, she said crossly, "Put that newspaper down. Your breakfast is ready." Then, when he didn't put the newspaper down, she put the food in front of him, a breakfast of bacon and eggs, homefries, chocolate éclairs, coffee.

Putting his newspaper down, he began to wolf down the food, making a lot of little sounds of pleasure as he did, such as, "Mmmmm, y-mmm, y-mmm."

Watching him, I firmly believed he was trying to eat himself to death and that my mother was in on it.

"Tell me why, Matthew," my mother said.

Seeing that she was using French, something she didn't do when Major Danny was present, I asked, "Why what?"

Wiping beads of perspiration from her upper lip, she asked, "Why are you getting married?"

I answered in French, saying, "I love her, Mama."

With his mouth full, Major Danny said, "Goddamnit, speak English! Don't be so rude!"

Smiling, as if she were glad he was irritated, she said in English, "Daniel, would you like more to eat—how about some nice pork sausages?"

"No," he said. "I can't hardly finish what I've got. Besides, you know what the doctor said."

I kept my eyes on the door, expecting Wanda.

My mother was asking, "Matthew, what does Wanda's father do for a living?"

"He's dead," I said, keeping my eyes on the door.

Chuckling, Major Danny said, "Well, bein' dead is a helluva lot better'n being' on welfare. So, what he die of—syph'lis?"

Angry, I said, "He died fighting for his country. He was a hero, just like my father. A real hero, not a phony one like you!"

"Don't call me a phony—you fuckin' beanpole!"

Interrupting, my mother said, "It doesn't matter now, if her father was a hero, or not. Why argue about it?"

Red in the face and coughing, he said, "Well, hero or not, my son's not gonna marry his slut of a daughter—a gold-digger, to boot!"

Losing it with anger, I yelled: "I'm not your son, you evil, stupid man! Can't you get it through your fat head that I'm not your son!"

"Well," he yelled, snarling and coughing, "I'm tickled to death you ain't my son! And I'm happy—yes, happy—you two assholes are gettin' married, 'cause you deserve each other!"

Looking at me, my mother said, "Marrying now would impede your progress, my dear."

Still angry, I asked, "Progress? Is that what it's all about—progress?"

"No, no," she said quickly. "Please don't misunderstand me."

Still coughing, he yelled, "You bet your ass that's what it's all about—progress, blood, sweat and tears and money! That's what makes the world go 'round!"

"Daniel, please take your medicine."

"Fuck the medicine! Well, I'll say one thing for that whore—at least she knows what's important in life—money! But you, asshole, ain't nothin' but a good-for-nothin' sissy!"

Crying now, my mother said, "My son's not a sissy and he's not a good-for-nothing. He already had a book published, and ..."

"You call that squirrely little book a book? I wouldn' be able to wipe my ass with it, even if I wanted to. It's nothin' but heresy against war—goddamn sissy stuff! For Christ's sake, Anne, let 'im be a man!"

"A priest is a man. Now that he's finished his undergraduate work, I want him to be a Jesuit."

"A Jesuit?" I asked, smiling inappropriately. "That's news to me. When did you decide I should be a Jesuit?"

"It's a secret wish of mine. I've had it for a long time, Matthew."

"Well, okay," Major Danny said. "Let 'im be a priest. I guess that's better'n nothin'. Come to think of it, some priests are okay guys and invest on the side and make tons of money, just like the Vatican does. And come to think of it, again, I once knew a chaplain in the army who screwed more women than three battalions. But, sorry to say, I get the feelin' that Matthew here won't amount to a small pile of dogshit, no matter what he does! All he wants to do is paint those stupid pictures and write those stupid poems, and finger his guitar and piano—and that's not all he's fingerin', considerin' that slut he's got. I'm sick and tired of it. I can't take it, Anne. God knows, I tried to make a go of it with you two, but all I ever got was resistance. Resistance! This is my house! I'm orderin' you and your sissy son to get the hell out of it! Go on—get out!" Then, as he began to fight for breath and grab his neck, he said, "Anne, please call someone. I'm havin' another attack."

Just before he fell, I grabbed him and laid him on the floor, saying, "Try to relax, Major Danny."

With tears rolling down his cheeks, he looked at me and whispered, "Where's your mother?"

"She's calling an ambulance," I said, trying to put his knees up but not succeeding because they were too heavy. Then, with my emotions gone wild, I started to cry.

Putting his hand on my arm, he said, "You're a good man. I'm sorry it didn't work out." Then, just before he passed out, he said, "You may not believe me, but I love you and your mother."

The ambulance came and took him away. I went up to Wanda and told her Major Danny had another heart attack and was taken to the hospital. She was dressed and sitting on the edge of the bed with no expression on her face.

"I know all about it," she said, getting up and going down to the car.

Going with her and opening the car door for her, I asked, "Are you okay enough to drive?"

Getting in, she said, "I'm fine. I'm not a wimp, like you!"

"I'll go with you, okay?"

"Suit yourself."

And in the next moment, we were on the slippery road, with Wanda speeding recklessly. "Take it easy," I said.

"Shut up, you nothing!" she screamed. "Major Danny was right—you're nothing but a nothing!"

Seeing her face all twisted with what I guessed was hatred, I asked, "How much did you hear?"

With the road coming up too fast and wet, she yelled: "I heard every goddamn word, last night and this morning... every cruel, violent, hypocritical, greedy, goddamn word! And I agree with the fat-ass mayor—it is all about money!"

Her eyes were no longer fresh and moist and blue. They had changed to dry rockets of hate, zeroed in on me now, when I said, "Yes, it is all about money."

"You wrecked it for me, Frenchy—my chance to be somebody!"

"I'm sorry," I said, seeing a hateful, slimy smile grease her lips. Then, as the car slipped and swerved, her rocket-eyes detonated and hit me with hate, and hate ran all over me, weakening me to the point where I didn't want to live any more, and I whispered, "Wanda, I can't live without you."

"Tough shit!" she yelled.

We were on the main highway now, and it was dark and foggy, so apropos for a miserable morning of hate, and I accepted it just as I accepted what I believed she was trying to do—kill us. Casually, I began to welcome death, and after her defilement of my love marked my heart with a dye, the color of pus, my mood had been completely changed by the involuntary, defensive reaction. Sitting back in my seat, I looked over at the anger and hate on her face and began to laugh, inappropriately, of course.

"What the hell are you laughing at?" she yelled.

"I don't know," I said. "But I feel great."

"Well," she said, swerving the car on purpose. "I'll give you something to really laugh about!"

"Wanda, I can't live without you," I said, laughing my ass off, still feeling good, waiting calmly for the end that had already begun. Then, after the car hit a tree, I felt her hot blood splatter all over me.

## chapter 6

I HAD nightmares in the hospital. The first one was about my wading in the shallows of the Dark River where Wanda and I had gone fishing. Around my neck was the end of the blue ribbon she'd worn around the waist of her long, white dress, and the ribbon was tied in a bowknot. I felt like a French poodle, with a grin of confusion. Words of love and hate were assembling in my head, but I couldn't understand or express them. Just as I saw my mother on the shore, she jerked the leash-ribbon. I obeyed and let myself be pulled towards her, and now I saw that she was wearing Wanda's white dress. When I was near, she smiled and asked, "Matthew, do you really love me?" Desperately, I tried to say I loved her, but the words wouldn't come out. In despair, I cried bitter tears, but they too remained locked inside me. Finally, my mother quit pulling and just stared at me, as I stood there in the shallow water staring at her. Finally, she said, "I can see that you are filled with pain and tears. I order you to turn yourself inside out and talk about yourself. My dear, it's my solemn duty as a mother to interfere in your life and save you; and it's my duty to make amends for my sins, by offering to God and the Jesuits the life of my only begotten son."

I wanted to tell her that she'd promised not to interfere in my life, but the words wouldn't come out. Then, suddenly, she vanished, and I closed my eyes and started to grind my teeth in the pain of loneliness for her. After an eternity of grinding with loneliness, I opened my eyes and saw Wanda. She was sitting in all her naked glory on the shore where my mother had been sitting. With no expression on her face, she picked up the ribbon-leash, that looked more like an umbilical cord now—and led me to the place by the Dark River where she'd acted so weird and demanding. Then, just as we had done that morning, we laid naked on the quilt of many colors. Soon however, there was a sudden, blinding flash, and afterwards, I could see her standing above me with her long legs spread apart and her hands on her hips. Looking up and thinking it to be a symmetrical and very intimate moment, I stared, and stared, until I reached up and, gently taking her hand, guided her down to rest beside me again. Blue-grey wisps of fog blended with the red and gold of sunset. As I kissed her lips, a gentle breeze carried the smell of pine and the flute music of Mozart's "Tempo di Minueto" and Wanda's voice, as she asked, "Matthew, do you really and truly love me?" Then, just as I was about to say yes, the gravity of the sun's disappearance changed my mind. Cold and miserable for me now, I looked up at the stars and begged them to fall on me. Finally, I said, "No, Wanda, I don't love you." And in the next moment we were at her house, where she, in her white dress and blue ribbon, sat alone at her kitchen table drinking whiskey from one of my mother's fine, crystal glasses. I stood by the door with a large knife in my hand. The knife looked like the hunting knife with which Maurice Martineau had threatened my mother that night he was killed. Looking at me with a nice smile, Wanda toasted me with the glass held high; then, after downing the whiskey, she beckoned with the empty glass for me to come to her. Gripping the knife hard, I started towards her but stopped suddenly and said, "I'm not going to kill you, if that's what you want. I'm not going to ruin my life over the likes of you—you slutty gold-digger!" "Kill me!" she said. "I won't take no for an answer." And then suddenly brilliant flashes of lightning came through the windows and illuminated her dress and the smile I loved so much. My head imploded in agony, and all the sounds I'd ever heard deafened me, all the things I'd ever seen blinded me, and all the courage I'd prayed for came to help me turn the knife on myself, so that with one quick thrust I'd be able to end it all. Then, as I held the point of the blade to my chest, Wanda rushed to me and stopped my hand, thus saving me from myself. And I was weeping on her shoulder now, and she whispered, "You'd rather take your own life than mine. Now I know that you really and truly love me...."

Late in the afternoon on the day of the accident, I awoke from my nightmare world to the hospital world. I was dizzy and had a large bandage on my head. My mother was there. She told me that Major Danny was dead. "I could have been a better wife to him," she said, without tears.

"In his own way, he loved us," I said. "He told me he loved us, just before he passed out."

"I suppose he did love us, but he loved power and money more."

"It seemed that way."

"In case you're worried, your friend Wanda is all right, except for some cuts and bruises. Her mother came and took her to Bad Axe. Matthew, I don't want to interfere in your life, but I think God wants you to become a Jesuit priest."

Closing my eyes, I said, "Please, not now, if ever."

"I understand, dear. Rest now. I must go and make arrangements for the funeral." Then, after kissing the bandage on my head, she said, "I shall return soon. I have some important things to say."

After she'd gone, a doctor came, examined me, and told me I'd be there for awhile. The idea of being in the hospital during the funeral didn't rupture my mind. It meant I wouldn't have to listen to a lot of eulogistic bullshit and maybe pass out. Not that I was completely adverse to attending the funeral—it was just that I didn't want to pass out and steal the show from Major Danny. That was my thinking, just before a lady in a striped uniform came and gave me fresh water and a crooked straw. When she was gone, a nurse came and stuck me with a needle, saying, "Now relax your butt, and you won't feel a thing. This is just a little something to make you sleep."

I fell asleep and had another nightmare. I was in my bedroom at home, with Wanda standing at the foot of my bed. In a kind of kaleidoscope of many different shapes and colors, she was snarling at me and, as her lips and torso twisted every which way with what I guessed was hate and aggression, she said, "La Fleur, I'm hot for your money and body." Then, as she ran her hands over my nude body, she said, "I'll take your body, first."

Pulling the quilt of many colors over me, I screamed: "Get the hell away from me, or I'll call the police! Get out—go!"

She went but didn't go far. With lips sidewinding like rattlesnakes, she took one step back and said, "That's no way to treat a lady. Okay, take one last look at me, lovebug, and see what you'll be missing."

I didn't want to look but did. Everything about her naked, gyrating body was repulsive to me as I yelled: "Stay out of my life, you trollop!"

She began to expand and contract like an accordion, and violent gusts of whiskey-stinking air attacked me. Dizzy and almost overcome, I nevertheless kept my eyes on her now, just in case she might resort to physical violence. As moonlight was filtered in through lace curtains and ran all over her as she massaged herself in front of a full-length mirror, I thought that she must have been in heaven once, before God threw her ass out on the street. And now, I could see her red, hating eyes protruding from her skull, as she seemed to be looking for something. That was when I blurted out: "Hey, Wanda, you've got some white frosting on the ass of your skirt, and it's shaped like a horseshoe!"

Losing her temper, she jumped up on the bed, sat on my chest, pinned my arms down and bit my neck, saying, "Mmmm!"

I was terrified. I firmly believed that I'd be turning into a vampire any second. Pushing Wanda off me, I got down and knelt by the side of the bed. I prayed I wouldn't become a vampire, but in my heart, I knew it was too late, that I'd already become one. Then, with huge tears of hopelessness, I begged God to forgive me for all the sinful things I'd done with Wanda, the gold-sucking vampire. Weeping and gnashing my teeth, as the sun crawled across the floor and threatened to burn me alive, I was aware of the prayer-beads of sweat popping out of my body. Then, a foul wind caused the curtains to rant and rave at me, and I screamed: "Unbearable!"

I awoke to the beauty of Elsie Quinn, of the sandtrap. She was sitting in a chair by my bed, asking, "What's so unbearable, Matty?"

"I was dreaming," I said, feeling the sweat on my body go cold. "Nice to see you, Elsie."

"Do you feel any better, Matty?" she asked, smiling with her perfect teeth.

"Yes, I do. I feel all right."

Serious now, she said, "I wish I did."

"What's the matter, Elsie?"

"Oh, Matty, you've got your own troubles. I'm not about to tell you my tragedy."

"Tragedy?"

"Well, maybe I will tell you. Maybe if you hear my troubles, you'll feel even better, being grateful it didn't happen to you. Do you think you'd feel better if I told you?"

"Tell me and we'll see, Elsie."

"Well, Matty, since you were at my house and we jammed on our guitars, lots has happened." Then, after drinking some of my water through the crooked straw, and after brushing several drops of water from her white blouse, she returned to her chair, asking, "Sure you're up to hearing about it?"

Seeing she wore no makeup and that her long, blonde hair was a shade darker, I said, "What happened? Get it out."

"Maybe I better not."

"For God's sake, Elsie—get it out!"

"Well, if it'll make you feel better by being grateful you're alive, I'll talk about it."

"Go ahead, make me feel better."

Taking my hand, as if to steady me from the shock, she said, "My parents were killed in a car accident two weeks ago. They were on their way to Tawas to get me some stuff for me to take back to college. This fall I was finally going to graduate school. I would've gone last fall, but I wanted to stick around and help out with the money at home. Whenever I can, I work over at the hospital as an aide. My dad got laid off from bricklaying, because of the recession. But then he got a job scraping and painting boats at the marina and things looked good, so I was going back to school, on a scholarship, without room and board and clothes, of course."

Seeing her cry and wipe tears away with the backs of her hands, I said, "I'm sorry, Elsie. Does this mean you're all alone—you've got a brother, don't you?"

Composed again, she said, "Alf was home for the funeral—Alfred's his real name. He's in the Marines, and he had to go back to California right afterwards."

"Will you be going back to Michigan State?"

"My music teacher wants me to, but I don't think I'll go anywhere—at least not this fall."

"What's your music teacher's name?"

"Mr. Osborne. He lives in Detroit. Do you know him?"

"No. Elsie. Do you mean you've been going all the way to Detroit for your lessons?"

Laughing, she squeezed my hand and said, "I've been going to him for years, Matty. When you want something, you'll sacrifice your ass off."

"Sacrifice...."

"You got it, Matty."

After another suck of water, I said, "It's not easy being without your parents, is it?"

"No it's not. One day they're here, and the next day they're not. God, I'll never forget when I got the phone call, telling me they were dead. I got crazy and wanted to kill myself. I was going to call Chief Morely up and tell him there was a robbery going on at the house. Then, when he came speeding in the driveway, I was going to throw myself under his wheels. Can you imagine my pulling off something like that, Matty?"

"No, Elsie, I can't."

"Well, I would've, if I didn't drink some whiskey and pass out for awhile. And then when I woke up, I had to go look at my dead parents. The troopers came and got me. And that's not all. After my parents were in the ground and Alf went back to camp, I didn't give a damn about anything, except booze. I started swilling it down, like I was an alcoholic fish. How do you like that, Matty?"

"That's not like you—drinking so much, and all."

"Well, I did. That's the way it was. I was like one of those gargoyles in a fancy fountain, where water's always running through it—only it wasn't water running through me. Know what I mean, Matty?"

"I know what you mean."

"Matty, did you ever feel like you're being sucked under a pile of shit and can't escape?"

"All the time."

"I don't understand it. It's been that way all my life. I've never been really happy—but I'll tell you this, Matty: I'd be happy for the rest of my life, if we could be together and talk, like we're doing now."

"It's been a nice visit, hasn't it?"

Crying again and drying her eyes with a tissue this time, she said, "After they died and were buried, and I was drinking too much, I went to a shrink."

"A therapist?"

"That's right. I only went to him once, because he almost drove me completely nuts. I'd tell him something, and he'd ask how I felt about it. 'How do you feel about it?' he'd ask. He must've asked that a thousand times. And then he'd get behind me and talk, and I got nervous because I couldn't see his face. Then he prescribed some pills, and I took them. They smoothed out my brain so much, I was like a zombie. Believe it, Matty, I couldn't think. Then, after I quit taking them and was able to think again, it was like a steel plow plowing up my brain. Then, for awhile, whenever I began to think, I'd fall asleep. Thank God I'm normal now."

"I'm glad, Elsie," I said, not patronizing her.

"Hey, Matty, when are you getting out of here?"

"Maybe next week."

"Well, if you feel up to it, maybe we can jam again at my house."

"That would be nice. We'll see," I said, studying her and liking her but not without a little envy. I wished I could be more like her. I liked the way she kept her inside, outside, and I wished I could do that. And I liked her easy smile, her gentle blue eyes and her beaming face.

"How were your grades at school, Matty?"

"Pretty good."

"Know what? I got all A's all the way through high school and college, but you'd never know it, would you?"

"I know enough to know that you're very talented and intelligent," I said, guessing that she'd brought up her accomplishments and, because of her extremely difficult situation, was having trouble hanging onto herself.

"Thanks, Matty," she said with tears welling in her eyes again. "That's the first time somebody told me I was talented and intelligent. What do you think of that?"

"Didn't your music teacher ever tell you that you were talented and intelligent—or your teachers at school?"

"They just said I was talented. Well, guess I better be going." Then, smiling again, she asked, "Do you feel any better now, after hearing my tragedy?"

"Yes, I do," I said honestly. "It made me feel good that you think enough of me, to confide in me."

"Well, guess I better get my ass out of here," she said, kissing my cheek. "I see the nurse's coming."

Elsie left, and the nurse came in and stuck me with another needle, saying with a smile, "Time for a little nap."

"Are all these needles necessary?" I asked.

"You want to get better, don't you?" she asked, leaving the room before I could answer.

I fell asleep and had another nightmare. With wings tipped with blood, a squadron of white butterflies were swooping down on me, touching and hurting me, and making me burn. In burning pain now, I believed God had let the sun out too far and had sent the butterflies to torment me and make me burn for my sins. Then, in a quick moment of ease, in which I felt no pain, I thought God had changed His mind and was now showing mercy by giving me the power of flight. Knowing that I was able to fly like a bird, I took off for the nearest cooling and saving river, the Dark River, the very river I'd been so afraid of in the past.

Coming to rest on top of a towering bridge above the water, I looked down through the darkness and saw small, dim, yellow lights dancing on the water and smiling up at me. Then, suddenly, a heavy gust of wind changed it, and a whirlwind of putrid air began to rise and torment me, making me feel once again that God had turned against me. Hopeless now, I began to chant: "World, world, go away, and don't come back another day." Then, after I'd chanted those words maybe a hundred times, I looked up at the starlit sky, stretched out my arms, and through wellsprings of burning tears, begged God to remove all the veils of space and time for me, and my terrible loneliness.

Nothing was removed. However, as the moon receives a reflection of the sun, I received a faint reflection of God's love, which was as murky and deranged as my love for myself. Nothing had changed, it seemed. Feeling disillusioned, unloved and unloving, I looked down at the yellow lights and saw that they were dancing again, this time doing some sort of skip-hop folk dance. Choosing what seemed to be the deepest part, and for which I had the greatest fear, I jumped, and as soon as I was under, I abandoned myself.

Dead now, stretched out in a coffin, I had a smile of satisfaction on my face. For one thing, I'd made the ugliest coffin possible, using old cardboard boxes of the poorest quality and stinking of dead rats; and second, I'd finally succeeded in killing myself. So there I was, with a perpetual smile on my face, laid out in my old army jacket and dirty khakis and with my bare feet covered with an overlay of dead leaves. I slowly looked around the room, which looked like the library at home, and with my arms folded neatly on my chest, I saw my mother, Major Danny, Morely and Wanda. They were weeping and beating mea culpas on their chest. It was my mother who spoke first, saying in soft, exquisite French, "Matthew, my dear son, it was love at first sight when you were born, and now it's love at last sight, until I see you in heaven, if I get there. Matthew, do me a favor and tell God I'm sorry I didn't succeed in making you a Jesuit, in order to make amends for my sins. Oh, my dear, dear son, have we looked in each other's eyes for the last time?"

"Well," Major Danny said, looking as if his fatal heart attack did him some good, "I see good-for-nothin' Matthew has finally achieved somethin' in buildin' that cardboard coffin—even if he did do a piss-poor job of it."

"I agree, brother," Morely said, scratching his crotch. "It is a piss-poor job. I wonder if he stole the cardboard."

I began to hear music, and I knew intuitively that it was Elsie in the Music Room playing the piano, with her fingers, like feathers, running over the keys and playing Mendelssohn's *molto sostenuto* with simplicity and élan. Then, when she'd finished, she came into the library and, looking at Major Danny and Morely, said, "Listen, you creeps, don't say Matthew's workmanship is piss-poor. It's of the highest quality, just like he is!"

Wanda, who was over by the French doors, looked at me and, with all of her strength and beauty, and wearing her white dress and blue ribbon, came to climb into the casket with me, and as we lay side by side, soft fingers of fog came in and carried us out into a new and spectacular sunrise. Then, as Elsie played passages from Mendelssohn's *The First Walpurgis Night*, when all of the witches and devils hold a great festival, Wanda said that I smelt like a dead rat and pushed me out of the coffin. And now I was falling, and yelling, "Help, help, help!"

"Matthew, Matthew," my mother was saying, when I awoke. Then, after giving me water, by way of the crooked straw, she said, "Dear, you were having one of your terrible nightmares."

"I'm sorry," I said, feeling saturated with cold sweat. "I didn't know you were here."

"Of course you didn't," she said, sitting near my bed and smiling. Then, smiling even more, she said, "I've got good news. Do you remember my speaking of a Richard Fowler, the Englishman who fought and worked side by side with your father in the Resistance?"

"Vaguely."

"He was present when your father was killed. Well, I've spoken with a private detective, who says he would be able to find him. Mr. Fowler can tell me what happened that night. He was a witness. He can tell us who killed your father. I must have closure."

"There's no such thing as closure."

"Well, maybe not, but I do want to know what really happened. I feel I must."

"How is Morely taking Major Danny's death?" I asked, but with my mind still on my mother. I was worried about her. I wished she'd move on with her life. I didn't like her not letting go of the past.

"Morely's upset, but I don't think it's over Daniel's death. He's upset because Daniel left me seven million dollars and all he left Morely was a new shotgun—just like his father did—but this time, there was a box of shells for him to blow his brains out. That's a terrible thing Daniel did to his brother, isn't it?"

"Yes, it is," I said, watching her take a laced handkerchief from her purse and dab the tears from her eyes.

Stiffening all of a sudden and growing pale, she said, "After what I did, I have no right to condemn."

"What is it, Mama?"

After blowing her nose hard, she looked at me and said, "Of all people, I've had the unmitigated gall and arrogance to play with the truth."

"What is it, Mama?" I repeated.

As if imprisoned in another world and talking to herself, she said softly, "It was so unlike me. In my youth, I was filled with courage and truth. At the University of Bordeaux, I spoke passionately of human souls being saturated with the deadly doctrines of the Nazi monsters of war. In an Underground newspaper, I warned people that they could be destroyed if they fed upon the Nazi's false ideals and the poisonous slogans and symbols that go with them. And those innocent, hungry souls who did feed upon such things, lost their innocence, and were hungrier than before…"

"Why are you talking like this, Mama?" I asked, alarmed at her grave state of mind.

Apparently aware of me now, she looked at me and said, "You'll see. Hear me out."

"Yes, of course," I said, my head beginning to throb with pain again.

"And now I must speak of something I should have confessed a long time ago," she said, composed and even smiling a little. "Matthew, I won't try to justify my actions, but in the way of explanation, let me tell you what's been inside me all my life. It's like a dark river, mysterious and intense, and defying all control at times. When it's intense, I can see no beauty in life. There's no hope inside me, it seems. No renewal or growth in my life. It's maddening. You don't understand—how could you?"

I understood but said nothing.

With her voice soft and low, she said, "Now I must tell you about Daniel and me. Now, more than ever, I must. Daniel's death has made me feel very mortal, but in case you wonder how you would have found out, if I died before Daniel, let me say that shortly after coming to America, I gave a sealed letter to my lawyer, Mr. Klingen, to be opened only by you, after my death."

Heartsick and confused, I said, "Don't talk like this!"

She went ahead and told me how Major Danny had arrived in Bordeaux in the spring of 1951 and began his investigations for the CID. Drugs were coming in by ship, she said, and were being sold to, and sold by, American soldiers in Bordeaux and Landes de Bussac. She went on to say that Major Danny usually wore civilian clothes and lived in a hotel near the University of Bordeaux. "His hotel was also close to the arena," she said, "where the ice show from America performed. We were there one evening, and Daniel sat behind us. Do you remember, Matthew?"

"Yes, and he kept making stupid jokes in broken French—badly broken!"

Serious, she said, "But I enjoyed the jokes. The laughter was good for me. I began to feel that I might be happy and beautiful again. But after, when you said you hadn't enjoyed yourself because you missed your father, I felt bad again. You did that all the time. Whenever you saw me getting on with my life and enjoying myself, you'd mention your father, as if you wanted to keep me in mourning."

"I'm sorry, Mama," I said, knowing there was truth to what she'd just said.

Holding up her hand, she said, "Don't speak, not while I still have the courage to tell you everything. Yes, after the ice show, Daniel invited us for a supper, but I declined, saying we had to get up for Sunday Mass the next morning. Then, when you were at a store window and looking at a doll—the same doll I bought for you a few days later—Daniel invited me for lunch on Monday. So, I defied you and accepted the invitation—not thinking of Maurice.

"I met Daniel on Monday in front of his hotel, but only to tell him about Maurice, who was out of town again. Because the stores were closed for lunch until two o'clock, many people were on the streets. I didn't want Maurice's friends to see us, so I asked Daniel if we could get off the street. He suggested nearby Café Orleans, but knowing that many of Maurice's friends went there, I said no. That was when he suggested we go somewhere in the French automobile he had at his disposal.

"It was a warm, spring day. He drove to a small restaurant in the country. During our omelets, he spoke of his mansion in Point Stevens, Michigan. He said he wasn't married, and I told him that my husband had been killed during the war. But I didn't mention Maurice. I just couldn't bring myself to do it. Oh, Matthew, I was so impressed with his warm and kindly attitude.

"We spoke of little things, then, until he said that he'd inherited enormous wealth from his father, who had been a brain surgeon before he died of heart failure, just as his mother had. He had tears in his eyes, and I felt great compassion for him. I began to compare him with Maurice. Daniel was good and decent and well-mannered, I told myself. Maurice was hard as stone and a drunk. Daniel was sincere and honest. Maurice was a liar and a thief, and a drug smuggler, among other illegal activities, and he was violent. He'd boasted many times about killing people, even policemen. It wasn't surprising that his life was only an extension of his life in the Resistance, when he'd go on raids and kill people. More than a few times after telling me of his violent activities, he'd say it was just like the good old days during the war. Then he'd laugh like a maniac.

"Days went by, and Daniel asked me to marry him. That's when I told him about Maurice, and I said it was over between Maurice and me. I told Daniel I would marry him and that I'd tell Maurice when he returned. Daniel said he was happy I'd chosen him over Maurice. Then, the very next day, he asked me about Maurice's criminal activities. Daniel said he'd seen Maurice's name on a report in his office. When I asked him if he knew about Maurice before we met, he said no. I took him at his word, thinking he was honest and truthful, and that I was in love with him. Oh, Matthew, he seemed so good.

"Anyway, that same day, he asked if Maurice kept money hidden in our house. That made me very upset. I was filled with fear. I didn't want to go to prison and leave you alone, so I told him about the money underneath the floorboards in my bedroom. He asked me then why I'd gotten involved with such a man, and I told him that he didn't know what it was like being a European woman during, and after, the war. Then I said I hoped that American women would never have to go through what we did, especially if they have children.

"He told me not to say anything about the money. He said he was going to confiscate the money and keep it for your education. He said we have a right to the money, because it was stolen. I wanted to ask why we couldn't use some of his money, seeing he was wealthy, but I didn't, because I didn't think it proper to ask such a question. Oh, my dear son, in my heart I knew it was wrong, but the dark thing I told you about, prevented me from thinking of the consequences. Then, aside from that, there was you. Oh, Matthew, I wanted so much for you.

"Two days later, Maurice returned and said he knew about Daniel and me. He was drunk and out of his head, and again he boasted about killing people. He even showed me the knife he'd used to cut their throats. I ordered him to leave the house, but he refused. I told him he wasn't welcome in our lives. Then, after he called me bad names, he said he was the one who killed your father, so he could have me. I called him a killer, but in my heart, I didn't believe he'd killed your father. I believe Maurice had only said that, so he could get back at me for leaving him for Daniel.

"After more cognac, he fell asleep on the sofa in the living room. That was when I called Daniel and told him about Maurice being drunk and out of control. After I hung up the phone, Maurice came at me with the big knife, saying he'd just heard me talking with Daniel. His eyes were glazed with madness, and he said he was going to cut out my tongue. Just then, I saw you. You were peeking out from your bedroom. I didn't want him to harm you, so I ran out into the storm that had been raging, and Maurice ran after me.

"While Maurice chased me around his car, Daniel drove up, alone, and grabbed Maurice from behind. Because he was so drunk, he dropped the knife and didn't struggle very much. Daniel continued to hold Maurice around the neck, while he yelled at me, telling me to pick up the knife and stab Maurice. I refused, and then Daniel knocked Maurice unconscious and left him on the hood of the car. Then, taking my hand, he put the knife in it and forced it into Maurice. Several times, he held my hand with both of his and stabbed Maurice. I was paralyzed with fear and was too weak to stop him. Then when I saw Maurice's body, with his face in the mud, my mind left me completely.

"It was a dark moment for me, and I've relived it every day since. And I've come to believe that Maurice wouldn't have killed me, and that he didn't kill your father. But I don't know. Somehow, I must find the truth. I can't help feeling that I killed someone I'd loved for ill-begotten money. And I believe that, even if I didn't force the knife into Maurice's heart, I was still responsible for his death. I betrayed him, by leaving him for Daniel the way I did—behind his back, like a coward. And I know that Maurice never would have threatened me with a knife, if I hadn't called Daniel that night. And I know that I should have had nothing to do with Daniel, after he said we should keep the money. And, one more thing: I know I should have remained in France, for St. Joan of Arc puts a curse on a Frenchwoman who leaves France, for good.

"Oh, Matthew, I wanted so much for you, but regardless of what I wanted, I shouldn't have followed the criminal way. I should have told the authorities about Daniel, not married him and let him build a fortune. Why wasn't I able to be honest and truthful? Do you hate me, Matthew? I know you must. Tell me how you feel."

"Well, I don't feel like dancing," I said. Then, closing my eyes, I felt nothing but anger for her having defiled herself and my love for her. Opening my eyes, I looked out the window and watched the sun going down and evening coming on; and, as I watched, soft music began in my soul, and I was a child again at the rosebud of my mother's breast, while being soothed by a lullaby. Looking at the misery in my mother's eyes now, I felt a warm, spiritual milk inside me, making me realize my mother's love and respect for me. She had told me the truth, and for me, it was much more than a confession of a crime. It was a gift—a valuable lesson. She'd been true to herself, regardless of the possibility that I might hate her for what she'd done. And now, as the sun disappeared, I had only love and respect for her, and, in seeing my mother's soul, I'd found my own, which was also imperfect. Kissing her on the cheek, I said, "I love you, Mama. Now, if you'll permit me, I'd like to get some rest. It's been a busy day."

## chapter 7

I WAS home from the hospital, but I still felt the effects of the concussion. I'd been crazy before the accident, but now I was falling off the edge.

I thought I wanted to be a Jesuit priest, telling myself that becoming a priest would be best, for my mother, and for myself. Deep down in my heart, I told myself, the idea had always been there, but I just didn't want to look at it. So, after thinking I was not too old, I decided to go to the seminary, soon.

However, as days went by, the decision to become a Jesuit was like a curse I'd put on myself—the curse of being able to lie to oneself without a shred of knowledge that it's a lie, which of course, is insanity. In other words, I was well on the way to hell, not heaven, for insanity forever, is hell.

I began to lock myself in my room, saying to my mother and Suzette that I wanted to be alone and meditate. I used the word meditate often, as if it were a surgical knife to be used to cut away a cancerous world. My mother, after hearing of my decision, agreed that I needed isolation and meditation, in order to get on the road to salvation and perfection.

I got on the road all right, but, of course, I was headed in the wrong direction. This morning, for example, I was at my bedroom desk, staring out the window and trying to find enough inspiration to think about God and write a poem about Him. Meditating, so I thought, I kept fixing my eyes on God's creations in the backyard. I saw morning shadows give definition and character to the spacious lawn, arrogant weeds, old tree stumps. Going to my pencil and paper, I tried to write a poem about these things and how they related to God, but I failed. All I could think of was, that all that I saw, was God, and that if I put that down on paper, someone might see it and call me a pantheistic heretic.

A huge, yellow cat was out there now, crouched and ready to spring up at a sparrow that was perched on a low branch of a maple tree. I quickly opened a window and threw a book at the cat, chasing it, and the sparrow, away. Overcome with guilt for what I'd done, I cursed God for allowing me to do such a thing. Then, feeling guilty for having cursed God, I cursed myself. I was a mess, but I didn't think about doing anything about it, just as I didn't think about doing something about the physical mess around me.

Crumpled-up balls of paper were on the floor, along with broken pencils, clothes, and other things such as a half-eaten candy bar, with bugs on it. As to my personal hygiene, it wasn't close to being up to standard. My blue robe was stained from drippings of food and beverages, and my pajamas were stained and stinking of sweat and urine. No doubt about it, my life had a lot of slack. I didn't bathe or brush my teeth, and I didn't care if I ever did again. And, of course, I didn't play the piano or guitar and I didn't paint. The last time I'd had anything to do with music was when Elsie and I had played our guitars last summer and the last painting I'd done was a portrait of Wanda, which I'd completed just before the accident and was still in my room.

And now I didn't care if I ever wrote a poem about God. There was something more important to me: Grief. First, I told myself not to grieve over what happened with Wanda. Over and over again, I told myself not to grieve over breaking up with a traitor who wanted to sell herself for money, as a prostitute would. Repeatedly, I told myself not to grieve over losing her—that it wasn't my fault. Then, in trying to find a reason for her cruel and twisted actions, I came up with the idea that she'd behaved in such a way, just because I didn't return her two hundred dollars.

Deciding not to be a patsy any longer, I began to escape from guilt by focusing on grief, itself, and by trying to debase its dignity. As if I were the devil giving a lecture to mourners at a funeral home, I told myself that grief's nothing but a poison drug used by jerks. That only the ignorant and stupid grieve because they don't have anything better to do. You've got your future to think about! I said to myself. Then, as I saw the yellow cat return and stalk another bird, grief slipped back inside me again—this time, worse than before, because with it came the memory of the fishing trip and of Wanda's saving those "little fishies."

But I didn't give up. This time, in my fight against grief, I used red wine, and it worked just fine, until, that is, I saw Wanda's portrait, still on its easel in a far corner of the room. Going to it, I studied her smile and recalled how hard I'd worked on that smile and had finally gotten it just right, an easy, loving smile filled with warmth and love for me alone. Lighting a vigil candle now, I placed it in front of the painting. The candle was in a red vase and red began splashing her face. I imagined it was blood, and that it was now splashing on my face, in my eyes, inside me, poisoning my guts. It was unbearable. I was terror-stricken.

But again, I fought back. Picking up the half-empty wine bottle, I threw wine in her face, her eyes, her smile of love and, after I'd thrown the last drop, I slumped to the floor and tried to die. But, as luck would have it, my life went on without me, and I found myself whispering, "She was greedy, cruel, hypocritical and violent and not once did she say she loved me."

Sitting at my desk again, I began grieving now, just for the sake of grieving. Smiling inappropriately, I told myself that if you can't beat it, join it. Grief became a nipple of self-pity for me, and I sucked the poison with pleasure. Finally, however, I got the idea of sharing my grief—it just popped into my head, like a visitor from Bedlam. I wanted someone else with me, so I could exhibit my grief, as if it were a work of art, like a rich soufflé. Rushing to the phone, I called Elsie.

"How you feeling, Matty?" she asked, waiting by the door in an old sweatshirt, blue jeans and a big smile.

"Okay, Elsie," I said, thinking that she was more beautiful than ever. I was glad I came.

"Come sit and have a Coke," she said, already moving towards the kitchen. Then, returning, she handed me a Coke, sat down next to me on the sofa, and said, "I was surprised you called."

After a drink, I said, "So was I."

"Well, what have you been up to?"

Trying to adjust to her cheerfulness, I said, "Nothing, Elsie."

Looking me over, she asked, "Why is your hair so wet?"

Running my hand over my head, I said, "I just took a shower."

"Well, that's something you've been doing, isn't it?"

"Well, maybe I have been doing something, besides taking a shower."

Smiling, she asked, "And what might that be?"

Squirming and looking at my hands, I said, "I've been trying to write some poetry."

"What did you write?"

"That's just it, Elsie, I tried but couldn't get anything down. I guess I'm carrying too much grief."

Massaging my neck and shoulders, she said, "Tell me about it."

"I would have sold my soul for just one line of poetry."

"Why didn't you?" she asked, still massaging, going to my back now.

"Lucifer wasn't around."

"Damn! He's never around when you need him."

"Elsie, I feel warped, and that my soul is howling at the moon."

"Shee-it!"

"One minute I'm sucking at my bitter heart and in the next, I'm pissed off at Wanda for turning out to be such a shithead."

"That she is—a shithead."

"Elsie, I can't seem to do a damn thing. Wanda, I guess, took all my strength."

"That selfish bitch!"

"It's like she's dead and buried, and I keep digging her up."

"Exhumed people make me bleed."

"I've got to forget her."

"I'll help you, Matty. There's a nice sandtrap in my bedroom—remember the sandtrap?"

"How could I forget?"

"You rejected me," she said, finished with the massage and looking in my eyes. "I can't say I blame you, Matty—the way I threw myself at you. I probably scared you away."

Looking out the window at the bright, autumn day, I said, "It wasn't a good time for me, Elsie."

Moving closer, she took my hand and asked, "Will there ever be a good time, for us?"

Excited by her warmth and the sweet scent coming from her body, I blurted out: "I don't think I'd reject you again."

"You mean?"

"I'm ready for anything."

"Now you're talking, Matty," she said, pulling me to my feet. "And wait'n see—it'll be good for us, all peaches and cream."

And it was all peaches and cream and good. Then, however, as I lay looking at the ceiling, I got depressed. I couldn't help it. I couldn't help feeling selfish and guilty, because I'd had sex with her without a shred of love for her. Then, trying to think tough, I told myself that I only had to like her and respect her, not love her. But it didn't work. Anxious and ashamed, I got out of bed, put my pants on, and went over by the window. Looking at the falling leaves, I told myself that I didn't want to get involved again.

"What's the matter?" she asked.

Not turning around, I said, "I'm sorry, Elsie. I'm sorry I took advantage of you."

"Sorry? What the living hell you got to be sorry about? Are you sorry you nailed me? Well, Matty, for your information, I wanted it—bad!"

Naked, she came to stand behind me but didn't touch me. Seeing her reflection in the window, I saw her brush tears from her eyes with the palms of her hands. As I turned around, I closed my eyes. I didn't want to see her blue eyes crying in pain. I didn't want to see her naked body, all peaches and cream and tears. "I'm sorry, Elsie," I said again, opening my eyes but not looking directly at her.

Hiding her face in the crook of her arm, she rushed back to bed. Pulling up the sheet over her, she said, "Get back in bed, please."

I sat on the edge of the bed and put on my shoes, saying, "I thought I could get involved, but I can't. I don't want to get hurt again, but most of all, I don't want to hurt you."

"I love you," she said, resting her head on my leg. "I'd never, ever hurt you, Matty. I've been crazy about you, since the first time I saw you—when you fell off your bicycle in front of the mayor's statute, a long time ago. I just want you to know that."

I looked at her and, for the first time, I felt something that was much more than a feeling of friendship. It was something I'd never felt for a woman, and it made me feel warm and clean and good. I was terrified. Then, as fog rolled into fog inside my head, I said, "Before I came here, I was thinking of becoming a Jesuit."

"A priest?"

"Yes."

Pulling my head down and staring in my eyes, she whispered, "Is that what you're going to do?"

Hiding my face in my hands and weeping, I said, through mucus and tears, "Elsie, I'm only in my twenties, but my life is all bullshit."

Taking my hands away, she kissed me on the cheek and said, "I know how it is, Matty. It's not easy for you." Then, after putting on an old, frayed, pink robe, she took my hand and led me out into the evening and sat me down on steps of her back porch. Sitting down next to me, she said, "Relax and breathe in some fresh air. Enjoy the moon and stars."

"I'm nothing but a big baby," I said, drying my eyes with the sleeves of my army jacket. "An asshole."

Laughing, she said, "Matty, cheer up."

Looking at her, I said, "You're right. I shouldn't be telling you my troubles."

"Go ahead. I don't mind. I told you my troubles, didn't I? That's what friends are for."

"But my troubles add up to a lot of adolescent shit, compared to yours,"

"Turn off the ass-kicking machine, Matty."

"It's just that the world is too much for me."

"Well, maybe you're too much for the world. Ever think of that? At least the world around here. You've had so many experiences, and I've heard you've published a book of poetry. God, if I'd achieved a book of anything, I'd probably feel that I was too grown-up for the world around here."

"No, Elsie, you wouldn't. You'd never feel too grown-up for anything. Look at yourself. You're not like me. You don't take yourself too seriously. I do. You don't suck for approval. I do. You're always growing, Elsie, and you're always ready for the dark. You went through the terrible experience of losing your parents, but you talked about it. You're wide open, and you know how to laugh. You're really something else! You've learned how to swim warm in the icy waters of adversity, and you don't lie to yourself, like I do. You're honest, intelligent, and a very talented musician. When you're down, you get up and do something about what put you down. You're a fighter. And you don't suck for sanity, like I do, while wallowing in insanity, intentionally."

"Is that what you're doing—sucking and wallowing?"

"Look at me. I'm all fucked-up. I lied to myself about wanting to be a priest, when in my heart I didn't want to be one. Then I started playing the head game, and I told myself it wasn't a lie that I wanted to be a priest—that I'd just thought it was a lie. See what I mean?"

She began to cry. Then, taking my hand, she said, "I'm not crying over you, Matty. I know you'll come through it, and with great style. I'm crying because of the nice things you just said about me. Nobody ever said nice things like that to me, ever. Did you really mean them?"

"Of course I meant them."

Smiling, she said, "You know, I got all A's all the way through high school and college."

"You told me, Elsie."

"Then why do people call me a dumb blonde?"

"I wouldn't call you that—I know better."

"You know, as long as we're being truthful, let me tell you a little secret. I feel like a failure."

"A failure? You're anything but a failure."

"Yes, I am, because I'm afraid, Matty. I'm afraid."

"Afraid of what?"

"Now, please don't laugh—promise?"

"I'll try not to."

"Well, when I got this last scholarship, I was so afraid that I peed myself. Matty, I see you're laughing. You promised not to."

"I didn't promise."

"I'm not going to tell you."

"Okay, I promise," I said, straightening out my face.

"Okay, I'll tell you. I got the scholarship, and after peeing myself, I started hallucinating, and it hasn't stopped. I see myself graduating from school with honors, and then I see myself on a concert stage, playing my ass off and getting a lot of applause. Then I'm rich and famous—a success—and that's what scares me. I'm afraid I might get to like it too much and destroy myself. I'm afraid I would begin to sell my soul for gold and fame, and forget my music. See what I mean?"

"That doesn't make you a failure now, before it's really happened. As I said before, I believe you're always ready for the dark, and I feel that the light of a healthy concern for the future is your way of getting ready."

"Is that what I've got—a concern? Then why did I pee my pants?"

"Elsie, how the hell do I know? Maybe you were just excited."

"Do you pee yourself when you get excited?"

"No, but I used to wet the bed, right up until I was about twelve."

"You did?"

"Yes. Elsie, don't worry. It's all in your head. You'll handle it, like you do everything else."

"I suppose. Maybe my feeling of failure's like a dream, like the dream of success, only different. With God's help, I'll get through it—and He's already helped, through you, Matty."

"I wish God would help me out a little."

Suddenly, she got angry. "Now, that's one helluva thing to say!" she said. "You, of all people, should know He's helped you plenty, but you have no gratitude. And there's some things you've got to get for yourself—such as willing yourself some faith and guts!"

Angry, I said nothing more and ran home. Going to my room and locking the door, I buried myself in the novel, *Crime and Punishment*, by Feodor Mikhailovich Dostoevski. Then, at daybreak, I fell asleep, wishing my name was Feodor Mikhailovich La Fleur....

Pounding on the door, my mother woke me up. After I'd let her in, she said, "I want you to get dressed and come with me. I'm going to a meeting at St. Joseph's. After that, we'll be going to the dress rehearsal at the Community Center."

"Rehearsal for that damn Halloween show? I'd rather stay here and meditate."

"No more meditation. I don't want you to meditate yourself to death. Besides, it will do you good to get out of this room for awhile.

And, speaking of this room, you will clean it up the first thing tomorrow morning. It's a pigpen!"

"But…"

"No but's. Get dressed and we'll be on our way, after you have a bowl of soup."

Looking at my bedside clock, I saw that it was almost seven. I'd slept all day and into the evening. I got dressed, and after I said no to the soup, we left.

By the time we arrived at the basement auditorium of St. Joseph's Church, Father O'Grady was just finishing his plea for Thanksgiving food for the less fortunate. Then, after a short prayer by Father Tom Beale, the new priest in town, the social part of the meeting began.

There were about two hundred people cramped into the place, and the air was not fresh. Hot and noxious fumes permeated the air and made it unbearable for me. I wanted to leave but didn't. My mother kept a watchful eye on me, as she sat in a corner with Widow Stevens and Ellie Mills, the schoolteacher. Going to the refreshment table, I took a cup of ginger ale and, as I hurried to a chair by the door, I hoped no one would come up and talk to me. But it wasn't to be, because as soon as I was sitting, Max Fork, the greasy president of Christian Citizens Organization (CCO), came up and said, "Hey Matt, I heard you're goin' into the sem to be a priest. Good idea." Then, after we shook hands, he went away, smiling like a politician, greasy-like.

Trixie Roper was next. Standing in front of me now, she said, "Hi, Matty. Guess who's servin' refreshments and cleanin' up?"

"You," I said, managing a smile.

"You guessed it. Want some more of what you're drinkin'?" she asked, twirling the ends of her red hair.

Drinking up and handing her the empty cup, I said, "Okay, I'll have another ginger ale."

I watched her bounce away and thought about her. Her real name was Theresa, and I hadn't seen her in years. I thought she looked nice, with her red hair done up and her well-developed body all decked-out in a light-green dress that matched her eyes. But, in no way, was I about to tell her she looked nice, for fear that she'd take it the wrong way. In eighth grade, I recalled, I complimented her on her winning a spelling bee, and she told everybody I'd asked her to go steady. Then, after I set the record straight, she said she'd broken up with me, because I was too stupid and conceited. She was beautiful, I thought now, watching her making her return trip, but extremely presumptuous and strange, in her earlier years.

"Here's your ginger ale," she said, standing in front of me and giggling a little. "And I brought you some food."

Having not eaten all day, I took the paper plate of food, saying, "Thanks, Trixie." Then, because she seemed to be waiting for me to eat, I took a plastic forkful.

"Unbelievable! Yeuck! How in the hell can you eat those baked beans and potato salad?" she asked, frowning and shaking her head.

"Why'd you bring the food, then? Is there something wrong with it?" I asked, looking down at the food.

"Well, it's not poison, if that's what you mean. I wouldn't've brought it if it was. It's just that Widow Stevens puts too much gas in her baked beans, that's all."

"I take it you don't like baked beans, Trixie."

"Don't like the potato salad neither—too much gas."

"What's all this gas business?" I asked, thinking that she hadn't changed a bit.

"Gas? Well, I've gotta watch it. I'm a Go-Go dancer now over at Devil's Den."

"You mean Devil's Outhouse?"

"That's the joint," she said, giggling again and dancing away.

I drank the ginger ale and threw the empty cup and plate of food into a nearby trash barrel.

Trixie returned and asked, "Can I bring you something else—oops, sorry 'bout that—there is nothin' else 'cept the widow's shit. There were some cookies, but the Indians at 'em all."

I hoped she'd leave. Wincing and putting my hand to my head, I said, "Trixie, I've got a terrific headache. I think I'll just close my eyes and rest 'til my mother's ready to leave."

Putting her hands on her hips, she said, "Well now, we'll just have to do somethin' 'bout that headache, won't we? I'll get some aspirins."

"No," I said, "I'll be leaving soon and I'll get some at home."

"Well, okay, but I'm worried 'bout you, Matty. I can see that car accident with Wanda didn't do you any good."

Putting her hand on my arm and lowering her voice, she said, "Speakin' a that bitch, I heard she's back in town. Did you know that?"

Feeling as if I were free-falling without a parachute, I said, "No, this is the first I've heard of it."

Squeezing my arm, she said, "Well, she is. And if I was you, I'd get a new girlfriend—me, for instance!"

"Thanks for the offer, Trixie, but I've got someone."

"Who?"

"You don't know her. She's not from around here."

"Somebody you met at college, right?"

"Right."

"Well, I tried," she said, "No harm in tryin', right? Well, gotta get goin'. Gotta clean the damn place up. See you, Matty."

Alone now and not wanting to be intimidated by the news about Wanda being back, I put my mind on the people around me. Max Fork was staring at his father Oswald, who was staring at Larry Roper, Trixie's father. Oswald and Larry had once been in business together, until, according to Oswald, Larry cheated him out of five hundred dollars, destroying their lumber business and their friendship. That had been two years ago and since then, Oswald threatened to cut Larry's heart out and make him eat the rotten thing. Looking elsewhere, I focused on my mother, who was still sitting in a corner with Widow Stevens and Ellie Mills, the schoolteacher. Wondering why she'd picked those two old hags to sit with, I moved to a seat closer to them and listened-in.

Widow Stevens, dressed in a black dress, was saying, "Hey, Ellie, go fetch me some of my baked beans—that is, if there's any left." Then, after adjusting her wire-rimmed glasses, she squinted and said, "You better hurry your fat ass over there, 'fore they're all gone."

Heavy Ellie didn't move. She only looked over at the refreshment table and said, "I can see from here, Clarissa, that there's plenty beans left. Looks like they ain't hardly been touched."

Nervously clicking her dentures, the widow said, "Then go get me some, and bring me some of my potato salad, and a few cookies while you're at it."

Looking at the table again, Ellie said, "Looks like your potato salad ain't hardly been touched, neither. You're in luck, Clarissa."

"Then goddamnit, get over there and get me some, 'fore I have to get up and do it myself!"

Ellie lumbered over and returned with a paper plate loaded with beans and salad. Putting the plate in the widow's hands, she said, "Here, Clarissa, enjoy."

"Where's the cookies?" the widow snapped.

Sitting and catching her breath, Ellie said, "Sorry, Clarissa. Trixie Roper told me that the Indians ate all the cookies."

"Those damn Indians—don't they have cookies on the reservation?"

"You're part Indian, ain't you, Clarissa? Is that why you like cookies?" the schoolteacher asked.

"I like cookies, like everybody else. And, no, I'm not part Indian—not any more, I ain't."

"You ain't part Indian any more—how come?"

"For a schoolteacher, you ain't got the brains of a louse, Ellie. I'll say it once, and I ain't gonna say it again. When you marry somebody, then you take on his nationality, like I did when I married Egwon. But you wouldn't know that, because you ain't never married, Ellie. You're an old maid, and you ain't never even got close to a man. That's right."

"What nationality are you now, Clarissa?" Ellie asked, smiling.

"I ain't sure. Maybe I forgot," the widow said. Then, looking at my mother, she said, "You didn't get to know my Egwon, did you Anne? You hadn't migrated from France yet. Well, my Egwon was quite a man. That's right. He did the vacuuming and dishes and anything that was to do around the house. I didn't have to lift a finger. There was no call for me to hire a maid, like you did, Anne. But I suppose now that Major Danny has passed, you ain't got your maid, or cook—or do you?"

"I've let the cook go," my mother said casually. "But I believe you already know that, and I believe you know I still have Suzette."

"Well," the widow said, eating her beans. "I just wondered if what I heard is correct. And I'm wondering now if our beloved mayor ain't up in heaven wondering why you still have a maid."

"My having a maid is none of your business, Mrs. Stevens," my mother said calmly.

"Well—pardon me!" the widow said, spitting a bean on my mother's cheek. Then, not bothering to say anything about the bean, she said, "Well, come to think of it, you'll be better off keeping your maid, because your precious Matthew won't be lifting a finger to help. That's right."

"Matthew's not lazy. Where in the world did you get that idea?"

"Now, Anne, don't go flying off the handle," the widow said.

"I'm not flying off anything," my mother said, smiling a little.

"I only mean that your son will be going into the seminary and won't be home to help you. Why do I get the impression he's not cut out for the priesthood? Now, don't get me wrong. He's a nice fellow, but ain't he too old?"

"I don't believe there's an age limit, Mrs. Stevens," my mother said, still smiling.

"Well, Annie, maybe there ain't—can I call you Annie?"

"No."

"Well, no matter," the widow said, eating potato salad, clicking her dentures rapidly. Then loudly, she said, "Annie, that ain't the main reason I don't think your Matthew is cut out for the priesthood. I hear he's been sleeping around—ain't that right, Ellie?"

"It certainly is, Clarissa—and with more than half the women population of Point Stevens."

"You see, Annie," the widow said, pointing her plastic fork at my mother. "It's the truth."

"No, I don't see," my mother said, still smiling.

"Well, no matter," the widow said. "But as patriarch of this town, it's my duty to keep track of evildoers, such as fornicators."

"That's matriarch," Ellie said. "Clarissa, it ain't patriarch, it's matriarch."

"Goddamnit, Ellie, shut up and mind your own damn business! Now, as I was saying, if, by some stupid accident, your son does become a priest, I'm gonna see to it that he ain't assigned here. You see, besides being morally deformed, he ain't a good enough politician, or business man. Why, he might turn out to be another Father O'Grady, who never did come around to our way of thinking. Father O'Grady is a disgrace and embarrassment. Thank God we have Father Tom Beale now, to oversee that old booze-hound O'Grady."

Still smiling, my mother said, "I'll say goodbye now, ladies. I hope you enjoy the rest of the evening, as much as you have, so far."

"Don't get sarcastic, Annie!" the widow snapped, spitting another bean on my mother's cheek. "I was just trying to shed some light on the situation—and, while I'm at it, those millions the mayor left you should go to Morely, his own flesh and blood. That's right!"

After my mother had hurried over to me and was in front of me, I asked, "Why do you keep those beans stuck to your face, Mama? Let me remove them."

Quickly stopping my hand, she said, "Leave them alone. I don't want to give her the satisfaction of seeing you remove them."

"Why in the world did you sit with them? You know how they are."

"It was part of my penance," she said, turning and going to the Ladies' Room.

## chapter 8

"Mama, why did you insist on being in the Halloween show?" I asked, as we walked to the Community Center for the dress rehearsal. "Every year you've told them it just wasn't your cup of tea—so why now?"

Taking my arm, she said, "Don't make such long steps. Slow down."

Slowing down, I asked, "And why are you going to be the red tulip? If I recall, the red tulip gets stepped on."

"It's my duty."

"Your duty?"

After a pause, she said, "It's my duty to make amends for my sins, by humbling myself in such a way."

"Who told you that?"

"I told me that."

"Then why do you insist I watch? I could be home meditating."

"Enough about your meditating! Matthew, I don't believe you're going to be a priest—am I correct?"

"Yes."

"Then, as I said before, I'm not going to interfere in your life. Be a bum all your life. Do as you please, and I'll do the same, without your interference. Is that understood, dear?"

"Understood, Mama."

We were at the Center. She rushed backstage to change into her tulip costume, and I took a seat in the back of the small auditorium. A few minutes later, the performers came onstage, wearing all kinds of weird things that, I guessed, were designed to terrify. There were grotesque paper-mache heads, rubber masks, deformed trees and flowers, fierce-looking ducks and spiders, a mean, squinty-eyed weasel with grapevines all over its body, and a crocodile with fake blood dripping from its jaws, and a lot of other stupid things. All together, there must have been about sixty of those creatures up there, and many were talking, laughing and playing grab-ass.

I didn't want to watch but did. I couldn't help myself. Wanda was there, and I was curious about her. She was standing just below the stage, wearing a blue sweater and plaid skirt, and Morely was at her side. I assumed, by the way they were looking at the creatures, pointing, and moving creatures around, that Wanda was the director, and Morely was her assistant. "Okay," Wanda finally said. "Let's get settled down and get the show on the road." Then, after watching Morely hit his leg with a swagger stick, she said, "Please, quiet on the set!"

"You heard her—quiet on the set!" Morely yelled, hitting his leg again.

When the creatures were quiet, as they were now, it looked to me as if they were having a hard time controlling their laughter, and I could see why. I thought it was probably the way Morely was dressed. His outfit consisted of a khaki shirt and britches, leather boots that reached up to his thighs, and a pith helmet that kept falling down over his eyes. Also, he had a holster and gun, the size and shape of South America, on his hip.

Wanda was saying pleasantly, "We all want this show to be a success, don't we?"

My mother, a voracious-looking red tulip, was the only one who responded, saying, "Indeed we do, Wanda!"

"Well," Wanda said, "we'll have to work hard tonight, won't we?"

"We'll have to work like hell tonight!" my mother yelled.

I couldn't believe my mother, a beautiful, elegant, French lady, now sounding like a red tulip might sound if given half an ounce of vulgarity. If my father could only see and hear her now! I said to myself, feeling a little embarrassed.

Wanda was pointing her ear at a small band in the corner. "Could you please be a little more quiet?" she asked, smiling.

"Sure could," the drummer said, with a drumroll.

It was getting warm and stuffy. I removed my army jacket, after I saw

Wanda remove her blue sweater. Then, watching her closely, I saw her carry the sweater over by the north wall and place it on a chair. "Quack, quack!" some weird duck yelled. "Take it off, Wanda—take it all off! Quack, quack!"

"Who's the dirty asshole who yelled that obscenity?" Morely yelled, slapping his leg with the stick. "Well, whoever it was, better wise up or go home!"

Returning to the creatures and pointing at a tree, she said, "Quit scratching the surface of Wicked Princess—would you, please?"

"Who's scratchin' surfaces?" Morely yelled.

"Please, Morely, let's get on with it," Wanda said.

By this time, I was almost sure that Wanda had changed for the better. I was impressed with her poise, perfect posture and a lot of other things I'd not seen before, but I was mostly impressed with her gentleness.

Lawyer Ted Flax made his entrance into the auditorium, saying loudly, "Sorry, everybody, that I'm unavoidably tardy." Then, after taking a place onstage, he pirouetted, asking, "How do you like my new Batman costume? I had it imported all the way from Gotham City."

"Hey, Flax! Morely yelled, hitting himself. "How come you're Batman, all of a sudden? You were assigned to be an evil duck!"

"I don't wanna be an evil duck. I wanna be Batman."

"But Batman's a good guy," Morely said. "And we don't allow no good guys in. I confess you look okay, but you ain't followin' orders."

Putting a smoking pipe between his teeth and rattling it, Flax said, "Well, it's a matter of interpretation, whether or not I'm good or bad, isn't it?"

"Flax!" Morely yelled. "Just 'cause you're a big-shot lawyer, that don't mean you don't have to follow orders like everybody else!" Then, removing his pith helmet, he pulled out his red-checkered handkerchief and, snarling, wiped his narrow forehead, the inside of his helmet, and then replaced it on his head, saying, "You're a pain in the goddamn ass, Flax!"

"And so are you—so there!" Flax yelled, sticking out his tongue. "At least I don't look and act like a bulldog!"

"Please, gentlemen!" Wanda said, looking at Flax, then at Morely. Then, looking at the cast, she asked, "How many of you practiced the assigned noises?"

When she put her hand over her mouth, I felt she was giggling and trying to cover it up. It was the first I'd seen her giggle, innocently and spontaneously, metrically and sweetly. Thinking that the giggle was probably addictive, I told myself to beware.

"Dear Wanda," Flax was saying. "What noise shall I make, now that I'm Batman?"

Poised, Wanda asked, "And what noise would you like to make, sir?"

Flax made a loud pipe-sucking noise, and asked, "Will that do?"

"It'll do," Wanda said, smiling.

"Well, I don't like it!" Morely said. "It sounds like a rotten fart!"

"Oh, Morely, let's get going with this." Then: "Okay, everybody, sound your noises—begin!"

In my mind, the winners of the most stupid noises were: The gorilla, who made loud grunts, and the creature with the head of a wolf and the body of a sheep, who howled and bleated almost simultaneously. I had to admit, I was impressed.

When the noises were finished, Wanda, after she stopped giggling, said, "Fine."

"Louder!" Morely yelled. "You gotta be louder!"

Looking at Morely, Wanda said, "I thought it was excellent. But, as you say, it could have been louder."

The cast started acting up again, making their noises louder without direction to do so. I began to enjoy myself, listening to all that bleating and howling and grunting and screaming and moaning and groaning and disgusting pipe-sucking. It wasn't the noise that I enjoyed, especially. I enjoyed the defiant, mutinous conduct coming from the motley creatures. In any event, the noise continued and continued, until finally, Morely took charge. Firing his gun into the air, he yelled, "If you don't stop, you'll get the next round right between the eyes!"

There was a warped silence, and it remained right up to the moment that, slowly but surely, an empty beer can rolled down centerstage and exploded a bulb in the footlights. There was another warped silence then, until someone yelled: "Hey, Morely, was that loud enough for you?"

Picking up the can, Morely asked, "Whose can is this? You lunatics know there's no drinkin' in ranks! Confess—whose is it?"

Taking the can, Wanda said, "Morely, sir, the show must go on." Then, holding the can at arm's length, as if it were a dead skunk, she deposited it in a trash barrel and returned to the cast.

Scotty MacDonald, who looked like a killer turtle, was waiting for her at the centerstage. "Miss," he said, frowning, "I have a complaint. Mister-r Flax has no legitimate r-right to use his pipe to make noise. It's a r-real pr-rop. We wer-re definitely infor-rmed that r-real pr-rops would not be per-rmitted. So, if he's per-rmitted to per-for-rm on his pipe, then, by all that's r-right on this teeming ear-rth, I should be per-rmitted to play my bagpipes. So, now ye have it, don't ye?"

"You certainly have a legitimate grievance, sir," Wanda said politely. Then, after looking at the rest of the creatures, she asked, "Does anyone else have a grievance?"

A worm spoke up, saying "I wanted to be a robin."

Pointing his swagger stick at the worm, Morely said, "You takes what you gets, Clarissa!"

"I've got an idea," Wanda said. "Why don't we postpone the grievance time until after the rehearsal." Then, looking at the band, she said, "Okay, boys, take it from the top!"

When the band started pumping out a polka, and Wanda started a lot of fanny-perking, a gorilla began chasing white-sheeted ghosts, until the ghosts were jerked into the air by means of unhidden cables. But, the gorilla, looking fierce and determined, was not about to be defeated. Jumping up and grabbing the ghosts, the gorilla threw them on the floor, one by one, and began kicking them, making the ghosts scream and moan and groan, until, suddenly, other creatures came on, biting each other, kicking, scratching, wrestling, and making their assigned noises. And it got so violent that the head of a vulture was knocked from the body of a zebra, and Dracula fell and broke off one of his magnificent eye-teeth. But, Dracula, seemingly undaunted, got right up and, with his remaining eye-tooth, began biting the necks of all those women who were wearing wilted, ugly daylilies all over their body. And then it seemed to be nothing but rotten luck for the gorilla, for the ghosts recovered and began beating up the gorilla, and anything else that got in their way. However, the resurgence of the ghosts was short-lived, for just as they produced large razor straps from inside their dirty-white sheets, the gorilla was at them again, wrenching the straps from them, throwing them on the floor to lay belly-up at centerstage. At that point, the curtain closed.

But, it wasn't over. When the curtain opened again, Batman was alone at centerstage, saying, "Hark! It was Nostradamus who predicted that a world séance would take place, during which all the Great Personalities of the past would reappear. That event is about to take place right now, with the Great Personalities exposing themselves, as they never have before. Come on, Great Personalities, don't be bashful—expose yourself!"

One by one, or in pairs, with name-tags, they came. Rhett Butler and Scarlet O'Hara came on, both screaming "I don't give a good goddamn!" Next, Josephine and Napoleon entranced, fondling each other. Mussolini was eating Cleopatra's hair, which was loaded with something that looked like tomato sauce. Catherine the Great, holding up a large, wooden bowl, was yelling: "Borscht! Let them eat Borscht!" Then laughing hysterically, she poured the borscht all over someone labeled Potemkin. Adolph Hitler, with a world balloon in his arms, was kicking St. Joan of Arc. Christopher Columbus kept grabbing at Queen Isabella's purse. Things began to heat up then. Marc Anthony hit Mussolini with a bowl of spaghetti, Marquis de Sade burst Hitler's balloon with his sword. Removing her head, Marie Antoinette threw it at Robespiere. Then finally the red tulip, my mother, made her sorry entrance, looking weak and fragile and ready to submit to anything. I hated it. She seemed without pride, beauty, elegance. Flopping down on the floor at centerstage, she lay there belly-up and motionless, with her face turned to the audience. Her face was that of a sad clown's. Then, when the band struck up a loud rendition of "Tiptoe Through the Tulips", the Great Personalities, in single file, trampled on her, singing, over and over:

> "Tiptoe, on the tulip
> In the garden.
> Beg your pardo,
> You old lardo."

Finally, they formed into a circle around my mother and began stuffing popcorn into her rouged and distended mouth, yelling: "Eat, eat, eat…"

The curtain closed, and reopened immediately. Looking at the creatures, Morely yelled, "I'm gagging. I'm gagging! You all act like a bunch of sissies! You gotta get more violence in it! You gotta stomp on that old moneybag!"

Some guy yelled: "Hey, Bulldog—maybe we should all get guns like yours and put the poor tulip out of her misery!"

They were laughing and pointing at Morely, and that seemed to be enough to cause Morely to pull his gun and fire off four rounds into the ceiling. When some ceiling fell down and knocked Morely's pith helmet off, everybody, it seemed, laughed, except Wanda and me. I could tell Wanda was crying, with her hands covering her face and her body trembling. I wanted to go to my old friend of the leaky, green rowboat and console her, and I would have, if she didn't run from the building, screaming, "Oh, God, why is there such violence in the world?"

I was worried about Wanda. I went to her house but found no one at home, so I went to Devil's Den and took a table in Nancy's section of a large room filled with a perfumed, red mist. I had never been here before. I thought of it as a hell one might see in a movie, or a painting, but it wasn't the hell of anxiety inside me now, making me feel as powerless as a Mickey Mouse watch, wound too tight and unable to tick.

Nancy came to the table, wearing only a red wig, half an apron, and sparkling red shoes that turned up at the toes. "Welcome to Devil's Den," she said, smiling. "Is this a social call, or do you want a drink?"

Looking at her naked breasts, I asked, "Have you seen Wanda?"

"No, but she said she might come in. Do you want a drink, or don't you?"

"I forgot my wallet."

"Don't worry 'bout it. My treat."

"Thanks."

She went to the bar and returned with a red, tall drink. "I brought the specialty of the house," she said, grinning. "It's called a Devil's Kiss."

As soon as she was gone, I tried to relax in my plush, red, leather armchair and sipped my drink. After a few sips, I told myself that I was glad I waited. Then, about halfway into the drink, my ears began to ring and my vision got blurry. However, mysteriously, my mental condition seemed to improve. I seemed to be more aware of my surroundings and, looking around, I saw the place now as a beautiful amphitheater of hell, with me right in the middle.

Up one level and all around me, there were red gazebos, with naked, smiling, dancing women inside. Squinting, I thought I saw Trixie Roper, dancing and smiling at me. Looking around again, I saw that each gazebo was tagged on top with a glowing image of the devil. He had big eyes, a red face, and a long, stiletto mustache that turned up at the ends. I imagined now that his eyes were staring at me, in a hard and fast recruiting way. However, instead of fear, I experienced a warm feeling of intimacy with those eyes, and a pleasant feeling of warp and wantonness. Yet, even with this hallucinatory flush, I believed my mind was working better than ever and improving. I asked myself three questions: Why does the devil look like a man? Why does the devil have a stiletto mustache? Would I look good with a stiletto mustache?

Whammied but eager for more, I listened to the loud, furious sound of bongo drums and watched multi-colored spheres of light whirling in the red mist. Then, turning my attention to the dancers, who were now bursting into flames as they danced, I could feel the flames of hell lick my soul. The dancers danced on and like perpetual candles of hell lit up my hour of salvation and, when I let it pass me by, they laughed. With a smile in my heart now, I welcomed the teasing odor of musk and allowed it to seep into my senses. Closing my eyes, in an effort to better appreciate it all, I felt certain I'd remember this moment for the rest of my days, especially in impotent moments of regret. Then, knowing I had a smile on my face, I fell asleep and had a nightmare of repentance.

In the nightmare, I felt a great need to tell Fr. O'Grady about my sick soul. Hurrying over to the rectory at dawn, I rang the doorbell and waited in torment. Finally, the old priest came and took me to a small room, where he said, "You're a mite early, lad, but I'll hear what you have to say—but be quick about it!"

The priest sat at a heavy, wooden desk and drank from a large, golden goblet, which smelled of whiskey and coffee. I sat on a metal stool near a wall of books. Wishing he'd offer me some whiskey, laced with coffee, or otherwise, I lowered my head and said, "Unbearable."

After a gulp of the brew, he said, "Look up at me, lad, and tell me what it is that's so unbearable."

Sitting on the stool, I felt like a dunce without mind or virtue. Looking up, I saw a long stream of spit-bubbles coming from the man's mouth, heading towards me now, slow but sure, and threatening me. Then, as the sun came through the stained-glass windows and caught the bubbles, and filled them with all kinds of holy colors, I gnashed my teeth, ducked the flying bubbles, and said again: "Un-bearable!"

"No, don't be doin' that with your teeth, so early in the mornin', lad!" he snapped. "Best, you be tellin' me what's so damn unbearable!"

Breathing deeply and deciding that half a confession is better than none, I lowered my head again, saying, "Father, I'm being tormented by impure thoughts and desires."

"So," he said, after slurping his brew and belching, like an old car trying to start on a cold morning. "So, that's what is so unbearable! Damnit, look at me when I'm talkin' to you!"

Looking up and seeing a whole squadron of colored spit-bubbles coming at me, I took off for the door, saying, "Thank you, Father, but I've gotta go now."

"Sit!" he yelled. Come back here and sit your skinny arse down!"

I returned to the dunce stool.

"Tell me lad, do you do a whole lotta whiskey-drinkin'?"

"No, Father."

Looking at his goblet, he said softly, "Drink will do it to you, every time. It'll bring on all the devils of impurity—take it from me, lad. Best, that you not drink too much."

Because I hadn't told him about my intimate relations with Wanda and Elsie, I began to feel that I'd committed the worse sin of all—the abominable, mortal sin of omission. With that sin eating away my soul, like cancer, I began to cry.

"'eesus, Mary and Joseph, lad-- quit that damn blubberin' and get holt of yourself!" he yelled. Then, after taking another swig, he said, "You know, Matt, me boy, it would be best if you were to put your sights on becomin' a priest of God, like your dear mother wants, instead of thinkin' of doin' it to naked women. You'd make a fine broth for the Church. Now, be off with you, and quit busting your arse over a few thoughts and desires. You'll worry yourself to smithereens, if you're not careful. And remember, lad, it's the doin' it that counts. You know that as well as I do. Now, off with you, and my regards to your dear mother."

When I saw him lower his head and stare into his drink, sadlike, I took off, feeling gratitude and respect, but also feeling sad that the old gentleman was doing all that drinking and blowing spit at the world....

When I awoke from the nightmare, Wanda was sitting across from me at the table. She had a look of perplexity on her face, as if she were a holy person trying to determine if my soul was worth saving, or not. Groggy, I said, "You're here."

"Yes," she said, smiling. "Are you all right?"

Before I could think of an answer, Nancy came with a cup of hot coffee and accidentally splashed some on my hand. "Oops!" Nancy said. "Sorry 'bout that!"

Wanda, jumping up and grabbing a piece of ice from one of the drinks on Nancy's tray, rubbed it on my hand, saying, "This should help."

"Thank you," I said, fully aware of her sweet breath of body.

Nancy brought more ice and wrapped it on my hand with a towel, and Wanda hurried me out of hell's recreation room into the cool night and down the street to a restaurant, where she fed me a cheese sandwich, and it was nice when her fingers slipped into my mouth a few times. Then, taking my good hand, she led me to her house and, when we were there, she asked, "Would you like to come in?"

Standing there, like a telephone pole without wires, I said, "Maybe I should, to get my bearings."

And when we were in and sitting on the sofa drinking coffee, she said, "Whatever they put in those drinks over there, should be made illegal—and probably is."

Looking in her eyes, I found myself falling into spiritual glue, but I didn't resist. While a familiar scenario played in my head, that of our lying by the fire in Major Danny's cabin far into the night, making love and listening to the drone and licks and thwacks of the Dark River, her defilement of my love was nowhere in sight. I took her hand now and said, "I love you," but, in the next instant, a chill of pride ran through me, making me realize that I'd been wronged by her. Then, after my pride cast the hypocritical stone at her, and I told myself she'd sinned in the worst way, I went to her room and, falling asleep in her bed, I hoped she wouldn't join me.

In the morning, I found myself at her kitchen table, with two poached eggs and a cup of coffee in front of me and with Wanda sitting across from me. I knew who I was, but I wouldn't let myself in, just as I knew who she was, but wouldn't let her in. I didn't want my feelings stirred up, in any way, by anyone. In fact, I didn't want any feelings, or to even be human any more, choosing now to be an ear of corn, a radish, or a stone lying in a field somewhere—anywhere but here, in a sewer of dishonesty, in which we both were trying to swim but couldn't, because of all the shit—because of her dishonesty to herself and me, in doing what she did, and because of my dishonesty to myself, in being here with her and not wanting to be here.

Wanda broke the awful silence, saying, "You were talking in your sleep last night, Matthew."

Just then, Nancy came out of her bedroom, smiled at us, got coffee, returned to her bedroom.

"I'm worried about you," Wanda said. "You were talking in your sleep, just like you did when we went fishing."

I wanted to say something, but not about my sleeptalking. I wanted to say something nasty, with a lot of sarcasm—sarcasm that would burn her, as if it were pus-colored wax, and mark her forever as a gold-digging trollop. But, as I was trying to think of something, I saw my eyes undulating on the black sea of coffee, and it made me seasick. That was when I looked up, happened to see her eyes, and falling into a sea of blue, I began to swim joyfully, as if I were going home after a long and miserable voyage. However, after a quick feeling that I was drowning, I rescued myself from that deep sea of blue and put my eyes on the poached eggs and their scum-cataracts. Repulsed now by the eggs, I closed my eyes and tried to mediate myself to death.

"You scared the hell out of me last night," she was saying. "I didn't know what to think. You were yelling: 'I hate the bastard! I hate the bastard! I'm going to kill him! I'm going to kill the man who killed my father!' Then you'd moan and groan and grind your teeth and then get on that horrible cycle of hatred again, yelling that you were going to kill the man who killed your father."

Embarrassed and heartsick, I couldn't look at her. I jumped up and left the house. Finding refuge in the small park across the highway, past the familiar bench, I went to a wooded area, not quite so familiar to me. Then, coming to a wooden bridge, I crossed over and soon found myself wandering on a small, deserted island, surrounded by a moat of stagnant, slimy, stinking water. Almost overcome with nausea, while sitting on an old tree stump and staring at dead leaves, the dull tattoo of death began beating inside me, and I welcomed death, as I would an old friend. Feeling feverish and exhausted, I slumped to the ground and lay on my back, in surrendering to the awful loneliness of dying alone. Then, after telling myself I'd even welcome a sewer rat to come and sit with me, I looked up at the blue sky for what I thought was the last time and whispered, "Take me...."

With my eyes closed now, I could feel a soft, cool hand on my burning brow. I thought of myself then as a dehydrated dog turd, and that a beautiful butterfly had come to rest on me. Opening my eyes, I saw it was Wanda. She was smiling and saying, "Hi, Matthew."

Staring at her, I asked, "What are you doing here, walking your dog?"

Chuckling softly, she said, "You know I don't have a dog."

"How did you know I was here?" I asked.

Helping me to my feet, she said, "I looked through my window and saw you come here." Then, chuckling again, she asked, "Is this all you have to do—take a nap on the ground and mess up your army jacket? Let's go back, and I'll wash all of your clothes. And, I want to talk."

Returning to the house, she put my clothes in the washer and gave me a blanket to put around me. Eating chicken soup at the kitchen table, she asked, "Do you remember that blanket you've got on?"

"Yes," I said, not looking at her. "It's the quilt of many colors from the cabin. How did you get it?"

"I stole it," she said, smiling. "You see, after the accident, and I'd returned from Bad Axe, I went to the cabin, picked the lock, and took it for a souvenir."

"Why?"

Taking my hand, she kissed it and said, "Matthew, I have something to tell you."

Withdrawing my hand, I said, "I think you've told me all I want to know."

"No," she said, taking my hand again. "It's all different now. I'm different."

"Stealing a blanket is different?"

"You can have it back, if you want it."

"I don't want it. It's probably contaminated."

"Please, listen to what I have to say."

"I'm listening."

"Well, since the accident, I look at life much differently. For one thing, I'm grateful to be alive. Before the accident, I didn't care if I lived or died. I was that fucked-up. Anyhow, then came the accident, and I survived, and thank God, you did too. And now I know why I survived. It was because there was love inside me—not love for myself, coming from me, because I didn't have any. What was inside me, was the love you gave me, and at my mother's, while I recuperated, I saw that love, as well as my mother's. But, most of all, it was your love that made me believe—that if some nice guy like you loves me, then I must be worth something. Matthew, it was enough to save me. Thank you."

Smiling now, I said, "But you stole the blanket—is that what you call, being saved?"

"Nobody's perfect," she said, smiling along with me.

Laughing now, I said, "We had a few laughs, right?"

Not laughing, she said, "I'll never forget."

"What are your plans, Wanda?"

"There's so much I want to do," she said, her eyes clear and warm and showing excitement. "With the help of my mother and aunt, I'm going to business school. Someday, I'd like to own my own business."

"A drugstore?"

After a good laugh, she said, "I'd like to go into real estate, but owning a drugstore isn't a bad idea. You know, believe it or not, I've started repaying what I figure I borrowed from the drugstore. Just yesterday, in fact, I gave the clerk ten dollars and told him I found it on the floor. That's the best way I can think of to repay—any ideas?"

"Sounds good enough to me," I said. Then, after she got my clothes from the dryer, I put them on in her bedroom and returned to the table, saying, "We'll be good friends, right?"

"Matthew," she said, taking my hand. "I love you dearly, and I always will, as a friend—a beautiful, precious friend."

Seeing tears run down her cheeks, I said, "We'll keep in touch, right?"

"I hope so."

Going to the door, I felt good, thinking that what we had was over—especially the bad part—and that something new and wonderful had begun.

Coming to me, she pulled my head down and kissed me. Then, while we gave each other a big hug, she said, "And don't forget to take care of those little fishies."

"I won't," I said, vowing never again to keep a fish I caught. "See you around, Wanda."

"See you, Matthew."

Then, feeling as if I was in some kind of nether world beneath the sea, I made it home.

## chapter 9

THE doorhammer sounded like rapid gunfire in the cold evening air. Over the sound of Gussie's barking, my mother said, "Matthew, please answer the door. Suzette has gone to a movie. It must be Mr. Baxter. I'm donating some furniture to poor Indian families. He's going to pick it up and distribute it for me.

I knew Charlie Baxter, the American Indian, who taught American history at public school. He was a good friend of my mother. They learned from each other whenever they could. She learned American history from his point of view and he learned French from her. Major Danny had approved of their relationship, saying, "Plenty votes to be got from those redskins!"

Opening the door, I saw Charlie and his friend Philip Dawson waiting in the snow. Charlie's wife Kateri was in the cab of his old pickup and had their daughter in her arms. After I invited her to go inside the house, she went in. Soon after, the two men and I started loading the truck with the furniture that had been in the basement long before we came from France. Then, just as we were about finished, a large group of people came up the driveway and stopped in front of the house. I could see now that there were about thirty of the worst troublemakers in town, with Widow Stevens and Ellie Mills right up front. Among the others, there was Larry Roper, whom Oswald Fork had called a swindler and wanted to cut his heart out and make him eat it. There was Rudy Houle, the new mayor. Tate Krouse, the used car salesman, was there, and so was Ted Flax, the lawyer, who of course was wearing his Batman outfit and yelling: "Hey, injuns, where you going with that furniture?"

"That's right!" Widow Stevens yelled.

I could see Morely in his squad car on the highway, facing us. His interior lights were on, along with his headlights that broke the falling darkness along with the porchlight. I could see he was laughing and eating pizza. Clouds thickened and a strong wind came in from the west, making it difficult for us to finish loading the truck. Charlie slipped and almost fell, and Larry Roper yelled: "Take it slow, you drunken Indian!"

Just then, Elsie came walking up the driveway. Staring at Larry Roper, she yelled: "Shut your filthy mouth, Roper—and that goes for the rest of you!" Then, breaking through the mob and going up on the porch, she yelled: "You people have no business here!" Go on home where you belong, and take your hate and ignorance with you!"

"You bitch, Elsie Quinn!" Widow Stevens yelled. "You go home, you stupid blonde! All that money the mayor left belongs to Morely, and so does the furniture! We have business here! We're here to protect Morely's rights! Not a stick of this furniture's gonna leave here 'til Morely contests the will and testament—that's right!"

"There's nothing to contest, you old fart!" Elsie yelled. "Morely got his share!"

Morely yelled from the squad car: "You call a shotgun and box of shells, and a note tellin' me to blow my brains out, a share?"

The moon came out, took a look around, and quickly disappeared again.

The mob began throwing sticks and stones and snowballs at us, and some twenty more people arrived and joined in. Trixie Roper was among this last group, and she was yelling: "What's the matter, Matt, you skinny homo—ain't we good 'nough to invite in for tea?"

There was a lot of laughter, and when it subsided, Morely yelled: "You're a homo, Matt, and everybody knows it—my brother told us all about it!"

A black car pulled in the driveway. Fr. O'Grady and Fr. Tom Beale got out, and Fr. O'Grady yelled: "What in hell is this all about?"

The crust of the mob broke off and disappeared, followed by Morely, who left a lot of rubber speeding away. When the rest of the mob was gone, the priests smiled at us and took off. Then, after we finished loading, Charlie and his friend checked the load and left with Kateri and the child.

Elsie went home, and my mother and Gussie went to bed. As soon as Suzette came home from the movie, I went looking for Morely. It wasn't clear, at all, what I'd do when I found him, but the thought that I should punch him out did cross my mind. I wanted to hurt him, only because I believed he'd been behind all the trouble tonight. That much was clear.

I went to the police station but changed my mind about going in, telling myself that if he wasn't there, I'd have to explain what I was doing there, and regardless of what I'd say, Morely would be tipped off that I'd been there. Then anyone, even Morely, would conclude that I was looking for Morely, to smash his face, because of what happened tonight. So, with that kind of head-game going on inside me, I headed for Belda's Bar, where I suspected Morely would be before the night was over. Rushing the shoreroad now, I suddenly didn't feel lost, with no place to go but inside myself, where I'd feel gutless and alone, once again. I knew where to go, what to do and who to do it to, and I knew I'd found guts enough to do it.

Once inside the bar, I saw that Belda Bird wasn't there, but that her bartender, Pete Zelig, was. I ordered a draft beer and said, "Mr. Zelig, I have business with Morely. I checked the police station but didn't see him."

Zelig, short, fat and hairy, put a beer in front of me and said, "Well, you come to the right place. He'll be in, sure as sin—you can count on it. How's your mother?"

"Okay, she fine," I said, keeping my eyes on the door. Then, looking down at the glass of beer, I decided not to drink it, for fear that it might take the edge off my anger.

"That she is," Zelig said, "A fine lady, your mother. I see her in church a lot."

Zelig went to serve his other patrons, Belda's Regulars, as they were known to be, just as they were know to have bloated bodies and brains. Not wanting to look through this moment to the next, when Morely would show, I cut down on my anxiety by focusing on the Regulars. Ooly Barnstrom was a Regular and was sitting at his regular table by the juke box, waiting for some music so he could dance his little jig. Jimmy Door was sitting by the door on his regular stool, and Meg and Sid Potter were on their regular stools at the middle of the bar, looking as fat as ever. Sid Potter was saying, "Meg, you sure look swell in your new orange suit."

"Well," Meg said, looking in the rose-tinted mirror behind the bar. "Thank you, hubby, but I don't want to look swell, I want to look swelled." Then laughing and wheezing and primping her orange hair, she said, "Zelig, bring two bags of chips, and a couple more beers."

Zelig hurried the chips and beers and said, "Here you are kids, enjoy."

Sliding his chips over to his wife, Sid said, "Meg, I've made up my mind. I'm goin' on a diet."

I could hardly believe what I was witnessing. It was as if I were having another nightmare, or some other kind of subconscious aberration.

"Sid's a traitor!" Jimmy Door yelled.

"Sid's a Judas!" Ooly Barnstrom yelled.

A black cat jumped up and scratched Sid's face.

Sid swung at the cat and fell off his bar stool.

Sailorboy, looking fat and sassy in his sailor suit, rushed from the kitchen, yelling: "Now hear this! Now hear this! Sid's chopped liver from now on!"

Fighting off the cat, Sid got back on his stool, saying, "That cat's dangerous."

"You're the dangerous one, Sid!" Meg said.

The cat jumped up again, missed Sid, and knocked over a glass of beer, breaking it.

At the sound of the glass breaking, Ooly jumped to his feet and started to do his jig, yelling, "Yip, yip, yip!"

Sailorboy yelled: "If it's diet ye want, it's diet ye git! Shoot the bilgerat! Slash 'is spinnaker! Slit 'is throat from ear to ear! Put 'im in the brig, until 'e's sober! Hang 'im from the tops'l yardarm! Make 'im walk the plank!"

"That's enough!" Zelig said, pointing at Sailorboy. "One more word out of you, and you're goin' overboard!"

"Give 'im fifty lashes!" Sailorboy continued. "Wrap 'im up in a tarpaulin jacket!"

"Okay," Zelig said. "You are definitely overboard from here, until further notice. Get out, but before you do, clean up that glass."

"Aye, aye, Sir!" Sailorboy said, saluting. Then, after cleaning up the mess and getting a glass of what I thought was rum, he sat at Ooly's table, yelling, "Full speed ahead!"

Turning to his wife, Sid said, "Sailorboy just stole Ooly's chair—a real troublemaker, that sailorboy!"

Squinting meanness at Sid, Meg said, "No, you're the only troublemaker aroun' here!"

Obviously, Sid couldn't take the pressure. He ordered two bags of chips and said, "Guess I've got some catchin' up to do, right Meg?"

Just as Zelig put the chips in front of Sid, Morely walked in. Taking a stool by the front door, he crowded Jimmy so much that Jimmy was obviously forced to take a stool by the back door, next to me.

"Whiskey, Morely?" Zelig asked.

"Make it a double!" Morely said, trying to fit himself on the stool. Then, growling, he asked, "Can't Belda get any bigger stools?"

"She's tryin' to," Zelig said, putting the whiskey in front of Morely.

"After throwing the whiskey down his throat and slamming the empty glass down on the bar, Morely said, "Do it again, Zelig, an' make it a triple this time. I need it. I just come from a riot over at the French peoples' house."

Seeing the whiskey drooling from the corners of his mouth, I yelled: "Hey, Morely, you're getting your jowls all wet!"

Looking surprised at seeing me, with his bloodshot, yellowish eyes opening up wide, he said, "Well, well, if it ain't mommy's boy!"

I wasted no time. "Lap up your whiskey, dogface, and I'll give you a Christmas present—a good punch in the jowls!" I said, getting off my stool.

Grinning, he said, "Why, you skinny bastard, you couldn't punch your way out of a paper sack!"

Removing my army jacket, I said, "Maybe not, but I think I can punch through your ugly face!"

"You two get outside, if you're gonna fight!" Zelig said. Then, after Zelig went into the kitchen, Belda's Regulars hurried outside.

I realized this would be my first fight, and I further realized that painting pictures, writing poetry and playing music hadn't prepared me for this moment of violence. Then, thinking of the past animosity we'd shown each other, I felt that this fight had been coming for a long time—

maybe even before time, when it had been arranged in heaven, or, like a bad marriage, in hell. In any event, the moment was here, and I promised myself I'd do my best.

Morely struck the first blow, by hitting me in the stomach. Then, when I doubled up in pain, he threw me over a table, as if I were a bag of dirty laundry. Grabbing an empty bottle, he broke it off at the neck and pointed the jagged top at me, saying, "I gotta a Christmas present for you, too—take a good look at it!"

Staring at the jagged weapon and then at his gun, I knew I was in deep trouble—that if I wasn't ripped open, I'd be gunned down, or even crushed to death, if he decided to sit on me. In any case, I knew I'd die. It was that simple, but again, I promised myself to do my best. Quick and loose for his size, he pointed the jagged glass at me again and, grunting loudly, threw himself at me. However, I was able to step aside, grab his arm, and give him a hard knee to the testicles, making him drop the broken glass, bend at the middle and hold his crotch. Then, as I watched, surprised at my strength, something primitive inside me told me to finish him off, but I didn't, because something else told me that maybe I'd crippled him for life. So I just stood there until suddenly he came at me again, swinging his fists wildly and missing. Then, seeing a lot of openings, I was able to land a few blows to his head and body—mostly his body, because I could hardly miss—and that made him stagger back against the bar. More confident now, I began to butt him in the face, until he grabbed my long hair and twisted and pulled, until my eyes watered so much I was blinded. Then, laughing and still yanking my hair, Morely turned me and pinned me against the bar, and then he began to hammer my face with one hand and squeeze my throat with the other. But, somehow, I found enough strength to ram his face, grab his throat with both hands and squeeze, hard, until he started to grunt and wheeze and grind his teeth, in what seemed to be his way of dredging for more power from within himself. And, without a doubt, he received that power, for now he had a deathgrip on my throat, forcing me to let go of his and be only concerned with getting air in my lungs. I began to breathe now in whistling gasps, pitched with the high-frequency tone of fatality, until, alas, I couldn't breathe at all.

Death was invading my premises, but I didn't surrender. I resisted, just as my parents had done when they'd resisted the Nazi barbarians.

I promised myself I'd never allow this barbarian bastard to kill me, by forcing me to suffocate in my own blood, mucus and tears. Then, it was a moment of salvation for me. My vomit began oozing out onto Morely's hands and onto the shirtsleeves of his beloved uniform. Apparently weakened by the foul and treacherous gruel, he eased his grip on my throat. Then, with my throat no longer constricted, I let him have a full shot of gruel in his eyes. "You fuckin' dirty pig!" he yelled, before backing up and tidying himself up.

Again, I just stood there staring at him, instead of putting him away, and as sure as God made cockroaches, he came at me again, this time with a bar stool. I was able to get my head out of the way, but the thing hit my back, making me wild with anger now, a raving lunatic under a full moon, a lean-and-mean fighting machine, strong enough to shove him back against the juke box, where I battered, butted and kneed him, until Morely, also wild with anger, and with lunacy showing in his bulldog eyes, charged me, yelling: "I'm going to kill ya! I'm gonna kill ya!"

"Not if I kill you first!" I yelled back, wishing my voice hadn't been so squeaky-high and that what I said hadn't been so childish.

And it was suddenly all kicking, scratching, ramming, biting, until we began throwing chairs, stools, bottles, dirty glasses and spittoons. And he tried to throw the juke box at me and I tried to throw the shuffleboard at him but settled on throwing just the metal discs, which immediately started bouncing off the fat fellow and enraging him so much that once again he yelled: "I'm gonna kill ya! I'm gonna kill ya!" Then, throwing another disc, I yelled: "You'll have to kill me, because that's the only way you're going to beat me—you heathen!"

And now, as we caught our breath—as in a sort of Christmas truce— the word heathen began burning inside me, like a bad case of heartburn. I couldn't believe I'd just called him a heathen, and I couldn't believe it, because I loved heathens, I told myself. Then, in a punch-drunk moment next to the shuffleboard, I wondered: Who was the first person to call someone a heathen? Are heathens good guys or bad guys? Where have all the heathens gone?

The intermission was ended when Morely, snorting and growling and snarling, came at me again. I was rested some, and fairly alert. This time, it was a round of toe-to-toe, with flying fists, bobbing and weaving and jabbing, until, with a loud growl, he lowered his mammoth shoulder and drove me up against a wall. That was it for me. As I hung there on the wall like an animal trophy, feeling certain that the end of my life had come, I watched in acceptance, as he cocked his arm and clenched his huge fist, getting ready for the kill. Then, through bleeding, swollen lips and cracked teeth, I began to whisper, "Oh, my God, I'm heartily sorry for having offended thee, and I detest all my sins, because I dread the loss of heaven and pains of hell…"

"I'm gonna kill ya! I confess, I'm gonna kill ya!" Morely was saying, in contrapuntal growls. "You better pray, you skinny bastard!"

Ending my prayer, I looked in Morely's eyes and saw something that told me he wouldn't hit me again. Doubt is what I believed I saw, doubt, once registered in a forgotten book of reason, but shining now in the darkness of Morely's mind, like a searchlight in a cave, and telling me that he was human, after all, and that he had just recalled a suggestion from that book of reason, which said, "When in doubt, don't kill anyone."

So, in that violent web of a moment, it was doubt that saved my life, making me smile and say to myself, Never underestimate the power of doubt.

And Morely, after lowering his fist, said with a sincere smile on his swollen lips, making him even more grotesque, "Matt, you are one crazy son of a bitch, to fight with me. Say, how'd you like to join the police force?"

Thinking that I'd just heard the sweetest words this side of heaven, I passed out. The next thing I knew, Morely was pressing cold towels on my face, as I lay on the shuffleboard. He was saying, "I wanna confess to causin' trouble for you and your mother. I'm sorry and won't do it again. Forgive me my trespasses, Matt. It's just that I got nuts, when your mother didn't marry me, like I wanted her to."

"Thanks for the apology," I said, trying to keep afloat. I'm grateful Morely."

"By the ways," he said, giving me a friendly punch on a sore spot. "You don't have to call me Morely. Call me Bulldog, like my friends do."

"Okay, Bulldog," I mumbled through a cold, wet towel, before passing out again....

When I awoke, I was at home in bed, lying in a lake of cold sweat and staring at the ceiling. After surrendering to the cold house with a defective furnace, I went back to sleep.

At noon, Suzette brought me soup and attended to my wounds. She didn't ask how I'd gotten all smashed up, but she did tell me that my mother was on her way to Norway.

"Norway?"

Shaking her head and putting a smile on her pretty face, Suzette said, "She's unbelievable! She said to tell you that she heard from the private detective about Richard Fowler, the man who fought with your father in the Resistance. And she said she'd call you, as soon as she got there."

"Well," I said, trying to smile but not succeeding. "I guess I'm lucky she didn't see me like this."

"Very lucky."

A couple of days later, my mother called me from Molde, Norway. Excited, she said, "I finally met with Richard Fowler. He's just as I remembered him. Tall and slender, with his green eyes filled with good humor. Still a very handsome man."

"Why did you go there?" I asked, still groggy from the fight.

"How many more times do I have to tell you? I wanted to know who killed your father, for your sake and mine. Richard was with your father, the night he was killed."

"So what did he tell you?"

Going into some detail, she told me about the meeting with Fowler, that while they were in the dining room of her hotel having fish and salad, she told him about Major Danny passing away and that she was very worried about me. "I told him about your nightmares," she said. "I told him about how you cry out in your sleep, that you want to kill the man who killed your father. And Matthew, I told him that you are filled with hatred for this man and that I don't want hatred in your life. I told him, that if you knew the true circumstances of that awful night your father was killed, then the hatred would go away."

"So, that's what you talked about? I can't believe this!"

"Believe it. I was doing it for your own good."

"What is the matter with you?"

"Nothing now. Please, listen to all I have to say, and then condemn me if you wish."

"Go ahead."

"Well, dear, Richard said he didn't know all that happened that night your father was killed, but he did say that an ex-officer of the German army would know. He said that man is an Austrian and lives in Salzburg, and Richard said that the man helped him escape, when he was a war prisoner in Norway. When I asked if I could meet with this Austrian, Richard said he'd arrange it, if I wished. Then, because I'd brought your book of poetry along, so he could see what was inside of you when you were younger, and what's still inside you, I gave it to him."

"Oh, God, what next!" I said, wishing she'd quit.

"He liked them all, Matthew, but he especially liked the one about the monster."

"The monster?" I asked, not recalling any monster.

"I have it right here," she said, "Shall I read it, so you can be reminded of your beautiful poetry?"

"I don't want to hear it."

"It will be good for you, Matthew. Perhaps it will help you to get on the right track again." She read:

"'War is the eternal insanity—
the sick solution of the madman
who waits in the darkness.
Hate is in his heart, a
bullet in his gun. He pulls
the trigger, the deed is done.
My father is dead.
My heart has lost its way.
Love is gone.
Endurance has flown away.
Faith is no more.
Hope has become a hopeless whore
mocking my impotent soul…
mocking me.'"

It seemed to me that someone else had written it. "Is that all you have to say about the meeting?" I asked, anxious to get off the phone and lie down.

She went on, saying, "Richard advised me to drop the idea of you and me meeting with the Austrian. He just couldn't understand how you could harbor hatred for someone you don't know and have never seen. Then he said we both need a good psychiatrist. I was more than a little irritated, and I said that a doctor would probably advise us to meet with the man, face to face, and talk about it. Then, after he said it depends on the doctor we'd go to, and his credibility, we left the table, went to the lobby, where he said, 'I'm sorry if I was a bit hard on you, Anne. Please, don't be angry.' And I told him I wasn't angry any more and that I'd said to myself, what he'd said, many times—that I should drop it, and that we should see a doctor. After we said our goodnights, we went to our rooms, and as I lay in my room, unable to sleep, I told myself good intentions were not enough—that perhaps the meeting with that Austrian would do you and me more harm than good. I don't want to take the chance right now, so I'm dropping the idea. Tomorrow I'll go to Paris for a few days and then I'll be home to be with you for Christmas."

"I'll be glad to see you," I said, for lack of anything better to say, in a moment of throbbing pain.

"Goodnight, Matthew. I hope I'm doing the right thing. I love you, dear."

"Goodnight, Mama. I love you, too."

## chapter 10

MAJOR Danny's father had somehow gotten enough money together to build the house of his dreams, a gabled mansion fashioned after those in Muskegon, built by lumber barons at the turn of the century. And Major Danny had said that Dr. Ben Horton had loved to spend time in the library, with its fine paneling and exquisite French doors, which opened up to an expansive backyard, enclosed by tall Norwegian pines, and now covered with snow.

It was almost Christmas. Gussie and I were home alone. Suzette had gone to Montreal to be with her folks for the holidays and my mother was still in Paris. After two flights had been canceled because of bad weather, I'd encouraged her to stay until after Christmas. "It'll do you good," I'd said. "You'll be able to visit with relatives and, besides, I'll be busy helping with the music at church. Suzette is in Montreal, and you'd be alone a lot."

"I'd have Gussie with me."

"Mama, please."

"All right, but I'll be with you in spirit. Are you sure you can manage without me?"

"Yes."

"Will that nice Elsie Quinn be helping with the music, too? I like her. Have her over for a supper, after Midnight Mass."

"I'll ask her."

"I'll call you every evening. It will be morning here."

So, that was how it went with my mother, and I was glad she agreed to stay in Paris. I wasn't feeling well, at all, since the brawl, and I probably wouldn't be much company for her.

Sitting at the desk near the French doors, I looked out at the sun and shadows playing on the snow and tried to relax. But, it just wasn't the time for relaxing. There was too much distraction. Besides my aches and pains, I was immediately distracted by an enormous squirrel that had come to sit just outside the French doors. The squirrel was sitting up on its hind legs, juggling a black walnut. With my imagination disabled, as well as my body, I saw an arrogant expression on its face, one that said: "Hey, asshole, I'll bet you can't juggle anything!"

Intimidated, I told myself that I loved squirrels, but not this hostile bastard. Then in anger, I threw a cup of coffee at the squirrel, but the cup didn't break, nor did the glass in the door. I was very weak.

When the squirrel was gone, I tried to relax again. Ignoring the mess on the door and floor, I put my feet up on the desk and watched the wind gather snow and throw it against a large woodpile in the back of the yard, a woodpile stacked neatly with a layer of snow on top. Watching the woodpile endure the violence of the blowing snow, I told myself that somehow I would endure the violence and vulgarity of the world. I would be strong and without fear. But, for all my positive thinking, it didn't work, for I began to see something else in that pile of wood and in myself. I saw passivity, not endurance. And, as for myself, I realized that somewhere along the line I'd become passive and all the sad and beautiful melodies of my life, and all the joys, sorrows, laughter, tears, things of beauty and ugliness had become as dead logs inside me, unburned, rotting, useless without constructive purpose, and stinking of dead, passive waste.

I recalled how I'd expressed in my poetry how it was to be a child of war. I thought about my painting, playing music, composing, but that had been years ago, and since then I'd done nothing with my life except, as Major Danny said, "Piss it away." Why, I asked myself, had I become a warp in my own existence? Why was I always working towards one, tragic end, my destiny—suicide? Sure, Albert Camus had been correct in saying, "Suicide is something planned in the heart, like a work of art." Then, just as I decided to leave this world without any more fuss, I heard a dog bark, sounding far away and in trouble. Thinking it was Gussie out there in the cold, lost, I hurried into my new lumberjacket and new pair of leather boots and left the house.

Heartsick, hatless, and cold, I leaned against the wind and hurried into town. Being too early for the stores to be open, the streets were deserted, except for a man in a sweatshirt and an old pair of tennis shoes. The man was small and looked old, dirty and cold as he walked through the small park near St. Joseph's Church. Turning my attention to finding Gussie, I searched around buildings and trees, but with no success. Walking with the wind now, I thought of how Gussie's little cocker rump would fluff, whenever we walked together with the wind. Panic began sucking inside me, like a leech, so I hurried my search, calling her name, always calling, until I found myself at the foot of Major Danny's statue, where I tried to whistle, but, because my lips were almost frozen, my lips wouldn't work for me. Turning against the wind again, icy snowflakes, like needles, blew in my face and eyes. Suddenly, with my vision impaired, I thought I saw her over by the bank, but after running there, I found nothing but a trashcan moving back and forth in a tire track. Disheartened once again and telling myself that could have been Gussie lying in that tire track, dead and with her mouth open, I moved towards St. Joseph's Church. Sitting on a bench in the small park across from the church, while the wind diminished, I wept. Then, as snowflakes fell slowly, covering me with a thin blanket, I fell asleep. And I slept until I became aware that someone with stale, boozy breath was trying to remove my lumberjacket. Opening my eyes and heating up a few degrees, I saw the older man I'd seen earlier. Grabbing his arm, I asked, "What the hell are you doing?"

"Hey pal, let go of my arm," the man said. "Jeez, pal, I thought you was dead, but you ain't dead, right?"

Looking at the man's torn, blue, summer pants, dirty sweatshirt, and rotten tennis shoes, I said, "No, I'm not dead, yet."

"Well," he said, smiling without teeth. "You woulda froze to death if I didn't come along. That means I saved your life, right pal?"

Ignoring the probability that he was right, I asked, "Where are your winter clothes?"

With his toothless smile, he said, "Got drunk and sold 'em right off my ass—whataya think a that?"

"You must be freezing."

"Wowee, you are one, brainy fella," he said sarcastically. "Whatya doin' out here, coolin' off that brain of yours? Of course I'm freezin'—freezin' my fucking ass off!"

"Well, you won't survive with what you've got on," I said, thinking now that, when the Salvation Army store opened, I'd buy him some warm clothes.

"Who gives a rat's ass!" he said. Then, staring at my leather boots, he asked, "Those combat boots?"

"No."

"Well, from here, they sure as hell look like combat boots. You wouldn't kid a guy, would you? Hey, pal, you been in the army?"

"No."

"Well, feast your eyes on an army man. Know what? I was a captain in G2 Intelligence durin' the Second Big One—do you believe it?"

"If you say so," I said, looking around for Gussie, always looking and losing hope.

"You don't sound like you believe me. Okay, smartass, I'll show you my discharge to prove it—and it's laminated, too!"

Taking what he gave me and looking at the discolored old thing, and not knowing if it was a discharge or a laminated laundry ticket, I said, handing it back to him, "Real nice."

"Hey pal!" he said, putting the laminated thing back into his old, torn wallet. Then, holding the wallet up and looking at it, he asked, "How much you want for the combat boots?"

"Not for sale," I said, still looking for Gussie.

"How 'bout that lumberjacket?"

"I couldn't sell these things," I said, shaking my head. "My mother gave them to me." Then, as I watched him shiver, stomp on the ground and blow in his hands, I must have had a seizure—a kind of seizure of impulse—during which I removed my jacket and boots and gave them to him, saying, "Merry Christmas, pal."

Removing his rotten tennis shoes and throwing them on my lap, he said, "And Merry Christmas to you, too, pal."

Putting on the tennis shoes and finding that they weren't too tight because of all the holes in the sides, I asked, "You want to come home with me, thaw out, and eat something?"

With the boots still unlaced and his head buried in the jacket, he said, "You can go now! Just leave me the fuck alone and take off!"

"Well, if that's the way you feel about it, I will take off," I said, getting up and heading for home to get warm clothes, slipping and sliding in the rotten tennis shoes, feeling heartsick and cold. Then as soon as I arrived home and opened the door, Gussie was there to greet me and scold me, wanting out.

Wet and feverish, I took Gussie out and, afterwards, took a few aspirins and changed into warm clothes. After cleaning up the mess I'd made in the library and after throwing the tennis shoes in the garbage, I stretched out on my bed. My head was a belltower and the bells were ringing without mercy, and I cried: "Oh, God, I can't take any more!" Then, ever so gradually, the pain in my head subsided, and silence, like a breath from God, restored my soul, until soft music, like the heartbeats of God, began playing in my head. And, as Strauss's "Rosenkavalier Suite" played in my mind, other things began to happen there, as well. My mother, wearing the blue ballet slippers she'd worn long ago, came to dance for me, as I, as a small child, sat on the living room floor of our home in Bordeaux. She was beautiful, with her blue eyes bright and her long, dark hair playing down the back of her slender body, complemented now by black tights with a pink ribbon around the waist. Dancing, she kept her smile on me, as I sat there laughing and clapping my hands and hoping she'd never stop. But, when the music stopped, she stopped and, putting her long, slender hands on her hips, she smiled and said, "Now, my dear boy, we must go outside and help Papa with the rose bushes." And I, watching her put on a green chemise and other shoes, wished with all my heart that the music would play again, so she would dance again...

The brass doorhammer sounded, and Gussie barked. Following the dog to the door, I opened up to see Elsie, standing in the snow and smiling. She was dressed in a white ski-outfit, red mittens, a shiny pair of red, leather boots and around her blonde head she wore a red knitted headband. Handing me a poinsettia, she said, "Merry Christmas, Matty."

"Merry Christmas, Elsie," I said, showing her in and hanging her jacket by the door. Then, after kissing her, I said, "Thanks for coming."

Adjusting her white, turtleneck sweater, she said, "Your mom called me yesterday and made me promise I wouldn't leave you alone for Christmas—fat chance I'd leave you alone, right Matty?"

We went to the kitchen, where I put the plant on the table and asked,

"You hungry?"

"I could eat a little something."

"Well, you fix it, and I'll start a fire in the library fireplace."

A few minutes later, while we ate chicken sandwiches and drank tea on the leather sofa in front of the fire, Elsie said, "I see your cuts and bruises are getting better. I hope you get some scars. I love scars on men's faces."

"And I love scars on women's faces—gives them character."

"Matty, if I'd known that, I would've worn my scars that day in the sandtrap. I knew I'd forgotten something. And I would've worn them today."

"Will you ever get out of that sandtrap, Elsie?"

"Nope, never will,-- got any sand around here?"

"No, so keep your clothes on, at least for now."

"Laughing, with tears flooding her eyes, she said, "You're good for me, Matty."

"Because I make you cry?"

"These are tears of joy. I'm happy to be with you. Matty, are you glad we're friends?"

"Yes, of course."

Serious now, she said, "After that day in the sandtrap, I was so ashamed of myself, that I was going to run away. I thought you'd never be able to respect me. Know why I didn't run?"

"Because you wanted to take your piano, and it was too heavy to carry."

"This is serious, Matty—don't be so silly."

"I'm sorry," I said, straightening my face to serious.

"That's better. Well, I didn't run, because I was too nuts about you. Know when I first got nuts about you? Did I tell you that already?"

"If you did, I've forgotten."

"Matty, I've loved you ever since I saw you fall off your bike, ass-over teakettle, right in front of Major Danny's statue. That must be at least ten years ago."

"Did you laugh?"

"No—I swear I didn't," she said, laughing.

"But you're laughing now, aren't you?"

Covering her mouth with her hand, she mumbled, "I'm sorry." Then, after a few stifled giggles, she asked, "Can I come back here with you, after we finish with the music at Midnight Mass?"

"Sure."

Now looking at the guitar over in the corner, she said, "Maybe we could play a little guitar—you know, to sort of pass the time, until we go to church."

"Okay," I said, getting up and getting the guitar. "You go first."

"Oh, Matty, please—you go first, because it's your house and your guitar."

Without saying anything more, I sat on the sofa again and, after running a few chords in my key, I decided to sing, while I played:

> "There was a goat,
> so big and fine,
> who ate three red shirts
> from a farmer's line.
> The farmer took him,
> to a railroad track,
> and there he tied him,
> on his back.
> The train came along,
> the whistle blew,
> the goat, he knew,
> his time was due.
> He gave an awful
> shriek of pain,
> coughed up the shirts,
> and flagged the train."

Smiling through tears, Elsie said, I'm so glad the goat was saved. Did you write that, Matty?"

"No, I didn't write it, and I don't know who did," I said, playing chords and thinking of what to sing now. Then improvising, I sang of my love for the woods and wild flowers, of fishing and my fear of the Dark River, of the hunger in my soul for love and peace, and finally, of Elsie. Looking in her eyes, I sang:

"Elsie, I find refuge
in you today, as my
day and dreams
fly away.
I find refuge in
your smile.
I find refuge in your eyes.
I find refuge in your heart,
today.
Aujourd'hui. Aujourd'hui."

After I'd kissed her and gave her the guitar, she played with a soft, classical touch, and looking in my eyes, sang:

"Lie naked in the sand
with me. Love me.
Love needs no reason,
and has no shame.
Lie naked in the sand
with me.
"Feel the sun and sand.
Feel the warmth of love.
Wake, and sleep no more
in the darkness of
yesterday.

"Sing, sing of the
long, sad night. Sing
of that which made you
sleep, and sing of the love
that awakens you.

"God's dream of life
was born in you-- that you
love and be loved
in return.

> Lift up your heart
> with mine and lie
> naked in the sand
> with me… with me,
> my love, with me."

We sat in front of the fire a long while in silence, before I went upstairs and changed into my blue blazer and grey, flannel pants. Then, after we stopped at Elsie's, so she could put on her red dress, we went to the church, and as soon as we arrived, it was Morely "Bulldog" Horton who greeted us out in front. He was wearing the lumberjacket and boots I'd given away, earlier. The jacket was too small, of course, but the boots seemed to fit. "Where'd you get the nice jacket and boots?" I asked, realizing it was the first time I'd seen him out of uniform.

"You like 'em?" he asked, grinning. "I bought 'em from an undercover agent for the F.B.I., for fifty dollars. That little, old fella had a lot of things he didn't need any more."

"Nice," Elsie said. "Jacket's a little tight, isn't it?"

"It'll stretch," Morely said, tugging at the jacket and going into church.

When we left church, it was snowing. After going to her house and picking up a small Christmas tree, loaded with homemade ornaments, we went to the cemetery, where she placed the tree on her parents' grave. After bowing her head, when she probably prayed, she looked at me and asked, "Do you think the tree is too much?"

Seeing her tears, I said, "Not at all. It's beautiful, what you did."

Looking up into the falling snow, smiling, and stretching out her arms, she said, "When I was a little girl, my mom told me that each snowflake is an angel's smile, and I believed it."

"And you still do, right?"

"Of course," she said, laughing. "Why not?"

Taking my hand and leading me from the cemetery, she asked, "What do you believe about Christmas, Matty?"

Taking her arm, I said, "That's a good question."

"Tell me, do you believe Christ was born God?"

After thinking for a moment, I said, "Elsie, you might not like it, but I'll tell you. I believe a child was born in Bethlehem, and that his name was Jesus. Whether or not that child was born God, isn't important to me. However, what is important to me is that the child is remembered with love by so many people, in a world that needs love, desperately."

"I like that. It's okay with me, if you feel that way."

"I'm glad it's okay with you, Elsie," I said, chuckling.

"Be serious!" she said, laughing.

Arriving at my house, I took Gussie out, while Elsie made hot chocolate. When I returned, I built a new fire in the library. Then, as we were getting comfortable, the phone rang. It was my mother. "Merry Christmas," she said. "I'm still here in Paris."

"Merry Christmas, Mama."

"How did the music go at church?"

"Good," I said, yawning.

"Did you have a supper yet?"

"No, Mama. We just got back."

"Oh, is Elsie there with you?"

"Yes."

"Fix her a nice supper, Matthew. She's such a nice young lady."

"I will."

"What will you cook?"

"Salmon cakes."

"Matthew, if you have soup, use the porcelain bowl. And don't forget the salad and French bread."

"No, Mama."

"Well, prepare what you wish. I don't want to interfere. Greetings to Elsie. She's such a beautiful young woman and very intelligent. You may not think so, but she is. Well, I know you're busy. I'll call again tomorrow. It is morning here. I wish we were together, dear."

"I do, too."

"God bless you, my dear son."

"Goodnight, Mama."

"Goodnight, Matthew."

I hung up and fixed something to eat, salmon cakes and salad. After eating, we went to the Music Room, where I showed Elsie my mother's collection of porcelain figurines, displayed in a Queen Anne curio. "When I was a small boy," I said, "I used to be jealous of these pieces. When my mother made a fuss over them, I hated it. Do you understand?"

"Yes, I understand," she said, smiling and putting her arm around my waist.

Moving on to a painting I'd done, we stopped and looked at it, a landscape filled with animals and trees, and the moody Dark River. "I did it a long time ago," I said, "when I was about sixteen."

"It's beautiful," she said, squeezing my arm.

When we were at the piano, she raised the cover and, after running a few scales, asked, "Shall I play one of my favorites, of all time?"

"Okay, Elsie, tear my heart out."

And that was what she did. She tore my heart out, with Franz Liszt's Pester Karneval and, when she finished, I applauded, and she twisted a finger in the dimple in her cheek, curtsied, fluttered her long eyelashes and said: "You ain't hoid nuttin yet!"

"Laughing, we went to another painting, and I said, "This is my conception of a day with my family, before my father was killed." It was a scene taking place on the grounds of our home in Bordeaux, with its graceful trees, white house, and a gazebo covered with red roses. Inside the gazebo, as I sat on a branch of an apple tree, my mother and father were looking up at me. I was waving at them, but only my father was waving back. My mother was just sitting there, with an expression of fear on her face. "What do you think, Elsie?" I asked.

"It smiles," she said. "Matty, your paintings have a smile—a mysterious smile."

"Well, I guess all smiles are mysterious," I said, guiding her back to the library. Then, after we were seated in front of the fire, I asked, "Are you tired—shall we retire to our sandbox?"

"Not yet, Matty. Let's just sit for awhile. I love it, Matty, I love it. I'm so happy I could pee my pants!"

"Go ahead."

"I just might—watch out!" she said, laughing. Then, with a serious expression, she said, "I'm sorry I said what I said in my bedroom that day—that you should get some guts. You've got plenty of guts, fighting with Bulldog."

Smiling weakly, I said, "Those aren't the kind of guts I need."

"Hey, Matty—guts is guts!" she said seriously.

"Maybe you're right."

"How could I forget? I mean, when you said you were afraid to get involved. At the time, I thought you were afraid, but now, after looking back, I can see you had a lot of guts. Yes, you were probably afraid, but you did something about it. You didn't love me, and you didn't want to hurt me, or yourself. Right?"

"Something like that."

"Just think: You could've gone on and on screwing me, and then what?"

"I don't know."

"Well, I don't know either, Matty, but I have a feeling it would've ended in disaster. Know why?"

"Why?"

"As time went on, you would've respected me, less and less. And that goes for me, too. I would've seen you didn't love me, and could never love or respect me, and that would've made me feel bad, and as small as a grasshopper's turd. So, you see, you did the right thing by weaseling out of it. Even then, I guess I knew in my heart that it was the right thing, and now I'm sure. You see, Matty, I'm not as dumb as some people think. I got all A's in school."

"How many more times are you going to tell me that you got all A's?"

"Don't be mad at me, please."

"I'm not mad," I said, laughing. "I was just kidding. I could never get mad at you."

Smiling again, she asked, "What're you going to do with the rest of your life, now that you've graduated?"

Getting up, going over by the French doors, I watched the heavy snowfall and said, "I don't know, and I don't much care."

Coming to me and taking my hand, she said, "Well, at least you know what you don't want to do-- become a priest."

"You're right about that."

"Look at me, Matty, and don't fly off the handle at what I say. Look at me."

"I'm looking," I said, looking.

Expressionless, she said, "When the time comes, you'll know what you're supposed to do, and that's going to be what you feel God wants you to do with your life. Day by day, keep doing what you feel is right. Keep in touch with yourself and God and follow your heart. If you believe that God wants you to sit in the sun all day and breathe in the beauty of nature, then do it. If you feel He wants you to write poetry, paint pictures, and play music, then do it. If you feel He wants you to look at your pain and mistakes, and learn from those things, then do it. But, damn!—move on and keep doing something. We makes our mistakes, takes our lumps, learn from our mistakes, and move on. Well, I've said my piece. Take it or leave it."

"What's happened to you, Elsie? I've never heard you talk like that before."

"Me? You want to hear about me?"

"Is there more about you that I don't know about?"

"A whole bunch. For one thing, you don't know what else I did, when I went to Detroit for my music lessons. After the lesson, I went to the Institute of Arts and looked at the beautiful things. I never told people I did that, because I was afraid they'd think I was strange and weird, besides being a dumb blonde. I cared too much what they thought, but now I couldn't care less, because it's none of my business what people think of me. I just try to do the right thing and let it go at that. Anyhow, when I first saw those masterpieces down there, nothing happened inside me. But, when I kept going back, I began to think about all the dedication, passion, and suffering that went into creating those beautiful things. Then, gradually, I began feeling something inside me, that seemed to relate to all that dedication and passion and suffering. When I looked at all that form and color and harmony, I could feel it working inside me. Do you know what I'm trying to say, Matty?"

"Yes, I know, and I know something else—something I didn't know until now, but often wondered about. Elsie, when you play the piano, guitar, sing—or even if you're just talking, or not talking, the souls of those artists shine through."

"Well, maybe you just hit the nail right on the head. I believe those artists suffered for something good, and true, and beautiful. They were driven to work like hell, and fight, for the freedom to do what they felt they ought to be doing. They inspired me, I guess, in all that I did, and do, especially in my work with suffering children. Matty, did you know that for years, I've been working as a volunteer at a hospital, in the children's ward?"

"No, I didn't."

"Oh, Matty, if I had a billion eyes, I don't think I'd ever be able to see the reason for a suffering child. There was this little girl. Her name was Barbara and she was dying of leukemia. Well, it was July and one day she said she wanted Christmas. Then, after we asked her what she wanted for Christmas, she said, with a big smile, 'Christmas. That's all I want—just Christmas.' You see, I guess Christmas meant life to her and joy. It broke my heart. Well, we put up a little tree and sang carols and she gave us all a big hug and kiss. She was so happy. I'll never forget it, and I'll never forget the day she died. I was there with her, and for some reason, I felt she'd given me her heart, to keep safe in my heart. Her mother was there, when Barbara faded away, but she was drinking and hysterical. Oh, Matty, I want to keep my heart clean for Barbara. I want to be honest and become a good person, before my blood has burned away, like Barbara's. But I need your help, Matty. I need another human being. It's not easy for me. My life has never been one of confidence. I need your gentle smile in my life. I need your music and words to help me cope with the harsh, ugly echoes in my mind. There are things I can't look at all by myself. I need someone I can trust—someone who also has harsh and ugly echoes. When my guts run out on me, I need someone to help give me courage and make me smile. I need you, Matty. Is that one too many needs?"

A train whistle sounded in the distance, before I said, "I have the same needs."

"I'll be there for you, Matty."

"And I'll be there for you, Elsie."

## chapter 11

E<small>LSIE</small> was on the phone, saying, "Matty, could I ask you to get away from your work tomorrow and drive some people over to Glennie. The annual excursion is tomorrow. It'll do you good. It'll do us both good."

"I forgot all about it. Sure, Elsie, I'll do it. What time, where?"

"At eight in the morning, at the small park in front of St. Joseph's—okay?"

"I'll be there."

"Good. Then I'll see you on the boat. I love you."

"I love you too, Elsie."

Returning to the piano, I couldn't believe it was June already. Since Christmas, after being inspired by Elsie, I'd remained at home, and except for seeing Elsie at her house for a couple of hours each day, I'd worked on my music, painting, and poetry until music became most important for me and seemed to demand most of my time. So, I'd forgotten the excursion, that being an annual event of boating down the Au Sable River, the Dark River, on the River Queen, a paddle boat, now docked at Glennie, a small town about fifty miles to the west of Point Stevens. My mother seemed pleased that I was going.

The next day was warm and sunny. I was fifteen minutes late, when I arrived at the park and found no one there but Trixie Roper. Not relishing the idea of being alone with Trixie, I fought off the impulse to return home and drove over to her. Rolling down the window, I asked, "Want a ride to Glennie, for the excursion?"

"Well, she said, looking around. "If you're the only one here, I guess

I'll have to accept."

"Hop in."

So, there she was next to me, as pretty as ever, and as snotty as she'd become, saying, "Can't you get this station wagon to go any faster? Thirty miles an hour is for the birds. The speed limit's fifty, you know. We'll never get to that goddamn boat. I could walk faster."

Remaining at peace, after dismissing the idea of telling her to get out and walk, I nudged the accelerator and said, "This is it for fast, Trixie. I can't afford a speeding ticket."

"A rich guy like you? Shit you can't. Must be nice to be able to afford a nice station wagon like this."

"It's my mother's."

"My boyfriend's got a beautiful sports car. It'll do a hundred, without even tryin'."

Not really interested, but wanting to keep her off my driving, I asked, "So, who's this guy with the fast car?"

"Just a guy," she said, twisting the ends of her long, red hair.

"Is he from Point Stevens?"

"No."

"What's his name?"

"Chick."

"Chick who?"

"Fuck off, will you!"

"Well, you're the one who brought him up."

"Okay," she said, staring in her large leather bag, "now just mind your own business."

"Where does he live?" I asked, with an ominous feeling unsettling me now.

"Boy, you are one nosey bastard. If you must know, he lives in Loon Lake-- satisfied?"

"What does he do for a living?"

Laughing, she said, "Still the same curious shithead, aren't you? Okay, I'll tell you about him—but only 'cause I'm proud of him. He's very handsome and has a college degree and I love him. And he loves me, with all his heart'n soul—he told me so."

"What did he get his degree in?" I asked, seeing that her mood had changed suddenly from snotty to almost friendly. I was getting interested now. It was as if my instincts were sniffing, as if I were a police dog.

"Chemistry," she said, her mood changing back to down.

Looking at her staring at the leather bag between her feet, I asked, "What's in the bag?"

"Jesus Christ!" she yelled, her green eyes wild and protruding. "No more goddamn questions—okay?"

Seeing her anger and defiance, I told myself that she'd changed for the worse. I recalled last October, when she'd served me ginger ale and a plate of food. Glancing at her, I saw she was chewing gum now—Juicy Fruit, by the smell—and she wasn't offering me any. I saw too that she was having trouble focusing her eyes. I asked, "Something the matter with your eyes, Trixie?"

Snotty, she said, "Not a damn thing's wrong with my eyes. Just shut up and drive."

"Is Chick going to be there today?"

No answer.

"Are you high on something, Trixie?"

"Stop the goddamn car, I wanna get out!"

Not about to let her out, I said, "I'm sorry. I only asked . "Maybe I'll want some, when we get there."

That was enough to change her mood again. Smiling, she said, "You know, come to think on it, you just might want some. I heard from Nancy Hunter that you're a real party-guy, sometimes." Then, opening her bag, she said, "Well, feast your eyes on this, Matt!"

Glancing again, I saw a large plastic bag of what I guessed to be marijuana. "Is that pot?" I asked.

"We're really gonna get stoned. I hope you'll join us. Chick'll be there. He's a real hip guy and so are you, when you wanna be."

"I can dig it," I said, laughing, seeing now that her head was back and her eyes were closed. I was glad she was resting, so I could think of what to do. I didn't want her to get into trouble—at least, not deep trouble with the law. And I didn't want her falling off the boat. Trixie, regardless of what was happening to her, was still an important part of my life. In sixth grade, when I'd first come to America, she hadn't made fun of my accent, as many of the kids did, and was always there to help me with my schoolwork. And it was in sixth grade, when she'd put the first valentine on my desk, sending me a message of love. And she'd done the same the next two years, with the same message, but then stopped, probably because I never put one on her desk, or even acknowledged hers. I was shy, and she was popular, so much so, that by the time we reached high school, she was a cheerleader, and I was a square with an inferiority complex. However, although she was busy, she sometimes crowded me into her schedule. At school dances, for example, she always asked me to dance, choosing me from the bunch of sticks leaning against the wall, and I'd always stepped on her feet, being tall and clumsy—just as I was now, in trying to figure out how to keep her out of trouble.

"I must've fell asleep," she was saying, stretching and yawning.

In a casual, snoopless tone, I asked, "Did you say Chick is going to be on the excursion?"

"Yeah, he'll be there. Did I tell you he wants to take me to California?"

"Well, no you didn't tell me. Why's he going to take you there?"

"To marry me—that's why."

"He doesn't have to take you there to marry you. He could do that in Point Stevens."

"Who the hell wants to get married in Point Stevens?"

"But, why California, Trixie?"

Laughing, she said, "Don't laugh, clown, but Chickie knows people there, in the movie business. He said, with my talent for dancing, he could get me in the movies."

I didn't laugh, of course. I was worried, and skeptical about Chick's motives. "When you leaving?" I asked casually.

"Next week."

"Do your parents know?"

"I'm twenty-six, and I'm my own boss. What the hell my parents have to do about it?"

"I just wondered."

"Well, my father knows, and he's all for it. He wants me to be a movie star and make a lot of money."

"What about your mother?"

"She doesn't know, I guess, and I'm not gonna tell her."

"Don't you get along?"

"We get along okay, and she probably wouldn't raise hell, if she found out I was goin' to the coast. I don't know, it's just that you don't know where you stand with her—and it's been that way all my life. I'll never forget, for instance, when I was just a kid. She sends me to the store for a big bottle of pop, and when I came back with it, the stupid thing slips out my arms and breaks, right in front of the house. Then she comes out, with her stupid broom and dustpan—Christ, I think she took 'em to bed with her—and then she cleans up the mess from the sidewalk, and doesn't even yell at me for breakin' the damn bottle. In fact, she gave me more money to buy some more pop. See what I mean? You don't know where the hell you stand with her. Now, if my pa saw me break that, he would've beat the livin' hell out of me, like he did whenever I did stupid things like that. But not my mother—not one word about it. And, when I was in bed that night, with my eyes closed and not sleepin', she kisses me on the forehead, and, you know, that's the only kiss I got from her, in my whole life. She's a weirdo, I tell you!"

"Maybe you just can't recall the times she kissed you."

Squinting at me, she said, "You know, for an intelligent guy, you're very stupid, Matt. You're supposed to kiss people, when you know they can tell you're kissin' them, just like you're supposed to say nice things to kids growing up. My mother never did, at least not when I was awake."

"Some people have a hard time expressing their feelings."

Poking me in the ribs, she laughed and said, "Some people, like you, right?"

"I'll admit to that. Say, did your father ever say nice things about you, to you?"

"He has no trouble with expressions, but it's all bullshit with him, and anger."

"I heard Oswald Fork's going to cut your father's heart out and make him eat it."

Laughing, she said, "So, you know about him swindlin' poor, old Oswald. Well, if you ask me, they're two of a kind. It was just a matter of who was gonna do it to the other one, first."

"I guess."

"And most of the people in town ain't clean, neither. Lots of hypocrites aroun'."

"Know who you sound like?"

Laughing, she said, "Wanda Ross, right?"

"Hold on, I should've said it was the way she used to sound. Since the accident, she's very different—a nice person now."

"I'll bet. You know, when you took up with her, I got so goddamn jealous I couldn't see straight."

"Jealous?"

"Get off it, Matt. Ever since sixth grade, I've had a crush on you."

"I didn't know that."

"Bullshit, you didn't know! Anyhow, you took up with Wanda, and now you're with that stupid blonde—Elsie Quinn. But I don't give a shit. It's over between us, Matt, 'cause now I'm nuts about Chickie." Then, after we were in the parking lot in Glennie, she said, "Will you just look at that old garbage barge—ain't she a beauty?"

"The River Queen? Old, is right."

"See you later," she said, as soon as I'd parked.

We were under way, and the feeling of impending disaster, like chokeweed, began growing inside me. I felt sure it had to do with Trixie, but I said nothing about it, not even to Elsie, at the moment. Uppermost in my mind was to keep an eye on Trixie, but it wasn't easy. It was obvious she'd changed her mind about letting me in on the marijuana party, because she would disappear when I got near. Finally, after maybe twenty minutes, I told Elsie about the marijuana and the ominous feeling inside me. "I can't help it," I said. "I just don't want her to get into trouble and maybe go to jail."

"I just saw her upstairs," Elsie said. "Let's go and check."

Climbing to the upper deck, I saw her. She was aft, in front of the paddle wheel, and next to her was a short, dark, burly man of about fifty, and right in front of those two was a group of about twenty young people. Then, as Elsie and I stood by a railing and watched, I could see that Trixie and her friend were selling small plastic bags.

"Good God!" Elsie said, nudging my arm. "Do you know what's happening, Matty?"

"They're selling pot, I guess."

"That's not pot," Elsie said, "unless it's been dyed white."

Looking again, I said, "That's not the stuff Trixie showed me, when we were coming."

"Let's go see what's happening," Elsie said. "It's probably heroin." Then, without waiting for me, she ran to Trixie, grabbed her arms, wrenched a large paper bag from her, looked inside and threw it overboard.

"You rotten bitch, Elsie Quinn!" Trixie yelled. Then, whining, she turned to her boyfriend and yelled: "Chickie, you gonna let her get away with that?"

After the group of young people took off, Chickie yelled: "You fuckin' bitch! You had no right to do that! That smack is private property!"

Although the group of young people was gone, others had taken their place in front of Elsie and the other two, making it almost impossible for me to get through.

However, being taller than anyone in front of me, I could see what was happening. Without anyone trying to stop them, Chickie and Trixie were pulling Elsie over to the starboard railing. "Let her go!" I yelled, slowly pushing my way through. "For God's sakes, somebody help her!"

No one moved to help—in fact, some people in the crowd were laughing, maybe thinking it was all in fun.

Finally, I broke through, but it was too late. "Elsie!" I yelled, seeing her splashing and trying to swim in a desperate effort to clear the wake left by the paddle wheel.

"Matty, help me!" she screamed, now free of the wake and being carried downstream by the swift and treacherous current.

Seeing her in the water, like a wounded and helpless bird, it was a matter of a split-second before her struggle became my struggle and the meaning of my life became the saving of my soul by trying to save her. And I knew that if I didn't try, then I would lose myself, and her drowning would be my drowning, for all eternity. So now, with her fear in my heart, I jumped into the forbidding waters of the Dark River—the river that had bullied me for so long. Then, by thrashing and splashing and keeping the marker of her blonde hair, spread out on the water, in view, I managed to clear the wake and finally reach her. She was unconscious, limp and heavy, but somehow, I got her to the shore of cold mud. There, I tried to revive her but failed.

I looked in the box of death and didn't recognize her. She had on a blue dress, with a fluffy, white collar that hid her long, slender neck. Her swollen lips were smeared with orange lipstick and something pinkish was plastered all over her face and even up into her hair. It was too much for me. I rushed from the funeral home and began to walk the shoreroad. Morning fog and the smell of burning waste came at me in loops and swells. I wanted to hide, but I could think of nowhere to go but down inside myself, where there was nothing but confusion, anger, and soulsickness. My throat was sore, and my eyes burned without tears. They'd made her look like a clown, I told myself. Then, thinking that booze would deaden my emotions, I headed for Belda Bird's Bar, to get as drunk as possible, for as long as possible...

"Well, well, if it ain't Honey Pole," Belda said, grabbing my arm at the door. "Why, I ain't seen you since the moon went over the mountain."

"Hello, Belda," I said, looking around. "Where are your Regulars?"

"Too early for them, except Sailorboy. He's in the kitchen, eatin' breakfast, before he goes behind the bar for awhile. You wouldn't believe it, but he's a good bartender when he's sober."

As she led me to a table, I thought about the last time I'd been in here, when Morely and I had the fight. I hoped she wouldn't mention it, especially today. Then after we were at a small table in a dark corner, and she left to check on Sailorboy, I recalled another night, maybe five summers ago, when Belda had tried to talk me into going up to her private chambers. But, after I told her I had cancer, she retreated. I hoped now that she'd forgotten that, also.

Belda Bird wasn't young, nor old, not small, nor large. For me, today, when Elsie's cries for help were still sounding in my soul, Belda was just right, and if she were to ask me up to her chambers again, I had a feeling I'd jump at the chance—anything, that would help remove Elsie's cries and the agony of guilt I felt. Watching her now, as she talked with Sailorboy and seemed to be showing him where things were located, I saw that her body was trim, and that her face was all handpainted, like a beautiful movie star's. But the exterior beauty wasn't what interested me most. I believed it was the beauty inside her that excited me, and made me think of it as a refuge for my tired and suffering spirit. She was devoted to truth and was wise, caring, loving, extremely compassionate, and honest. But, by no means was she a living saint, and she would come down hard on anyone who even suggested that she was. She readily admitted that there was a coarse quality about her and that a bug got up her ass at times—but only when someone showed lack of honesty, love, or compassion. Now, sitting across from me at the table, she showed no signs of coarseness, or ill-temper, saying, "Nat La Fleur—what a nice surprise!"

"That's Matt," I said, hoping I wouldn't offend her by correcting her. "Matt."

"I'm sorry, Honey Pole. Okay, Nat is out, and Matt is in. Didn't want to hurt your feelin's none—that's the truth." Then, after staring at me for a moment, she asked, "Well, Nat, what you want to drink?"

Not wanting to correct her again, I said, "I'll have what you're going to have."

"Hey!" she yelled, reaching over and slapping my arm. "This's a special occasion—let's have a big, good ole boilermaker. It'll do wonders for me—and it'll be good for your cancer."

Wishing I hadn't lied about having cancer, I said, "Okay, a boilermaker it is—what's a boilermaker?"

"A shot'n a beer, Nat," she said, getting up and going to the bar. Then, when she returned with two shots of whiskey and two draft beers, she said, "It's on the house, and there's plenty more where these come from."

Not wanting to look like a wimp, I threw the whiskey into the glass of beer and drank half; then, after clearing my throat, I said, "Nice dress you've got on, Belda. It's a nice shade of blue."

"Honest?" she asked, smiling and showing sparkling, white teeth.

"Honest," I said, smiling along with her.

"The dress is green, not blue."

"So it is," I said, taking a sip of my drink.

"They call it teal blue, but it looks blue to me, too. Glad you like it, Nat." Then, after running her fingers over her lowcut neckline, she asked, "Don't show too much of me, up here, does it—too much cleavage for you?"

"No, not at all."

"I'm in pretty fair shape, for bein' in such poor health, right?"

I didn't know you were in poor health, Belda."

"Bad heart, failing kidneys, disappearing liver, painful piles. Nope, Nat, I won't be here much longer. It won't be long before I join my four ex-hubbies, buried out back in my private cemetery, just below my private chambers. My first hubby—that makes it five—ain't buried with the others. He's buried in the Pacific Ocean, along with the rest of the guys who were on that four-pipe destroyer, sunk by the Japanese during the war. Then, pointing her ear at me, she asked, "What's that you're hummin', Nat?"

"Humming? I'm not humming, Belda—honest."

"Well, whatever you're doin' with your mouth, cut it out. I don't want you to be makin' noises with your mouth when I'm tryin' to tell you somethin'."

"I understand," I said, watching her get up and go to the bar again.

Returning and putting more drinks on the table, she sat and said, "Well, I think it's time I told you the truth about yourself, Nat, and you better give a listen." Then, after throwing down another whiskey, she coughed and said, "You're messin' up on your life, Nat. I can tell by your eyes that your life's in shambles. Christ, you're scattered all over the place, like the sawdust on this here floor. You don't know who the hell you are. You're tryin' to be somethin' you ain't and you're tryin' to have somethin' you ain't got—like cancer. Is that the truth, or ain't it?"

"I've gotta be going, Belda," I said, getting up.

"Sit!" she yelled, her eyes looking like big, black balloons, ready to burst. Then, after I was seated again, she said, "You see, I know every single thing that there is to know about the people in this town. You lied about the cancer, didn't you?"

"To tell the truth, yes, I lied."

Smiling, she said compassionately, "Well, we're all titled to a couple lies in our life. But, that's not what I was getting at. Why did you come here today?"

"I'm not sure."

With tears in her eyes now, she said softly, "You came here 'cause of that Elsie Quinn, who died. You wanna get drunk and screw me, to try to forget you didn't save her. You failed, but you tried your ass off tryin' to save her and you almost drowned. Shit, Honey Pole, so get honest with yourself and get a handle on it."

Feeling the drink, I said, "I've really gotta be going, Belda."

"Are you gonna getta handle on it—all that fuckin' guilt you're carryin'?"

"I'll try, but I don't think I'll be able to. I should've saved Elsie. I'm a failure. I can't help it. I hate myself."

"Where you goin' when you leave here?"

"Home."

"I want the truth!"

Panicked, I drunkenly thought she'd caught me in another lie. Big bubbles of sweat began popping out on my face, bursting and stinking. I could feel the roots of my hair begin to ache and burn. "Okay," I blurted out. "I'll tell the truth.. I'm gonna go to Hawaii, and from there I'm goin' to Chicago, Los Angeles, France, and New York."

"New York? Christ, hey, Honey Pole, doncha go there. New York ain't for you. I was there once, in an honest effort to find happiness. I wanted to act on the stage—it's the God's honest truth!"

"I believe it, Belda," I said, my head hanging and my eyes closed, in my trying to manage my dizziness.

"I was nothin' but a kid—a truthful, kind, lovin' kid. Well, after I couldn't get a job on the stage, I started workin' in a whorehouse, just so I could get enough money for a bus ticket back here. Know how long it took me? It took my three years to save enough to come back here, and now, here's where I stay, 'til they bury my ass out back with my four hubbies—hey, now don't let me mislead you, 'cause there's another one in the Pacific Ocean, under all that water, and that's Jinx Crowley down there, bigger'n life, no doubt, like he was in life. I honestly hope Jinx's happy, but to tell the truth, I don't think he is—not without me beside him. Know what, Nat Baby, I just might be buried with ole Jinx, after all, after I ship the other four out there, of course—that's the only sensible thing to do. Then, we can all be together, happy and cozy under all that ocean—what do you think?"

Not lifting my head, I said, "Damn good idea, Belda. Going out there would be a lot easier than having the ocean shipped here."

Laughing, she said, "I love you, Honey Pole. I love your style—just like mine, honest and fun-lovin' and kind, and it's good to have you aroun'. So, why the hell you gonna go to New York, and all those other places for? You'd think you'd wanna stay here with me, drinkin' and drinkin', 'til you see the snakes and die. Hey, I just thought of somethin'. If you stay here and die, I'll see to it that you get buried at sea, with the rest of us. Would you like that?"

"Good idea, Belda."

"Honest?"

"Honest."

"Then you'll stay?"

"I'll stay," I said, looking up in time to see her smiling.

"Guess what?" she asked, frowning now.

"What?" I asked, smiling.

"It'd be better if you did have cancer, 'stead of what's inside you. You told me you hate yourself for failin' to save Elsie. Well, that means you're a hatin' person. I thought as much. To tell the truth, I was suspicious of you the very first time I seen you. You don't have an ounce of love for yourself in your damn heart. In fact, you're full of hatred!"

Looking in her dark, angry eyes, I said, "But I love my mother."

"No matter. It only takes one hate to fuck things all up. And, come to think of it, how come you think you can love anybody else, if you don't love yourself? It don't work out, unless you love yourself, first, shithead. If you hate yourself, then you gotta hate every goddamn creation on the face of the earth. Hey, asshole, you unnerstand what I'm talkin' 'bout?"

"I unnerstand, Belda."

"Then, one final word on the subject: Listen, you skinny son of a bitch, don't you dare bring your hatin' ass aroun' here anymore—unnerstand?"

"I unnerstand, perfectly."

"And one additional thing: We ain't gonna let you be buried at sea with us, not with all that goddamn hate. You'd be pollutin' up the whole ocean, includin' ole Jinx and us. O-kay, Mr. Hatred, now you get your hatin' ass the hell out of here and don't come back 'til you don't hate yourself no more! Beat it!"

I was quick about leaving, and when I was outside, I staggered and stumbled towards home, feeling confused and sad over her scolding me and throwing me out. Then suddenly, I thought I knew why she'd acted that way, hostile and mean. It was part of her act, to help her get her points across. With that in mind now, I had a new respect for Belda, and gratitude for her trying to help, and because she'd allowed me to see what a fine actress she was. I felt privileged.

However, by the time I got home, and I'd sobered up some, I no longer felt privileged. The misery in my soul had not lifted. Arriving home and finding no one there, I unhooked a bunch of keys from a nail by the back door, started up the station wagon and drove down U.S. 23. Stopping at Pee Wee's Bar, where I was ready to stay for the rest of my life, I went in and ordered a glass of beer. Having been here before, I knew what to expect.

Pee Wee, an ex-boxer and bantam-weight contender about twenty years ago, was doing his thing. With his shaved head all oily and shiny, like a peanut, and now reflecting the colors from the bar lights, he was bobbing, weaving, jabbing, and uppercutting the foul air. Then, just as he was really getting into it, grunting a lot, there was the sound of polka music and laughing coming from upstairs. Quitting his shadowboxing and looking at the ceiling, Pee Wee yelled: "Hey, youse up dair, show a liddle mercy!" Then, looking at me, he smiled and said, "Havin' a good time up dair—couple stupes tied da knot."

Now, wanting desperately to be where there was music, dancing and laughter, I finished my beer and went upstairs to the wedding reception. With no one at the door, checking, I had no trouble crashing it. Then, after drinking just one highball, it happened. My mind tilted, and suddenly I was out there with the polka dancers, spinning, bobbing, weaving and ringing the bunch of keys I'd taken from home, which included the key to the station wagon. Continuing to bob, weave, and spin around, I rang the keys above my head, around my body, and between my legs, always in tempo with the music. Then, moving from the dance floor, I jumped up on top of a table, stomping now, ringing the keys, spilling food, knocking over drinks, until I jumped down to the dance floor again, this time to be alone at the middle of the floor, with people gathering in a circle around me and some of them yelling: "Go, man, go!" And now I was bobbing and weaving and ringing my way to an open window, where, with my spirit saturated with compulsion, I climbed out on the sill, yelled "Geronimo!" and jumped. Then, after hitting the sidewalk and rolling over, as a paratrooper might, I lay on my back, laughing and ringing the keys, until the huge cache of tears inside me burst, and my agony spilled out.

A Michigan State Trooper came, picked me up and drove me to a hospital, where I was treated for cuts and bruises and strapped to a bed. The next morning, with a dim sense of reality, I told a doctor that I wanted to go home.

## chapter 12

I was in a young psychiatrist's office, saying once again, "I want to go home."

Fumbling with my driver's license, he said, "Tell me about yourself, Matthew."

Seeing the man getting ready to write in a notebook, I just sat in front of his desk and said nothing.

"O-kay," the pale young doctor said. "How about dreams? Do you have any recurring dreams?"

"I used to have nightmares, but I haven't had any lately," I said, seeing him writing and not looking up.

"O-kay, Matthew, and what were those nightmares about? Can you remember?"

Now cooperating, so I could go home, I said, "Sometimes, I dreamt I wanted to kill someone. Yes, I wanted to kill the man who killed my father—but I don't any more. Can I go home now?"

Writing, crossing out and writing again, he said, "Let's see, you wanted to kill the man who killed your father. O-kay, who do you want to kill now, besides yourself?"

Shaking, and with nervous sop running from every pore, I said, "Nobody."

"Have you ever attempted suicide before?"

"No."

"Do you get sexual pleasure from jumping from high places?"

"No. Can I go now?"

"Have you ever jumped from a high place before?"

Jangled, I said, "Just once."

"O-kay, Matthew, now we're getting to the crux. Tell me about it—would you do that for me?"

"Well, it was just a dream. I jumped from a high bridge, over the Dark River."

"Why—why did you jump, Matthew?"

"I don't remember. I just jumped, that's all. What's wrong with that?"

"You're angry. Why are you angry?"

"I'm not angry. Can I go now?"

"Now, how did you happen to be up on that high bridge, in the first place?"

Wiping sweat from my face with both hands, then wiping it on my khakis, I said, "I flew up there—okay?"

After writing, he asked, "And how did you fly up there—by helicopter?"

"I flew like a bird."

"O-kay, and where were you, before you flew up there, like a bird?"

"In bed. Can I go now?"

"Matthew, tell me this: Why did you leave your warm bed, to go flying around like a bird?"

"Well, butterfly wings, covered with blood, kept touching me, and hurting me."

"I see. And did you jump from the high bridge, to escape those bloody butterfly wings?"

"No! I jumped so I could join some dancing lights, down on the water. The lights were yellow."

"Let's see now—dancing, yellow lights. Go on, Matthew."

"But I didn't try to kill myself."

"Go on."

With my mouth taking on a life of its own, I said, "I didn't want to kill myself. I wanted to live. Well, sort of half and half. I don't remember all."

"Go on, Matthew."

"Well, I jumped, went under and died."

"How did you feel, when you were dead?"

"Dead, but very much alive. I remember that much. I was in the coffin I'd made out of cardboard boxes and it smelled like dead rats. Okay?"

"O-kay," he said, getting up, getting a cup of coffee, and not offering me any. And sitting again, he wrote in his notebook, ripped out a page, rolled it into a ball, and threw it at me.

The paper ball missed me, but I got very angry. I wanted to get the ball, throw it back at him and put a dent in his face. But, just in time, I thought it wouldn't be the prudent thing to do, if I wanted to go home. Then, with my mind tilting again, I got the idea that he'd been testing me, to see if I was a violent reactionary. Thinking now that I'd passed the test, I snickered, guessing that it was inappropriate.

"What are you laughing about?" he asked, looking at me closely.

"I wasn't laughing," I said, looking at him closely, expecting him to throw another paper ball at me. But, instead, he knocked over his cup of coffee-- making it seem like an accident, I told myself. Then, as the scalding, hot coffee spilled off the desk and onto my legs, I forced myself not to move, or wince, or blink, or show anything in my face that would hint of violence. I just sat there, like a long stick, successfully ignoring my inflamed body and mind and asking, "Can I go home now?"

Also ignoring the coffee spilling onto me, the doctor asked, pointing his long ink pen at me, "Where were you, before you became suicidal and jumped from the window?"

"A bar."

"What's the name of the bar?"

"I don't remember."

"How many drinks did you have?"

"One."

"And before the bar, where were you?"

"Another bar."

"What's the name of that bar?"

"I don't remember."

"How many drinks did you have?"

"Two."

"And before that bar, where were you?"

The wall of silence went up, and the tragic incident of Elsie's death was locked inside me, to become another dark thing in the dark place in my soul.

"Matthew!" he was saying, rapping his knuckles on the desk. "Hello! Where were you, before you went to the bars? Were you doing something illegal?"

No response.

"Damnit to hell, where were you?"

No response.

"O-kay, smartass, you're already up for drunk-and-disorderly conduct. Do you want that I should recommend worse?"

No response. I was determined not to go where he was demanding I go. I thought of lying, but I didn't want a lie to be associated with Elsie, in any way.

"O-kay, punk, you asked for it," he said, getting up and leaving the office. Then, when he returned, accompanied by a big man in a white coat, he said, "You'll be going for a little ride this afternoon, Matthew. We've contacted your mother."

That afternoon, I was taken to the State Hospital.

Heavy gusts of wind and rain battered the windows and lightning ripped the darkened sky. Patients screamed for mercy or sobbed with what seemed to be despair. Some sat silent in corners with their chins on their knees and their hands pressed hard against their ears. Some were on benches, or underneath benches. Others were pacing the ward, seeming completely unaware of the storm, as they seemed to be visiting with imaginary friends, or fighting with imaginary enemies. There was also laughter, quiet and innocent, as an infant's in reverie, and angry-like laughter, as wild and loud as the storm. And also, climbing always higher, there was the shrill laughter of fear. Finally, there was the cruel, mocking laughter coming from two attendants, sitting on a bench laughing and pointing at those who were afraid. As I sat alone on a bench, I wasn't afraid, nor was I laughing at those who were afraid. I was busy harboring a dark place in my soul, which I refused to try to illuminate, look at, talk about, today. I would refuse today, just as I had yesterday, but tomorrow it might be different. I hoped so, because I wanted to get out of here. I wanted to look at the dark things and talk about them, but I didn't have the guts.

The storm moved on, and the afternoon sun moved in. I looked down at the blue denim sack that I held on my lap. The small sack with a drawstring contained my toothbrush, a small tube of toothpaste, a small notebook, and a pencil stub. Last week, when I was admitted, I bought the notebook from Mr. Eddie, an attendant, who kindly threw in the pencil stub for nothing. I had wanted the notebook and pencil, so that I might write something about my painful, maddening past. But not today, I told myself, focusing now on the two attendants, sitting on a bench and not laughing any more.

Young Mr. Eddie, whom I paid ten dollars for the notebook was saying, "Good idea, Mr. Bob."

Lighting his pipe, the old supervisor said, "That's right, you throw a new pipe in the backyard and leave it there for a couple years, to age. Then, you really got somethin' to be proud of—get the point?"

"I get the point, Mr. Bob," Mr. Eddie said, with his ear close to his boss's pipe-scabbed lips. "It's like a miracle, a natural miracle, right, Mr. Bob?"

"Well, I wouldn't know about that," the grey man said, as he wiped his bifocals with the tail of his dirty, white shirt. "All I know is, that a couple years ago, I got a new pipe and lost it in my garden." Replacing his glasses, he continued, saying, "And last spring, I digs it up by accident, when I'm puttin' in my tomatoes." Then, after stuffing his shirt back into his pants, he asked, "And guess what?"

"The pipe was full of worms?"

"Damnit, that's not the point!" Mr. Bob snapped, as if Mr. Eddie had just failed kindergarten. "The point is, it smoked good, and now it's the best pipe I've got. That's the damn point!"

"Is it the one you're smoking now—all stained and rotten-looking?"

"Hell, no. I wouldn't bring a good pipe like that aroun' this hellhole. I keep it home, safe, and just smoke it on Sunday."

Chuckling, Mr. Eddie said, "Might say it's your Sunday-best, right, Mr. Bob?"

"You bet it is."

"I get the point."

A rancid smell began to permeate the ward and the dinner wagon was rolled in for those patients not permitted to leave the ward, which included me. The assigned patients immediately passed out the metal trays and the attendants walked around and made sure everybody ate. If someone didn't eat right away, an attendant whacked him on the head with a big, heavy key, swung down on the end of a long, metal chain, the kind of chain used a lot for bathtub plugs. And that was what Mr. Eddie was doing now, whacking the head of a heavily medicated old man, while he yelled: "We'll shove it down your goddamn throat, if we have to!"

The main course was Swedish meatballs, with sides of rice, string beans and applesauce. After removing the contents of my denim sack and putting it all in my pockets, I dumped the food into the sack and waited. Shortly after, Mr. Bob came to me with his dangling key and, looking at my empty tray, yelled: "Hey now, will you lookit that? The beanpole ate all his maggot shit again!"

After Mr. Eddie saw to it that all the trays were collected and the wagon was gone, he unlocked the toilet door. I hurried to the toilet, flushed down the food, returned to my bench, and waited for bedtime. And it wasn't long before Mr. Kitty, the night man, relieved the other two attendants. Mr. Kitty stank of whiskey. He always stank of whiskey, along with other stinking things, usually differing from day to day. Today, he stank of whiskey and fish, maybe sardines. Yesterday, it had been whiskey and Limburger cheese. He was short, fat, and had red hair, which complemented his green eyes and the green hue of his skin, his most salient feature. His temper was bad, and his voice was shrill, especially when he sang, yodeled or yelled. At the moment, he was yelling: "Okay, you pigs, get the hell out of the toilet, so I can lock the door!" Then, as patients came out and got a whack on the head with Mr. Kitty's big key, he yelled: "I don't see that fuckin' Old Man—where's Old Man?" Clenching his fists now, he yelled: "If he done it again, I'm gonna kill the bastard!"

And obviously Old Man had done it again, because after Mr. Kitty went into the toilet, Old Man's small, wasted body came flying out, and after landing hard on the cement floor, with a sickening thud, it just lay there, as if it were a corpse. And, as if that weren't enough, Mr. Kitty began kicking Old Man, yelling, "Somebody go in there and wash that fuckin' chalk picture off the wall!" Then, after several patients went in there, Mr.

Kitty quit kicking, and yelled: "Old Man, I wanna know where you get that goddamn chalk from—tell me, or else I'll kick the livin' shit out of you!" And, when Old Man stuck his tongue out at the attendant, he kicked him again, until he seemed exhausted, and yelled: "Some of youse search this old chalkbag!"

After searching Old Man, two of the patients handed a few pieces of colored chalk to Mr. Kitty, with one of them saying, "This's all he had on him-- want me look in his underwear?"

"No," Mr. Kitty said, breathing heavily and heading for his cubbyhole office, "you might get the clap!"

I was the one who carried Old Man to a bench by the windows and began to massage his battered body. But he would have none of it, and yelled: "Keep your bony hands to yourself, you weirdo!" Then, after he ran across the ward and sat on the floor against the wall, he just stared at me.

Embarrassed and angry, I got up from the bench and began pacing the length of the ward, telling myself all the while that I'd hit the first fruitcake that got in my way. And then I got in my own way, when the dangling, denim sack got tangled between my legs, causing me to trip and fall a long way down. I refused to pick myself up, and I would've stayed on that cold, hard floor for the rest of my life, if it weren't for Mr. Kitty, of all people, who helped me to my feet, saying, "You gotta be careful, asshole, and you better mind your own business. See what getting involved gets you? You helps the old bastard, and he calls you a weirdo. No gratitude, that's his problem. I trys to be nice to him, and he draws stupid pictures on my walls. Just be careful of that old fart!"

After Mr. Kitty walked away, leaving his foul odor behind and yodeling like a cowboy who'd been out in the sun too long, I returned to my bench, until bedtime, when Mr. Kitty unlocked the dormitory door and passed out medication in front of the door. I was last in line, and he gave me a pill, the size and color of a large lima bean. I put it in my mouth but didn't swallow it, something I'd done since coming here. Then, when I was in bed, and the lights were out, I reached down, put the pill on the floor, and smashed it with my shoe.

In the morning, the ward doctor tried to get me to talk about my past, but I refused to talk about anything. I just sat there in his office and stared at my hands, until he put his arm around my shoulders, walked me out to the middle of the ward, and left me there. Feeling stranded, confused and helpless, staring at the bench I usually sat on, which was now occupied by Old Man, I felt I had nowhere in the world to go and would have to remain where I was, forever sweating cold and feeling like a clown in State pajamas and a purple robe two sizes too small for me.

It was Old Man who finally rescued me. Taking my hand, the bent old fellow led me back to the bench I'd come to consider my own, the place where I spent most of my time with my private thoughts and phantoms. I was pleased now to be sitting next to Old Man, seeing the twinkle in his blue eyes and the glimmer of a smile on his thin lips.

Instantly, I began to feel less insecure. Then, just as I managed a faint smile of my own, he took off to help with trays, leaving me to look out the window, fidget with my sack and feel sorry for myself.

It was Mr. Bob who gave me my tray, shoving it onto my lap, saying, "Here you are, beanpole, eat your lunch."

I refused to eat, hoping with the odds that Mr. Bob would whack me on the head with his big key. But he didn't. After looking at me and waiting for maybe a minute, he shrugged his shoulders and walked away, leaving me to feel rejected and then angry at him, the uncaring son of a bitch who didn't think I was good enough to whack, as he did the other guys who refused to eat. Then, as I looked down at the meatloaf and chocolate pudding, a timely nudge of reason made me realize, that if I didn't start eating, I'd never get out of here. So I ate it all, and when Old Man came to collect my tray, I spoke the first words, since coming here. "Thank you," I said, smiling.

"It must've been the chocolate pudding," Old Man said, walking away. Then, when he returned, he asked, "What did the nutcracker have to say to you today?"

"Nutcracker?" I asked, scratching my head.

"You know—the doctor. Did he tell you anything about your mind?"

"Nothing."

"What did you tell him?"

"Nothing," I said. Then, in trying to keep the conversation alive, I asked, "What does he say to you?"

Laughing, he said, "He tells me that I'm crazier'n a shithouse rat."

Trying to be as casual as possible, but not indifferently detached, I asked, "Are you?"

"Hell, no," he said, sitting down next to me. "Why, there's not an insane bone in my body."

"Then, why do you draw those pictures on the toilet walls, knowing that Mr. Kitty will beat you up?"

Showing he was excited, he asked, "So, how'd you like the last one—of Mr. Kitty eating a big piece of chalk? Sort of chalk on chalk, wasn't it?"

We laughed, before I said, "It was great, but you just do it when Mr. Kitty's on duty."

Serious now, he said, "Yes, only when he's on duty—because he's a filthy, cruel, rotten bastard, that's why." Then, after pulling out a white rag from inside his shirt, he jumped to his feet and began polishing the bench, saying, "However, the main reason I draw on the walls is: I have to act crazy so they'll keep me here. You see, I have no other place to go. Believe me, it's not easy acting crazy."

Feeling he was happy talking about himself, I asked, "What did you do, before you came here?"

Still polishing, he said, "I was a stock broker, and a good one."

"Are you planning to stay here for the rest of your life?"

"Hell, yes. I'll be here, until the closing bell rings for me."

"And so where you from?"

After shaking out the rag and replacing it inside his shirt, he sat and looked at me for maybe two minutes, before he said, "I'll answer your questions, because I trust you. But, don't betray my trust, young man, by repeating what I tell you—unless, of course, I give you permission. Is that clear?"

"Yes, sir."

"Well, I'm from New York City, originally. When I was a boy, I used to work at my father's fruit stand, until my father shot and killed a policeman and was electrocuted at Sing Sing. You see, that cop had stolen an apple almost every day, for ten years, and so finally my father blew his top. Unfortunately, I was at school at the time, so I didn't see that corrupt cop get it. So, after my father was gone, I lost faith in humanity and became a stock broker. Then, after I got rich as a king, and after my wife, Gypsy, ran away with a contract man for Murder Incorporated, I went mentally bankrupt. I somehow got to Detroit, where I bought some apples and threw them through the windows of a police station—headquarters—and they caught me and sent me here. Well, whataya think of them apples? Hey, just a little joke."

I was going to ask if the story were true, but, just in time, I told myself: You just don't ask a question like that, in a place like this. So instead, I said, "Fantastic!"

Mr. Kitty came in and unlocked the toilet and Old Man and I went in. Then, right away, Old Man drew another picture, this one showing Mr. Kitty in a pink diaper, sitting on the floor and sucking his thumb, and it wasn't long before Mr. Kitty rushed in, looked at the picture and threw Old Man out on the floor again. But, this time it was different. I hurried out and stood between Mr. Kitty and Old Man. Swinging my denim sack back and forth, I stared at the attendant and said, "Don't kick Old Man!" Then, surprisingly, Mr. Kitty backed off, locked the toilet door and walked away, singing like a screech owl, "Somewhere Over the Rainbow."

After that, I didn't see quite so darkly. I began eating regularly, mopping the floor, passing out trays, taking my medication and doing it all with a good attitude. I got caught up in things, thinking of myself as just one of the gang. It was as if I'd become addicted to the lifestyle, but more to Old Man, whom I followed around now, like a lanky Russian wolfhound, listening to his stories and philosophy. Then one day, I contributed something about me, saying, "I worry about my mother a lot. Last fall, for instance, she began to change, for the worse. She insisted on being in a Halloween show, as a red tulip, and had people stepping on her and throwing popcorn at her. I felt rotten about it. There was something very sinister going on inside her and I didn't know how to handle it."

Polishing the bench again, maybe thinking about a takeover, the retired stock broker said, "Well, I guess it's safe to assume that your mother was in a fluctuating, downward spiral. Tell me more."

"Well, as I said, she allowed herself to be trampled on, right up there on the stage, for the whole town to see. Then, afterwards, she told me she'd been doing penance, but it looked to me, that she'd lost all her pride, beauty and elegance."

Placing his hand on my shoulder, Old Man said, "Could be, she was finding her pride and beauty. You see, true pride and true beauty, and even elegance, the by-product, are found in acts of humility, sacrifice and penance. Don't worry. It looks like all she was doing, was paying her bills, so to speak. It's a fact of life. Proud and beautiful women pay their bills. My dear mother always paid her bills, especially the ones of the spirit. My son, you've got a lot to learn."

We were interrupted by the smells and sounds of the evening meal coming. After Old Man and I separated to pass out trays, and after I ate my own meal of beef stew, beets and Jello, I went over by the windows and, for the first time, wrote in the notebook. I wrote about how Elsie'd died, and how I'd failed to save her. Then, while I tried to make some sense and harmony out of it all, surges of anger and guilt shook my body, and I quit.

When Mr. Kitty came on duty, strange, perplexing, and zapping things happened. During the toilet break, when Mr. Kitty found no mural on a toilet wall, he rushed to Old Man and, with a worried look on his face, asked, "Are you sick or something, Old Man?"

"No," Old Man said, sitting on our bench and smiling.

Then, going to his cubbyhole office and returning, he gave Old Man several pieces of chalk he'd confiscated and said, "You can do it anywhere. Please, draw me like you did yesterday, like I'm milkin' a cow. It makes me think of the farm I grew up on. Please, you can draw me, and we can erase it and you can do it again tomorrow—okay?"

"If I'm here tomorrow," Old Man said seriously. "I just might be out of here, before you come on duty."

Old Man got up and drew the picture on the wall behind the bench, and Mr. Kitty wept.

After Mr. Kitty went to his hole, I looked at Old Man and asked, "Are you really leaving?"

"I might," he said, smiling, getting up and going over by the windows with me. Then, as we watched the sunset, he continued, saying, "I've learned something, my friend. I've learned that I've got to accept the reality that I did my best while I was out there. It's been deep in my heart, but I chose to cover it up with guilt. I told you about my father, and what he did. Well, all these years, I've blamed myself for not being there to stop him. That's bullshit, blaming myself. It's taken a long, long time, but I finally accept that. I finally say to myself, in truth, that I did my best with what I was given. As to my leaving, I don't know. I didn't admit it, but I have a daughter out there. She lives in New Jersey, and she wants me to live with her." Then, turning to me and looking up, he asked, "What about your, Matthew?"

"What about me?" I asked, looking out the window again.

"You still don't want to talk about yourself, is that it? I've told you a lot about me, but you've said little about yourself, if anything."

I removed the notebook from the denim sack, saying, "I'll be finished with this notebook soon, and I'll give it to you. It's about my life."

Looking at the notebook and smiling, he said, "Filling up that dinky notebook might just be your way out of here. That's it, Matthew, let it all out, anyway you can. Then, tell the nutcracker about it, like I'm going to do."

## chapter 13

It was sunny but cool. We'd just met at four in the afternoon in front of my apartment. She wore a blue blazer over a white blouse and blue dirndl and, in lowcut, white shoes, she came up to my shoulders. "You look beautiful today, Herta. How's your mother?"

"My mother is good, and she sends her greetings. And you look beautiful, also," she said, taking my arm.

Walking across a bridge over the Salzach River, on our way to Tomaselli's for ice cream, I looked down at the white shirt and khakis I'd worn yesterday. Then, after making a mental note to change my shirt and put on a sports coat before the operetta, I asked, "Shall we have ice cream or shall we have dinner, first?"

"I leave you to choose." she said, looking at me and smiling.

"Well, where would you like to have dinner—or did you have dinner at noon, as most Austrians do?"

"Yes, I had dinner. Now, I must have another dinner, or something. I'm hungry."

We laughed, and then I asked, looking at my watch, "Is Peter's Keller all right?"

"I leave you to choose," she repeated.

We went to Peter's Keller, a restaurant below the Fortress of Hohensalzburg, near the catacombs and Festspielhaus. When we were seated, I looked at my watch again, asking, "What are we going to do after we eat?"

Smiling, she said, "First, we eat, then we shall see—no?"

Seeing her scanning her menu with enthusiasm, she seemed more delicate and smaller in her high-back, baroque chair. Looking at the menu, I said, "I think I'll have the Hungarian goulash." Then, looking at my watch, I asked, "How about you?"

"I shall have the chicken," she said. Then, leaning to me, she asked, "Why do you look at your watch so many times?"

Hedging, I said, "I don't know. I guess I don't want us to be late for the performance."

Looking at her own watch, she said, "But it's only twenty-after-four. The performance is not until eight o'clock."

"I'm sorry, Herta. It's just that I have no idea what we can do until then. I'm sure you've seen Salzburg many times. You live here."

"But, I haven't seen it with you," she said, smiling. "If it's too early, do you wish for me to return home, until later?"

We laughed, and I said, "Of course not."

The waiter came and took our order. After he returned with two glasses of white wine, we toasted each other's health and drank. Looking at the ring on my little finger, a small ruby that her father had left me, she asked, "Do you like the ring?"

"Yes, I like it very much. It must've been in your family a long time. I can't guess why your father left it to me."

"My mother gave it to him when they were young, before they were married."

Running the ring around my finger once, I asked, "So, where did you say you're taking your internship?"

"I'm at Unfall Krankenhaus, in Vienna. I'm working with Dr. Lawrence Beohler, the famous orthopedic surgeon. How goes it with your work?"

"Okay now, but for awhile, it was difficult."

"Do you ski, when you have time?"

"Yes," I said, getting more comfortable. "I go to Kleinarl, or St. Johann, near Bischofshofen. I went to Kitzbuhel once, but I found it too expensive."

"St. Johann?" she asked, looking excited. "Yes, I've gone there many times. And, also in the summertime. Very beautiful."

"Maybe we could go there, before you return to Vienna—

tomorrow?"

"Yes, that would be much fun. I shall come early. We can spend the whole day. I'll bring something for us to eat."

"And if you'd like, we could come back here and see Jedermann at the Festspielhaus."

Reaching over and putting her hand on mine, she smiled and said, "First, St. Johann, then we will see."

After the food arrived, and we began to eat, I asked, "Where shall we have coffee—here, or somewhere else?"

Smiling again, she said, "But we have only begun to eat. Must we decide now?"

"Herta, I'm sorry. I guess I'm a bit nervous."

"Is it because you haven't been to dinner with a lady in a long time?"

"That's probably it."

"Well, that makes two. I can't remember the last time I was to dinner with a gentleman, or even with a non-gentleman."

We laughed and went about eating our meal. Afterwards, as I looked at her and found what seemed to be warmth and blush on her face, I had the courage to ask, "Would you like to come to my apartment, for coffee?"

Excited, she asked, "Could we? I'm very eager to see the place of a maestro."

"I don't know about maestro, and the apartment's a dump. However, I'll get some Austrian pastry along the way—you know, to brighten up the place."

"Wonderful!"

We left and, after I picked up the pastry, we went to the apartment. "This is it," I said, leaving her by the piano, while I put the pastry in the kitchen. Then, when I joined her and saw her looking at my paintings, I said, "I see you found some of my work."

"Yes," she said. "This is of your father, with my father's remembrance card in the corner."

Seeing tears in her eyes, I said, "Yes."

"War has brought them together. War and death."

"I feel as you do, Herta, that they are victims."

Wiping her eyes with a laced handkerchief, she pointed to Elsie's portrait and asked, "Is she another relative?"

"No," I said, hoping she wouldn't ask about her, just yet.

"Do you have one of your mother?"

"Yes, but she's got it in Paris. Come and sit, and I'll get the coffee and pastry."

Looking at Elsie's portrait again, she asked, "Is she a friend?"

"She was a friend."

"I see."

"She's dead," I said, going to the kitchen and putting on coffee. Then, after I brought the pastry and put it on a small table near her, I said, "She was a very talented musician."

"Were you to be married?"

"We never talked of marriage, but I suppose we would have been married," I said, going to the piano. "Do you play?" I asked, lifting the cover from the keys.

Coming to me, she said, "No, but I like to listen, if it does not thump too much."

"Would you like me to play?" I asked, glad not to be talking about Elsie.

"Yes, please—oh, yes."

"Any favorites?" I asked, looking at sheets of music.

"Chopin, I love it, if it does not…"

"Thump?"

"You choose—thump or no thump."

Discarding Chopin's Polonaise in A, I played Berceuse in D-flat, Mazurka in C-sharp minor and finished with Chopin's waltzes in C-sharp minor, G-flat, B minor, and A-flat. Turning to her now, I waited for her reaction.

Saying nothing, and with her face like stone, she was crying.

"Did I do, or say, the wrong thing?" I asked, concerned.

"No, nothing wrong," she said, going to the kitchen. Then, while we fixed coffee for ourselves, she said, "I'm sorry. I'm such a silly goose. You play so beautiful and I cry my eyes off."

Taking her into my arms, I asked, "Why are you crying, then?"

After blowing her nose, she said softly, "I cry, because I think of my father. He loved Chopin. I would sit on his knee, when I was a small girl, and we would listen together to Chopin coming over the radio. I loved my father very much."

The phone rang.

It was my mother, calling from Paris and saying, "It's only me."

"How are you?" I asked, somewhat abruptly.

"Have I called at a bad time? Do you have company?"

"Yes," I said. "It's Herta Müller . We're going to see Merry Widow at the Festspielhaus."

"How nice. Well, I won't keep you. Say hello to Herta for me. She's such a nice lady—and so beautiful! By the way, I have a surprise for you. I have a job. I'm a counselor. I help women with their lives. Yes, I'm very happy about it."

"But, you have millions, Mama. Why a job?"

"No, no, no. I won't touch it. I'm giving the money to an important cause. You said you don't want any of it. Have you changed your mind?"

"No, I don't want any of it. Mama, I must go now."

"I'm happy you and Herta are together. Ask her to give my regards to her mother. Well, also my best to the Merry Widow, and tell her that your mother envies her, for being so damn merry."

"Will do, Mama."

"I love you, my son."

"I love you, Mama."

After I'd hung up, Herta asked, "How is your mother?"

"She's fine, and she sends you and your mother her greetings."

"She's a fine lady and so…"

"French?"

"French."

Sitting on the small sofa now, drinking coffee and eating pastry, I said, "Herta, my mother was somewhat lost in America. She gave me the impression that she didn't want to be there, that she wanted to be in France. When we both got our citizenship, she wept, but I don't think it was because she was glad to be an American."

"She didn't like America?"

"Don't get me wrong. She loved America, but as I said, she wanted to be in France."

"How about you, Matthew?"

"I don't want to live in France. I want to return to America. It's home for me, now. In fact, I still have a house to go to, when I return."

"When will you return, Matthew?"

"I don't know. Maybe next year."

"I see."

We did the dishes and went to see Merry Widow. Afterwards while waiting for her bus, I asked, "What about tomorrow? Will we be going to St. Johann?"

"Oh, yes," she said, excited. "I'll come to your place. It will be early."

"Early is fine," I said, seeing her bus coming.

She kissed me on the cheek and was gone, leaving me her smile to light my way.

Back in the apartment, I sat on the sofa, ate pastry and thought about the house in Point Stevens, and about the day my mother was ready to sell it to Morely for one dollar. I'd been in town, buying a new suitcase for my trip to Salzburg. Then, when I returned home, I found Morely in the kitchen with my mother, eating strawberry tarts and drinking wine. "Hi," I said, sitting down with them and grabbing a tart. "What you up to?"

"Just wanted to come over and inspect this place, before I buy it," Morely said, with his mouth full.

"Inspect it?" I asked.

"That's right," he said, before drinking wine.

"But you're only going to pay a dollar for it." I said, smiling and shaking my head.

"Business is business, Matt, no matter what you pay."

"I guess you're right," I said. Then, turning to my mother and winking, I said, "You know, of course, it has a defective furnace."

With a startled look, he said, "Well, now that's gonna cost me—really cost me. What else's wrong with this ole' joint?"

"Joint?" my mother said, I'll have you know, this old joint would cost a million dollars, if I put it on the market."

"Well," he said, picking lint off his uniform. "I didn't mean nothin' ignorant, or nothin'. I was just wonderin' how much it's gonna cost me to fix up the place. I know you're bein' good to me, Anne, and I appreciate it."

Seeing that he was trying to be sincere, I said, "Maybe you'd like to look around."

"I confess that I would like to look around," he said, lumbering through the doorway. Going into the Music Room, he stopped in front of my mother's Queen Anne's curio and asked, "What you gonna do with all this stuff, when you leave—give it to the Indians, like you did all that furniture?"

"I'm taking it with me," my mother said crisply.

Going into the library and stopping in front of my painting of a sunrise, as seen through the forest of pines near the Dark River, he saluted the painting and asked, "Does that picture go with the house?"

My mother quickly said: "No, Morely."

"How 'bout the furniture?"

"Sorry," she said. "This place will be empty, by the time anyone moves in."

"You gonna take all this to France with you, Anne?"

"Some of it," she said. "The furniture I'm giving to Charlie Baxter and his friends."

Narrowing his eyes, he growled.

My mother was saying, "Suzette's taking some things to give to her parents in Montreal."

Shaking his head, with a mournful expression on his face, he sat down in an armchair by the fireplace and, pointing, said, "I bet that's brandy over there on the table."

Sitting next to my mother on the sofa, I asked, "How'd you know it's brandy?"

"Just an educated guess," he said, trying to adjust in the chair.

"Would you like a glass?" my mother asked. "I'm sure you would. Matthew, would you mind? Bring us all a glass—better still, bring the decanter and put it on the coffee table."

After I gave him a glass of cognac, Morely said, "Bet you can't guess what I've been up to."

"Not in a million years," I said.

"Well, I put an ad in the paper, for a wife," he said, smiling like sin.

"That's wonderful, Morely," she said. "May I ask why you haven't been married before?"

"Seein' you asked, I'll tell you. It's 'cause I couldn't find anybody like my mother. She was a lady, just like you, Anne. She was good to me, and always laughin'. I was just a little-bitty boy, but I can remember her laughin' and her body'd shake like a little butter churn churnin' butter. She was the only woman I ever loved."

Seeing tears well in his eyes, as he poured himself another brandy, I said, "Don't worry, there's someone out there for you."

"You could have tried to love someone else, couldn't you have, Morely?" my mother asked.

Downing another brandy, he said, "Well, I tried to love you, Anne, but you wouldn't let me."

Seeming flustered, she said, "I'm sorry, but…"

"Aw, that's okay," he said, trying to cross his legs; then giving up, he said, "You'n me'r from two different worlds. I know that. It's like oil and water don't mix, right?"

"Maybe," she said gently.

"More cognac, Bulldog?" I asked, taking up the decanter.

"Matthew!" my mother said sharply. "I'm really surprised at you. Don't ever call Morely that name again!"

"That's okay, Anne," Morely said. "All my friends call me that. You can call me that too, Anne."

"Well," she said firmly. "I like Morely, just fine."

Drinking cognac and smiling, he said, "Getting back to my love life—well, maybe I didn't want a wife, 'cause I didn't want to mess up my life, 'til now. You know, like Cuddles Crawfort did. Ever hear of him?"

My mother and I shook our heads no.

"Cuddles is dead now—God rest his stupid soul," he said, pausing then and staring in the cold and empty fireplace.

"What happened to Mr. Crawfort?" my mother asked.

"Well," Morely said, picking up the decanter of brandy, taking a swig and letting it rest on his lap. "I confess, I investigated him, person to person, and found out what really happened. He was a good man, that Cuddles, and it's a shame he got involved with Tickles Tamegoat.

Anyways, one day, Cuddles gets married to Tickles, who I confess, I never heard of, before she came to the weddin'. Anyways, not a week went by, after the weddin', that Tickles didn't break Cuddles's heart. Then finally, she ran away into thin air, with nothin' on her back but the clothes Cuddles had boughten her, which included a pair of purple panties he'd boughten her for a weddin' present. Well, to make a long story short, he went lookin' for her and couldn't find her, 'til he called me in on the case. Then, it was exactly Easter Sunday mornin'—a beautiful day—when we spies her purple panties from my squad car. Holy shit!—if youse'll excuse the expression—there they were, as big as life, hangin' out to dry, on the clothesline of Cuddles's worst enemy. I won't mention who that worst enemy is, but I'll give you a little hint. He wears a sailorsuit all the time, and hangs out at Belda's Bar. Anyways, that's what killed Cuddles, 'cause a month later, he died of a busted heart. A very strange case and it's been in my files all these years."

"Very sad," my mother said, shaking her head slowly.

"How do you know the panties belonged to her?" I asked.

Quickly, he said, "Seein' you asked, I'll tell you. I got a warrant, and we investigated. We busted in the house and caught'm red-handed, so to speak."

"What happened to Tickles?" I asked.

"What could I do?" Morely said, shrugging his shoulders.

"Where is she now?" my mother asked.

"Well," Morely said, finishing off the brandy. "I investigated on my own time, and found her livin' over in Loon Lake. I talked to her, and it was like an unconditional surrender. She confessed to marrin' Cuddles for his money—the disability check he got every month, 'cause he got wounded in Korea."

"What happened to the poor man?" my mother asked.

"He got one of his arms blown off. I think it was the right one, or was it the wrong one?"

"You mean the left one, Morely," my mother said. "My God, that poor, poor man…"

"I guess my head is gettin' a little dizzy," Morely said, "from talkin' 'bout Cuddles and what happened. But I'm not dizzy 'bout one thing: Cuddles got a military funeral, with a twenty-three gun salute—I counted.

Well, gotta get back to work," he said then, getting to his feet with my help and staggering to the door. Then, turning halfway, he said, "I think I'll pass on the house. Too expensive to keep up, with everything broke down and heavy taxes, and all. But, thanks for showin' it to me."

The next day, Morely agreed to act as caretaker for the house, for one hundred dollars a month. And, after we left Point Stevens, my mother called him frequently, to check on things, I supposed.

## chapter 14

She came at daybreak, wearing a green sweater and blue dirndl. Taking a large, leather bag from her shoulder, she put it on the floor of the living room and said, "Good morning."

"Good morning, Herta," I said, shaking her hand. "As you can see, I'm not fully awake and still in my robe."

Laughing, she said, "I'll spritz you with cold water, to get you awake."

"No spritz, please," I said, putting on a pot of coffee. Then, moving towards the bedroom, I said, "I'll be just a minute."

"Do you have some pastry left?" she asked.

"No, sorry," I said, leaving the bedroom door open. "I ate it all last night."

"So, so…"

After putting on a clean, blue shirt and khakis, I left the bedroom to find Herta watching the sunrise from a window seat. Bringing coffee, I joined her, saying, "I see you like sunrises."

Making room for me on the window seat, she said, "Yes, I like sunrise more than sunset. Sunset makes me feel so…"

"Melancholy?"

"Thank you. Yes, melancholy."

"It's the same with me."

"I'm not very sad, however. I only think serious about something. But, even the sunrise can make me do this."

"Like this morning?"

"Yes, just before, I was thinking of something serious."

"May I ask what?"

"Yes, of course. I have no wish to keep secrets. I thought of how much time and work I have given to become a doctor. Then I thought of you, and what you said about returning to America. And, carefully, I asked myself, is it good for me to get involved with emotion, at this time. Then, a strange event happened inside me. A little Zwergerl was laughing at me and saying, 'Hee hee, Herta, you already are involved with emotion.' Do you see my serious problem?"

Taking her hand, I said, "Yes, it's a problem for both of us."

"And do you wish to hear what else I thought serious about?"

"Yes."

"I thought about your Elsie, and I felt it was good that you didn't tell me more about her, at this time. And, I told myself not to ask about her ways, at this time. You see, I do not wish to be self-conscious, and try not to act like her. I would, first, like to show myself with freedom. Then, Matthew, I thought of how warm and happy I feel, when I'm with you. Your gentle, sensitive spirit moves my deepest feelings, and when you touch me, my heart begins to…"

"Thump?"

"Yes, thump!" she said, laughing.

Going into the kitchen and rinsing out our cups, I asked, "And so, does your mother approve of us being together?"

"Yes, very much."

"It must be lonely for her, now."

"No, not at all. At least, I don't believe it is. She has a position in a travel agency, and she likes very much to be with people."

"My mother also has a job."

"It is good they work. They are still young. So, now we must go. Soon, there will be another train to St. Johann."

After putting on my tan jacket, I asked, "Do we have to bring anything from here?"

Opening her leather bag, she said, "See, I have everything here, food, a flashlight, serviettes, and so much more."

"I can see that," I said, laughing. Then, after slinging it over my shoulder, I said, "It's heavy. How in the world did you manage to carry it?"

"I'm strong," she said, smiling and making a muscle in her arm. "Very strong woman!"

We laughed and left for the Bahnhof, and in a few hours, after riding a local, we were in St. Johann and riding a chair lift up to a small Gasthaus on top of a mountain. Then, sitting outside the Gasthaus, we drank orange soda, ate chicken sandwiches, and watched in silence as shadows moved slowly over the Alps. It seemed obvious that, together, we'd caught onto the quiet rhythm of our day, with its gentle breeze, mountains, songs of birds and brooks, the meadow below, the land, trees, the blue, the grey, the brown and green, all in perfect harmony with our quiet breathing and the music of our beating hearts. It was I, who finally said, "It's quite a day!"

"A day of peace," she said softly. Then, taking my hand, she looked in my eyes and said, "It is so good to be with you. I don't know what it is. You make me want to smile. Before you came to my father, I wept all the time. Then, when I saw a deepest sadness in your eyes, and saw you were able to smile, I felt better. Your smile in sadness made me smile, as it did my mother and father. He told us what you said to him, that he was too chewed-up to shoot. It was an importance for him, at that time, and for all of us. It told of your heart of compassion. I wished so much to speak with you that day, but I could not find the words to say. But, even then, in my heart, I knew that someday we would be together." Then, after removing a green scarf from her bag and tying it loosely around her neck, she asked, "So, what do you say to what I have said?"

It was sudden. Just as I told myself that I loved Herta, quick shadows of fear and shame came from a dark place within me and darkened my day, and all the beauty and peace I'd experienced only a moment ago was not enough to stop a flood of tears. Putting my hands to my face and weeping, I said, "I'm sorry."

"What is it with you, Matthew?" she asked, putting an arm around my shoulders.

Getting to my feet, I asked, "Could we go?"

"Yes, of course," she said, showing alarm. "Perhaps, if we walked down, it would be good for you."

Taking her bag, I said, "Walking would be good. I'll be all right.

Maybe it's the altitude."

As we descended on a winding dirt path through the forest, she pointed out and named all the kinds of flowers that graced the waysides. Then, coming to a Gasthaus, we went in and drank apple juice in a cool, quiet corner, and she said, "I'm sorry that I made you nervous, telling you what is in my heart. I didn't wish it in my heart. It just got there."

"I had no right to lead you on."

Angry, with what seemed to be tears of frustration, she said, "No one leads me! I am not a goat! My mother does not lead me! My brothers do not lead me! I listen to advice, but I make my own choices! I have my own mind, and heart, and soul!"

"You're angry. I'm sorry I made you angry."

"You do not listen, Matthew!" she said, shaking her head back and forth. "I speak, but you do not listen. No one leads me! No one can lead me to be angry. I must make myself angry—yes, now I have made myself angry, because I have made a fool of myself!"

Seeing her crying softly, I reached for her hand, but she excused herself and went to the restroom. Angry at myself now, for allowing fear to ruin the day, I felt like an infant, once again. A short time ago, we were on a mountain top, sharing a moment of peace, and now it was a moment of disaster. Drinking my apple juice, I wondered how I could tell her that I was in a mental institution.

When she returned, her smile was tight on her lips, and her green, silk scarf no longer hung loosely around her slender neck. The scarf was tied with two hard knots on the side of her neck, as if to show me as the hangman who'd put it there. Standing, she reached into a pocket of her dirndl and pulled out a twenty-schilling note, saying, "This will be enough for the Apfelsoft. You paid for the orange drink, on the mountain. I will pay now."

Sullen, I said, "If that's the way you want it, okay." Then, forgetting to take her bag, I followed her out.

Once again, on the winding dirt road, she pointed out flowers and called them by name. Then, after picking some, she asked, "Would you be so kind and carry my bag?"

"My pleasure," I said, taking the bag and smiling.

Standing close and looking in my eyes, she asked, "Why did your mood change so fast? Is there something very much the matter?"

No response, and with that silence, my soul went dark, and I was lost, once again, unable to speak, to laugh, to love, to work, to hope, to dream. But, as he did the first time, Old Man came to me and said, that if I didn't open up and be truthful, then I'd be stuck for the rest of my life with only myself, my worst enemy. Then, as I took her hand and walked slowly down, it was Old Man who spoke to me, loud and clear, in my mind: *Now's the time to tell her, while she's here with you. Now's the time to tell her what's in your heart. Now's the time, before she slips away, like the light of day. Tell her, before the long nights and short days come again to find you alone, agonizing over past and possibility, and over a dreary and lonely now. Now's the time to tell her, and have a little faith. Wake up, my friend, and with the realities of truth, beauty and love within your soul, stand up to a world of war, insanity, and insecurity. Life thumps sometimes, my friend, and it's not necessary that you take it alone. It's the law, Matthew—the natural law born in you—the impulse of your human nature—to seek out and befriend another human being. You were given another chance. You're holding the hand of someone you love and respect-- someone with the kind of spirit that's an extension of, and complementary to, your own spirit. During your love-starved days, Elsie came to you, Elsie, a singer of sad songs, not strange to your heart. Daphne chased Apollo, and then Apollo chased Daphne. But God had other plans for her, and you were left without her music to hear, her lips to kiss, and without her spirit to nourish the small seeds of love you had left in a heart torn by war and loss. Wise up, my friend, this could be the end of a maddening past. You have in your hand someone else who knows about the insanities of war, loss, and destruction. She's a woman of substance, of compassion and understanding, like my mother and yours. Reach out. Speak of the dark within you. By doing so, you will open to the light. Now is the time to tell her, and for God's sake—don't whine!*

"Aller Anfang ist schwer," she was saying, as we walked across the meadow below the mountain.

"Yes," I said, taking shorter steps and slowing down. "All beginnings are difficult."

Obviously not giving up on me yet, she asked, "And what do you say about that saying, when it is said about us?"

*Tell her, Matthew, tell her. Tell her, damnit, tell her!*

Swimming in the lukewarm waters of evasion, I said, "You have your work, and I have mine. Would there be time for us? And, as I told you, I'll be returning to America."

"So, so," she said, looking down and getting in step with me. "But, to put love in time and place is to corrupt it. Love must stand without regard to time and place. Time and place are only tests for love, and love will survive time and place, if not neglected." Stopping then, and stepping in front of me, she removed the ruby ring from my finger and showed me the inscription inside. Reading it, she said, 'Liebe.' Love. Only one word-idea, standing alone. Love, to be given freely and accepted, without reservation, or regards to place or time. That is all I wish for us—a love to cherish and care for, no matter what we do, or where we are, together, or alone. Do you have a thought on it?"

*Tell her now!*

Still in front of her, I closed my eyes and said, "I wish I didn't have to tell you this, but I know I must." Then, in a meadow of green grass and wild flowers, and with the world hushed, as the sun descended, I opened my eyes and the door of my heart and said, "I was in a mental hospital. I tried to save Elsie from drowning, but failed. I got drunk, jumped from a window, and they put me in a mental hospital. I might flip out again at any time."

She smiled, repeating, "Flip out. I must remember that." Then taking my hands and squeezing them gently, she said, "It does not matter to me, how you were. It only matters how you are today… only today, every day. So now, if you wish, we shall return to Salzburg and eat. I have very much hunger for Hungarian goulash."

"And I'd like some chicken."

"I shall perhaps be fat someday. Will you object?"

"I don't know. Do it, and find out."

Laughing, we held each other, and she whispered, "Matthew, do we have something good?"

"Better than good."

As we walked, I placed the ring in her hand, saying, "I got your father's message. I want to return the ring to your mother."

Putting the ring on her finger, she said, "Yes, I'll give it to her. It belongs to their world."

"Why do I get the feeling that your father knew what I'd do with it?"

"He did know. He told me that you would not keep it." Then, with tears on her cheeks, she stopped us, put my face in her hands and said, "Ich liebe dich, Matthew."

"I love you too, Herta."

"I shall go with you to America, if you wish."

"We'll see."

In Salzburg, we went to a small, elegant restaurant with plush furniture, rose-tinted mirrors, small art objects in subtly-lit niches, and oil paintings on the walls. Changing our minds, as to what to eat, we agreed to have Brennender Hunnenspiess, a kind of flaming Hungarian shish kebab. While we ate, we listened to a combo play soft music and watched a few couples dance. The last time I'd danced was when I'd stepped all over Trixie Roper's feet in high school. I definitely didn't want to get out there now and make a fool out myself, especially not tonight. Then, when the music stopped, I breathed easier.

Finished with the meal, we just sat there with our wine, looking at each other and smiling, until she looked at the wall across the room and said, "That's the best oil painting of Fortress Hohensalzburg I've ever seen."

"Thank you," I said. "I did my best."

Looking surprised, she asked, "It is your work?" Then, after going to the painting and returning, she said, "So, so, it is your work. I didn't know you sold your paintings."

"Only when I'm starving."

"Did you paint it from the Kapuzinerberg?"

"You have a good eye."

"Tell me, Matthew—why didn't you go to the Paris Conservatory, for your music?"

"It's less expensive here."

"You said you have a house in Mich-igan?"

"Yes."

"Someday, we might live there. No?"

"Herta, thinking it over, next year, when you're finished your internship, we can talk about it. The house? Well, it wouldn't be difficult to talk my mother into giving it away, with the condition that it be used as a music school, or art school—anything of the arts. I'll talk to my mother about it. As far as we're concerned, I want to show you the country, first, and then we can decide where to live."

"And we would also have a place, here."

"I suppose we could do our work in both countries. Just a dream to pursue."

"Now I know that I love you, for sure."

"Why's that?"

"You have dreams, Matthew."

"Dreams. There are dreams and then there are dreams."

"What do you say with that?"

"Only that, there are good dreams and bad dreams."

"The bad dreams are finished, Matthew."

"Yes, I believe so," I said, kissing her.

The music began again, and she said, "I saw you staring at the dancers, just before. You must love to dance. Would you wish to, now?"

Trying not to be rattled, and a stick, I asked, "Would you like to dance?"

"Yes, but let me warn you, first. I'm not good at it. Most, I danced with my father, and look what happened to him."

After laughing, I kissed her again and said, "Maybe we should forget about dancing."

"No!" she said, getting up and pulling me up. "You like to dance very much, and now I will learn to like it."

We were the only ones out there. Then, surprisingly, it became one of the most pleasant experiences of my life. I was a success, and I knew she had everything to do with it. Warm and supple in my arms, she made me feel warm and supple, and I began to believe that dancing was all that it's cracked up to be and not the drudgery I'd thought it to be. Moving freely and expertly, we twirled, dipped and sashayed all over the place—and not once did I step on her feet, nor did she on mine. "A miracle!" I said, when the set was over. "Considering that we were the only ones out there, we did all right. Were you nervous?"

Breathing hard and laughing, she said, "With you holding me, I could take the pressure."

A waiter brought a bottle of white wine and said, "Please, this is a gift from the manager, in appreciation for your fine dancing."

As the waiter poured the wine, I said, "Maybe we should go on the road with our act."

"I don't understand."

"Maybe we should become professional dancers."

"So, so, no, I don't think so," she said, laughing. Then, after looking at the label on the wine bottle, she said, "Look! The manager makes a joke. The wine is called Flohaxl. Do you know what that means?"

"Flealegs. My God, he's insulted us!" Then, looking around, I saw the manager's grinning face by the door. Smiling and raising my glass to him, I toasted him, before touching my glass to Herta's and saying, "Here's to love."

"To love," she said. Then, after we drank, she asked, "Do you know the manager? He seems to know you."

"Yes, he helped sell my painting to the owner. Nice man." Then, after we settled in for some serious wine-drinking, I said, "It's all different now."

"How so?"

"Love makes it different and better, of course."

"We are in love. It is destiny."

"Definitely."

"Matthew, how do you see us, with our love?"

Staring in my wine and acting as if I were a drunken prophet, I cupped my glass with my hands and said, "I can see it all."

"And what do you see, my tipsy Hellseher?"

"Flealegs, and they're growing."

"Please, tell me what else you see."

Still staring into the wine, I said, "I see a beautiful young woman."

"Yes."

"She's with a skinny young man."

"Yes."

"And they both have flealegs."

"They don't."

"They do."
"Where are they, and what are they doing?"
"Wait."
"Yes?"
"They are standing in a valley, under a tree. They have just come down from a mountain of fear and sadness, and they're now in a shaded meadow of peace and love…"
"And what else, my Hellseher?"
"In the hush of dusk, they declare their love for each other, while Shubert sings, ever so softly:
'In schattigen Talen,
das schweigen die Qualen
den liebenden Brust.'"

"'In shady vales, silenced are the tortures of a loving breast,'" she whispered.

## BOOK TWO ANNE

## chapter 15

My dear son and I were in Bordeaux. We had come here after Matthew had spoken with Hans Müller, who was dying of cancer at his home in Austria. We had come to visit the grave of Henri La Fleur, my first husband and Matthew's father. It was evening. As we stood silent by the grave, a warm, gentle breeze and the red afterglow of sunset seemed to forbid us to speak. Staring at the grave, I thought of change—that deep, dark essence of the human heart that comes to separate us from those we love, leaving cold finality to remain, as our reluctant heart moves on with the rush and flood of lesser things. And now, as my son put his arm around me, there were my tears, dark blue rivers returning to the sea.

Placing roses on the grave, I thought of the rose bushes Henri and our son had planted and cared for. I felt blessed that I had been given time with Henri, with so many moments of love, laughter and respect. I'd known him. I'd witnessed his courage and loyalty and endurance. I had experienced his infectious, dry sense of humor, his warmth, gentle touch, his passion. Closing my eyes, I recalled the first time we had walked together.

It had been an unusually harsh winter. The pine trees in the forest near Landes de Bussac were covered with snow and the snake of a creek ran through glassy tunnels of ice. He kissed me and told me that he loved me, and the warmth of his sincerity had opened my heart, as it did now in remembering. And now, with hot tears breaking from the corners of my closed eyes, and with sobs climbing up and away, I cried out: "Damn you, Henri, you should have been more careful!" Then, ever so softly, I said, "However, I still love you, dead as you are, and I always will."

My son continued with his arm around my shoulders and said nothing. With my eyes open now, I smiled at the memory of him teasing me when I told him I was pregnant. "Well now," he said, wriggling his mustache and squinting his dark eyes. "So it's a premarital pregnancy, is it? Well, I suppose all I can do now is to quote my old friend, Friedrich Nietzsche, who said, 'Mon Dieux, as yet, woman is not capable of friendship. Women are still cats and birds, or at best, cows. For too long hath there been a slave and a tyrant concealed in woman. On that account, a woman is not capable of friendship. Ergo, she knoweth only love. In woman's love, there is injustice and blindness to all she doth not love. Everything in woman is a riddle, and everything in woman hath but one solution. It is called pregnancy.'"

"Merde!" I screamed. I slapped his face and bit his arm. "Merde! Merde! Merde!"

He stared at me and quoted again, maybe Dante: "Whom the devil employs, he first makes mad."

"Merde!" I screamed again, chasing him around and around until we fell into each other's arms, and I said, "I thought you'd be happy."

Holding me gently, he kissed me and said, "I love you dearly, Anne Villon, and I'm the happiest man on earth."

Soon I became Anne La Fleur, and then God gave us Matthew.

And now, staring at Henri's grave, I realized that I had lusted after the essence of my life and had found it in my love for Henri. And there had been nothing more important in my life than my love for him and my son. In no way, then, had I been willing that Henri join the French Resistance and fight the Nazis. Yes, I had opened the door of my heart to love, but by so doing, I had also opened it to pain. "He's gone now," I whispered. "He has vanished like a puff of his cigarette smoke. He has gone into remembrance with his acts of goodness—his masterpieces of life. Au revoir, Henri...."

Soon after, we left for my apartment on Rue de Ponthieu in Paris. It was the apartment I would return to after we settled things in Point Stevens, Michigan. On the second day, after my son had taken a walk, he returned to find me sitting on my new sofa listening to music by Edvard Grieg and crying. Sitting down next to me, he asked, "Mama, what is it?"

Clearly, I recall saying, "I'm remembering when we were at your father's resting place. The sun was going down and the birds were finished singing for the day. And I was thinking about life. A graveyard is a perfect place to think about life. It was a moment of peace for me, and a moment of deep gratitude to God for His allowing me another day and for giving me you, Matthew. My soul no longer cried out for anything, in that moment. Oh, Matthew, I have so much to do."

"Like getting married to Mr. Fowler?" he asked, with sarcasm twisting his face.

"How could you ask that?"

"For one thing, the music of Norway that you're playing."

"No, no, just the opposite. I'm saying farewell to Norway, and to Mr. Fowler." I said firmly, wanting to remind him that we had promised not to interfere in each other's lives. But then, just in time, I thought his irritation was due to his meeting with the man who had killed his father, so I let it go at that.

"You're no longer friends?" he asked, smiling ugly.

I didn't want to lie, so I chose a mental reservation, saying, "Just friends. That's all it has been, and will ever be, for you see, Mr. Fowler is still married to his dead wife. He isn't able to move on with life. And that suits me just fine. Oh, Matthew, I have so much to do. I'm free. I'm out of the shadows of the world. No longer do I play hide-and-seek with life. No longer do I close my heart to the Will of God. I'm aware of my nature and I'm going to live in accordance with it. The fire in my blood cries out for the good, the true, the beautiful. I'm a new woman. I'm no longer just flyash!"

"Good for you!" he said, yawning and going to his bedroom.

His yawning is what did it. I was glad now that I had chosen the mental reservation and told myself that I would do it again if it concerned my affaire d'amour with Richard Fowler, or anything else that would interfere in his life by making him worry about me. I didn't care if he would call me evasive. Then, I wasn't about to tell him, or anyone, all about myself. I was sure that to do so would make me feel like a dried-out dishrag that is worn and torn from being squeezed too much. Besides, I had told him enough. I told him about the dark thing in my soul that turned me into a criminal when I didn't prevent Maurice Martineau's murder and the stealing of Maurice's ill-begotten money. Yes, I told that to my son and to Father O'Grady in the confessional, and then I had done penance mainly by dressing up like a ferocious red tulip and by letting people stomp on me in a Halloween spook show. After that, I felt beautiful and clean, but I did not feel fulfilled as a woman of the earth, as I had felt when married to Henri. Daniel Horton, or Major Danny, as everyone else had called him, had done his best to fulfill me, I suppose, but, with all due respect for the truth, he was more interested in fulfilling himself—an opposite of both Henri and Richard.

After Daniel, my second husband, died, I devoted most of my time to my son. He was having frequent nightmares, during which he would call out that he wanted to kill the man who had killed his father. Feeling certain that Matthew would not go to a doctor, I did what any pseudo-psychiatrist would do. I diagnosed the condition and concluded that if he met the man face to face and talked, then he would be cured, perhaps. Thinking back now to when my Henri was killed by an officer in the German army, I knew Richard Fowler had been present. I employed a private detective to find out the whereabouts of Richard and was advised that he was in Norway. This had been about a year before I took Matthew to see Hans Müller , when I left Matthew and my dog, Gussie, in the care of Suzette Robert, our maid, and went to Norway just before Christmas and didn't make it back for Christmas because of bad weather. And there was another reason, before the bad weather, that prevented my returning to Michigan for Christmas. This reason involved Marsha Lowden, an old friend who had become a CIA agent, and the kidnapping of my dear niece, Gabrielle—a tragedy I shall turn to, perhaps, after my visit with Richard Fowler, who, so the private detective said, was also a spy, or maybe even a double-spy.

In any event, after arriving in Oslo, I had taken a train up the Trondheim Line to Lesjaskag, where I took a hydrofoil to Molde on the Northern Sea. It was evening when I checked into the hotel on the waterfront that Richard had suggested while we spoke on the phone just before I came. After a bathtub soak, and after I'd put on a white sweater, dark blue slacks, and a tan trench coat that made me feel that I was the one who had graduated from spy school, I went to sit on the glassed-in veranda to wait for Richard. Drinking coffee now, I recalled what Richard had said to Henri and I during the war. "I hate war," he said, after dinner at our house. "I can't help thinking of myself as a bloody fool, playing a child's war game. But then, of course, I realize it's about life and blood and death." Then, when Henri asked about his wife, he'd said, "She died a horrible death in Norway." And that was all he wanted to say about his wife. Now, looking across the darkening fjord from the veranda, I hoped he would speak more of her someday, but I promised myself not to push it. I also hoped, of course, that he would advise me about my son and tell me where I could find the man who killed Henri.

Church bells began ringing and seemed to be bringing people out, including myself. After buying herring and bread from a vender's booth on the waterfront, I found myself being pulled into the stream of people heading towards a white wooden church about a quarter mile away. However, when the procession passed by the church and I found myself standing alone in front of the church, I decided to go in to see what it was like.

Sitting in the back, I enjoyed a moment of peace. A red-orange glow of sunset illuminated stained-glass windows and most everything else, including Viking symbols and the small replica of a Viking ship hanging by very thin wires from the ceiling.

Looking to my right, I saw sunset colors on a badly burned airplane propeller hanging on a wall. The propeller was made of wood and had a small swastika at its center, and directly above it there was a badly burned wooden cross. It seemed to me right away that these things were sad souvenirs of a barbaric bombing. Then, continuing to sit and look, I saw a God-sees-all eye staring at me from the ceiling. Quickly looking away from the penetrating eye, of course, I focused on a large oil painting hanging on a wall to my left. The painting showed three young women sitting on large stones by some water—maybe the sea. An arrogant-looking blonde, sitting higher than two brunettes, was dressed in a long, white gown and was pointing up at a cerulean blue sky. The two brunettes were sitting on jagged stones and were dressed in faded blue dresses that were ready for the ragbag. The lowly brunettes' faces were filled with fear, and with bare, overworked-looking arms, they reached out to the blonde one, as if imploring her for help.

After looking at the painting for maybe ten seconds, I told myself that the artist had a great prejudice against brunettes and left the church in a kind of stupid anger. Crossing the road to a raised roadside garden, I sat on a bench, wanting to get cool and collected before returning to the hotel. Autumn flowers were in bloom and it was a moment of peace for me. Suddenly, however, just as I was adjusting to the soft flow of peace inside me, an old woman with a small boy entered the garden. When the boy started squealing, I got up to leave, but the woman shoved a box camera at me, and saying something in probably Norwegian, made motions that I should take their picture. I obliged, of course, and just as I was finished and the woman and boy went away, Richard Fowler appeared, sat on the bench with me, kissed me on both cheeks and said, "So, here you are."

Looking into his green eyes, I smiled and said, "Yes, here I am."

As handsome as ever, with the sides of his hair greying, wearing brown, corduroy knickerbockers with a black, turtleneck sweater, he said, holding my hands, "Anne, it's really you. You're even more beautiful."

"Thank you, Richard. You look well, and you look very handsome in your turtleneck. Thank you for allowing me to come."

"Nonsense," he said, his green eyes smiling. "If I'd known where you were, I would have insisted we get together for a nice visit."

"I heard you are with CIA, Richard, or am I being too nosey?"

"Who told you that?" he asked, frowning a bit.

"A private detective I hired to find you. I'm sorry if I did the wrong thing."

"Not you, but the detective did, I suppose. No matter. I'll be retiring soon."

"Could we go to the hotel? It's getting cold and I'm hungry. All I've had is a little herring today."

We went to the hotel and into the dining room, where we ate salad and steak, and after we'd finished, Richard said, "You told me on the phone that your second husband passed away. Again, I want to offer my condolences. You haven't had it easy, have you, Anne? First, Henri, then your American husband."

"No, it hasn't been easy, but it's worse for my son."

"Yes, I remember him… Matthew. He was a tall and intelligent lad."

"He still is. He has finished university... cum laude."

"Wonderful... yes, indeed."

A pretty waitress brought coffee, and Richard, after asking me if he could smoke, lit his pipe, a dark, mean-looking thing curving down with a large bowl at the end. Through a cloud of smoke, he said finally, "You said it has been more difficult for Matthew."

"Yes, and I'm worried about him. You see, he is filled with hatred for the man who killed his father, and for a long time now, he has been having nightmares and crying out in his sleep that he wants to kill that man. Richard, I don't want hatred in his heart. I believe if he talked to the man and found out the true circumstances, then the hatred would disappear."

"So, you have come to me, knowing that I knew the man, even before he was assigned to Bordeaux."

"Yes, and I too would like to know what happened that awful night when Henri was killed. Can you help?"

"Anne, I wish I could tell you what happened that night, but I don't know—not for sure. You'd have to speak with the former officer of the German army who was involved. Hans Müller is his name, an Austrian who lives near Salzburg."

"Could you arrange a meeting?"

"If you really want it, I'll ring my old friend up tonight."

"Old friend?" I asked, confused. "You are friends with this man?"

Smiling, he said, "I can see I have some explaining to do." Then, looking at the door, he said, "Anne, let's get out of here and walk a bit."

Leaving the hotel, we walked along the waterfront. As the moon played upon the water, I asked, "How could the man who killed my husband be your friend?"

"Allow me to give you a bit of a history lesson, all right?"

I didn't respond. I jerked up my coat collar and looked down at his dirty hobnail boots.

He spoke then of the Norwegian people, who had resisted the German army during the occupation from May, 1940 to May, 1945. He spoke of the ten thousand Gestapo agents who were unable to break the will of the people. He spoke of the Norwegian teachers who had refused to indoctrinate the children with Nazi ideals, so that the Nazis had to bring in their own teachers. "Returning to 1940," he said now. "English Commandos had come in June, right after the Germans, but it had been a bloody disaster—technically, that is. However, psychologically it was a rousing success, for it served as a morale booster for the Norwegians when the Germans were victorious everywhere. You see, at least some resistance came, before they walked into Paris."

With both sadness and anger, I said, "Yes, I can recall the day they occupied Paris."

Turning his back to the wind that had come, he lit his pipe again and said, "I was here, Anne, when they came." Then, when I began to shiver, he put his arm around me, saying, "You've had a tiring day, and you're cold. What I have to say can wait."

Toughing it, and liking his arm around me, I said, "No, I want to hear about it now."

"Well, if it isn't too much, I'll continue. You see, before they came, I'd already been here a year. As an electrical engineer, like your Henri, I helped give farmers electricity—those who'd not had it before. It was similar to what Henri did in the Bordeaux region, before he went with Post, Telegraph, and Telephone. Right. Well, after the Germans came, my wife Mary and I joined the Norwegian Resistance, and in the spring of 1943, we were captured. As you know, Mary was killed, and soon after that friends helped me escape. We then began tapping Colonel Hans Müller's communication system—yes, the very same Hans Müller who was in France later on. You see, Anne, by tapping into the communication system, we were able to intercept messages from the Germans and then send out false messages in order to confuse them as to the whereabouts of the Resistance Fighters. Fortunately, then we were able to destroy a heavy-water plant, used to develop atomic energy. Just after that, I was captured again."

Holding up my hand, I said, "I'm sorry, Richard. I'm freezing. I would like to return to the hotel, where I would like to hear more."

"Right."

Returning to the hotel, we went to the bar. While drinking a glass of wine, I removed a book of poems from my coat and said, "Maybe you would like to read Matthew's poems. Before I forget it, I want to give this to you. You may gain some insight as to what might still be inside him."

Taking the book and lighting his pipe, he said, "What a nice surprise! Indeed, I'll read his work. Then, thumbing through the pages, he asked, "How old was he, when he wrote these?"

"He put them into a book when he was sixteen. He was working on them through his younger years, of course."

Stopping at a page, he read aloud: "'War is the eternal insanity/ the sick solution of the madman who waits the darkness/ Hate is in his heart/ a bullet in his gun/ He pulls the trigger/ the deed is done/ My father is dead/ My heart has lost its way/ Love is gone/ Endurance has flown away/ Faith is no more/ Hope has become a hopeless whore/ mocking my impotent soul… mocking me.'"

After a moment, I asked, "Do you think the poetry is too dark for a young boy?"

"Not if the boy has just lost his father," he said, lighting his damn pipe again. "Let me think about it. In the meantime, let's have another glass of red wine."

"Yes, I'd like another glass," I said. Then, after he'd ordered, I placed my hand on his arm and said, "Richard, I'm sorry I interrupted your story."

After the wine arrived, he said, "As I was saying, right after we sabotaged the heavy-water plant, I was captured for the second time. And then the most extraordinary thing happened. Colonel Hans Müller saved my life. You see, after I was taken to his office one day, he told me that he was being transferred to the Bordeaux area in order to repair some underground cable. I must say, his telling me this really surprised me. One just didn't give this kind of information to the enemy. I was immediately suspicious of his motive, of course, and I thought he was up to something. But, as you will see, it turned out to be to my advantage—quite…. More wine?"

"No thanks."

After he got another glass, he continued. "As I sat there in the colonel's office, he asked about my work in helping farmers get electricity. When I didn't answer, he began speaking to me as a colleague, telling me technical things about his work in Norway—and he even talked about his schooling in Vienna and his friends. Then, to beat all, he talked about his wife and three children. Then, seeing no harm in crossing the barrier,

I talked about my wife and about the miserable way she'd died. Anne, after I spoke of Mary, the man actually wept. Incredible! Then, after he was composed again, he spoke of atomic energy—what good it could do for mankind and what harm it might cause if used the wrong way. To my surprise, then, he went to the telephone and told someone— a pilot, I assumed—to drop me in the Bordeaux area, where he would soon be transferred. Hanging up the phone, he looked at me, smiled and said, 'I'm putting you where I can keep an eye on you. And I'll take care of the men who murdered your wife.' So, you see Anne, that is how I like to remember Hans Müller."

"But didn't he kill my husband?" I asked, almost regretfully.

"Yes, I believe he did, but I'm not sure. It was dark. We were loading ammunition on a farm truck in Landes de Bussac. I can recall Henri and Maurice Martineau were arguing. Perhaps it was about Maurice's pilfering supplies. He was always stealing something. I must say, he wasn't the most trustworthy of human beings, nor the most humane. For the least probable cause, he'd slit your throat. In any event, the Germans arrived and suddenly Henri appeared in the light coming from the Germans' truck. A single shot brought Henri down. The rest of us took to the woods and were not caught."

After a brief pause, I said, "You must hate the men who killed your wife."

Smiling, he said, "No, I harbor no hatred. Mary wouldn't want that inside me."

"I wish my son could hear you say that."

Taking my hand and looking in my eyes, he said, "My friend, I advise you to drop the idea of meeting with Hans. Frankly, I can't see how your son can hate someone he has never seen and doesn't know. Good Lord, after all these years—move on, Anne. Get a good psychiatrist for him and move on."

Irritated and defensive, I said, "A doctor would advise us to meet with the man and talk about it!"

"It would depend on the doctor, wouldn't it? One might advise it, and another might not."

I left the table in anger, and he followed. In the lobby, he said, "If I was a bit harsh, I'm sorry."

"Richard, I understand what you said in there, and I've said the same thing to myself many times. My show of anger was uncalled for, and I'm sorry."

"You're exhausted. Sleep on it, and if you still want me to contact Hans, I'll do it. When will you be leaving here?"

"If I decide against the meeting with the Austrian, I shall go to Paris tomorrow. I want to spend time with my sister-in-law, Halona Villon, the widow of my brother, Jean, who was killed in the war. Then in two weeks I shall return to Michigan. I want to be with my son at Christmas."

Smiling, Richard said, "I know Halona and I also know your younger brother, Vachel. I know you all."

"Yes, Halona has spoken of you, come to think of it. I told her I knew you during the war. CIA wasn't spoken of."

"By the way, Anne, what's the name of that private detective of yours, and I wonder how he found me."

"He's an international from Detroit and he speaks many languages. Lamont Bradford is his name. He talked to Halona, and she said that when you're in Paris, you often go to Willi's wine bar on rue des Petits-Champs. He said someone there, who had been tipsy, mentioned that you are a CIA agent."

"Well, I suppose it's no secret after all these years. And, as I said, I'm going to retire soon."

"Do you spy on people?"

Laughing, and then after he lit his pipe, he said, "I'm sure I can trust you to keep a secret—secret in large quotation marks… I'll just say that I'm a link between the British MI6 and the CIA. Now it's time for bed. If you need me, or if you get up earlier than I, please knock on my door. I've taken the room next to yours."

After saying goodnight and giving each other a hug, we went to our rooms. In bed now, I thought about Richard and how he was able to prevent hatred from ruining his life. I prayed that I would be doing the right thing, if I met with the Austrian and would bring my son later on. Then, after deciding to go to Austria, I thought of the warm hugs Richard had given me. Yes, I told myself, it was the hugs that did it! I hurried to his room and we gave each other something wonderful to cheer about....

Moonlight flooded the room and the sounds of night were few. I lay beside him and watched him sleep. I loved to watch him sleep and feel something good coming from his spirit that spoke of his strength and life of service in helping the world become a better place. Then, with tears, I thought about myself and how very much I was like a Chagall painting in which incomplete people float in space. I felt like one of those people, incomplete and floating in space....

It was morning. After hard rolls and coffee, we went for a walk. Going to the end of a long pier, we stood in silence for a long moment, before he said, "The sun shows no compassion. It's too warm for this time of year."

With a tired smile and tired humor, I said, "We made the weather warmer last night."

"So we did, didn't we?" he said, smiling and putting an arm around me.

As we looked over the fjord to the mountains on the other side, I said, "Richard, I think I'll go to Austria to see that man. Then at a later date, if I think it would help my son, I'd bring him to see the man."

"Right. I'll call Hans. Would you want me to go with you? I have to see some people in Vienna next week. Could you possibly wait until then?"

"No, as I said, my time is limited. I'll be all right. Don't you think?"

"Yes, of course. If I could, I'd leave with you today. Sorry."

"No need to be sorry." Then, staring into the water's glare, I said, "You know I love you, don't you."

After turning me and kissing me, he said, "And I love you."

Returning to the hotel, I said, "Damn it all, I wish things were different. I wish there was no Cold War and that you weren't an agent. Just a moment ago, I felt so good and confident. Now I feel rotten."

"Anne, you're exhausted. And you've had a lot of pain, haven't you?"

"You're right. I am exhausted and my ear aches."

"No doubt, your ear aches from listening to a lot of bullshit coming from me."

Laughing, I said, "Please don't make me laugh. For some reason, I want to feel miserable. Is it possible to feel miserable and love someone at the same time?"

"I do it all the time."

Laughing again, I squeezed his arm hard and said, "All night long I looked for something in my life to be warmly aware of and look at with pride, but I could find nothing but failure and death and destruction. And yes, pain. Somewhere along the line, I lost my soul. How could I fall in love with no soul, Richard?"

"I do it all the time."

Ready to cry, I stopped him and said, "Please don't laugh at me."

Taking my shoulders, he looked in my eyes, saying, "My dear, you still have your soul, and don't be surprised when it appears soon. Then you will marvel at all the beautiful things you see—priceless souvenirs to give you comfort for the rest of your days, eternally."

With tears and a smile, I whispered, "That's your great gift, Richard. You have the power to replace fear with faith in someone. You've just made me feel that, after all, I may be worthy of heaven."

"How's your ear?"

"Better—much better, thank you."

We walked in silence for a moment, until I got up nerve enough to ask: "What was Mary like? How did you meet?"

His green eyes smiling now, he said, "Yes, I'd be delighted. I love talking about Mary. I must say, her brief life was first-rate and has greatly influenced my life. She was an orphan, you see, and she often said she wasn't adopted because she was too wild and had one leg that was shorter than the other. According to her, at the age of sixteen, the people who ran the orphanage pronounced her the most incorrigible girl in London because of her absolute obsession with animals of all kinds. Numerous times, she said, they told her not to bring stray animals back to the orphanage, but time after time, she disobeyed them and returned from her domestic duties in private homes with stray dogs and cats and with just about everything else. Once, in fact, she brought back an injured monkey and tried to hide it in her room. But, as with the others, she had no success. She was nineteen when I met her in my father's bookshop and it was love at first sight. Her hair was the color of ripe strawberries in sunshine and her eyes were deep blue and filled with passion.... As I told you, Mary and I were in the Norwegian Resistance. After we were captured, she was tortured, raped and shot to death—right before my eyes.... I harbor no hate, as I said, for those responsible. They are dead now—shot by Hans himself, before he left for France. Mary is buried here, where I live most of the time.... Well now, here we are at our luxurious hotel."

"Luxurious?"

"Comfortable."

"That's better," I said, already on my way to my room to pack my small suitcase.

Richard called the Austrian from my room and told him I was coming, before he showed me love and tenderness in bed, as I did him. Lying on his back now and staring at the ceiling, his mood seemed to darken, and in an abstract way, he said, "I must get on with my life. Mary would have it that way. It's time I realized that I wasn't responsible for her death by allowing her to remain in Norway and fight in the Underground."

I was confused. I had thought that he had gotten on with his life long ago. I wanted to ask about it, but I didn't. Within ten minutes, I was gone from Molde. Traveling back down the Trondheim Line, I was glad Richard and his dead wife weren't with me. Then, just before Oslo, I damned myself for being jealous of a dead woman, especially a woman of courage who had suffered so much.

## chapter 16

Tired and apprehensive, I sat on a bench by the River Salzach in Salzburg. I tried to relax, but it wasn't to be. A band concert started up across the river, and the sounds came across the water in dissonant swells. I wanted the meeting with Hans Müller to be over. As soon as I arrived last night, I had called him from my room at the Goldener Hirsch Hotel. After being friendly, he said, "Tomorrow, at midday, meet me at Bahnhof." looking at my watch now, I saw that it was time to go meet the man. I took a streetcar and was at the train station five minutes early. Finding a small, unoccupied table near a front window, I sat and got coffee. It wasn't long before a distinguished-looking man in a grey suit came to the table and asked, "Are you the one?"

Smiling at him, I said, "I'm the one."

Smiling, he said, "Yes, I can see now. I was told how you look." Then, after shaking my hand, he sat and ordered tea.

I was very nervous and shaking. I thought my toes would fall off. When I thought about the new white dress I bought today for the occasion, I felt like a silly goose. Funny, I'd gotten all dolled-up to meet the man who killed my husband. "Is the tea good?" I asked, looking at the tablecloth.

"Good," he said in French. Continuing then to speak perfect French, he said, "Richard told me why you have come. I would have invited you to my house to talk about it, but I didn't want to upset my wife. I have talked to her about it several times—too much. Do you understand?"

"Yes, of course. Sir, I'm not here to judge you. I only want to hear what happened the night my husband was killed."

Softly, he said, "I shall do my best. To begin, I had much respect for your husband, both as an engineer and as a man. What happened that night was darker than war, if such a thing is possible. An informer gave us a telephone message. He would not give his name. He told us of the truck with ammunition in Landes de Bussac. We went there right away. It was very dark. The only light came from the lights on our vehicle. Suddenly, there was someone coming at me. I was very nervous and I shot him. It happened so quick. Yes, I killed your husband. I do not deny it. However, when I thought about it after, I concluded that he was pushed into the light. I knew your husband, Henri, and I had spoken with him many times at Post, Telegraph and Telephone. I am very sorry. That is all I know about the matter. He is always in my mind. He was the only person that I have ever killed, except the two who raped, tortured and murdered Richard's wife, whom I considered monsters, not men. I say again: I'm sorry. Please forgive me, Madame La Fleur."

Wiping tears from my face, I said, "I believe you, sir, and I forgive you. I believe I know who pushed my Henri into the light. He is really responsible. He is also dead. You may call me Anne."

"And please call me Hans. Thank you for your forgiveness… So, today is Saturday. Anne, would you come to our house tomorrow for the midday meal. I would very much like you to meet my wife and daughter. My two sons are away at school."

"Yes, I'll come, but I won't be able to stay for very long. I want to get back to Paris."

"Shall we pick you up?"

"No, I'll take a taxi. Give me your address, please. By the way, I have a son who is in America. Someday in the coming year, may I bring him here to meet you?"

Already busy writing down his address with detailed directions and drawings, he looked at me for a moment and said, "So, now he has grown up without his father. My God, I'm so sorry. Yes, of course, please bring him. I must ask for his forgiveness, also."

"Thank you, Hans. You are a good man."

A few hours later, after a nap, I went to a nearby Gasthaus to eat. Being Saturday night, the place was crowded. Finally, I found a place at a long table with several other people and a schnauzer. At first, I thought it was just what I needed to keep out thoughts of myself, Richard, Hans and even Matthew for the moment. I was getting too serious and dark, I believed, and my spirit was going up and down too much. I felt I was like that yo-yo thing my son had when he was a boy, with mostly someone else playing the string.

The atmosphere at the restaurant was thick with barking, smoke, loud music, singing, laughing and a lot of other important things. A pretty girl in a low-cut dirndl took my order for Hungarian goulash and tea, and while I waited, I listened to the music and studied the musicians—three fat men in leather pants with wide grins on their apple-like faces, who all played several instruments, alternately playing the zither, accordion, piano, trumpet, flute, drums, tuba and violin. And, as if that weren't impressive enough, they sang on key most of the time with well-trained voices, in spite of all the quick moves they made in their tight-fitting Lederhosen.

I was eating goulash and drinking tea now, as I glanced now and again at the schnauzer and the people at the table. Across from me, there was the older couple with the schnauzer. The man was small. She was huge. His hair was white, and he had a large white mustache that curled up at the ends—like Emperor Franz Joseph's. Her hair was blonde with white roots, and her mustache curled down at the ends—like their schnauzer's. Hardly an inch above his strawberry-like nose, his blue eyes were small and clear. Her blue eyes were big and glassy. He wore a wrinkled white shirt, blue tie and a grey suit with green lapels. She wore a red dirndl, blue apron, and a wrinkled white blouse. He was sitting still and grinning at me, while she was standing and waving a stein of beer in the air, keeping time with the music and spilling beer on the old gentleman, who didn't take his eyes off me.

The old goat kept staring at me and now he was puckering his ash-blue lips and kissing the air between us. I wanted to just laugh it off, but I couldn't manage myself. I got angry and nervous and spilled some goulash on my white dress. Then, after giving the old man a scolding look and after not bothering to clean the dress, I paid the bill, put on my trenchcoat and left, only to be met by a cold-blowing rain outside. Inside, my mood had darkened, but now, walking in the cold rain and opening my mouth to it in order to wash away the spicy taste of goulash, I felt giddy but good. I slept well that night, knowing that I was passing some kind of endurance test on my own.

Dressed in my dark blue suit, I bought a mixed-bouquet of flowers and got into a taxi. The sun was shining, and it was warm. After ten kilometers, or so, we were on a dirt road and stopped in front of a large iron gate. The gate opened and when we were through it closed again, automatically, as far as I could tell. Following a long, circular driveway, we stopped then at a large stone house. I got out of the taxi and went to the door. I was a little nervous, for a reason I didn't have time to look for or worry about. Before I could find a bell or knock, the door opened.

A lovely blonde woman greeted me with a handshake and a bright smile. She was petite and elegant in a black-embroidered dirndl, white apron and a white blouse that had a small back cameo fixed at the neck. Her hair was cut short, and her blue eyes twinkled in the sun. "Welcome," she said in English. "I'm Alysia, Hansie's wife." Then, after taking the flowers, she said, "Thank you for the lovely flowers. Please, enter."

As soon as I was inside, Hans came to greet me in English and lead us to the dining room. And it was then, as I walked beside Alysia, that the name *Hansie* echoed in my head. Alysia had referred to herself as "Hansie's wife" and obviously had thought nothing of it. Now, however, I found it somewhat disturbing that the man who killed my husband—and had suffered so much guilt for so many years—should be called Hansie. Yes, I found it incongruous and a little obscene that the man who killed those men who had raped and tortured and killed Mary Fowler should be called Hansie—and that the man who had been so courageous in setting Richard free, should be called Hansie…

Alysia was saying, "Please sit." Then after we were seated at the ornate table with an embroidered tablecloth, a young woman entered the room and Alysia said, "This is our only daughter, Herta. My dear, this is Mrs. La Fleur."

"Hello," I said, extending my hand.

"Grese Gott," Herta said, blushing and shaking my hand, and then leaving the room, saying in English, "Please excuse it. I must get the food."

Watching the young woman leave the room, with her long dark hair and tall, slim body, I said, "She's beautiful, very beautiful."

"We're proud of her," Alysia said, smiling. "She will go to Vienna tomorrow. She will be a doctor of medicine. Our two sons are away at school. They will be engineers, like their father."

Just then, Herta returned with a small wagon loaded with food and beverages. After putting it all on a buffet next to a wall, she said, "Please eat."

As soon as we had food and drink at the ornate table, and just after I'd taken a mouthful of Erdapfel Puffer, or potato pancake, and Pariser Schnitzel, well done, Hans asked, "And so did you sleep well last night—at what hotel do you stay?"

Maybe taking up time until I finished chewing and swallowing, Alysia said, "I condemn us for not asking you to stay with us."

Finally able to speak, I said, "The Goldener Hirsch Hotel. Yes, I slept well, and I'm glad you didn't invite me. Please, let me explain." Then, after a gulp of coffee, I smiled and said, "It gave me a chance to go out to one of your restaurants. The food was good, and there was music and excitement. The musicians were extremely talented and there was a woman who must have thought she was a conductor. For her baton, she used a stein of beer, and when she waved it around, she spilled beer on her husband's mustache—at least, I think it was her husband."

We laughed, and after talking about things that wouldn't stick in my head, we finished eating and I said, "I must be going."

"I'll get the car," Hans said. "We'll all go to the airport with you."

To be in Paris in bad weather is like getting a kiss without a squeeze—but there is always that kiss. It was raining when I arrived in the late afternoon. Going to my apartment on the Rue de Ponthieu, I lit a fire in the fireplace and settled in with cookies and hot chocolate. It wasn't long, however, before my peaceful moment was ended by a phone call.

"I've been trying to reach you. You should tell me when you leave town. Did you leave town?" my sister-in-law Halona said.

"What's the matter?" I asked, surprised by the amount of anger in her voice.

"Gabrielle has been kidnapped," she said, calm now. "I called to let you know and to see if you're all right."

"How do you know she's been kidnapped?"

"J'nine and Marsha Lowden told me the bad news. They are here now."

"I'll be right over."

I dressed and got a taxi. Staring at Notre Dame Cathedral as we headed for the West Bank, I thought of Halona and of the trouble she'd experienced in her life and was still experiencing. She was a Mohawk Indian who had married my brother Jean during one of his visits to Montreal. Then on June 14, 1940, she and Jean and their two small daughters, J'nine and Gabrielle, along with thousands of other Parisiens, had left Paris with what belongings they could carry and headed south. Walking the roads, the fleeing crowds had of course unintentionally blocked the German push from Paris to Augouleme, about three hundred kilometers to the south. Then, in order to clear the roads, the German Luftwaffe used cannon and machine guns. While Halona and Jean hid in a ditch and protected their daughters with their bodies, Jean was killed. And from that moment on, Gabrielle, the older daughter, had blamed herself for her father's death, saying that if he didn't use his body to protect her, he would still be alive. Halona had been in her early Twenties, and after Jean's death, she went on to study and eventually teach philosophy at University of Paris at Sorbonne. And it was at a café near Sorbonne that I met Marsha Lowden, on one of my visits to France while married to Daniel Horton. Marsha had been one of Halona's students and J'nine's friend. Halona, in her fifties now, lived in one of the apartment buildings along the Seine, not far across from the Louvre. Her place was elegant, with antique furnishings and masterful paintings, and when I entered, I hoped that my son would someday paint something for Halona.

In the next moment, after warm greetings, the four of us were sitting at the table in the dining room with tea in front of us. Right now, nothing was being said, perhaps because of the gravity of the situation confronting us. I took a moment to study J'nine. I hadn't seen her in a few years and was amazed at how much she was getting to resemble her mother. Although her hair was long and Halona's was cropped short, she had her mother's dark eyes, high cheekbones, and smooth, reddish skin. Then, studying Marsha, whom I also hadn't seen in several years, I saw the contrast. Marsha's shoulder-length hair was blonde, her skin was fair and her eyes were bright blue. Also, Marsha still had her tall, trim figure beneath her dark blue suit, while J'nine was getting a little too squat for her small frame, wrapped in a white dress that was too tight....

Halona, in a black dress with a strand of pearls around her neck, looked at me with swollen eyes and said, "J'nine called me from her apartment in Lyon, and then she called Marsha, who was in Torremolinos, Spain."

Marsha interrupted, saying, "Actually, it was I who called J'nine, I wanted to let her know I was coming to Paris, so we could get together."

"That's right," J'nine said, "And that's when I told her about Gabrielle—that her latest boyfriend got her high on drugs and sold her."

"Sold her?" I asked, not understanding.

"It's true, Aunt Anne," J'nine said, nodding her head. "Gabrielle fell in with the wrong crowd some time ago. Now she's been sold to some guy called Otto Schmidt. From what I could gather, he's been doing pharmaceutical business in France."

"How do you know this?" I asked.

"The police picked up the boyfriend, and he spilled his rotten guts. A friend at the police station told me. He said, that just outside a brasserie on St. Germaine, the boyfriend forced her into a car and he and Schmidt and two other men took her to the airport, where Schmidt's private plane was waiting."

"Where are they now?" I asked.

"In Bordeaux, at the old family homestead. When Grandmama and Grandpapa died, Gabrielle went to live there."

I looked at Halona and said, "I thought you sold the house. You told me that you sold the house. You told me that you sold it."

"I told you I was thinking of selling it," Halona said. "But I didn't. I just couldn't bring myself to sell it. Jean and you and Vachel were born there, and besides, Gabrielle begged me not to sell it. She and J'nine spent so many summers there when they were small, and Gabrielle wanted to live in it."

Looking at J'nine again, I asked, "When did all this take place?"

"Over a week now."

"My God!"

"We didn't know about it until a few days ago," J'nine said, sobbing now.

Marsha spoke up, saying, "If the police move in, there is a good chance she'll be dead."

"But there is a chance that we can get inside," Halona said. "Stop the hysterics, J'nine, and tell her!"

Straightening up, J'nine said, "Gabrielle called me at my lab in Lyon. She said that some man wanted to make me a lucrative offer… that he needed a chemist, and that her boyfriend, Claude Buchard, had told the man about me. By the way my sister sounded, I knew she was in trouble—emotionally and probably physically."

"When did you get the call? I asked.

"Let's see… today's Saturday. It was Wednesday. Pardon. I'm a little mixed up. It was two days after one of Claude Buchard's girlfriends went to the police and told them that Buchard had been bragging around that he'd sold Gabrielle for a lot of money. That's when the police picked up Buchard, after he returned to Paris."

Marsha said, "Schmidt probably doesn't know about the confession, putting the finger on him."

"That's right, Marsha," Halona said. "He probably thinks he can do what he wants, but he has robbed the wrong nest!"

"Yes, he has!" I said. Then, looking at J'nine, I asked, "What did you tell your sister about the lucrative offer?"

"I said I'd think it over and call her back. Then I told Uncle Vachel about the kidnapping and the call. He said he'd check on Schmidt and call me back. When he did, he said that the police knew about Schmidt, that he was into experimental drugs, but that they had nothing on him, until now, with the kidnapping. Uncle Vachel asked me to play along, so I called Gabrielle and told her I was interested in the offer. She called back and said Schmidt would like to interview me in Paris. Tonight I'm going to meet with him at the Kaspia."

"You mean we are going to meet with him," Marsha said. "A lot of Russians go to the Kaspia."

"Will the police arrest Schmidt tonight?" I asked.

"Vachel says it's too risky," Halona said. "Vachel said that there may be someone watching, who would probably call Bordeaux and have Gabrielle killed."

"He's probably using my sister as a guinea pig," J'nine said. Then, looking at Marsha, she asked, "Are you sure you want to come with me tonight?"

"You didn't have to ask that," Marsha said. "I love Gabrielle as much as you do. And, frankly, I'd like to be the one who sends this Schmidt guy to hell, where he belongs."

I knew Marsha meant what she said. Since I'd first met her, she had come to mind often. She was from Michigan, but I had never contacted her while I lived there because, knowing that she traveled a lot, I didn't expect she'd be home. Besides, I was quite busy looking after my son, or fighting with my American husband, Daniel—fighting silently in my heart and mind, mostly when it came to his sleeping with other women. In no way, was I about to lower myself by talking about his whores.

Concerning Marsha, she got married during the Korean War, and after her husband, Frank Rhodes, joined the Air Force and was sent to Casablanca, she went to join him. She was but a child, when in the early spring she left by troopship, the USNS H.F. Hodges, from New York. She was one of several wives going to be with their husbands who were stationed throughout Europe. The women and officers occupied cabins on the forward deck, while the enlisted people were down below. Sergeants and corporals kept a watchful eye on the women and officers, especially at night, when there was dancing in the deck lounge. When word got out that the officers were seducing wives, the non-commissioned men took guard duty. Marsha said that she had enjoyed the sea air so much, that she was outside on deck much of the time. She said that the sea began to dominate her life, and she began to feel submissive to its power. And then it happened, she said. On the night before arriving in Casablanca, she was on deck talking to an officer about the possibility of a storm. Then, because of a sudden list of the ship, she found herself falling into the officer's arms. Immediately, a guard ran up to them and, after taking their names, reported them for having sex. Then, after she told the commanding officer what really happened, he laughed and said, "Yeah, I know, and the Pope's got ten wives."

After word about the incident was forwarded to her husband, his reply was that he didn't want her to join him. She was forbidden to get off the ship and was told she'd be returned to the States. Feeling humiliated and angry, she said she wouldn't accept that "garbage" and, when people got off at Naples, she sneaked off with them. Making her way to Paris, she settled in a small apartment on the West Bank and began taking courses at Sorbonne, where she met Halona and J'nine. After her divorce, she learned about existential philosophy from Halona and went about making life as meaningless as possible, because, as she put it: "It helped me endure the pain my husband inflicted upon me, without giving me a chance to explain."

Taking back her maiden name, Marsha had continued on in Paris, studying and hanging around such places as Les Halles, Montparnasse, Le Rubis, Palais du Louvre and Jeu de Paume on Place de la Concorde, where she said she couldn't get enough of looking at impressionist paintings. Sometimes, J'nine would be with her, and one day, after lunch on a sightseeing boat on the Seine, J'nine took her to Aux Deux Magots on Saint-Germain and introduced her to Jean Paul Sartre, a friend of ours, and on the next day, she took her to Willi's, a wine bar on rue des Petits-Champs, where she met my brother, Vachel Villon, one of the English owner's best customers.

She began spending time with Vachel, and one night, while having dinner at L'Orangerie, Vacehl persuaded her to go to Langley, Virginia and become a CIA agent. Afterwards, speaking confidentially to Halona and me and J'nine—confidentially and freely—she said that she'd pursued her job as an analyst with "zeal" and learned several languages including Russian and Mandarin after spending hundreds of hours listening to language tapes in small cubicles with headsets clamped on her ears. She went through tough physical training and learned how to read newspapers, including Pravda and Izvestia, and roadmaps, railroad timetables, telephone directories that indicated who was new to a city and who had left. She learned about microfilm and worked the translating machine. She learned about machinery and read journals. Then she became a field agent, working undercover as a travel agent. "Flimflam!" she'd often say to us. "My life is all flimflam!" But not for a moment did I ever believe that she didn't realize that every bit of the flimflam was necessary, because of the lives involved. And I further believed that she realized that her being a travel agent was highly suspect in her world of deception, and therefore dangerous. She had courage, plenty of it! And I envied her now, as I watched her empty her large, black purse on the table.

Marsha was saying, "Before we get caught up in projections, I'm going to get busy and get out the authentications I might need." Then, after opening the false bottom, she removed a French passport, replaced it with her American passport, along with two other passports which I couldn't identify, closed the false bottom, replaced the items, including a small cosmetics bag, and said, "Flimflam. It's all flimflam—but worth it, right? Now, I'm Renee Martin again. I have relatives in Lyon and work there with J'nine, as her assistant. How's that, J'nine, so far?"

"Sounds good," J'nine said. "I'm sure Vachel will approve. You know, I think I'll call Vachel right now. He must have a plan in mind." Then, after she left the room and returned, she said, "Uncle Vachel said he'd fill us in after we've met with Schmidt tonight."

"Say, I've got an idea," Marsha said. "Why don't we all go to Pont de l'Alma and have a boatride on a nice bateaux-mouches. We can relax, and it'll help us think."

"And we could have canard au sang," J'nine said.

"No boatride, and no duck!" Halona said sharply. "Do you two think that we're on holiday?"

"Your sister's life is at stake," I said, looking at J'nine sternly.

"No one knows that better than I, Aunt Anne," J'nine said seriously.

"I thought Vachel was going to retire," I said, looking at J'nine and smiling now.

"Uncle Vachel is a long way from retiring," J'nine said.

"Did you hear about the coat hanger, J'nine?" Marsha asked, chuckling a little. "No? Well, he was in Vienna and he and Sepp Gruber found a coat hanger in a trash barrel at the airport. The barrel was loaded with stuff from a Russian Aeroloft commercial that had landed. Vachel said he sent it to Washington to be analyzed and they found out the bomb load and range of Russia's long-range bomber. He said that after they made the wings, they melted the shavings and made coat hangers. Vachel said the people in Washington used spectro-analysis and chemical testing."

After wondering if Marsha was a blabber-mouth and talked like that when she was with just anyone, and after I told myself that she was much too smart for that, I looked at J'nine and said, "You're a chemist, J'nine. I'm sure you found that interesting."

"Yes, Aunt Anne, I found the story interesting, but unless our lab in Washington has other information, there is no way to tell the range and bomb load from analyzing the metal from a coat hanger."

"You should know," I said.

"Well, the fact is, that by using a spectrometer and breaking down the chemical composition of the hanger, and then finding the wave lengths of each element in the alloy, the only thing they could determine is that it was Russian. And they certainly wouldn't be able to determine it was a long-range bomber, because the same metal is used in fighter planes and other things."

Halona brought pieces of cold chicken, bread, and strawberry sherbert. "Sorry, daughter," she said, placing it on the table. "It's not canard au sang, but it will have to do."

"Marsha," I asked, not expecting a straight answer, "What was Vachel doing in Vienna, besides looking in trash barrels?"

Without hesitation, Marsha said, "He was looking for Nada Kreuger. She's with us, and Vachel wanted to find out what she'd gotten from Hildegarde Benjamin, also know as Red Hilde. Nada... my God, she's really something! She's an agent provocateur and, in the Fifties, she broke plenty of communist heads in East Germany during the Worker's Rebellion. Now, I hear she's with German spy, Reinhold Gehlen, who also does work for us, I believe." Then, turning to J'nine, Marsha asked, "J'nine, if you're not going to eat your sherbert, can I have it?"

Pushing the sherbert over, J'nine said, "Just like old times—begging for my dessert, like a pesty puppy."

"You two are unbelievable!" Halona shouted, slapping the table with the palm of her hand. "And at a time like this, you choose to clown!" Then, when it was quiet, she stared at the table and said, "Gabrielle has been in emotional bondage for years, as many women are, spending hopeless days and years in misery. For some time now, I've thought of doing something for these women. God willing, I shall find a way, soon."

"Gabrielle has always felt responsible for Papa's death," J'nine said.

"Guilt'll do it every time," Marsha said.

"For whatever reason, or reasons," Halona said. "Gabrielle fell, and I feel I have abandoned her. And there are many more like her that have been abandoned..."

Like streams of water flowing into desert places, nourishing them and helping them bloom, ideas flowed into my head and heart, making me feel beautiful again. "I have some suggestions," I said slowly, collecting my thoughts. "As you know, Halona, in America, I was married to a cruel and abusive man who seemed to show kindness only when he wanted to gain money, power or sex. Anyway, he died and left me a lot of money. Along with others that you would surely enlist, I would be willing to finance places of care, protection, and education for women who need a new start in life. And, God willing, we could do it soon. Our staff... well, it could be made up of Academicians, including you, Halona; Neutralizers, who would deprogram and reverse destructive states of mind; Doctors, who would revitalize them physically and emotionally. AND would be the name of our organization—a conjunctive force between that which would bring death to a soul and that which would bring a useful and reasonably happy life.... Halona, what do you think? What do you all think?"

After a moment of silence, Halona said, "I'm impressed, deeply. But it's no surprise, Anne, for you have always impressed me deeply."

"I'm also impressed," Marsha said, smiling.

"Me, too" J'nine said.

It was then that something began burning inside me—perhaps, feelings that I had lived with most of my life, that had grown cold. In any event, as if I were young again, I began quoting what I had never forgotten—a compulsion made me do it. "Resist!" I said, my eyes closed, my head held high, my body more erect. "Resist those who would enslave us and our precious children. We must take up the staff of freedom from those who have fought and died for freedom before us. Just as before, the ravens are hovering over us."

"More!" J'nine said, encouraging me.

"Yes, please," Marsha said, opening my eyes with her words.

"Continue," Haloma said. "You know more. I've heard you. It was a long time ago."

"There was a song," I said. "It was called 'The Song of the French Partisans,' and my husband, Henri, taught it to me. 'Friend, do you hear the heavy wings of the ravens over the plain? Friend, if you fall, a friend comes out of the shadows in your place.'"

After a moment, J'nine looked at Marsha and said, "During the war with the Nazis, my aunt worked on an Underground newspaper—didn't you, Aunt Anne?"

"Yes," I said, delighted that J'nine knew such a thing. "In December, 1940, the first mimeographed copy of Resistance came out. Although it was just a simple piece of paper, with print on both sides, it said it all. 'Resist!' it said. 'This is the cry in all of our hearts. But you feel yourselves isolated and disarmed, and in your chaos of ideas, opinions and systems, you look for where your duty lies. To resist is to keep your heart and your head. But it is above all to act, to do something which yields positive results through useful and reasoned action. Many have tried and have been discouraged, seeing themselves powerless. Others have formed groups. But often, their groups have found themselves in turn isolated and impotent. Patiently and with difficulty, we have sought one another out and have united. The method? Form groups in your homes with those whom you know. Those whom you designate will be your chiefs. With discernment, enroll resolute people and staff them with your best. Strengthen and comfort those who doubt and those who no longer dare hope. Every day, gather and transmit information which can be of use to your leaders. Practice an inflexible discipline, a constant prudence, an absolute discretion. Beware of lightweights, those who talk too much, and traitors. Never boast, never make confidences. Steel yourselves and face up to your own needs. Our committee, in order to coordinate your efforts with those of unoccupied France and those who fought alongside our allies, will command. Your immediate task is to organize so that you may, on the day when you receive the order, take up combat again. We have only one ambition, one passion, one wish: To accomplish the rebirth of a France that is pure and free.'"

Somber, Halona said, "Those ideas worked, didn't they, Anne?"

"Yes," I said. "And the spirit of those words might be applied now. We must resist the hatred and cruelty in the world, or we all will become enslaved and lost. And we must realize, that a good heart and experience will bring light and hope to the shadows of ignorance and hopelessness in the lives of those poor women who would come to us, or whom we would seek out. We must do something for the cause of freedom, for those who have suffered and find themselves powerless in heart and mind. There is so much at stake. I feel a duty to show them a chance for life, to protect them and to nourish what hope and sense of freedom they may have left, until they can be self-reliant. However, we must be careful, to not put their minds in a suit of armor, thus defeating the positive things we set out to do. By nourishing and protecting the Continuum of Love, we should be able to break the Continuum of Hate in their lives. If you all agree, we have work to do."

"We'll talk about it," Halona said. "Now we must work to free my Gabrielle."

Looking at Marsha, then at J'nine, I said, "I'm going with you two tonight."

"To the Kaspia?" J'nine asked, looking somewhat shocked.

"To the Kaspia," I said, smiling. "How about you, Halona?"

"I'll remain here, in case there's a call."

"The more, the merrier," Marsha said. "Let's talk, and get our stories straight. Your aunt's coming is no big deal. I don't believe Schmidt knows that we know he has kidnapped Gabrielle. Call Vachel and tell him to fix it with your chemical company, that I'm your assistant."

"Credentials?" J'nine asked.

"If he asks, I'll just say I left my ID at home. We'll be all dressed up and I'll be carrying a small purse with nothing in it but cosmetics. My trusty weapon will be strapped to my leg, as usual. If he tries to feel me up, he'll find it and may die of a heart attack."

## chapter 17

I borrowed a light blue dress and a dark blue coat from Halona. J'nine wore a black dress and dark blue coat. Marsha wore a red dress and black coat and she had a large automatic pistol strapped to the inside of her left thigh. We arrived at ten. The Kaspia was a Russian enclave on Place de la Madeleine and was noted for its beluga and volka. It was also noted, I knew, for its location, because one could get a spectacular view of Madeleine Church from there. As soon as we entered, a short, grinning man in a brown suit came at us. He was middle-aged, and he had a large bald spot in the middle of his brown hair. Marsha whispered, "He's got the tonsure of a monk."

"And the teeth of Dracula," J'nine whispered.

Coming to us, he spoke broken French, as he put out his hand to J'nine and said, "You must be Gabrielle's sister, J'nine. You look alike. Yes, you're more beautiful than she said you were."

Smiling demurely, J'nine shook his hand, saying, "Good evening, sir."

Turning to Marsha and me, still grinning and showing a few gold teeth, he asked, "And who might these two lovely ladies be?"

"This is my good friend and assistant, Renee Martin. And please meet my Aunt, Anne La Fleur."

"It's a pleasure," Marsha said, extending her hand.

"Hello," I said, shaking his hand, loathing the little monster.

Turning and extending his arm, Schmidt said, "Shall we go to the restaurant and meet my friends? By the way, do any of you speak

Russian?"

Lying, Marsha said, "No Russian."

Lying through her teeth, J'nine said, "Sorry... no."

Truthfully, I said, "No."

"How about German?" he asked, massaging Marsha's back as we walked.

"No German either," Marsha lied.

"No German," J'nine lied.

"No," I said truthfully.

"I don't speak Russian, either," Schmidt said. "How about English? My friends and I speak English. They know no German, but the important one speaks French."

"Sorry, no English," Marsha lied.

"Only French," J'nine lied.

"Only French," I said, lying and feeling good about it.

"I'm surprised," he said. "I should think your education would have included other languages."

"A person can be educated, without learning foreign languages." Marsha said firmly.

"Of course," he said. "Of course. No matter. We can all speak French, except my friend's son."

I gave thanks to God that the episode about the languages was over. After getting it straight in my mind as to who spoke which and who didn't, I followed Schmidt and the others to a small table next to a wall where two men were waiting. The older-looking one had a short beard, yellowish and dirty around the mouth. He got to his feet to greet us. Smiling broadly, he said in French, "So, you have finally come. Please, sit."

Before sitting, Schmidt said, "These beautiful ladies are J'nine, the chemist, her assistant, Renee, and last but not less beautiful, Anne, J'nine's aunt. Ladies, meet my friend, Vladi, and his son, Casimir."

We shook Vladi's hand and then, seeing obese Casimir trying to get out of his chair, I held out my hand to him, saying, "Please, don't get up. It's too crowded in here."

After struggling every which way and grunting a lot, Casimir finally managed to get to his feet, shake our hands and say something in Russian.

I couldn't help feeling pity for the fat young man.

Keeping our coats on, as did the men, we all sat and looked at each other for a moment, before Vladi pointed at his son and said, "He speaks only seldom." Then, looking at J'nine, he said in French, "Otto tells me that you are a chemist. By the way, do you speak Russian?"

Oh no! I said to myself. Let's not go through the language thing again!

"They speak only French," Schmidt said, grinning. "All three of them."

"No Russian, no German, no English," Marsha said, smiling. "Do you consider us ignorant?"

"No, no, no," Vladi said, apologetically and seemingly on the defensive. "I only asked."

I began to feel pity for Vladi, already. After Marsha, J'nine, Vachel and I, get through with these guys, I thought, they'll need a lot more pity, if one can feel pity for monsters.

J'nine was saying, "Yes, I am a chemist. As you probably know, Mr. Schmidt here is going to consider me for a job." Then, turning to Schmidt, she smiled nicely and asked, "Have you changed your mind, Mr. Schmidt?"

Schmidt looked at J'nine with rape in his eyes--- at least, I believed it was rape. If I had something heavy in my hand, I would have knocked his gold teeth out.

Schmidt was saying, "Yes, I would like it if you would work for me. I heard you're a fine chemist."

"I'll work for you," J'nine said seriously. "But the money must be good—much better than I'm making now."

"Don't we all need more money," the German said, grinning and pouring volka for everybody.

Staring at me, Vladi licked his lips and asked, "What do you do, Anne, besides keeping yourself beautiful?"

Not at all flustered by an ugly man making a compliment, I managed a smile and said, "I'm a chaperone for these unmarried young ladies."

After everyone had laughed, Vladi, raising his glass and accidentally spilling volka on me, said, "Here's to you, kid. That's what the American said to a woman in the stupid movie, Casablanca. American movies are no good."

"I agree," I said, smiling through my anger.

Turning to Marsha, the clumsy Russian asked, "And so what do you do?"

"I'm a research assistant," Marsha said quietly. "I work for J'nine at Renaissance Chemicals in Lyon. I also want to make more money, Mr…"

"You can just call me Vladi," he said sharply.

"Yes, Vladi, sir," Marsha said, probably also disappointed that she didn't get his last name.

After drinking more volka, Schmidt and Vladi grinned at each other, and Schmidt said in English, "My friend, we will check the two out, if we decide to hire them. Don't worry. As I said, none of the women speaks English."

"If they check out," Vladi said in English, "I'll visit you and put it between their legs."

Laughing, Schmidt said, "Not before I do, my horny friend."

Looking at his son, Vladi asked, "How would you like to show one of these women what a good man you are?"

Sweating and blushing, Casimir struggled to his feet and headed for a nearby toilet.

Turning now to us, Schmidt grinned and said, "I apologize for speaking English. Privately, we have been discussing your futures. Vladi has suggested that you two ladies work for me."

"Well, we'd love to," J'nine said, "if the money is satisfactory."

"Oh, the money will be most satisfactory," Schmidt said. "Trust me."

"Well, now, we have something to discuss in private. Would you excuse us, please. Come, Aunt Anne and Renee."

The three of us women went to the Ladies Room but didn't go in. In front of the door and out of sight, Marsha said, "Looks like we're hired."

Pursing her lips, J'nine asked, "Did you catch what those creeps were saying in English?"

Filled with anger, I said, "They should get their balls shot off, and I'd like to be the one who does it!"

"Aunt Anne!" J'nine said, smiling and lifting her eyebrows. "I'm surprised you said that."

"Well, don't be surprised," I said, laying a hand on her arm. "And don't be surprised if I do just that, and more, for what he did to Gabrielle."

"Please, Aunt Anne, don't do or say anything that might spoil it and put Gabrielle in more danger."

Marsha said, "Come on, girls, let's go in and freshen up a bit."

Feeling a little hurt, that my niece would think I'd lose my balance and spoil it for everybody, I went into the Ladies Room. Standing next to J'nine now, as we both combed our hair, I caught her eye in the mirror and said, quietly but firmly, "Don't worry your pretty head about me—worry about yourself, spoiling something!"

Without more said, we returned to the table with bright smiles and, once we were seated again, J'nine asked, "What would our duties be, Mr. Schmidt?"

Vladi quickly put his hand on Schmidt's arm, saying in broken English, "Don't say too much, before their credentials are checked."

Looking at us, Schmidt said, "My friend has just told me that I should wait with the details. But, I will tell you that you will be required to travel, now and then. You see, I'm collecting herbs and roots from Asia, Africa and South America. They are for my unique project. I shall speak more about it, later."

"Interesting," J'nine said.

"And does it sound interesting to you, Renee?" Vladi asked.

"Yes," Marsha said, smiling.

"When would we start?" J'nine asked.

"I was hoping to take you to Bordeaux tonight," Schmidt said. Then, turning to Vladi, he said in English, "Before I let them touch anything, I'll wait for your report."

Watching his son lumbering back, Vladi said in English, "Perhaps I'll bring the report tomorrow, personally, and I'll bring Casimir along, so he can bounce on one of these beauties, too. He has never had a woman."

As the two men laughed, J'nine looked at me and shrugged her shoulders, ever so slightly, and I took it to mean she wanted my advice. "Well," I said, "If we're going to the Bordeaux tonight, we have some packing to do. When and where shall we meet you, Mr. Schmidt?"

Before Schmidt could answer, Marsha said, "J'nine, we will have to give a month's notice to our employer."

"That's right," J'nine said. "We could go to Bordeaux for the rest of the weekend, but on Monday we would have to go to Lyon and tell them we're quitting."

Crossly, Vladi said in English, "My contact will check them out tomorrow—Sunday. But if these two don't start with you on Monday, then there will be no deal!"

Grinning, Schmidt said, "Ladies, Vladi has just told me that you will be paid a large bonus, if you start work immediately. Please, he has my back against the wall. I have my Grumman Two waiting at the airport. Please give me a commitment now."

Looking at Marsha, J'nine asked, "What do you think, Renee—shall we quit, without giving notice?"

"I will if you will," Marsha said. "After all—a bonus!"

"All right, sir," J'nine said. "We accept."

"Then we will meet at Orly in one hour," Schmidt said. "One hour!"

We hurried outside and hailed a taxi, and once we were on the way, J'nine told the driver to take us to La Lousiane, a hotel on rue de la Seine.

"Why there?" I asked quietly.

"I'm staying there." Marsha said.

"Why don't you stay with Halona or me? There's plenty of room," I said.

"I make sure I stay there when I'm in Paris. It's in the outdoor-shopping district and nice and noisy, in case I want to talk in extra-private privacy. Know what I mean?"

"Yes."

"It's also cheap, and it's a chance for her to cut down on contingency funds—that's the real reason," J'nine said. Then, looking at me, she said, "Vachel told me on the phone that he'll be there, and we can talk while Marsha packs a bag."

We were soon at the hotel, sitting with Vachel in Marsha's room, with J'nine saying, "Uncle, we'll be leaving for Bordeaux tonight. Did you fix it with Renaissance that Renee Martin has been my assistant for the past three years? By the way, before I forget, someone will be checking records tomorrow—Sunday."

"I'll find out how that's possible, and who. Yes, it's all set, with Renee Martin."

My eyes never left my brother Vachel, a small man with great strength of character, always in his dark blue eyes. Seeing him there sitting erect, with his dark hair greying on the sides, I felt enormous pride and respect and love....

Marsha, packing, said, "Tell us the rest."

"Will you be there, too, Anne?" Vachel asked.

"Yes," I answered. "Why not?"

After looking in my eyes for a moment, he said something that I'll remember on my death bed, and even after that, probably. "Yes," he said, his eyes twinkling. "We will need your courage, to pull this off."

"Thank you, Vachel," I said, keeping my tears in check by blinking a lot.

"Now, let's get at it," he said. "You will be in the house in Bordeaux with Gabrielle, Schmidt and his men. I suppose it's important that you know this, first of all: There's a shotgun in the master bedroom upstairs." Then, looking at me, he said, "Anne knows about it, I believe."

"Yes," I said. "Our father kept it underneath the floorboards on the open side of the bed—that's not next to the wall. He put it there during the war. I hope it's still there…"

"I only hope it's not needed," Vachel said.

"There's always my weapon," Marsha said. "I'll have it strapped to my leg, as usual."

"Good," Vachel said. "Now, if you can, take our Gabrielle for a walk. The police and I will be waiting. I will be on a bench in the small park down the street. Marsha, if you can, sit next to me on the bench and pass me a note telling me about the chemicals inside the house—if you think there are a lot of explosives. Try to get research data, before he might destroy it if he thinks he's going to be caught. We'll all have to play it be ear and eye. If you can't take Gabrielle for a walk, try to stay by her—especially you, Marsha, with your weapon—and give a signal. If the window shade on the east side of the master bedroom is up, pull it down. If the shade is down, let it go up. If you're not in the bedroom, do it with any of the window shades. We'll be watching. One more thing: When

I'm on the bench, I'll be dressed as an old woman, and I'll be wearing a green coat and hat. Any questions or comments?"

With a wry smile, Marsha said, "You'll do just fine as an old woman!"

We laughed, and Vachel said, "So will you, if the grey hairs in your blonde hair show through enough." Then, as he was leaving, Vachel said, "Be extra careful. Remember, I'll be on the bench, with police around me, ready to take Gabrielle from you when I give the signal. God be with you. I'll see you tomorrow."

At dawn, we arrived in Bordeaux. Riding in a taxi, with Schmidt sitting in the front, we headed for the old homestead. J'nine, in the middle in the back, suddenly began acting like a tour guide—maybe trying to lull Schmidt into some kind of false security. "Bordeaux is really an important city," she was saying.

"How so?" the German asked, turning around.

"For one thing," J'nine continued, "it's a city of beautiful eighteenth-century architecture. Over there, for example, is the beautiful Grande Theatre, designed by Victor Louis. It's so elegant, with its ceiling filled with frescoes and with its gigantic chandelier made of Bohemian crystal. Have you ever been in there, Mr. Schmidt?"

"Yes," he said, grinning. "But soon I must see it again. We could perhaps all go together."

Passing through Bordeaux's central square near the Garonne River, J'nine said, "Look—another landmark? It's Place de la Bourse, and there's Town Hall, with its gorgeous gardens… and there's the Fine Arts Museum, with its many works of the fifteenth century."

"J'nine, aren't you overdoing it a bit?" Marsha asked, smiling.

"I don't think so," Schmidt said. "Let her be, Renee!"

"Thank you, sir," J'nine said, grinning at Marsha. Then, looking at Schmidt again, she asked, "And have you ever seen La Rochelle, Mr. Schmidt? It's not far from here."

Flashing his gold teeth again, he said, "No, my dear, I have never been there. Tell me about it."

"Well," J'nine said, chuckling at Marsha. "You must go there and see its historic harbor and fortresses. Just beautiful at night, when it's all lit up. It was built in the fourteenth century and was the last stronghold of the Huguenots, before it was captured by Richelieu. And I'm sure that you'll be interested to know that the Germans used the town as a submarine base during the war. Were you in the war, sir?"

"Not in the military—but I had a very important position in a munitions plant," the weirdo said.

"How exciting!" she said. Then, after I elbowed her ribs, she stopped talking.

Arriving at the house, we were met by two men, who were both tall and heavy. They wore dark suits, dirty-white shirts, and black, wrinkled ties. Both had a lot of dark hair. Frowning at the men, Schmidt said something in German and the men picked up the luggage and hurried inside.

A woman was standing just inside the door. She looked to be in her fifties, and she was pretty, with blonde hair cut short and penetrating dark blue eyes. Dressed in a white uniform, starched and spotless, she smiled warmly, shook our hands and said in French, with a German accent, "Good morning. I'm Nada Kreuger." Then, focusing on J'nine, she said, "You look like Gabrielle."

"Yes," J'nine said, smiling. "Could I see her now? I haven't seen her for awhile—since last Christmas."

"Of course you can see her now," Schmidt said. "Nada will go with you and my two assistants will carry your luggage up."

As we walked upstairs, the name, Nada Kreuger, kept sounding in my mind. Then, I knew where I had heard the name. Marsha had mentioned her, when she said that Vachel had been looking for her in Vienna and had found those coat hangers instead. Marsha had also said that she was an agent provocateur who "broke plenty of communist heads in East Germany during the Worker's Rebellion." I thought about her now and wondered if she was still on our side. Why hadn't Vachel told us she'd be here? I asked myself.

Once in the master bedroom, we saw Gabrielle lying in bed and staring at the ceiling. When the three of us started walking towards the bed, Nada grabbed Marsha and me by the arm and held us back, whispering, "Let only J'nine go to Gabrielle." Then, after walking us away from the door, she said, "If you are shocked I am here, I apologize. I have been with Otto Schmidt for a year now, acting as a nurse and gathering information about his work in using drugs to control minds. I came here last night, after I tried to reach Vachel Villon and was unsuccessful."

"He was with us," Marsha whispered. "And he's here now, waiting nearby on a park bench, dressed as an old woman, in green."

"Damnit," I said, irritated. "I wish you agent people would get on the same wave length more often than not!"

Marsha smiled at Nada, and said, "Anne is their aunt."

Nada smiled at me and whispered, "I promise we'll get it straight." Then, after scribbling on a sheet of prescription pad, she tore it off and handed it to Marsha, saying, "This goes to Vachel. I want him to know that there are some high explosives here. Take Gabrielle for a walk. I'll try to go with you, but I may not be allowed to."

"Gabrielle, Gabrielle," J'nine was saying, sitting in a chair by the bed. "Look at me. It's J'nine, your sister."

Gabrielle, dressed in a white silk robe, looked at J'nine for a long moment before taking her in her arms and saying with a voice that seemed dreamy and unnatural, "You have come to visit me. How nice!"

Tearfully, J'nine asked, "What has he done to you?"

As if she were a child in school reciting something she'd memorized, Gabrielle, with her dark eyes fixed cold on J'nine, said, "Mr. Schmidt has treated me with kindness. I feel happy."

I guessed what had happened, that Gabrielle had been given some kind of amnesia-inducing drug. And now, as I stared at her from a corner of the room, I could only see her as that little girl in a ditch in 1940, when her father had protected her with his body from German bullets and bombs. I easily saw through today's show of cheerfulness—so unnatural and overdone—to the little girl that had never stopped suffering guilt, making her easy prey for men who would take advantage of her, especially older men. "Oh, merciful God, help her!" I whispered, turning then to Marsha and seeing tears running down her cheeks.

Nada said loudly: "Perhaps we should take Gabrielle outside for a breath of fresh air. It's such a beautiful day!"

Turning her head, J'nine said, "That's a perfect idea. We could walk in the park, as Gabrielle and I did when we were children and visited our grandparents."

Seeing a shadow moving just outside the open door, I said, "We should get permission from Mr. Schmidt."

Entering the room, Schmidt said, "No need to ask permission. She is not a prisoner, especially not in her family's house. Gabrielle is the one who gives permission, just as she gave me permission to do work here, after her fiancé, Claude Buchard, asked for it. If she wants, she can go to the park or anywhere else.… By the way, Vladi called and he recommended that J'nine and Renee be employed. Isn't that nice?"

Smiling modestly, like a convent girl in front of a bishop, J'nine said, "Thank you, sir."

"And do you still want a job with us, Renee?"

"I'd love it!" Marsha said. "Does this mean we're on the payroll, as of today?"

Grinning, he said, "As of last night, my dear. We shall discuss money later today. Oh, yes, by the way, Vladi said that he will come here tomorrow. Isn't that nice? He has taken a special interest in you ladies, including you, of course, Anne La Fleur."

"And I'm sure we all are interested in him," I said.

"I'm so happy you feel that way," he said, leaving the room and going downstairs.

With him gone, J'nine and Marsha helped Gabrielle dress and then it was downstairs and out the door, with Schmidt and his men nowhere in sight. "It's going too smooth," Marsha said, walking with Nada and me a few yards behind J'nine and Gabrielle.

Casually looking back, I said, "We've got a problem. Schmidt's two apes are following us."

Not looking back, Nada said, "We may get hit in a crossfire."

"I don't want to chance it," Marsha said. "As soon as we get to the bench, I'll tell Vachel to call it off, for now. What do you think, Nada?"

"That might be better. I want to collect more data. We could come for another walk, later." Nada said.

"Let Vachel decide," I said.

Arriving at the bench in front of a large maple tree, Marsha sat down next to Vachel, looking like an old woman in green. When Schmidt's men stopped about thirty yards away and watched some boys playing soccer, she shoved the note Nada had given her into his pocket.

"Are those two ugly men with you?" Vachel asked, motioning slightly with his head.

"Yes," Marsha said. "And I think we should call the rescue off, for the time being. We might get caught in a crossfire. Besides, Nada has more data to gather."

Looking at Nada standing by the bench, Vachel smiled a little and said, "So, Nada, I finally caught up with you—or you, with me. All right, return to the house and come back this afternoon—whenever you can." Then, pointing up at the blue sky and smiling, he shook his head. "There," he said. "It's done. That was the signal for the police not to move in. Yes, we'll wait, and if the uglies follow you again this afternoon, we'll get them before they can do any harm."

A few minutes later, Nada said, "We should be going back to the house."

Gabrielle, lifting her head from J'nine's shoulder, said sleepily, "Yes, if we stay away too long, Mr. Schmidt will get angry. I wish we could stay, though."

With tears falling, J'nine said, "Gabrielle, we will come back here soon. I promise."

Returning to the house, we were greeted by Schmidt and his stupid grin. "Did you have a nice time?" he asked.

Gabrielle was the only one who answered, saying, "Yes, Mr. Schmidt."

"You all must have appetite to eat something," he said. "There is plenty in the refrigerator."

"I'll fix something," Nada said. "Marsha and Anne, would you be so kind and help me in the kitchen?"

When the three of us went to the kitchen, J'nine went upstairs with Gabrielle. Then, just as we were discussing what to eat, Schmidt and his men entered the kitchen, and Schmidt, holding the note that Marsha had given to Vachel, asked, "What's this?"

"A dirty piece of paper," Marsha said innocently.

Glaring at Marsha now, he said, "You gave this to the old woman in the park. Tell me what it says."

Suspecting that the police had gone and left Vachel alone, I looked over at the note and said, "It seems to have been written in a foreign language—maybe Chinese."

Marsha said, "I found it on the ground and asked the woman if it was hers. She didn't say anything—just put it in her pocket."

"One of my men say you put it in her pocket, Renee. Don't lie to me. I warn you!"

"We could go and ask the old woman," Marsha said.

"Forget the old fool," he said. "What does this message say?"

"I have no idea," Marsha said, obviously mocking him with a huge grin.

He grabbed her neck and slapped her face, yelling, "Tell me what it says, or you will be as dead as that old witch on the bench!"

"Wait!" Nada said, taking the note. "I shall examine it." Then, after looking at the note, she smiled and said, "Sir, it is nothing more than a child's scribbling. It is nothing of concern."

"Are you certain?" he asked, letting go of Marsha and scowling.

"Certain!" Nada said, before crumbling the paper and putting it in her pocket. "It is worthless to us."

Sheepishly now, he looked at Marsha and said, "Renee, please forgive me."

"Did you say the old woman is dead?" I asked, hoping with all my heart that it wasn't so, and that my brother was still alive.

"Yes, my dear," he said solemnly. "I'm afraid she met with a horrible accident."

"Your men killed her!" Marsha said.

Grinning and stretching out his arms, he asked, "Why are you making such a fuss over that decrepit old thing?"

Without a bit of doubt in my mind, I knew what I would do. Calmly, I smiled at Schmidt and said, "Excuse me, I shall go up and see to my nieces, all right?"

"Yes, of course," Schmidt said, grinning and nodding.

I hurried upstairs and got the double-barreled shotgun from beneath the floorboards in what was once my parents' bedroom. Then, after telling J'nine and Gabrielle to stay where they were, I hurried back downstairs and into the kitchen. Leveling the shotgun at Schmidt's head, I said quietly, "You killed my brother."

"Don't do it!" Marsha yelled. "Let us handle it!"

"Move out of the way, Marsha and Nada. I want to do this for Vachel and Gabrielle."

Suddenly, as Marsha and Nada moved away, Schmidt and his men came at me, and that was enough for Schmidt and one of his men to get their heads blown apart. The third man, on the floor now and in a corner, tried to draw his gun from beneath his coat, but Marsha quickly put a bullet in his brain.

The killing over, Nada secured research data and left the house, saying as she left, "I'll tell the police to come. Till we meet again, my friends, be happy."

"Until we meet again, Nada."

"Until we meet again."

Two days after Vachel was put in the ground beside my parents' graves in Bordeaux, Gabrielle died of a massive heart attack brought on by the drugs Schmidt had given her. Returning now from the funeral, after burying her next to Vachel, J'nine drove Gabrielle's old Renault through the streets of Bordeaux. Marsha was in the front with J'nine, and I was in the back. As we passed a city swimming pool, J'nine said quietly, "That's where we saw them when we came to visit our grandparents in the summer."

"Saw whom?" Marsha asked.

"The American soldiers from Landes de Bussac. They would come to the swimming pool and rent bathing suits, which were nothing more than pieces of cloth with no linings. Gabby and I, with our friend, Francine, went there often and laughed at them. We called them Jockless Wonders. They'd sit at the poolside tables, drink beer, and jump from the highest platform. They were always laughing. Some would sit at our table sometimes and try to speak French. One spoke well enough to be understood, and one day he asked how old we were. Francine and I told the truth, that we were fourteen. Gabby said she was nineteen, but she was only fifteen. He then asked Gabby to meet him at Café Orleans that night, and she said no. That night, however, she went and she continued to go there. That's how it started—the drinking and drugs and the whoring around."

"I'm so sorry," Marsha said.

Because of the unyielding mixture of sorrow and guilt running inside me, I couldn't bring myself to speak. I could only feel that the dark thing that had been with me maybe all my life had finally won—that it had, like a dark river, flooded my soul with darkness, and that my soul was now lost to me. I had killed someone, Otto Schmidt, and the act had been one of passionate, unrestrained vengeance—which is madness. It hadn't been enough that I had Schmidt and his men covered with the shotgun, which would have allowed Marsha and Nada to take over. I let the madness of vengeance take over, instead. Thinking back now, I recalled the slight moment in which I hesitated, when Marsha had yelled, "Don't do it! Let us handle it!" Yes, I believed, I could have stopped, but my will, almost completely inundated by the darkness of selfishness, allowed my passion for vengeance to rule. I had chosen the wrong way—the criminal way—again, just as I had when I did nothing to stop Major Daniel Horton from killing my lover, Maurice Martineau. I had not fought to prevent him from taking my hand and plunging a knife in Maurice. And I had done nothing to prevent Daniel from stealing Maurice's money, rationalizing along with Daniel that it was ill-begotten money, and saying to myself that my son would benefit—that I would do anything for Matthew. And now, as I sat silent in the living room of the house of my birth, I saw it for the first time, clear. The Dark Thing inside me—the raison d'etre for my sins of darkness—was Self, with all of its selfish motives and acts.

While J'nine and Marsha drank coffee and talked, I was now at a window, looking out at the autumn day and listening to J'nine. "I hate myself for not doing enough for my sister," she was saying. "Now it's too late."

"It's not your fault," Marsha said. "I have never had a sister, but I do know about not doing enough. When my marriage died, for example, I blamed myself for not doing enough and for doing the wrong things when I did do something."

"Did you love each other very much?" J'nine asked.

"I loved him, but now I know that he didn't love me enough," Marsha said, with a little laugh.

"Do you still love him—Frank Rhodes?"

"No... after all the years, love has finally died, and its last breaths were miserable, believe me."

I couldn't believe what I heard next, something very similar to what

I had just been thinking—about losing my soul. After some quiet sounds of cups clinking on saucers, J'nine asked, "How do you feel, after that mess with Otto Schmidt, and all?"

Slowly, Marsha said, "When I killed that man, I think I lost my soul."

"Don't say that!"

"It's true. And I think the work we're in has a lot to do with it."

J'nine said, "I'm trying to think of something fancy to say to you, but I can't think of anything that wouldn't sound hollow."

"I can't do it any more," Marsha said. "I'm going to pick up what's left of me, after I quit the Company, and try to live a little. I'm getting out of this loveless game, in which I have to be dishonest and ruthless and a lot of other dirty things, in order to win something from countries that will be our political friends tomorrow. As you know, the thing with Schmidt was different—but it ended making me feel about the same, down and dirty."

"I've felt like that for a long time," J'nine said.

"Time…"

"Time is on our side, Marsha. I'm sure time will return us to life and love."

"We're over forty years old."

"Just right, for a change."

"J'nine, I wish we could be like we were when we first met."

"God, yes…"

"We were at a café near the Sorbonne, with your mother."

"I remember that we laughed a lot," J'nine said. "What did we laugh about, Marsha?"

"Everything—what else?"

"It was fun—really fun?"

"And your mother said we were crazy."

"And we agreed to be friends, and our friendship has survived, Marsha."

After a moment, Marsha continued, saying, "Yes, I've thought about it, plenty. I'm quitting. I feel like a damn fool doing what I'm doing—worse than a fool. For a long time, I lived on patriotism, but now I'm less patriotic than ever. I don't know—maybe I was looking for some kind of reward and didn't get it."

"Mental hospitals are filled with people who expected rewards and didn't get them."

"I know what you mean."

"Stay where you are," J'nine said. "I'm going in the kitchen and fix some omelets. Aunt Anne, would you like an omelet?"

"No, thanks," I said.

"I'll go with you and help," Marsha said.

Alone now in the room, I continued to look out the window. Then, just as I noted that leaves had changed color and were falling from the trees, the moment of the killings caught me and held me. And once again, I could feel the power I had as I held the shotgun in the doorway of the kitchen. And once again,, I could see the mixture of fear and surprise on Otto Schmidt's face. And once again, I could hear the explosions and smell the burning gunpowder, and once again, I could see the bloody mess of brains and blood on the walls and floor. Finally, once again, I had the feeling I'd had in that awful moment, when the blood seemed to rush from my own body, leaving me feeling shrunken and cold. And now, as I became aware that the old, family clock was striking the hour of two, I opened the window in front of me and, as I listened to the haunting sounds of wind in willows, I told myself that I must survive the Terror of Change. Somehow, I told myself, I must survive by being open to more change, however vulnerable and afraid I might be...

"The omelets are ready," J'nine was saying, a smile in her voice. "I went ahead and made one for you, Aunt Anne. Cheese. Would you like it?"

"I'm sure I'll like it," I said, turning and smiling easily.

"Mine's a little burnt," Marsha said, frowning. Then, as we sat and ate, she asked, "J'nine, did your mother go right back to Paris after the funeral?"

"Yes," J'nine answered, her mouth full. "She rushed off. I asked her to come here, but she refused. She's very upset with what happened in this house. I told her that you can't take it out on the house—what happened here."

"Good for you, J'nine," I said, thinking then that the old homestead could fit nicely in a plan to help women like Gabrielle.

"I'll be leaving for America tomorrow," Marsha said.

"So soon?" J'nine asked.

"I was serious. I'm going to resign—sooner the better!"

"We can live on our retirement money," J'nine said.

"Let's get back to Paris," I said. "I want to get ready to return to Michigan in a couple days. I miss my son and little dog, Gussie."

We crossed over the bridge to the Right Bank, passed the Louvre, and walked through the Tuileries Gardens to a small café across from a Metro station. Halona was on her way to the Sorbonne, and she had asked Marsha and me to accompany her some of the way. She wanted another moment of conversation with us, seeing that we'd be gone when she got home. Yesterday, J'nine had driven her car to Lyon.

As we drank coffee at the café, Halona said, "I pray the weather clears, so you two can be with your loved ones for Christmas." Then, turning to Marsha, she asked, "What will you do after the holidays with your parents?"

"Retire," Marsha said with a smile.

"And then what?" Halona asked.

"I really don't know—maybe just sit on my butt."

"What do you think of what Anne spoke of—about homes and schools for troubled and disfavored women, like Gabrielle?"

Looking at me, Marsha smiled and said, "I don't know. She said so much and so well. I was overwhelmed."

Looking at me, Halona said, "Yes, once she gets going, it's full speed ahead. Right, Anne?"

"Maybe I should sell used cars," I said, getting the feeling that my talk about homes for women hadn't been taken seriously.

Marsha laughed, and then said, "Anne, I must admit, that when I got the impression that you were recruiting me, then something inside me told me to resist."

Laughing, with her dark eyes shining, Halona said, "Marsha, I got the same feeling. It's quite an irony, that all her talk about resistance, fired up resistance for her project."

"I wish I knew why," I said, downhearted.

"Well," Halona said seriously. "I suppose it's because you're asking us to go to war. And that's what it would be—a war... on several fronts, especially against the new Führers of the world. Anne, I remember so well what you once wrote in your Underground newspaper, which is pertinent now. You spoke of souls being toyed with and destroyed by the evil charlatans of the Third Reich who preached deadly doctrines, with the religious fervor of evangelists. You spoke of hungry souls becoming victims of words and slogans of destruction, dressed in sentimental, commercial trappings and distributed by the media, so that those hungry souls might devour their basically cruel and fabricated symbols. But, of course, those symbols and slogans, and even songs, were designed to make the poor souls hungrier than before, so that they might be easier controlled. Yes, Anne, much of your life has been spent in trying to help people resist the greedy power-and-money Führers of the world, who never quit trying to control our minds and hearts and souls with their arrogant religio-political ideals. And now, dear Anne, you have me beside you—and there will be many others. Gabrielle and so many others, will not have suffered and died in vain."

"What about you, Marsha?" I asked.

"I promise to give it a lot of thought," Marsha said.

Smiling now, Halona said, "Think also with your heart, Marsha. And remember what I told you when you were a student of mine. 'Don't sing of heaven, if you're looking at hell and doing nothing about it. And never say that there's no beauty in the world, if you don't go look for it.' Whatever you decide, my friend, please return—yes?"

"Yes."

"Until we meet again."

"Until we meet again."

Halona went to work, and Marsha and I returned to Halona's apartment, where I had brought my luggage. That afternoon, because of bad weather, our flight to America was cancelled, and it wasn't until after Christmas that we were able to depart.

Once on the plane, I recalled the phone call I had made to my son on Christmas Eve. Matthew had said that he was going to Midnight Mass with Elsie Quinn, and that they were going to play the music. Thinking of Matthew and Elsie together, when I had called, made me feel a little abandoned, even though I had encouraged their being together. But now, on the plane with a magazine in front of me, I hoped he would marry, so I could devote more time to helping abused and helpless women, once I returned to Paris.

## chapter 18

In one of his poems, my son had written about the Bird of Endurance and how it had flown away after his father was killed. Well, the Bird returned, or maybe it had never left. In any event, it was there for him when he needed it, as it had been there for me all along—a great gift from God, which I accepted gratefully—but not too gratefully, for it was hard to be grateful with pins and needles and swords sticking in my heart. And the latest sword thrust into my heart by Life was my son's getting sick, after Elsie Quinn died.

In the June following my return to Point Stevens, Michigan, my son Matthew went with Elsie on a riverboat excursion on the Au Sable River. Tragedy struck then, when a dope peddler threw Elsie overboard and Matthew, although he tried desperately, failed to save her. Then, after looking at Elsie's body at the funeral home, Matthew got drunk, intruded upon a wedding reception being held on the second floor of some building near Tawas City, and jumped from one of the windows. After the state troopers came and took him to jail, he was sent to a mental hospital for observation. I knew nothing about it, until someone called for me to pick up my station wagon, and I wasn't allowed to visit him at the hospital—not even a phone call. Shaken, with gratitude and endurance slipping away quickly, I went to Father O'Grady at St. Joseph's rectory. Fortunately for me, he was drinking. He seemed to do his best work when he was drinking, but then, he seemed to be drinking all the time—I could smell it—so I really had no way of comparing. Anyway, after we were sitting in the main office, I told him about Matthew.

"And so now you're broken-hearted. Is that it, Anne?"

Broken-hearted isn't the half of it, Father," I said, sniveling now in a superbly-laced handkerchief—one my mother had left me, and when that occurred to me, as I sat there, I cried hysterically, managing however to say, "I'm turning into pieces. It's like I'm being smashed by a heavy-handed demon, and I can't do anything about it."

Coming out from behind his desk, he put his large hand on my shoulder and softly said, "Now, now, go right ahead and blubber. That's it. As your confessor, I highly recommend it. Best you do it more often. It's good for the soul, if regulated. And, I do believe, it's good for the sinuses. Clears 'em right up. I try to blubber in the mornin', when my sinuses are hurtful and gummy."

"Gummy?" I asked, with laughter spilling out with my tears. Then, after he was behind the desk again, I said, "I don't know how much more I can endure, without losing my faith, Father."

With his piercing blue eyes, he stared at me for a moment, before saying, "Through the years, I've come to know you pretty good, Anne. You've survived the destructive forces of war. You've lost your dear and loving parents and, as you told me last week, both brothers are gone now. Then there's the first husband you lost—Henri, I believe—and the second husband, Daniel, the son of a bitch-- God rest his soul. Anne, do you like to walk outside, when there's a storm, with thunder and lightning?"

"As a matter of fact, I do," I said, wondering what he was getting at.

"By all that's holy, I thought as much. That's the bug in the middle of the pudding. You're one of those blessed ones who walks the line fancier than ever in a storm. To put it another way, when there's trouble at the door, you open it without pause and thrive on overcoming it. You see, my dear friend, you don't endure anything that would bedevil you. You get rid of it, as you would the bug from the pudding. But that's only my opinion, perhaps as worthless to you as a pinch of snuff, because I am not you, and I've not had one flinder of the kind of troubles you've had, in amount or weight. So there you have it. What do you think of my opinion of you?"

"I try not to give an opinion on an opinion. By the way, what's a flinder," I asked, laughing.

"My child, look it up!" he answered, laughing.

And so that's how my talk with Father O'Grady ended, with laughter and, of course, my feeling much better about myself and with more faith that it would turn out well, as far as Matthew was concerned. I prayed then, that if it didn't turn out to my liking, that I would have the strength needed to see it through and help all I could, as an instrument of God's will, not mine.

In a few weeks, Matthew came home, after he finally talked to a doctor, who then said he'd had an anxiety reaction and discharged him. Immediately afterwards, he said he wanted to go to Salzburg to study music and I said that I would return to Paris to live. We tried to sell the house to Morely, whom Daniel had left a shotgun in his will, along with shells and note telling him to blow his brains out, but Morely didn't buy it. Morely, hurt by what his brother had done, of course, after his father had left him a shotgun, with no shells and a note suggesting he blow his brains out, said the house had too many bad memories. However, the main reason he gave when he declined to buy was that the mansion would demand too much money in the way of upkeep. We agreed with Morely, and after we asked him to look after the place while we were gone, he said yes, for a monthly fee of one hundred dollars.

Matthew had been in Salzburg about a year, before I took him to see Hans Müller, who told him about his father's death and died of cancer shortly thereafter. I returned to Paris to help Halona get the necessary documents for our homes, which we obtained sooner than expected. So it wasn't long before we had unfortunate women in a house in Paris and in the old homestead in Bordeaux, which we called Gabrielle House. Surprisingly, it wasn't difficult to staff our homes with professional people, and even more surprising, it wasn't too difficult in getting financial support, in addition to mine.

During the busy year, Richard Fowler visited a couple times and talked about his dead wife a lot. I supposed he talked about her, because I had asked about her once—just once. Anyway, when he didn't even mention our future together, and that he wasn't about to resign from CIA duty, I knew our affaire d'amour was about to freeze, as far as I was concerned.

Also, during the year, Marsha Lowden and I kept in contact, both by letters and phone calls. In her last letter, she mentioned that she was working as a foreign affairs analyst for a news organization in Detroit. Then, in the same letter, she said that she was having "difficulties" with her ex-husband's wife. Thinking it over then, I came to realize that Marsha, knowing her as I did, would not have mentioned that she was having trouble, unless it was deep trouble and that she possibly could use some help. On the other hand, so I went on to think, maybe it's nothing of much importance. Just in case, however, I called her at her home in Troy, Michigan and received a detailed account of what was happening.

"It was a nice day," Marsha said calmly. "I like to get out of the office building on nice days, so I walked over to a nearby restaurant for lunch. Well, as I sat at a table by the front window eating a salad and watching people walk by, this woman staggers up to the window and starts with grotesque facial expressions, directed right at me. She was all in black, with a thick black sweater and black skirt, and she seemed drunk, or maybe high on drugs. Then, after giving me the obscene finger and a glassy-eyed stare, she went away."

"What did you do, then?" I asked.

"Well, after feeling sorry for her, I left the restaurant so that I might catch up to her and help her—who now, with her blue eyes and dark hair, seemed familiar to me. However, when I didn't see the woman, I went back to work and minimized the experience in my mind.... Anne, I guess I'm still a little nervous, after the experience with Gabrielle."

"Aren't we all?" I said. "Is that all that happened with the window woman?"

"Sorry to say, it isn't.... Anne, I hate laying this on you, but when I do, you'll see why. It involves a young woman, the daughter of my ex-husband. Damnit, I'm getting ahead of myself..."

"Take your time."

"Well, after work, when I was in the parking lot, on my way to my car, I heard someone behind me yell: 'Hey, Marsha, you dirty bitch!'"

"Turning around, I saw it was that woman. I asked her how she knew my name, and she said that we had gone to high school together, and that she was married to my ex. 'Sheila Barnes?' I asked, knowing who she was but still not recognizing her face."

"'That's Sheila Rhodes, if you don't mind, she said."

"'Yes, of course. Sorry, Sheila,' I said."

"Coming up to me, with one hand behind her back, she says, 'You didn't recognize me.'"

"'It's been a long time,' I said. I couldn't believe she'd changed so much."

"'Don't bullshit me, Marsha,' she said. 'Go ahead and tell me that you think I look like an old bag. And I do look like one, and it's because of you and Frank, your charming ex. You two just can't keep your hands off each other, can you?'"

"'Why, I haven't seen Frank in years,'" I said."

"'Liar!' she yelled, with her bloodshot eyes narrowing. I couldn't believe what was happening. 'And I suppose you two haven't been together every night these last few weeks, when Frank said he'd been out looking for our daughter, Cassy,' she said."

"'Your daughter is missing?' I asked."

"'That's right,' Sheila said. 'She ran away with a dirty refugee from Czechoslovakia—and Frank would've found her, if he didn't take time to screw around with you.'"

"Luckily, I caught a glimpse of the claw hammer in her hand," Marsha said. "And it was coming down on me. I wrenched the hammer from Sheila and threw her on the ground. As she lay there sobbing hysterically, I said, 'Stay right where you are, Sheila!'"

"'Are you going to have me arrested?' she asked in a squeaky little voice.'"

"'I might,'" I said. "'But first I'm going to take you to my house. Get up slowly and get in my car, the bluish Volkswagen.' Then, after we were in the car I asked her what would make her do such a thing, for any reason. Then, after she said she was desperate, I said, 'Desperate or not, you shouldn't have done it. There's definitely something broken inside you that needs to be fixed.' And so, after I repeated that I hadn't seen Frank Rhodes in years, the last time being just before he joined the Air Force and was sent to Casablanca, I said, 'Relax, and I'll take you to my house, and you can sober up.'"

"And Sheila said, 'As long as you don't take me to my house, I'll go anywhere. I can't live with that man!'"

"'So you don't know where your daughter is?' I asked."

"'No,' she said, her eyes closed. 'Cassy is gone.'"

"'You have another daughter, younger. Where is she?' I asked. Then, after she said her younger daughter, Tiffany, was at her mother's house, we said nothing more, even while I fed her soup and a baloney sandwich and put her to bed."

"So," I said, changing the phone to my other ear, "Their daughter is missing. How long has she been missing?"

"Anne, I really don't know. I didn't get a chance to ask Sheila. When I looked in on her the next morning, she was gone. Wait! She did say, that for the last few weeks, Frank said that he had been out looking for their daughter."

"A few weeks. Have they called the police?"

"I don't know."

"Do you want to help find her?"

"Anne, I don't think it's my place to stick my nose in. I know, the girl's life is what's important, most of all. But hear me out, please. I consider Sheila a friend, even though I didn't know her all that well in high school. Perhaps more of an ally, than a friend, when it comes to my ex-husband, Frank Rhodes. I want to help find the girl, but maybe it would be a horrible mistake, if I were to do something that would put me between her and Frank and wreck it for them, for good. Anne, I find myself in a dilemma, having to choose between two undesirable alternatives—to do nothing, or to help and maybe mess things up for them…"

"Marsh," I said softly. "Look at the reality in yourself. It will tell you that you're afraid to act, for fear of making a mistake. That is being afraid to live, my friend. No?"

"Yes."

Cheerfully, I said, "Now I know why you told me about your trouble in the letter. You want me to help."

"How did you know?"

"Marsha, I know a lot about you that you don't seem to know. One thing is: You're not very direct, when you want to ask for help."

"I'll admit to that."

"I could use a little change. I'll catch the next plane. All right?"

"Well, I could use a visit with you, regardless of whether we try to find the girl or not."

"Have a glass of sherry, Marsha, and by the time you finish it, I'll be there. Au revoir."

"Au revoir. Call me from New York, when you get in."

Hanging up, I smiled, thinking of Marsha as being blonde and bashful, not blonde and brassy, as she pretended to be sometimes. Then, I supposed, she would be too vulnerable, if she were seen to be blonde, beautiful and bashful. I appreciated her being honest with me. It helped me trust her, as I felt she trusted me. Less and less, did I find myself being evasive, but I didn't want to give up evasiveness all together. After all, I had worked hard to acquire perfection at it, and I wasn't about to discard it tout ensemble, because I knew it would come in handy, and it often did.

Sheila Rhodes came early, and she was having breakfast with Marsha and me. With scrambled eggs left untouched, she took a sip of coffee and said, "I'm sorry to bother you and your friend from France, but I didn't know where to turn."

"Eat the eggs," Marsha said, yawning. "Give me a little time to wake up."

"I can't eat a thing," Sheila said, wiping tears from her face with a cloth napkin. Then, turning to me, she whimpered and said, "Anne, as you can see, my life's in shambles." Then, after blowing her nose, she asked, "What do you do in Paris, Anne?"

Deciding to be evasive for the time being, I smiled and said, "I shop for clothes."

Pushing back strands of dark hair from her face, she said, "Wish I had the time to shop. I've been wearing these black things for ages. And I'd certainly like to get something like that white housecoat you've got on—it's beautiful."

"Eat your eggs!" Marsha said, preventing me from thanking Sheila for the compliment. "You'll need all the strength you can get."

"I know, I know," Sheila said, whimpering and taking a small bite of eggs.

"Have you been drinking?" Marsha asked.

"No, I haven't touched the stuff, since that awful day in your office parking lot." Then after blowing her nose again, she said, "Frank called this morning, just before I came here."

"And?" Marsha asked, sitting with her arms folded.

"He said Karl Zionchek called him this morning. He's holding Cassy for a ransom of one million dollars. And Karl said he's going to call again this afternoon."

"Is he the Czech your daughter ran away with?" Marsha asked.

"That's the one," Sheila said. "He used to be Cassy's riding instructor over at Bloomfield Riding Academy. When he came to our house with Cassy, Frank insulted him, kind of, and Karl went away in a huff."

"Do you think it's a revenge thing?" Marsha asked.

"I don't know what to think, Marsha. Maybe they're in it together, Karl, and Cassy. Maybe if Frank threatens to call the police, Cassy'll come right home, with her tail between her legs."

"When you got the call at your mother's, where was Frank?"

"Probably in his office."

"It's Sunday, Sheila. Would he go to his office on Sunday?"

"Sunday?" Sheila asked, hitting her forehead with the palm of her hand. "No, he never goes on Sunday. See what Cassy and Frank are doing to me! I don't even know what day it is. Why you want to know where he is?"

"When the call comes from Karl, I want to know where Frank will be," Marsha said.

"I'll call him and ask," Sheila said, going to the phone on the kitchen wall and dialing. Then, after a few moments, she hung up, saying, "No answer. I know he's not in church. He's probably with one of his whores."

"This is no time for that kind of talk!" Marsha snapped.

"I'm sorry. I know. I should be thinking of a way to save my daughter—if she has been kidnapped. What do you suggest I do, Marsha?"

"Well," Marsha said, glancing at me, then looking back at Sheila. "You could hire a private detective, or call the F.B.I. and hope for the best. If you want a private detective, there's a reputable firm in Detroit that's not filled with a bunch of gumshoe felons. But it will cost you. A lot of people may have to be bribed. If you want the F.B.I., I know an agent who lives in the area. Then, there's the police of course."

"Maybe a private detective, first," Sheila said.

"Do you think Frank would go for it?" Marsha asked. "It would cost a lot of money."

"To hell with Frank. He's broke. He's the only lawyer I know who doesn't have a bundle. Bad investments—that's what it was. I've got my own money, a trust from my parents. There's just one thing, though; I wouldn't trust anybody but you, Marsha. Would you look into it?"

"I'd rather not," Marsha said weakly.

"But Marsha, you've got all kinds of experience, and if Karl took her back to Europe with him, I'm sure you have contacts there." Then, looking at me, Sheila asked, "Isn't that right, Anne?"

"I have no idea who she knows, except me," I said.

Looking at Marsha and whimpering again, Sheila said, "Please Marsha. I know I don't deserve your help, but will you? Hey, I just remembered something. When Karl was at the house, he said he once worked in Vienna, caring for those famous Austrian horses."

"The Lippizaner horses?" I asked.

"Yes," Sheila said. "I believe those are the ones."

"Sheila," Marsha said softly. "I'll make a few inquiries and try to find out what's going on. Go home now and take care of your other daughter—and don't drink!"

"I promise I won't ever drink again," Sheila said, going to the door. "Thank you. Nice meeting you, Anne."

As soon as Sheila left, Marsha and I went over to Bloomfield Riding Academy and into the office of the manager, who stood and introduced himself as Chuck Bosinger when we went in. He was tall and thin and had bushy brown hair. He also had a crooked smile.

"I'm Marsha Lowden," Marsha said. "I'm a friend of Mrs. Sheila Rhodes. Is Karl Zionchek here?"

Still standing and smiling, he said, "Please, have a seat." Then, as we sat—he, behind his desk, and Marsha and I in chairs near the desk—he asked, "Would you like some coffee, or maybe a Coke?"

"No thanks," Marsha said, smiling. "We just had breakfast. How about you, Anne?"

I just smiled and shook my head no. I didn't want to speak, just yet, because of my French accent.

After getting a cup of coffee from the pot on a table in a corner, Bosinger returned to his desk, put the coffee down, and began to comb his bushy hair, while he asked, "What you want with Karl? Is he in some kind of trouble?"

"As I told you," Marsha said. "I'm a friend of Mrs. Rhodes, and I'm helping her find her daughter, Cassy."

"Are you with the Missing Persons Bureau?"

Laughing out loud, Marsha said, "Goodness no. I'm just a friend, looking for Cassy."

"Then it's Cassy you're looking for, not Karl," he said, his smile getting more crooked with each word.

"Her mother thinks that Karl might know where she is," Marsha said, looking down at the floor and blushing.

How does she make herself blush like that? I asked myself, while I watched Bosinger sit behind his desk again.

"Why didn't Mrs. Rhodes come and ask about her daughter?" he asked.

Looking up, Marsha said, "She's not feeling well."

"She's a drinker. Right?"

"I'm afraid so," Marsha said, shaking her head and wincing.

Getting up quickly, he asked, "Would you ladies like to take a walk around?"

Without saying anything, we just got up and followed him outside. Then when we passed a new black van, Marsha said, "Nice van. Must've set you back plenty."

"Sure did," he said, taking us both by the arm and guiding us around a mud puddle. Then, letting us go, he said, "Marsha, Cassy spoke of you, you know. I just thought of her saying once that you were married to her father once."

"That's once too often," Marsha said, getting brassy. "If you want to call it a marriage, then go ahead. I don't!"

"What would you call it?"

"A disaster. Hey, why did Cassy bring my name up, anyway?"

"I can't remember what all we were talking about. I just remember she mentioned you, as his first wife."

"What else did she say about me?"

"Nothing," he said, guiding us around another puddle. Then: "Oh yeah, she said that even without knowing you, she likes you. I didn't ask why."

Marsha, freeing her arm, as I did, looked at him, saying, "I don't know why she'd say something like that, when we've never even met, or, as far as I know, seen each other."

Laughing, he said, "She probably likes anyone who has disagreed with her father."

"Then you know him?" Marsha asked.

"He's been here a couple times," he said, shaking his head slowly and frowning.

"Then you know why I just called the marriage a disaster."

"Let's just say, I know that he's not the most pleasant guy I've ever met." Then, turning to me, he said, "Anne, I guess we sort of cut you out, Marsha and me."

In my best English, I smiled and said softly, "I understand."

Marsha was quick, asking, "Do you happen to know where Cassy is, Chuck?"

"Yes, as a matter of fact, I do," he said, taking her arm, and her arm only, leaving me to walk behind with their shadows, which was better than all right with me.

"Where is she?" Marsha asked.

"She's with Karl… in Vienna, Austria. In fact, I just got a letter from Karl. He says they're very happy and will be married soon."

Nicely, Marsha asked, "Could I see the letter?"

"Sure," he said, leading us into his office. Then, when he was behind his desk, he opened a drawer and pulled out the letter. "Here, read it for yourself," he said, handing it to Marsha.

"There's no return address on the envelope," Marsha said. "It's been torn off."

"I tore it off," he said, standing now and running his comb through his hair. "I'm sure they wouldn't want a lot of people knowing where they live—not right away. I'm sure you understand."

After reading the letter, Marsha said, "Thanks, Chuck. I'll tell Cassy's mother that she is safe. That's mainly what she wants to know."

Putting his comb in his hip pocket, he asked, "How about some coffee now?"

"Sounds good," Marsha said. "Black, please."

In my best English, I said, "Yes… black."

Giving us coffee in dirty cups, he said, "Poor kids. I hope it'll work out for them."

"So do I," Marsha said.

"Vienna's a beautiful city," he said. "I guess he's working where I first met him—at the Spanische Hofreitschule. He's terrific with horses. That's why I asked him to come work for me here."

Looking in her coffee, Marsha manufactured a blush and asked, "Did your wife go with you, when you went to Vienna?"

"Smiling and giving his wedding ring a twist, he said, "No, Jewel didn't go. It was a business trip, only. You know—in and out."

"How long you been married?" she asked, with another blush flooding her face.

"Several years," he said, smiling and looking at her legs.

I began to feel invisible.

"Getting back to Karl and Cassy," she said. "What did their friends say when they ran off like that?"

"Friends? I didn't know their friends. I believe they kept to themselves. But don't take my word for it, because I only saw them here, when Cassy came for her riding lesson."

Getting to her feet, she took his hand and said, "Well, Chuck, I'll tell Mrs. Rhodes that her daughter's okay. We thank you for your time and coffee and help. And if I ever take up riding, I'll be sure to ask for your advice."

"Nice meeting you both. Okay, Marsha, if you want to ride, come on over and ask for me."

We left, and as we rode back to the house, Marsha wondered out loud as to what sort of business Bosinger might have in Vienna.

"With any luck, we'll find out," I said.

Turning onto her street now and nearing her white, brick colonial, she slapped the steering wheel with both hands and said: "Shit! There he is."

"Who?" I asked, sounding like an owl.

"My ex, Frank Rhodes."

Standing next to the red Cadillac in front of her house, Frank Rhodes, dressed in a pin-striped blue suit and a red tie, looked younger and more handsome than I had imagined. Putting aside his flashy clothes and car, if one could overlook these things, his greying dark hair, tall and athletic build, and rugged facial features made him appealing, if not dignified-looking. Now, once we were stopped and out of the car, he came to us and said, "Good morning. Marsha, can I talk to you?"

"Is it about your daughter?" Marsha asked. Then, after turning to me, as if to introduce me, she turned back to Frank and said, "Your wife says she's been kidnapped. Is it true."

"Yes, and will you help us find her?"

"I'll try."

"Will you come over to the house, so I can tell you what the situation is?"

"You can tell me right here," Marsha said coldly.

"Okay... I love Cassy and want her back," he said tearfully. "Karl Zionchek, the man who took her, has called twice, so far. The first time, he asked for a million dollars, which I don't have. He told me to get the money tomorrow, Monday, and wait at my house for another call."

"Cash?"

"Cash."

"How much money can you get your hands on?"

"Marsha, I might be able to get half, if I'm lucky. I made some bad investments. I'll try to borrow it."

"Half might be enough. When Karl contacts you, tell him that you'll give him half now and half when your daughter is released.... They're in Vienna, Austria, you know."

"I suspected as much. Karl used to live there."

"Something else, Frank. Tell Karl that a family friend will pick up your daughter and give him the other half of the money, then, and not until then."

"What if he wants all the money—right away, tomorrow?"

"You said you were told to wait in your house with the money. That means someone will pick it up and then send it to Vienna. That means a partnership of some kind. Don't worry. It's probably expected—half now, and half when the merchandise is delivered."

"Who's the family friend, Marsha—you?"

"You'll know in due time. Just focus on what you have to do and say!"

"Marsha, Sheila thinks that maybe Cassy and Karl are in this together, extorting us."

"Well," Marsha said, laughing, "if they are, and get the money, then they're going to have one helluva good time, aren't they? By the way, do you have a photo of your daughter?"

"No, I don't have one with me, but I can get one."

"Good. Put one in your mailbox, and I'll pick it up."

"Okay…. Marsha, thanks. And I'm sorry I acted like I did, years ago."

"Forget it!" she said sharply, already moving to the house with me.

Marsha offered me a salad and a baloney sandwich for lunch. I declined the baloney sandwich. After lunch, while we drank coffee in the living room, I asked about Frank Rhodes, and how they had gotten involved.

"He was something else!" she said, laughing. "You know, I asked Frank about himself once, and he told me—dramatically, if not truthfully."

She told me, that Frank had won an academic scholarship to University of Michigan, where he became interested in dramatics—so much so, that when he took his degree in Liberal Arts, he wanted to go to New York and become a professional actor. However, Velma, his mother, objected, saying at breakfast one morning, "Fool, what in hell you wanter be an actor for, when you can marry some rich bitch, go inter business and help me out, for Chris's sake!" Then, while slapping the kitchen table, she yelled: "Look at yourself! You're a college grad, and you can't even put a loaf of bread on the table!"

"Well," Frank said, "When I get a break in New York, I'll be able to put plenty of bread on the table—bread that you will probably spend on more booze!"

With her bleached-blonde hair hanging in her eyes, with her pasty blue eyes filled with contempt, with her early-morning breath stinking of stale tobacco and alcohol, she shot sharp darts of spit into his face, when she yelled: "Go be a phony actor—but if you do, I never wanter see your face around here again! Your father left me high and dry, so now you may's well too! Get the hell out and take your duds with you.!"

Collecting all he owned in a small cardboard box, he tied a string around it and headed for the door. Then, stopping at the door, he looked at his mother and said, "May God help you. Goodbye."

"Don't forget!" she yelled. "I never wanter see your face again—you lousy bum!"

Closing the door and listening to the sound of dishes breaking against the door, he whispered, "Sober her up, will you God?" And then he hurried away from Swamp Road and headed for Woodward Avenue, whispering now, "I'm free. I'm free."

But his sense of freedom didn't last long, for the farther he got from the house, the more he grew afraid, so that by the time he'd reached the bus stop on Woodward Avenue, his sense of freedom had been overcome by fear. In fact, as he waited for the bus, he was filled with fear, being alone and adrift now, after being abandoned by his mother just now, after being abandoned by his father fifteen years ago, when his father divorced his mother and married a rich widow in Florida.

It was Marsha who came to help. Seeing him standing at the bus stop with his box of belongings, she stopped her new blue Plymouth and asked, "Where you headed, Frank?"

The idea of going to New York dropped out of sight, and he said, "I was going over to St. James Church to leave some old clothes for the poor."

"Hop in!" she said, smiling.

They went into Birmingham, and he carried all of his possessions into the vestibule. Then, after a few minutes, he returned to the car, still carrying his belongings. "Nobody around in there," he said. "I'll come back later." Then, getting into the car, he asked, "How about some lunch?"

"Swallows Inn?"

"I was just about to suggest it."

At the expensive restaurant in Birmingham, Michigan, they both ordered a Greek salad, and while they ate, Marsha said, "I didn't see you around campus this last semester."

"I kept pretty much to myself," he said. "Study, study, study."

"What you going to do now, Frank—go to grad school?"

"Actually, I don't know."

"Some of the guys are going into the military."

"Actually, I've thought about that—about joining up and going to Korea to fight for my country. And then when I get discharged—if I don't get killed—I'll use the G.I. bill for more schooling."

"What you thinking of being, a doctor, a lawyer?"

"A lawyer, actually. A corporation lawyer."

"Good for you, Frank."

"How about yourself, Marsha?"

"I don't have a clue, as to what I'm going to do."

They finished lunch, and Marsha dropped him off at his house, after agreeing to have dinner with him. Then, after he went in and apologized to his mother for having sassed her, he said, "Mother, you'll never guess who I had lunch with."

"The Queen of England," she said, laughing and coughing and wheezing.

"Marsha Lowden."

"The rich bitch?"

"Actually, she's not rich, but her parents are."

"Richer'n a honey bee's ass," she said, before a fit of coughing.

"You better see a doctor," he said, worrying.

"Don't tell me what to do!" she said, still coughing. Then, after going to the cupboard and taking a swig of whiskey, she said, "That'll fix it!"

And it did fix it, for good, for just after she sat down at the kitchen table again, she had a massive heart attack and died. When Frank found her, she was still sitting upright in her chair.

After his mother's funeral, which was paid for with the money from a small insurance policy she'd kept, he found himself alone, penniless, and with two mortgages on the house. It was Marsha who came to his aid again, by getting him a loan from her father, and it was she who agreed to marry him, after he told her he was going into the Air Force.

They were married in her parents' house by a Lutheran minister. Marsha wore a white dress. Her maids wore blue. About two hundred people attended, and they were not crowded. Sheila Barnes was one of those attending and it was she, of all people, who caught the bridal bouquet. After the wedding, they'd gone to Bermuda for a honeymoon, and during that time, Frank attended his wife with all the grace and care of a bull in a cow pasture. When they returned to Michigan, he went into the Air Force and was soon sent to Casablanca as an Intelligence officer. Then, after receiving the cablegram that told him Marsha had committed adultery on a troopship, he divorced her. A few years later, he was discharged and went to law school. He then married Sheila Barnes, the daughter of a wealthy car dealer, made millions of dollars by buying and selling real estate and stock. And, eventually, he made a lot of wrong investments and went broke.

When Marsha stopped talking, I asked, "Did Frank really tell you those personal things about himself?"

Smiling, she said, "He told me some. The rest? Well, let me put it this way: I just filled in the blanks."

"Merde."

## chapter 19

Early Monday morning, Frank came to the house. "I heard from Karl," he said, his voice unsteady.

"And?" Marsha asked, putting a cup of coffee in front of him at the kitchen table.

"I told him, half the money now and half when I get my daughter back."

"Go on."

"I said a family friend would pick her up. And when he asked for a name, I gave him yours—okay?"

"It's all right. I hope I won't be checked out too thoroughly. Frank, maybe I'd better step aside…"

"Let's wait and see," he said anxiously.

"But it's your daughter's life. If someone connects me with CIA, well, things may get out of control."

"Marsha, please let's wait."

Turning to me, Marsha asked, "What do you think?"

"It's a little too late to pull out now, isn't it? He has already given your name," I said, shrugging my shoulders. "Frank's right. Let's wait and see."

"What else did Karl say?" Marsha asked.

"He told me not to call the police, and to wait at home with the cash."

"How much have you got?" Marsha asked.

"I've already called friends. I'll have five hundred thousand by this afternoon."

"Are you sure?" Marsha asked, raising her eyebrows.

"Sure," Frank said, nodding his head nervously.

"Get the cash and go home, and wait!" Marsha said, pointing a finger at him. "And don't forget to leave the picture of your daughter in the mailbox!"

"Okay… When are you coming to the house? Should I call when I get home with the money?"

"No more phone calls," Marsha said. "Now go!"

"Do you think our phones are bugged?" Frank asked, getting up and moving towards the door.

"I wouldn't be surprised," Marsha said softly, remaining at the table. Then, after Frank had left and the phone rang, she said, "Anne, get on the extension in the living room and listen in. Two ears are better than one."

I went to the phone and waited until she yelled for me to pick up.

Chuck Bosinger was saying, "Hey, Marsha, I heard you're going to Vienna?"

"Who told you that?" Marsha asked, sounding like a little girl.

"Marsha, I want to talk to you. Will you be home this afternoon?"

"I'm sorry, Chuck. This afternoon, I have to go someplace."

"Where—over to your ex-husband's place?"

"Yes."

"What for?"

"To give him a big kiss," she said dryly.

Laughing, he said, "I don't think so."

"Neither do I. If anything, I'd like to give him a punch in the nose."

"Why are you going there?"

"Chuck, he said he'd leave a picture of his daughter in the mailbox. I'm going to get it."

"Why are you doing this, Marsha?"

"Because his wife is a friend. We were in high school together."

"I see."

"What have you got to do with this, Chuck?"

"Later, I'll tell you later. I've got important stuff I want to tell you. I like you, Marsha. You've got a head, you've got guts, and you're being loyal to a friend. I like that."

Warmly, as if she were about to nibble on his ear, she asked, "When will I see you, Chuck?"

"This afternoon, at Frank's," he said, then hung up.

The house was a rambling, red-bricked ranch in the heart of Bloomfield Hills, with the white mailbox located out front next to the road. After checking the mailbox for the photograph of Frank's daughter and not finding it, we went up to the house and rang the doorbell.

Answering the door with a drink in his hand, Frank said, "Sorry, I forgot the picture. Would you like a martini? Come in."

When Marsha looked at me, as if it were up to me to decide, I said, "It might not be wise to be here when someone comes to pick up the money—if he got the money."

"Frank, how much did you get?" Marsha asked.

"Five hundred thousand, from my banker-friends," Frank said. Then, looking at the glass in his hand, he said, "To settle my nerves."

"Bosinger, the horseman, said he'd be here," Marsha said. "That changes it. Let's go in. I want to see what the hell is going on. Okay?"

"Okay," I said. "I could use a martini, too."

"Your friend makes sense," Frank said, letting us in. "A martini would be just the thing right now."

After introducing Frank and me, Marsha said, "No drink for me, Frank."

Then, just after Frank got another glass from another room and poured me a martini from the pitcher on the coffee table in front of a large sofa, we sat and looked at each other in silence, with Frank on the sofa, grinning at us, as we sat staring at him from nearby plush chairs.

The doorbell rang. Frank jumped up and, after peeking out from a side of the drapes, turned to us and said, "It's Keith Stoltz and Cappy Duggan. What do those assholes want?"

"Who are they?" Marsha asked, not getting up.

"Two guys I met when I went to look for Cassy. She was working in a nightclub, so I heard, but I didn't find her. These two guys came up to me at the bar, introduced themselves, and said they'd keep an eye out for her and let me know if they saw her. Should I answer the door?"

"See what they want," Marsha said. "Maybe they have good news. If not, send them on their way."

As soon as Frank opened the door, the two men pushed their way in and threw Frank down on the sofa, where he yelled: "What the hell are you doing?"

Sitting on either side of Frank, the men looked at the black suitcase standing at the end of the sofa, and the tall, good-looking one said, "I'll tell what we're doing. We're waiting for somebody." Then, after sticking a pistol in Frank's ribs, he turned to the short, ugly one and said, "Cappy, close the drapes, all the way."

The one called Cappy closed the drapes and said, "Drapes closed, Keith!"

Looking at the suitcase, the one called Keith said, "Now take this suitcase and put it on the chair right across from me and Frank!"

Cappy put the suitcase on the chair.

"Now, open it!" Keith said.

Opening the suitcase, Cappy said, "Bucks, Keith—lots bucks!"

"Close it!" Keith said.

Cappy closed it.

"Put it behind the chair, closed! And now sit in the chair in front of it and shut up!" Then, after Cappy sat, Keith said, "Take out your switchblade and keep an eye on Frank and his friends. I've gotta go to the toilet."

"Can't I gun?" Cappy asked.

"No gun!" Keith said, leaving the room.

"Shit!" Cappy said, opening his knife. Then, when Keith returned, he said, "Gotta have gun. Better gun."

Sitting next to Frank again, Keith said, "No gun! You know what happened the last time you had a gun. The girl just sneezed and you blew her away. All that merchandise—wasted!"

"What girl?" Frank asked, his face flushed and his voice cracking high.

Snarling at Frank, Keith said, "Don't worry, Mr. Moneybags. It wasn't your daughter Cassy, our favorite stripper down at Whispers. We wouldn't let anyone waste that body."

"Is she still working there?" Frank asked.

"You know very well she isn't, asshole." Keith said.

"Where is she?" Marsha asked, smiling nicely.

Looking at Marsha, Keith said, "You must be Marsha Lowden. Our boss told us you'd be here. And this is your friend, Anne—right?"

Before Marsha could say anything more, Cappy said, "Hey, Frank, what drinkin'—martini? Gimmee some!"

"No martini!" Keith said, shaking his head at Cappy.

"How 'bout beer—got beer?"

"No beer, either!" Keith said, looking at the door.

Angrily, Frank said loudly: "If you jerks came for the money, take it and leave!"

Laughing, Keith said, "Sounds like Frank here has a little fire in his ass, after all."

Waving his knife at Frank, Cappy said, "Don't call jerks, Frank, or cut tongue out!"

"That's enough, Cappy!" Keith said, looking at his watch.

Looking at his own watch, Cappy said, "Boss late."

Keith snapped: "He didn't say what time he'd be here, so how could he be late!"

"Why didn't say what time?" Cappy asked, grinning.

"Just shut up!" Keith said, going then and parting the drapes, saying then, "No sign of him yet. Hope he doesn't have the wrong address."

Looking at the thugs in dark suits and no ties, I thought of them as killer clowns, and I had no doubt about their killing us. For the first time since they'd come, I was afraid—filled with fear, in fact, as I had never been before. My mouth was dry and had a bitter taste. Cold beads of perspiration dripped down my body from my armpits. My eyesight became blurred. However, without a doubt, I could still feel a strong will to survive at the very core of my fear, and it was getting stronger. Then, just as I was thinking of some way to defend myself, Frank acted heroically. Springing to his feet, he threw himself high in the air and landed on Keith, who was still looking out the window. Then, after knocking Keith down, he took the pistol from his hand, but unfortunately, it was too late. Cappy rushed over and, grabbing Frank's hair, put his knife to his throat, asking "Hey, Keith—slit throat?"

"No!" Keith said, getting up and retrieving his gun. "Just hold the bastard." Then, after hitting Frank in the face with the gun, he said, "Okay, Superman-- back to the couch, and I don't want to see you even twitch!"

Frank sat again, and the doorbell rang. Cappy rushed to answer, saying, "Prob'ly boss."

Quickly, Keith said: "Before you open the door, look through the peephole and see who it is!"

"Ain't got no peephole, Keith."

"Then peep through the side of the window!"

Peeping, Cappy said, "It boss."

As soon as Bosinger walked in, he looked at Frank and asked, "What happened to the creep's face—what's been going on?"

Laughing, Cappy said, "Keith gave face spanking with gun."

"He got out of line," Keith said.

Brassy now, Marsha said, "Serves him right, and he never looked better!"

Laughing and turning to Marsha, Bosinger said, "So, you approve of what happened to your ex, right, Marsha?"

Coarsely, through her teeth, Marsha said, "He asked for it."

"He try get Keith's gun, but I stop him," Cappy said. Pointing his knife now at Frank, he asked, "Want kill him, boss?"

"Don't be such an animal!" Bosinger said, frowning and looking at Marsha and me. "We've got more important things to do, right now. By the way, Cappy, don't talk like that in front of the ladies."

"Yes, boss."

Bitterly, Marsha said, "I'd like to see the sick dog put down, but not until after I return from Vienna. Chuck, will you ask him about the photograph of his daughter? I can't bring myself to even talk to him."

Laughing again, Bosinger said, "Hey Frank, what about it?" Then, after slapping Frank's face, he said, "You know, I should kill you right now, because of the way you treated Marsha when you were married. I don't know the details, but it looks like you did some rotten things to her."

"Don't kill him yet. When I return from Vienna, I want to see it," Marsha said.

"The picture is on the piano, the only one I can think of now," Frank mumbled.

"I'll get it," Marsha said, going to the piano, removing the photo from its large silver frame, rolling it up and putting it inside her tan trenchcoat.

"By the way, what's the picture for?" Bosinger asked.

"Didn't I tell you? I've never seen her. When I pick her up in Vienna, I want to be sure it's her."

"My associate in Vienna can be trusted!" he said sharply.

Putting her hand on his arm, and maybe feeling his muscles, she smiled and said, "I believe you, Chuck. I'm sure he can be trusted. You know, I'm very surprised that you're in this kidnapping with Karl."

Laughing, he asked, "Do you really think that Karl has anything to do with engineering this?"

"That's what I was led to believe."

"My dear, this is too big for somebody like Karl. It's very big—and my ass is on the block and will be chopped off, if I screw up. And, of course, your ass is on the block, along with Frank's and his wife's."

"That certainly is a lot of asses!" I said, trying to lighten the moment.

Laughing, Marsha put her hand on Bosinger's shoulder now, saying, "Take it easy, Chuck. I'm not about to screw it up. All I want is the girl, for her mother's sake. And… to show you where my loyalty lies, I'm going to let you in on a little secret."

"So what's the secret?"

"The money in the suitcase is all the money he's got. Frank Rhodes is broke. His wife told me."

"That's all he's got?"

"That's it."

"Very bad news! What you going to bring to Vienna—just your gorgeous ass?"

Smiling and rubbing his shoulder a little, she said, "I've got another secret for you. His wife said that she would make up the difference, but, if she can't come up with five hundred thousand, I'll get the money."

"You'd do that for your friend? I wish somebody would give me that kind of loyalty."

"Isn't your wife loyal to you?" Marsha asked.

"Jewel? She has to be loyal. She's my wife."

"I see," she said, rubbing his shoulder again, with a gentle, slow, circular movement. "Well, one can't have too much loyalty, so I'm offering mine, as well."

Looking in her eyes, he said, "You're okay, kid."

"What are you going to do with Frank?" she asked, stopping with all that massaging.

"I've got plans for him, and I think you'll approve. I'm going to take him out of the picture for awhile—at least, for awhile." Then, taking her arm, he went with her to stand in front of Frank. Releasing her arm, he removed a small white pill from his pocket and, after picking up what was left of the martini in the pitcher, he said, "Take this here pill, Frank, it'll quiet your nerves."

"What is it?" Frank asked.

"Just a little tranquilizer."

"Shove it!"

"Kill now, boss?" Cappy asked, holding up his knife.

"Yes, kill now!" Bosinger said.

"Okay, I'll take the damn pill," Frank said. Taking the pill then, he put it in his mouth and washed it down with the martini.

"Don't kill the jerk," Marsha said. "I couldn't care less, but my friend loves him."

"It's just a little something to keep him humble for a few days," Bosinger said. Then, after going to the phone and dialing, he said, "Sergeant, he'll be out front in two minutes." Then, hanging up, he went to Frank and asked, "How you feeling, sport?"

Frank's only response was a weak and fleeting smile.

"Look eyes!" Cappy said. "Turn white!"

"His eyes are rolled up inside his head," Keith said. "Cappy, you've seen this before—so what's the big deal?"

"Where are you, Frank Rhodes?" Bosinger asked.

Calm, with his eyes closed now, Frank said, "I'm in my family's old cinder-block house on Swamp Road in Bloomfield Township."

"What's it like in there?"

"It stinks bad. It stinks of rotting food and my mother's whiskey and tobacco smoke."

"What are you doing?"

"I'm lying on the couch and planning how I can climb the social ladder."

"Do you want to get away from the house?"

"I want to get away from the house."

"If you do, then go out and sit in the middle of the road. Some important person will come by to pick you up."

"I'm going out to sit in the middle of the road," Frank said, getting up and falling back down again.

"What's the matter—you drunk, Frank?"

With eyes still closed, Frank said, "I'm drunk."

"Where are you now, Frank—in jail?"

"I'm in jail."

"Do you go there often?"

"Often," Frank said, suddenly putting his hands on his face and sobbing.

"Go right ahead and cry," Bosinger said, laughing. "Crying is what makes you human, and feelings are what makes you real. You do want to be real, don't you, Frank?"

"I want to be real."

"You've lost someone, Frank—you don't remember who you lost, do you?"

"I don't remember."

"Okay, try to go outside again and sit in the middle of the road."

"Can I help him?" I asked, feeling my heart pounding in fear and anger.

"He'll be okay," Bosinger said. "Don't worry, Anne."

Hardly able to control my anxiety without screaming, I watched as Frank went out the door and sat in the middle of the road. In a few seconds then, it was over, when a police car pulled up alongside of Frank, and he was taken away.

Without saying anything more, Bosinger picked up the suitcase of money and left, followed by Keith and Cappy.

Soon after, we left, with Marsha saying, "Remind me to call George Bolton." Then, once we were on our way in her Volkswagen, she said, "George is with the F.B.I. and lives nearby in Huntington Woods. I want

George to keep an eye on Bosinger and his two killer-clowns. After we get Cassy, then he can pick them up. Also, I want to tell him about the police sergeant Bosinger talked to, just before he drugged Frank. There's a lot to look into and George will know what to do. I trust him… George Bolton, who played hockey for Michigan when I was going there to school."

As soon as we arrived at her house, Marsha called George Bolton, with no reminder from me, and then she made reservations for our flight to Vienna.

When she got off the phone, I called Richard Fowler and told him what Marsha and I were about to do and why. "Will you help us?" I asked, feeling anxious and exhausted.

"Marsha Lowden is a good one," he said. "Let's see… who else can we get?"

"Not J'nine," I said quickly. "Because of Halona's losing Gabrielle, I don't want J'nine involved, or even to know about it."

"I understand."

"You have contacts in Vienna, don't you?"

After a long pause, Richard said, "I'm thinking of you, Anne. Now that Vachel is gone, you have no one from your immediate family left."

"Never mind that," I said abruptly. "Do you have any ideas. We'll be in Vienna in a couple days."

"All right, here's what we'll do: As soon as this call is finished, I'll call a banker-operative in Vienna. His name is Klaus von Thalhofen, and he'll open an account for you for a transfer of funds. He and Vachel were great friends, and I'm sure he'll do anything for you, Vachel's sister. Tomorrow, call Klaus at Sparkasse Wien Bank, get the account number and take it to the bank, and they'll send the remaining five hundred thousand to the account in Vienna."

"We'll arrive at eleven Wednesday morning. Will you be at the airport?"

"I'll be there, but don't expect me to run and throw my arms around you—at least not straight away. Clearly, we must be careful. One final thing, love: Tell Marsha that Sepp Gruber will be waiting in his taxi."

"Thank you, Richard."

"Be careful."

We left to pick up Sheila, who was still at her parents' house with her daughter, Tiffany. Looking in the rearview mirror, Marsha said, "I thought so. Bosinger is following us in his black van-- remember the black van?"

"Yes, but maybe it's not him," I said hopefully.

"It's him. I can see his bushy hair."

Not seeming intimidated, she picked up Sheila and drove to Sheila's bank, where Sheila filled out an Application for Foreign Transfer. Then, after being told it would take two or three days for the American dollars to be credited to my account in Vienna, we left to have lunch at Swallows restaurant in Birmingham.

While we ate salad, Sheila, anxious but sober, said, "Frank called me and said he's in jail."

Acting surprised, Marsha asked, "What the hell for?"

"For being drunk and sitting in the middle of a road—not like him, at all."

"Will he get out on bail?" Marsha asked.

Tight-lipped, Sheila said, "They're going to keep him there, until he sobers up enough to stand in front of a judge."

"How does he feel now?" I asked, wanting to tell her what was going on.

Turning to me, Sheila said, "He said his memory is poor, and that all he can remember is that he brought a lot of cash money home in a suitcase. Bits and pieces are coming back, he says. I told him to see a doctor, as soon as possible."

"Good idea!" Marsha said.

"These are long, painful days for me," Sheila said, with tears in her eyes.

"You poor dear," I said, looking at Sheila. "We could leave, if you want." Then, looking out the window, I saw Bosinger in his van across the street from us.

"I'll be okay, Anne," Sheila said, blotting tears away with a tissue. "It's just that everything's so damn rotten right now. I've never felt so insecure in my life."

"Sheila, may I speak freely?" I asked.

"Of course."

"I've often felt like you do now. It seems we must learn to live mostly with the insecurities of life—with the broken dreams and broken hearts. It's hell on earth, but I believe we need it for growing."

"But there's more, Anne," Sheila said. "If you have children, you have to live with their agonies, too."

"You're right, Sheila," I said, thinking of my son. I know from experience."

Shaking her head slowly, Sheila said, "It was too much for me, I guess, and I tried to hide from it in a bottle. But now, I know that I only stunted my growth by not facing up to the challenges. And maybe I've stunted my children's growth, as well."

Marsha said, "It's about taking your lumps of guilt and moving on. We must do it, or become the walking dead. After a short time, kicking our own ass gets counter-productive."

"I'm finding that out," Sheila said. "Yesterday, when I kicked myself hard, I compared myself to a neon sign outside a honky-tonk bar. I felt that I was flickering and dying."

"And now?" Marsha asked.

"You know, in some weird way, Cassy has maybe saved my life. Thinking of her being held in harm's way, has made me live again. I feel that my life is meaningful now, and that I can do something to save my daughter."

Finishing our lunch, we left the restaurant and, after dropping Sheila off, we went to Marsha's house. Having another coffee, Marsha said, "I expect Bosinger any minute now."

Just then, the doorbell rang, and after Marsha let Bosinger in, he said, "It amazes me."

"Okay, what amazes you, Chuck?" Marsha asked with a smile.

"It amazes me that a tall, beautiful, rich blonde drives around in an ugly little Volkswagen."

"What should I be driving—a limo?"

Laughing and running his comb through his hair, he said, "I smell coffee."

"Take your jacket off and have some," Marsha said, before taking his leather jacket and hanging it on an antique rack by the door. "Have a seat," she said then, before going to the kitchen and bringing back another cup. Then, pouring coffee, she said, "If I recall correctly, Chuck, you drink yours black."

"You remembered!" he said, acting pleased as he sat alone on the sofa.

Sitting next to him then, Marsha asked, "What can I do for you?"

Stretching his long legs, he said, "You two have been busy. I know, because I followed you. I hope you don't mind."

"If you followed us, then you know we went to the bank with Mrs. Rhodes. And yesterday, I made reservations for a flight to Vienna. The money will be there, Chuck. How about Sheila's daughter, Cassy?"

Taking a slip of paper from his hip pocket, he asked, looking at me, "Are you going with Marsha, Anne?"

Before I could answer, Marsha said, "She sure is. She's my moral support."

"Good," he said, handing the slip of paper to Marsha. "I made reservations for two at the hotel where you'll stay at. I've written down the name of the hotel, along with the address of the apartment where the girl is. The girl will be waiting. Leave the money, get the girl, and get the hell out of there, fast. And remember, no tricks, no police."

Reaching over and placing his hand on hers, he said softly, "Be extra careful."

"I will."

"Good."

"Why the concern, Chuck?"

"I like you, Marsha. I guess I'm just a sucker for tall, beautiful blondes."

Smiling broadly, Marsha said, "I take it that your wife is…"

"That's right. She's tall, beautiful and blonde."

"Chuck, what does she think of all this?" Marsha asked, while pouring him more coffee.

"She's all for it," he said. "We're in this together."

Taking his hand in hers, Marsha said, "You told me that you'd tell me why you're doing this kidnapping."

"I'll tell you, if you really want to know, but let me warn you: The more you know, the more likely you get killed, if things get hot."

"You mean, you'd kill me, Chuck?"

"And Anne, too. Sorry. Let's hope things don't get screwed up."

"I see," she said, looking at me.

"You still want to know about our cause?" he asked.

Putting her hand on his leg, she said, "All we need to know is that the girl is okay." Then, removing her hand from his leg, she asked, "What guarantee do we have that the girl will be released and we won't be kidnapped?"

"No guarantee, but it's highly unlikely. My associate in Vienna is only interested in getting the money, for now. And he can get very nasty, if crossed. You know, if something happened to the girl, or even to Karl, then it would draw attention to us and our cause would be threatened."

"Chuck, I can't help it. I have to ask one more question. Why five hundred thousand here, and the same in Europe? It complicates things, doesn't it?"

Smiling, he said, "You don't want to know that—for your own good." Then, getting up and going to the door, he said, "Thanks for the coffee. I'll be here at three, to take you ladies to the airport."

"That would be nice, Chuck," she said, going to the door and shaking his hand.

As soon as he was gone, Marsha called her friend in the F.B.I. and filled him in. Then, after watching a little television and eating chicken thighs and rice, we went to bed. Surprisingly, I slept right through until eight the next morning, at which time, I showered and went down to find Marsha cooking pancakes and eggs, with nothing on but her bra and panties.

Bosinger came at three and helped us with our luggage. When we were on the way, he said, "You're in luck. The weather's beautiful. Got your passports?"

"Yes," Marsha said.

"How about you, Anne?"

"Yes," I said, sitting in the back.

"Ever been to Vienna?" he asked.

Marsha was quick to say, "Sure. We both worked for a travel agency once and got some good deals on trips."

With the airport in sight, he turned off the Ford expressway and said, "Well, this is it, ladies."

"I don't suppose I'll ever see you again," Marsha said, with her voice cracking, as if tears were caught in her throat and her heart was breaking.

"We might meet again—sure, why not?" he said.

Marsha wouldn't quit, saying now, "I guess this means that you'll never be able to show me how to ride a horse." Then, after picking away a few pieces of lint from her dark blue suit, she asked, "Did you quit your job at the riding school?"

"Yes, I quit there, but you'll do all right, if you want to learn to ride. There are a lot of good instructors around."

"Why not come with us, Chuck?" Marsha asked.

"I'm sorry, Marsha, I can't get involved with you, right now."

"Because of your wife?"

"Let's drop it, okay?"

"Okay, but if things don't work out with her…"

"Then I'll get in touch with you."

"Or you could let me know where you are, and I could join you."

"I might not be as far away as you think," he said, looking at her and smiling.

I hoped to God that she'd stop pumping for information, and she did. Instead, she kept working up tears and blotting them away, until we reached the terminal.

## chapter 20

Arriving in Vienna on time, we secured our luggage and went through Customs. Going out into a cold, drizzling rain, we buttoned our tan raincoats and pulled down our hats snug. In a matter of seconds, a taxi pulled up close, and the obese driver opened his window and asked in English, "Do you want to stay wet all your life?" Then, after he put our luggage in the trunk and we were on the way, he asked, "How you been, Marsha?"

"Busy," Marsha said. "Sepp Gruber, meet Anne La Fleur, Vachel's sister."

"It's very good to meet the sister of an old friend," he said, reaching around and shaking my hand, while at the same time shifting a lot of weight and keeping his eyes on the road as he went too fast in heavy traffic.

"It's good to see you again, Sepp," Marsha said. "Thanks for helping."

"For good friends, anything!" he said, smiling in the rearview mirror.

Marsha said, "While you're helping, maybe you can catch some political bad guys for The Company."

"It's getting more and more impossible to tell who is bad guy and who isn't bad guy," he said, pulling up in front of Hotel Europa. Then, after giving our bags to a porter, he said, "Big Ben is here, someplace."

After we checked in and were in our room, Marsha asked, "You know who Big Ben is, don't you?"

"I assume it's Richard," I said, putting our coats on chairs near the radiators. "I'm disappointed he wasn't at the airport to meet us, but I understand, of course."

"He probably was there," Marsha said, going to take a bath. "We just didn't see him, that's all."

After we both had a bath and were dressed—she, in a black suit and me, in my dark blue suit—we went down to the hotel's café and ate a lunch of Danish pastry and whipped cream. In our seat by the window, I looked for Richard, and when it seemed probable that he wouldn't appear, I said, "Let's return to the room. I want to call Klaus von Thalhofen at the bank." Then, in the room again, I found the telephone number for Sparkasse Wien Bank and called. After Thalhofen identified himself, I said, "It's Anne La Fleur."

"Yes," he said cheerfully, using English, "I have expedited it. Please come after two o'clock, after lunch."

"Thank you, sir," I said, hanging up just before the phone rang. "Marsha," I said, "shall I answer it, or will you?"

"I will. Think I know who it is—Bosinger. When will the money be ready?"

"At two o'clock."

"Chuck! How nice of you to call!" she said, before waving me over to listen in, thus fulfilling her adage that two ears are better than one.

"I thought I'd see how things are going," he said. "Did you have a good flight?"

"Yes, a good flight.... It's so good to hear your voice. Did you change your mind about joining us? Where are you?"

"Still in Michigan, I'm afraid. No, I don't think it wise to be with you, at this time—although I'm tempted."

"Well, at least you think enough of me, to say you're tempted. That's good to hear."

"Do you remember the instructions I gave you?"

"Yes, but something's come up. We called the bank about the transfer of funds and were told that we won't have to wait two or three days. We could get the money today."

"Good. Pick it up—the sooner, the better. I'll make a call and call you right back."

After she'd hung up, Marsha said, "I think it's good to play it as close to the truth as possible."

"The art of deception."

"I guess."

The phone rang again, and Marsha said, "Here we go. Come on, get your ear in here next to mine."

Bosinger said, "It's okay. When you get the money and leave the bank, there'll be a taxi waiting. The driver will help carry the money to the apartment. His name is Sepp Gruber. Be sure it's him. Ask, before you get in the taxi."

"Again," Marsha said. "What's the taxi driver's name?"

"Sepp Gruber!"

"Got it!" she said, with a little giggle escaping.

"What you giggling about?" he asked. "You sitting on a feather?"

"I always giggle when I'm light-headed from lack of sleep." Then, with a whine, she said, "Chuck, I'm scared—really scared."

"Well, it'll be over soon, Marsha. I know you'll do a good job. You've got guts. Just relax. Goodbye."

"Goodbye for now, Chuck. Miss you!" she said sweetly, before she hung up and laughed, saying, "Sepp Gruber gets around, doesn't he? I wonder how he was able to get close to those people."

"Well," I said, "you'll get a chance to ask him."

"Let's get out of this room," she said. "I'm getting a little anxious, aren't you?"

"I've never stopped being anxious."

So, with some time on our hands until two o'clock, we went downstairs and had coffee, with another Danish pastry and whipped cream, of course.

At two, we asked the doorman for directions and left for the bank, not far away. The rain had stopped, so we walked under a sky of blue and a warming sun. Focusing now on getting the girl, we agreed that we might also be kidnapped, and worse. Marsha had not brought her gun, which in the past, she had strapped it on the inside of one of her legs. So, with no plan of protection, and not wanting to deal in hypotheticals, we agreed on getting to the bank, getting the money and checking in with Sepp Gruber.

As soon as we stepped into Klaus von Thalhofen's office, I saw a pair of green eyes smiling at me. "Richard," I said, trying not to show too much surprise. "I knew you'd be here."

"You knew?" he asked, laughing and giving me a hug.

"Well, I almost knew," I said. "And I would've known for sure, if I'd had more time to think about it."

After introductions, the young banker said, "Please, sit. Anne, I'm very sad about Vachel. He was a good friend."

Considering him a handsome man, with dark eyes showing sensitivity and compassion, I said, "Thank you for your kind words."

Sitting behind his desk in a dark suit and tie, Klaus went on to say, "As I said on the phone, you can have the money today, if you want it."

"You're a good man, Klausie," Richard said, smiling and lighting his pipe.

Smiling back at Richard, Klaus asked, "So which face do you have on now, Fowler—your sincere face, or your butter-up face?"

"My own, personal face," Richard said, "Filled with respect for you."

"I'll bet!" Klaus said ironically. "Well now, let's get on with it. Two valises with the money are ready. Sepp Gruber, with his taxi, will help carry the money."

Marsha said, "He's gotten so fat, he can hardly carry himself. I'll carry them."

"Nonsense!" Richard said, laughing.

"Listen, Fowler—don't think I can't carry them. I'm in great shape."

"All right, you two, argue about it later," Klaus said, getting to his feet and going to a small closet, where he removed two black leather cases, saying, "Best if Sepp handles these. Marsha, don't underestimate the strength of that... large man."

Laughing, Richard said, "Sepp may just keep going with all that loot."

"Speak for yourself," Klaus said.

"How in the world did Sepp get inside with these bad guys?" Marsha asked.

"Persistence," Richard said. "After Anne called me, I went to the Spanische Hofreitschule and was surprised to find that Karl was still working there. Apparently, he and the girl could move about freely—but with one drawback, if you will. Karl told me this, and he also told me what the drawback was. Besides not telling the police, he would have to remain in plain sight of two Czech's, who would shadow him. And if he got out of line, Karl told me, then his family back in Czechoslovakia would be killed. Well, Sepp began to shadow the two Czechs, until eventually they got in his taxi. Then, after Sepp asked them if they knew of some way he could make some fast money, he was taken to their leader, whom they addressed as Herr Bird. The next day, Sepp was hired, to be on call, when needed, and Sepp was even given a small retainer fee, if retainer is the word. And, by the way, Herr Bird speaks German with an American accent and dresses like a hippie."

I asked, "Did you say that Karl and the girl can move about freely."

Richard said, "I suppose they want to keep things as normal as possible, until they get their hands on the money."

"Why don't we just rescue the girl and Karl, when they're on the way?" I asked.

"I told you. Karl has a mother and sister back home, and they will be killed. There's a better way."

Sitting behind his desk again, Klaus asked, "Anne, do you think Vachel would want you in harm's way like this?"

"I think he might," I said, thinking of how I had helped when Gabrielle had been kidnapped, without his asking me not to get involved.

"I don't think Vachel would approve," Richard said. "And I don't approve. Good God, I can't imagine what I'd do if you lost your life."

Smiling at Richard, I said, "You of all people, Richard, should know the value of life. 'You can't save your life,' El Cid said, and that means, to me, that I must spend my life in the best possible way. Do you agree?"

Looking in my eyes, he smiled and said, "Yes, I agree."

"Let's speak about protection," Klaus said. "Do you ladies have any weapons?"

Marsha said, "No, I don't think it wise. If they're discovered, it would complicate things."

"Get this!" Richard said. "We refuse to let you go, unless you have at least one gun between you. I happen to have one in my briefcase, holster and all."

Watching Richard remove a large pistol from his briefcase, I said, "Marsha, I think you should have it."

"Okay, if it'll make you feel better," she said, taking the leather-encased pistol and jamming it into her purse.

"Help will not be far away," Richard said. "Sepp will be with you, and I will be in the apartment across the hall. You see, for a generous fee, the tenants will let me have their apartment for a short while, and I've already rung them up and told them that it's for this afternoon. I guessed you would go, once you found out that the money is available. Listen now: As soon as you leave the money and get the girl and Karl, if he's there, then hurry across the hall with Sepp. Then we're off to the airport and to Salzburg in a small chartered plane."

"Why Salzburg?" I asked.

Evading my question, Richard said, "That's the plan. It's tentative, of course. We'll have to play it by ear, as Mickey Mouse said."

"Why Salzburg?" I repeated.

"The girl should be flown to Paris from here, don't you think?" Marsha asked.

"You, Anne and I will get off in Salzburg, and the girl will be flown to Paris," Richard said, acting cornered.

"Why so secretive?" I asked.

"Okay," he said. "I'll tell you this much more: I have a friend in Salzburg, who will help if the bad guys follow us."

"Why should they follow us, if they have the money?" Marsha asked. "And how will they know where we've gone? What's up with you, Fowler?"

Lighting his damn pipe again, Richard said, "Sepp will tell them where we've gone." Then, blowing smoke at Marsha, he said, "Trust me."

"Okay," Marsha said, "but I have more questions."

"I have a question," I said. "Could we get our things from Hotel Europa, before we go to the airport?"

"No need for that," Richard said. "Sepp has already picked up your toothbrushes, along with your spare girdles."

"Girdles? That's a laugh," Marsha said.

"You know that I don't wear a girdle," I said.

After laughter, Klaus said, "Fowler, I have a question. What kind of tobacco do you have?"

"You want some. It's a secret mixture."

"Of course—secret. Yes, I'll try it."

Taking a small leather pouch from his side pocket, Richard poured a generous amount onto the banker's desk, saying, "Enjoy it, Klaus." Then, turning to Marsha and me, he said, "Go now, and tell Sepp to come for the money. First, though, give us a hug."

After a hug from both men, I said, "Thanks for helping."

"Yes, thanks," Marsha said, after hugs.

"Take care," Klaus said, his face blushed.

Hugging me again, Richard whispered, "God be with you, my love."

Marsha and I left, and as soon as we were in the taxi and riding, Marsha lifted her skirt and strapped the pistol to the inside of an upper leg. "How do you pee, with that thing in the way?" I whispered.

Laughing, she said, "I manage."

Sepp Gruber was saying, "I'll take my time, so Richard will have time to get to the apartment on Linzerstrasse. I'll give you the Gruber's Tour."

After Ringstrasse, Rathaus Platz, the Konzerthaus, Prater, we came to the Spanische Hofreitschule, where Karl worked the famous Lippizaners, and Marsha asked, "Was Karl set up?"

"Yes, for sure," Sepp said.

Marsha persisted, asking, "Who's behind all this, besides Herr Bird?"

"That is what we will find out," Sepp said. "In time, we will know everything… I hope."

"I wish it was over," I said, then praying that it wouldn't be another bloodbath.

"It will be over soon after Salzburg," Sepp said. "Salzburg is a smaller city, and they won't be able to hide so good. And Julian Maier will be there to help, and maybe others."

Arriving at the apartment building and taking an old, noisy elevator to the third floor, we followed Sepp to the apartment and waited behind him as he knocked on the door. When there was no response, he opened the unlocked door and went in with the two satchels. After putting the satchels down and checking the rooms, he waved us in and pointed to the sofa in the living room, where we found Cassy sitting with Karl's head on her lap. Sepp immediately went across the hall to get Richard, and Richard rushed in saying, "Hurry, bring them to the other apartment!"

Once in the other apartment, Marsha pulled the photograph of the girl from her pocket and said, "It's her."

"Are you all right?" I asked, looking at the girl, who seemed to be in shock, or doped.

Surprisingly, she answered right away, saying, "I'm all right, I guess," Then, looking at Karl, she asked, "Are you okay, Karl?"

"Is okay," he answered, sitting in an armchair and smiling weakly.

"We should have them checked by a doctor," I said.

"You're right," Richard said. "But we don't have the time. In Salzburg…"

"They should be examined now!" I insisted.

"All right," Richard said. "Let's go to Emergency in Unfall Krankenhaus. Got that, Sepp?"

"Should I not wait for them to come for the money?" asked Sepp.

"You're right, Sepp," Richard said. "Wait. And tell them that we stole your taxi and went to Salzburg. Are the keys in it?"

"Here is the key," Sepp said, giving Richard a bunch of keys. Then, with a sad expression, he asked, "How will I be able to get to the hospital or airport, if you have gone there?"

"Take a taxi."

We left, and as soon as we started out for the hospital, Karl collapsed and remained unconscious. At the hospital, he was given emergency treatment, but it didn't revive him. The doctor said it was probably due to shock. The doctor also said that Karl would probably regain consciousness, eventually. Cassy, after being examined, was said to be "shaken" but all right for travel. However, after hearing about Karl, she insisted upon being with him. I spoke up for her and said I would stay with her in Karl's room, until it was absolutely necessary that we go.

Sitting alone with Cassy, as she stared at Karl and sobbed, I thought that she might want to talk about her bad experience. Yet, I wouldn't push it, if she didn't. Taking her hand and gently stroking her arm, I asked, "What happened, Cassy?"

Looking in my eyes and pulling herself a bit away, she asked, "Who are you?"

"My name is Anne La Fleur. I'm Marsha's friend, and I'll be your friend, if you want me to be."

With her blue eyes brightening, she ran her hand over the top of her long dark hair and said, "Marsha was married to my dad. I never met her, but I like her. It was good to see her just now."

"It must have been awful for you," I said. "I thought maybe you would like to talk to someone. I know I would."

"You would?" she asked, seeming now like a small child, innocent and curious.

Smiling with hope, I said, "Yes, I would. I'd talk about it until my face was blue."

With a little laugh, she said, "Well, I don't want my face to turn blue, but I'll talk about what happened. I can't believe all the things that happened, and maybe if I talk about it all, I'll believe it. Hey, Anne, what if I don't want to believe it?"

This is no ordinary girl, I told myself, and then I told her: "That's up to you."

"When Karl wakes up, I quit talking—right?"

"Right."

"I won't mind if you laugh at some of the things I say, because I know they'll sound pretty weird. In fact, right off the bat, I'm going to tell you one of the weirdest, okay?"

"Okay."

"Well, I was born with little bells in my blood. Do you think that's weird?"

"Do you, Cassy?"

"Yes, I sure do."

"Then, that's all that counts."

Smiling, she said, "I like you, Anne. And I like your French accent—it is French, isn't it?"

"Oui."

"Guess what? I speak French—high-school French. Could we speak French? I don't get many chances to speak with someone who speaks real French."

"Go right ahead," I said in French. "Speak away!"

And that she did, and speaking superb French, she told her story. Serious now, she said that the bells in her blood rang every spring, except last spring, when her best friend, Sidney, was murdered by her homeroom teacher, Mr. James "The Pain" Payne, whom Cassy considered to be the cruelest man on earth—even more cruel than her father and mother, who also were part of the world of stinking adults who get their kicks when they kill defenseless animals and other living things, including other human beings.

Last spring, just before her bells were due to ring, she had been good enough to bring Sidney to school, just to introduce him and show him around. But it didn't happen, because after she went to history and returned, she discovered that Sidney's cigar-box home was not on Mr. Payne's desk where she had left it. Instead, it was on the windowsill, with its lid open, and the sun had come around and dehydrated her beloved salamander to death. "You goddamn murderer!" she'd screamed at Mr. Payne, before running home and burying Sidney under an apple tree in the backyard. Then, after asking God to be good to Sidney, she went into "deep loneliness and depression," which lasted until summer vacation, when she began spending a lot of time with her riding instructor, Karl Zionchek, who worked at Bloomfield Riding Academy. Soon, she fell in love with Karl, and she began to introduce him and show him around. One day, she brought him home to her parents, Frank and Sheila Rhodes.

It had been Karl's brooding way that had attracted her, along with his long hair, dark eyes, foreign accent and his being twenty-four and a gentle person. But now, as she recalled, it was what she had found attractive in Karl, that her parents seemed to look upon as repulsive. As they sat in the living room, with her parents drinking martinis and she and Karl drinking ginger ale, it was her father who hurled the first insult. "Cassy, you look like crap in that black dress. Where's your good taste? The dress is too low in front," he said, "and shows all you got. And while I'm at it, that long hair running down your back makes the back of your head look like a horse's ass. You're a young lady now—be sophisticated!"

"Don't tell me how to fix my hair, or what to wear!" she said. "My hair's supposed to look like a horse's ass, because I'm wearing a ponytail!"

"Your father's right," Sheila said, finishing her martini. "You're a young lady now, and you should dress modestly."

With a snarl, her father stared at Karl, and asked, "So what's your excuse, fella—how come your hair's too long, and how come you never smile?"

"Long hair," Karl said, smiling broadly, "I like."

"Cassy told us you're from Europe," Sheila said.

"You're a refugee, right?" Frank asked. "Refugee from where?"

"I'm from farm outside Prague," Karl said, still smiling.

"That's in Czechoslovakia," Sheila said, like a smart-ass.

"How old are you, refugee?" Frank asked, frowning.

"I have twenty-four years," Karl said, smiling away.

"You're much too old to be dating our daughter," Sheila said, picking up her empty glass.

"Tell us about the motorcycle parked out front," Frank said. "And tell us about that dirty leather jacket you've got on."

Smiling, Karl said, "Cycle is good one. It is from Czechoslovakia, but I buy here. Jacket from my brother, who was killed by communists."

"What about the rest of your family?" Frank asked.

"Sister and mother still on farm. They could not escape with me to Austria."

"What about your father?" Frank asked.

"He was kicked by horse and died," Karl said sadly.

Laughing, Sheila said, "You're joking, of course."

"No joke. Is truth," Karl said, frowning now.

Moving on with the interrogation, Frank asked, "You escaped alone and became a refugee?"

Still frowning, Karl said, "Yes. I crossed into Austria at Mühlviertal. After many weeks, I was in Vienna. I was porter at Hotel Sacher, very good hotel. Then I got position at Rathaus Platz."

"What doing—killing rats?" Frank asked, laughing.

"I took trash from barrels in park. And then I got job I wished for, at Spanische Hofreitschule with Lippizaner horses."

"What doing, cleaning up horseballs?" Sheila asked.

"As trainer," Karl said seriously.

"Where are you living now?" Frank asked.

Cassy said, "He lives in Pontiac."

"Are you going to be an American?" Sheila asked.

"I don't know. I have just come."

"How in the world did someone like you get in at an exclusive riding academy?" Sheila asked, looking at the empty glass in her hand.

"Mr. Bosinger gave me position as riding instructor. He was in Vienna and saw me work with horses. He said come to America and work at riding academy. I am proud to work there."

"How nice," Sheila said. Then, looking at Frank, she asked, "Could I have just one more little drinkee?"

Ignoring Sheila, Frank stared at Karl and said, "If I were you, fella, I'd forget about dating our daughter. In fact, I don't even want you to talk to her."

Frowning, Karl got to his feet, saying, "I will go now."

Crying, Cassy walked with him to the door and said, "I'm so sorry, Karl. I can't believe my parents!" Then, after Karl was gone, she turned to her parents and shouted: "I definitely hate you!"

Fixing herself another martini, Sheila said, "Surely, dear, you can do a lot better than that refugee."

"Well," Cassy said bitterly. "Both of you could've done a lot better—take a good look at each other!"

"No more riding lessons!" Frank said. "I forbid you to see that bum again!"

Crying and sobbing, Cassy said, "First I lose Sidney, and now Karl. I hate you!"

"Sidney?" Sheila asked.

"That ugly salamander," Frank said. "Cassy, I told you I'd buy you another one."

"You see how insensitive you are!" Cassy screamed. "I was grieving over losing Sidney and you didn't say one kind thing to me! You don't care! You don't care about anything, except money and social standing!"

"I care," Sheila said. "How dare you say that I don't care!"

"Mother, your life is in no way about caring for others. It's nothing but a lot of drunken worries and hurries, and hypocrisy!"

"I resent that!" Sheila said, slurring her words.

"Don't worry, Cassy," Frank said. "Your horseball friend, Karl, will get another rich girl and then you'll see what he wanted from you."

Halfway up the stairs, Cassy turned and said, "Karl isn't like you, Father. That's how you got rich, isn't it? You slept with rich women, and you even married a couple—both suckers!"

Frank yelled: "If you believe that, you little turd, then you can hurry your ass out of this house, for good! Go live in a barn, with your horseshit Karl!"

At the top of the stairway, Cassy yelled: "That is exactly what I intend to do! And speaking of horseshit, isn't that what you slept in over on Swamp Road, before you married Marsha Lowden, and then my mother?"

"I want you out of this place—first thing in the morning!" he yelled.

"That's the first good idea you've ever had!" Cassy yelled, running into her room and locking the door.

And so the next morning at dawn, Cassy left the house, moved in with Karl, and got a job as a topless dancer at the nightclub, Whispers—all in one day. Then, when Karl said he was returning to Austria, she got a passport and went with him....

And it was on her eighteenth birthday, as cold autumn rain splashed the windows, yellowed and dirty with neglect, that she sat alone in their small apartment on Linzerstrasse. Sitting in a heavy, old rocker, she looked around and told herself that the apartment was a miserable, ugly, old prison, loaded with cancer-causing substances. And then, after a sip of coffee, she whispered, "I'm getting to be just like this place."

Going into the bathroom and looking in the yellowing mirror, she swept her long, dark hair up and stuck a few pins in it, wishing all the while that Karl would return from the "horsie home." In order to celebrate her birthday, he'd promised to take her to Hotel Sacher for dinner and then to Grinzing for music at the Heurigen. Impatient now, she called the Hofreitschule and was told that Karl had left about fifteen minutes ago. Deciding to meet him and walk back with him, she put on her black raincoat and matching hat over her new red dress and left. After walking down three flights of creaking stairs, she went out into a cold, wet evening.

As she neared Kartner Strasse, she saw Karl standing on a corner and talking with two men that she'd not seen before. Karl seemed to be arguing with the men, until he threw up his arms, as if in resignation, and walked away. And that was when Cassy ran up to him, saying, "Karl!"

Seeing her and taking her into his arms, he said, "How nice you come to meet me." Then, as they walked towards the apartment, he asked, "Do we still celebrate your birthday tonight?"

"Yes. As soon as you change your clothes, I want to go someplace," she said, wishing she had an umbrella.

"Good we celebrate," he said, seeming preoccupied.

"Who are those men you were talking to?" she asked stepping around a puddle.

"Old friends," he said cheerfully.

"They didn't look very friendly to me. They looked like a couple gangsters, trying to rob you. Karl, what were you arguing about?"

"It was nothing."

"Did you know them in Czechoslovakia?"

"Cassy, what does it matter? Yes, I knew them. Now, tonight we celebrate, and tomorrow I will not work. Just think: It will be Sunday all day tomorrow!"

Laughing, she said, "I wish it would be Sunday every day, so you wouldn't have to work."

At the apartment, he put on a white shirt, black tie, and a dark worsted suit. After she helped him into his black raincoat, they left for Hotel Sacher. However, because the wind was stronger and the rain had changed to snow, he said "Let's go to closer restaurant. I have good idea. Let's go to Maxim's."

"In Paris? Okay, let's go!"

"No. Maxim's here. Next time, Paris."

At Maxim's, they drank wine, ate Schnitzel, and watched the floorshow, a ballet with topless women dancing to Strauss waltzes. Laughing, Cassy said, "That's a long way up from my dancing topless at that nightclub, Whispers."

"I have not seen you dance, so I cannot compare, Cassy. I'm glad I didn't see you!"

When the show ended, Karl, with a worried look, said, "I love you, and I do not want anything happen to you."

Seeing his mood, she asked, "What's the matter? You haven't been the same since talking to those men on the street."

Evading, he smiled and said, "So, we have seen our first snow together. Very big juicy flakes. Sign of good luck!"

Seeing tears gathering in his eyes, she said, "Karl, tell me what's wrong."

"I wished to give you flowers and a gift for your birthday and I forgot."

"You gave me this dress, remember? That's not it. There's something very wrong that you're not telling me about."

"You must go home!" he blurted out.

Pouting, she said, "But it's early yet."

"I mean home, to America."

"Are you serious?"

"My love," he said. "Listen to what I say, and be calm."

"Be calm? You want to get rid of me and you tell me to be calm?"

"Cassy, you must listen and believe me. There is much danger here for you. I was not truthful, before. The men you saw me with are not my friends. They are my enemies. They want me to help them. They want for me to keep you like prisoner, until your father sends them money. They are Czechs, that is true—but they are not my friends."

"You're talking about getting ransom from my father?"

"Yes, they work for a man called Herr Bird. I don't think that is his real name. I've heard about him. He is a cruel and evil man who takes people in order to buy weapons, to sell to terrorists."

"Why me?"

"Because you are beautiful young woman. They take many young women. If they cannot get money from parents, they sell the women to evil and lustful people."

"I can't believe this!" she said, hitting her forehead with the palm of her hand. "If what you say is true, why not go to the police?"

Tearfully, he said, "If I do, my mother and sister will be killed. The same, if I don't help them take you, they will be killed."

"Karl, I'm sorry. It just doesn't make sense. If I do what you say and go to America, won't your mother and sister be killed, and you too?"

"I will say that you ran away, because I beat you."

"Oh God, you better come up with something better than that," she said, looking in his eyes for truth. "Karl, did you know about this in America, and did you let me come here, so you could use me?"

"No!" he said, taking her hand. "You must believe it. I will tell what I know, but let's go from here, first."

Outside and walking on a slippery sidewalk, she took his arm and said, "Tell me everything."

"The man called Bird, I think, has many connections in America and maybe everywhere in the world. When you were dancing in that place, two men saw you and found out you are from rich home. They were going to take you, but when they found out that you would be in Vienna with me, they waited."

Suspicious, she asked, "How do you know all this?"

"From the men that you saw me with tonight."

"Did they say who the two men at the nightclub are?"

"No."

"I wish now that you came to see me dance. Maybe now you'd know those two men at the nightclub."

"I didn't go to nightclub, because I didn't want to see you dance naked in front of other men."

"Then why did you let me take the job, in the first place?"

Thoughtfully, he said, "I wanted you to do what you wished. I wanted for you to feel like democratic woman. I didn't want to act like dictator."

Thoughtfully, she said, "If I go home, I might be kidnapped there. If I stay here with you, maybe I'd have a better chance. I don't care. I'm staying with you. I surely don't want to be kidnapped, but I also don't want your mother and sister killed."

"But…"

"I'm not leaving you, Karl, and that's that! We'll see this through together. Let's go to the apartment, get some things and run. Then we can have the police or someone protect your mother and sister."

"I don't think it will work. Let's go to apartment and talk about it more."

Arriving at the apartment, they were greeted by three men. The two just inside the door were the ones that Karl had been arguing with earlier. The third was sitting in an armchair, laughing now and saying, "You should lock your door. No tellin' who will come in."

"Jerks like you, you mean!" Cassy said angrily.

"Ah, yes, American women!" the sitting-one said, lighting a long cigar. "Their ass is always on fire!"

"You sound like an American," she said, squinting destruction at him, as she noticed the rhinestones on his black leather suit. "Who are you, and what do you want?"

Removing the black leather cap from his shining bald head, he said, "Let me introduce myself. My name is Bird."

"Bird?" she asked, chuckling. "You look more like a maggot!"

Laughing, he replaced the cap and, gesturing towards the sofa, said, "Have a seat, you two youngsters. We have some important things to discuss." Then, when they hesitated, he said in German, "Okay, sit'em down!"

Karl sat without a struggle, but Cassy jerked away, shouting in broken German, "Leave me alone!"

Karl said: "Please, don't hurt her. You don't have to hurt her."

"Let her stand, if she wants to," Bird said. Then, laughing again, he looked at Cassy and said, "With all that fire in your ass, I just might keep you for myself—that is, if your daddy doesn't come through with the bread. And, from what I hear, he just might not. You don't get along with your daddy, do you, beautiful?"

By the window now, watching the falling snow being illuminated by light from streetlamps, she said, "That's none of your damn business!"

Putting his burning cigar next to Karl's face, Bird, grinning with rotten teeth, said, "If I was you, Karl, I'd cooperate. All I gotta do is make a call to a certain party in Prague, and your mother and sister are gone."

"Leave him alone!" Cassy yelled.

"Don't get sassy, Cassy!" Bird said, going to her. "I might just take your pants down and spank you. Maybe you'd enjoy that—would you?"

"You're a sicko!" she said with loathing.

Karl said: "Cassy, be careful. He'll kill us."

"Karl's absolutely right," Bird said, removing a small photograph from inside his leather jacket. "And if you don't believe I'd kill you, then take a look at this. Come on, honey, move your sweet ass a little and look!"

"I don't want to look!"

"Don't be stubborn all your life," he said, getting closer. "Come see what happens to girls who don't cooperate. Come on—look!"

"I don't want to!"

"Don't want to! Don't want to! That's what this little pussy in the picture kept saying probably and look what it got her—cut and dead, man. Look—maybe she was a friend of yours."

Looking at the picture, she saw the nude body of a young woman lying in a pool of blood. Looking at Bird, she yelled: "You murdered her!"

"Did you recognize her? She was from Michigan, too."

"She was just like me, and you murdered her!"

"You'll end up like her, if you don't cooperate."

"You monster!" she yelled, swinging her fist and catching the side of his face, knocking the cigar from his mouth.

The two Czechs were quick. They grabbed her arms, and the bigger one asked in broken German. "Herr Bird, want us to tie her up?"

Rubbing the side of his head while he picked up his cigar, Bird said, "Yes, tie her up and put a piece of tape over her big mouth. Then put her on the couch with asshole."

Taking a roll of duct tape from his pocket, the smaller man taped her mouth, while the other one jerked her arms behind her and tied her wrists together with rope. Then, throwing her down next to Karl, one of them asked, "How about him?"

"Do we have to do the same to you, Karl?" Bird asked.

"No," Karl said, pushing hair from Cassy's eyes.

"Good," Bird said, looking at the telephone. "I will need you to make a call to her daddy."

## chapter 21

CASSY eventually fell asleep and was taken to the chartered plane, accompanied by a doctor that Richard had selected. Richard, Marsha and I followed the ambulance, and in about an hour, we were in Salzburg. With the doctor still with her on the plane, the plane took off for Paris, and the rest of us checked into the Goldener Hirsch Hotel. A little later on, the three of us went out to eat. It was the evening after the ordeal in Vienna.

The moon was full and silver and the stars were gold as they flickered in a darkening, blue sky. At the Winkler Haus, high above ancient Salzburg, a small orchestra played "Wine, Women and Song" by Johann Strauss II. Eating Schnitzel Parisien and drinking Gumpholzkirkner wine, we were silent, until Richard said, "It's still not too late for you two to pull out of this mess."

"We wouldn't think of leaving you here alone to enjoy it all by yourself," I said, chuckling a little.

"No, we wouldn't think of leaving you, old chap," Marsha said.

Serious now, I said, "Besides, there's the memory of what happened to my niece, Gabrielle, and what has happened—and is happening—to so many other young women."

After ordering coffee and lighting his pipe, Richard asked, "Anne, have you told Marsha what you and Halona are doing for ill-treated women?"

"She knows," I said. Then, fanning smoke away, I said, "Richard, would you stop blowing smoke at me!"

"I second the motion!" Marsha said.

"It's a conspiracy!" Richard said, placing his pipe in an ashtray. Then, after dishes were collected and coffee served, he lit his pipe again, saying, "You wouldn't want me to get nicotine fits, would you?"

"Just don't blow the smoke in my face!" I said.

"I didn't intentionally blow the bloody smoke in your face," he said, fanning his smoke away.

"I love it, when you two fight," Marsha said, laughing.

Returning the pipe to the ashtray, Richard said, "Let us put our irritations aside and get down to business."

"Let's..." Marsha said.

"Why are we here, Richard?" I asked.

"Well, first, I believe we're dealing with a small group, or cell, which is part of a subculture of thousands of such groups throughout the world who will do anything to finance their political causes—kidnapping, drug-smuggling—you name it. And the subculture is like a giant, regenerating lizard. A part may be cut off, but in a very short time, it is repaired. On another front, however, we may be dealing with a supplier group, whose only cause is to make money, by whatever means, and use some of it to buy material to sell to more violent groups."

"I told you about Bosinger," Marsha said. "His group seems to be connected to one, or more, over here."

Richard asked, "Marsha, are you certain Bosinger doesn't know that you were with CIA?"

"I'm not certain of anything," Marsha said, finishing her coffee.

"Richard, have you heard from Sepp about Karl?" I asked.

"Not a word. Sepp knows where we're staying. When Karl wakes up, Sepp will call."

"If Karl wakes up," Marsha said. Then, looking at me, she said, "I don't want to get shitty, Richard, but you didn't answer Anne's question as to why we're here."

"Waiting," he said.

"That's it?" I asked.

"You know, you can be unnerving at times," Marsha said. "As I said in Vienna, the kidnappers have the money, so why would they come looking for us?"

"You see," he said smiling. "They don't have the money. There wasn't a bloody penny in those bloody bags."

"What are you saying?" Marsha asked.

"Only that the satchels were filled with old newspapers. The money is still in the bank."

"Mon Dieux!" I said, closing my eyes. "You could have told us sooner."

The orchestra was now playing, "Tales From the Vienna Woods."

"Let's get the hell out of here!" Marsha said, her eyes on fire.

"What's the hurry?" Richard asked, chuckling.

"Never mind the bullshit!" Marsha said. "Let's go!"

We rode the elevator down, and once we were on the street, we headed for the hotel, slow-going because of the evening crowd in Mozart Platz. When we finally reached the hotel and went to our adjoining rooms, we saw the mess. Clothes were on the floor, along with bedding. Mattresses had been cut open, tables and chairs had been overturned. Looking in our room and Richard's, I said, "We've been invaded by wild animals."

Angrily pursing her lips, Marsha said: "The rotten bastards!"

Coming in from his adjoining room, Richard said, "The police will want fingerprints. We'll go elsewhere for the night. Leave everything but your toothbrush and flimsies."

"Flimsies?" I said. "You can do better than that, Richard."

"Flimsies?" Marsha asked. "What are we—a couple burlesque queens?"

"You'll be dead queens, perhaps, if you don't hurry!" he said, standing in the doorway with his toothbrush and a tin of tobacco.

Once in the lobby, Richard told the clerk not to touch anything until after the police lifted fingerprints. Then, on our way in a taxi, he told the driver to cross over the Salzach and take the street that runs behind the Mirabell Gardens. "I'll tell you when to stop," he said then.

"You speak the Austrian dialect pretty good," Marsha said, "Who taught you, Richard?"

"His Austrian girlfriends," I said.

"When he helped them out of their flimsies?" Marsha asked.

"My ladies don't wear flimsies," he said. "They wear nothing but smiles of satisfaction."

"I wish that was all I had to wear," I said.

Nearing the Mirabell Gardens and the Mozarteum next to it, Richard said, "I suppose you'd like to visit with your son, Anne, but…"

"I know," I said, with tears filling my eyes. "You don't think it would be a good idea and neither do I."

Turning to the driver, he said, "Stop!"

Going into a small hotel located behind the Mirabell Gardens, Marsha and I sat in the lobby, close to the desk, in front of which Richard was now standing, saying, "Hello, Julian."

"Hello, Richard," the greying, middle-aged clerk said. "When are you going to retire?"

"I'll retire when you do," Richard said, smiling warmly

"Then it will be soon," Julian said seriously.

"Soon for me, too," Richard said. "Believe me, Julian."

"Believe you? That'll be a day to mark, when I believe you." Then, looking around—no doubt to see if there was anyone else in the lobby other than Marsha and me, which there wasn't—he said, "By the way, Sepp called and said Karl is still unconscious. Sepp also said to watch out for Herr Bird-- that he's on his way here."

"We'll get the bastard and gather information about some terrorists, maybe," Richard said, about to sign the register.

Pulling the register away, Julian said, "Not a good idea. Don't register any names."

Smiling, Richard said, "Owl, you'll never change. You're always alert."

Smiling, Julian said, "You and me together again, just like old times, Big Ben." Then, when an older couple came in the front door, he said loudly, "Thank you, sir. As soon as your luggage comes, I'll have it brought up. I hope you and your daughters find everything satisfactory."

Continuing to use English, Richard asked, "Where's the lift?"

"It's out of order," Julian said, smiling with irony. "You'll have to walk up."

"Well," Richard said, looking at the keys. "At this time of night, walking up three flights of stairs is not very satisfying."

Putting his large, gnarled hand over his mouth, as if to stifle laughter, Julian said, "Jo jo," which I knew was Austrian for "Yes yes."

"Jo jo, your arse!" Richard said, signaling then for Marsha and me to join him.

Climbing the stairs, Richard talked about Julian's use of the word jo and what Julian had been trying to unleash, that being probably memories of when they'd worked together in Austria. "Jo," Richard said, "is an Austrian colloquialism for the German word ja, or yes, and we used it in the early Fifties." He went on to say then, that Vienna, like Berlin, had been separated into political zones, and he and Julian had worked undercover as thieves and scoundrels, dealing in the black market, peddling dope and doing a lot of other shady things. It had been no big deal for Richard, after what he'd been doing before, such as fighting in the Norwegian Resistance and then in the French Resistance. In fact, his Vienna days were fun, he said, especially after connecting with Austrian operative, Julian Maier, with whom he caroused and gathered information by frequenting the bars, mostly. Yes, Owl and Big Ben were quite a team, and especially good with prostitutes, with whom they never slept but did business of a different sort, which had to do with identification cards and tags. When prostitutes stole ID's from allied soldiers, in order to sell them to the Russians, then Julian and Richard would buy them, first. And then, in the early Sixties, they uncovered a plot to assassinate Khrushchev at a time when Khrushchev and Kennedy were working on a plan that would ease tensions between the two world powers. America would sell wheat to Russia which would help feed a lot of people and help the Balance of Payments at the same time. That was just before Kennedy was assassinated, when a young Hungarian woman asked Julian to supply some M1 carbines. "Richard," Julian had said. "I told the woman jo jo, and she kissed me and bit my lips." And then Richard had said, "You should know better. Hungarian women always bite you when they kiss you, if you say jo jo to them." Julian didn't supply the carbines, of course, and they helped apprehend the would-be assassins. But not without a price, for in the course of the arrest, Julian was shot in the stomach, and when he recovered, he was reassigned away from Richard. And Richard, whose cover was blown away, was retired by British Intelligence and soon after that, he was employed by the CIA.

And now, at the top of the stairway, Richard talked about our rooms, saying, "My room is here, with one bed. Yours, I imagine, has two beds.

Let's go see." Going then to the end of the hallway, he opened our door and said, "Yes, two beds, but the fire escape is too close, I think. It's close enough for someone to come in and grab you. You wouldn't like that would you?"

"Depends on who's doing the grabbing," Marsha said.

"Do you want other arrangements?" he asked, serious.

"We'll be okay," Marsha said, yawning.

"Marsha has a gun," I said.

"Well," he said, smiling. "In that case, if someone does grab you, you can enjoy it or shoot the bastard. Where is the weapon?"

Teasing up her skirt a little, Marsha said, "I suppose you want me to go all the way."

"Yes, let's have a look."

"No way!" she said, dropping her skirt. "My mother told me that I should never show my legs, when there's a gun strapped to one of them."

Shaking his head and smiling, he left our room, saying, "I'll be downstairs talking to Julian." And, so he told us later, when he got there, he found it deserted, including the bar. After pulling out his gun, he began to search for Julian. Eventually, in the supply room behind the bar, he found his old friend lying on his back near several cases of empty wine bottles. Bending over his friend, he said, "Julian."

"Look out, Richard!" Julian said weakly, obviously in pain.

Suddenly a hulk came smashing down on Richard, knocking the gun from his hand and leaving him pinned under a pile of stinking flesh, leather and denim. "Where's the money?" the stinking creature asked in American English.

Managing to look up, according to Richard, he saw that, besides having dark, teary eyes and a flabby mouth, the man had a jumbo-size bag of muscles. He was dressed in black denim, with a black leather jacket that had rhinestones all over it, gleaming white and forming phallic-like elongations. His face was stubbled with beard, and his bald head was shining bright, even in the dim light. Richard, whose throat was now in the grip of a large hand covered with a black, leather, fingerless glove, struggled to say, "Allow me to get up and I'll get the money." Then, after he was released, Richard got to his feet, opened his wallet and said, "Sorry, old chap, all I have is twenty Schillings, but you're welcome to it."

Slapping the wallet from Richard's hand, the man repeated: "Where's the money?"

Knowing the man was American by his accent, and by the way he swaggered, Richard said, "It's a bloody shame that they allow guttersnipes like you into a nice country such as this. Who in the bloody hell are you?"

"My name is Bird, and nobody calls me a guttersnipe and gets away with it!" he said bitterly. Grabbing an empty wine bottle then, he broke it off at the neck and lunged at Richard.

"Hold on, friend!" Richard yelled, easily dodging the glass weapon. Then, after kicking Bird in the face, he said, "Now, that should improve your appearance, Herr Bird."

Spitting blood, Bird said, "You goddamn limey—you'll pay!" Pulling out a switchblade knife then, Bird shouted: "Where you want it, limey?"

Richard, not seeing his gun in the dim light, nor having enough time to retrieve it, if he did see it, did the best he could. When Bird came at him with the knife, he grabbed Bird's arm and, locking it in his arms, snapped it at the elbow. Picking up the knife, Richard said, "Sorry."

"You busted my goddamn arm!" Bird squealed.

Just then, Julian picked up the gun and held it to Bird's head, saying in English: "Down!" And after Bird was on the floor, Julian said, "Richard, you take the gun. Give me the knife. Go check on the women."

After exchanging weapons, Richard hurried upstairs and down the hallway to our room. Seeing the door ajar, he went inside, holding his gun in front of him, and saw Marsha and me standing over the two men who were lying prostrate on the floor. With her gun in her hand, Marsha said, "We've got company."

"Shall I come back later?" Richard asked, chuckling.

Speaking loudly, Marsha asked, "What should we do with them?"

Winking at us, Richard said, "Shoot them!"

"No, please don't shoot us!" the bigger man said in broken English.

"Shoot us!" the smaller man said.

Putting the gun to the head of the one who had begged for his life, Richard said, "I detect a Czech accent."

"Yes, we are refugees from Czechoslovakia. Do you speak Czechoslovak?"

Continuing in English, Richard asked, "What are you doing here?"

"Money," the big man said. "We came for the money we have earned."

"Who do you work for?" Richard asked.

"We work for an American who calls himself Herr Bird. He is downstairs."

"Who does Bird work for?"

"We know of only Herr Bird—believe this! There are people in America, but we do not know them."

Looking at Marsha and me, Richard said, "We'll have them sent to Germany for more interrogation."

"Please—no Germany!"

Moving towards the open door, Richard said, "I'm going down to see how Julian's doing. Before I leave, however, let's lock these two in the bathroom."

"There's no lock," I said.

"We'll make do," Richard said, motioning with his gun for the two men to get inside the bathroom, and once they were in and the door was closed, we pushed a bed against the door. On his way out then, Richard said, "If you've gotta go, hold it—right?"

"No way!" Marsha said. "I'll use your bathroom."

"Don't separate from each other, ladies!"

"I've gotta go, right now!" I said.

"So do I," Marsha said, jumping up and down.

"Goodbye friends. Good luck! And don't hesitate to shoot them, if they act up."

"I won't" Marsha said.

"I wonder how many other women they've kidnapped," I said, "And how many young men, like Karl."

"We'll find out," Richard said, leaving the room.

And as we found out, once he was back downstairs, he saw that things were just about as they were before, with Julian holding the knife to Bird's throat as Bird squealed in pain. However, as he got closer, Richard saw that things were not the same. Julian was holding his chest and was having a hard time breathing. "Julian, what's the matter?" he asked, putting a hand on Julian's shoulder.

"My heart," Julian said, before passing out.

Catching his friend and letting him down easy, Richard put his coat under his head and, picking up the knife, said, "Bird, come with me—hurry!"

Looking into the barrel of Richard's gun, Bird quit squealing, got to his feet and said, "I need a doctor, too."

"You'll need an undertaker, if you don't hurry and do what I tell you!" Richard said, taking off Bird's belt and fastening it tight around his neck. Then, leading him, as if he were a dog on a leash, Richard went up to the desk and telephoned Dr. Reindl, designated by the CIA as a "safe doctor" to be called in an emergency in the Salzkammergut area. And Richard knew well that the Company was emphatic about calling such a doctor, when an agent was involved, just in case the agent, while unconscious, might give out the names of other agents. Reaching the doctor now, and being assured that he'd come soon, Richard locked Bird in a small utility closet and hurried to Julian, who was conscious again, asking, "Is the doctor coming?"

"Dr. Reindl is on the way," Richard said, adjusting the coat he'd put under Julian's head.

"Good," Julian said, clutching his chest and closing his eyes. "I think it's just a mild one, Richard."

"We'll see."

Soon, the doctor arrived with an ambulance and took Julian away. Richard , after calling a taxi for Bird's ride to the hospital, went to the utility closet. With his gun drawn, he opened the door and discovered that Bird wasn't there, that he'd escaped by way of an air vent at the bottom of a wall, that had been enlarged to accommodate his body. Looking for the chiseling tool, he found a metal handle that had been removed from a pail. Richard guessed now as to where Bird had flown to, and decided he'd gone through the kitchen and out the back door. But he had guessed wrongly, for just as he went to check outside the back door, he heard two loud gunshots. With sickening waves of anxiety running through him, he hurried upstairs and ran down the dimly-lit hallway, until he saw what was left of Bird. Sprawled on the floor outside of our room, with a kitchen knife by his side, Bird lay there with much of his head blown off. Looking through the door now, Richard found Marsha and me sitting on one of the beds staring at Bird and crying. Marsha, with her gun still in her hand, said tearfully, "After that experience with Schmidt in Bordeaux, I prayed that I'd never have to kill anyone again."

"He came at us with a butcher's knife," I said, knowing through experience how Marsha felt.

"Are the other two still in the bathroom?" Richard asked.

"Yes," I said.

Richard called his police contact and told him to pick up Bird's corpse and the two Czechoslovaks, saying then that the Czechoslovaks should be held until he, or a representative, contacted him. Next, he called Klaus von Thalhofen and asked him to make arrangements for the two Czechs to be taken to Bonn, Germany for further questioning. Last, he asked Marsha to call George Bolton, so the F.B.I. could pick up Bosinger and his associates. Soon after the phone calls, the Austrian police arrived, and soon after that, we returned to the Goldener Hirsch Hotel, where we got new adjoining rooms and went to bed, slept a few hours, and then went to see Julian at the hospital.

"I'm getting too old for this kind of stuff!" Julian said, sitting up in bed with his eyes opened wide, like an owl's.

"So am I," Richard said, adjusting the pillow behind Julian's back. "It's time we both got married and settled."

"Who's the unfortunate lady that you're going to marry?" Julian asked.

"Some floozy, with flimsy undergarments," I said.

"And so, what happened to the nappers?" Julian asked.

"Bird is dead, and the others have been spirited off to Bonn," Richard said.

"Just like the old days, Big Ben," Julian said, dozing off.

"Just like the old days, Owl," Richard said, kissing his friend's forehead. "Jo jo."

About three in the afternoon, after a short nap, we took a shower, with Marsha showering last and returning to find me hanging up the phone. "Who were you talking to?" she asked, her long blonde hair not looking so blonde now as it hung all over her face. Then, as she started dressing, she said, "You don't have to tell me, if you don't want to."

"Why shouldn't I tell you?" I asked, sitting on my bed in a blue terrycloth robe, with a towel wrapped around my head. "I called Halona." Then, after loosening the towel and going to stand in the sun coming in the windows, I started drying my hair with the towel, while saying, "Halona said that Cassy is better, and that she keeps asking for Karl."

"What did Halona tell Cassy?"

"The truth, that he's still unconscious," I said. "Cassy wants to go to him."

"Maybe it would be best if she did see him," she said, pulling down a white turtleneck sweater over her head.

Continuing to towel my hair in the sun, I asked, "Have you called her parents?"

"It's only been a couple days, since we left. You have to be careful with her parents…"

There was a knocking coming from the door between Richard and us. Peeking in from the adjoining room, Richard asked, "Can I come in, or shall I wait until you're naked?"

"Come in and feast your eyes," Marsha said, zipping up the side of her red plaid skirt.

Entering, he looked at me and said, "I love to watch women drying their hair in the sun."

"Pervert!" I said, noticing he had shaved and put on his brown sweater and knickerbockers.

"What can we do for you?" Marsha asked. "Or did you just come in to spy on us?"

"I want to update you ladies."

"So, update!" Marsha said, sitting down on my bed.

Richard sat in a chair by me and said, "First of all, Karl is awake and doing fine, so says Sepp. Second, Bird was indeed an American. His legal name: Mervin Fester. But more about him later…."

"As soon as possible," I said, "I want to know all about him."

"Why the extra-interest?" Marsha asked.

Stopping with my hair, I sat next to Marsha and said, "I want to get close to someone like him. I want to be able to see what's in his mind and soul. Along with Halona and J'nine, it's part of my life's work. That's what we do. Ever since Gabrielle died at the hands of one of those monsters, we've dedicated ourselves."

Taking his pipe out of his pocket, and then putting back in, Richard said, "Anne, when we go eat, I'll call and try to find out more about Fester. Right now, though, I'd better step out of the room, so you can put on your armor."

Watching him leave, Marsha said, "Richard, please, don't try to be funny. It doesn't become you."

Chuckling as he went, he said, "You'll find me in the bar, drinking, smoking and telling jokes."

We were eating omelets at the Glockenspiel Restaurant, and after the Glockenspiel bells in the tower across the street chimed the hour of four, Marsha said, "Richard, your work seems to have taken on a new dimension, in helping women help other women."

With no hesitation, he said, "My dear, it's a grave matter, and I'll treat it as such. It's a matter of subversion, and that's where I come in. Subversion affects all people in free countries, not only women. You see, I consider it to be my duty to protect the freedom of choice that we have within our intrastructure, which is intrinsic in a democracy, and very vulnerable. Sorry to say, those who would subvert this freedom of choice have made swift and insidious progress. In their untiring quest for power, they already control far too much money and power, and far too many minds."

I said, "I'm thinking of my niece, Gabrielle. Since her death, I've been doing all I can to help vulnerable women who have lost, or are losing, their freedom of choice."

Marsha said, "Otto Schmidt comes to mind, and his controlling drugs."

Richard said, "Drugs aren't the only things used to control minds. There are psychological methods and procedures. It's depressing. I wish I could do more. For years, I've been gathering information, dissembling it to some and passing on the so-called real thing to others. Lately, however, something inside me wants to connect with something else—with the spirit of goodness left in the world, which I consider, more and more, to be the real thing of life. And I feel, without a doubt, that I must get the connection with good and honest people, like yourselves."

Seeing tears gathering in his eyes and not wanting to embarrass him, I turned to Marsha and said, "I called my son, Matthew, but he wasn't home. I think he's busy with his girlfriend."

"Better call again," Marsha said. "We'll be leaving for Paris in the morning."

"I'll call from Paris," I said.

"I'll be leaving for Norway in the morning," Richard said.

"One more night in the beautiful city." Marsha said, looking out the window.

"Just enough time for a roll-in-the-hay with Anne," Richard said, laughing.

"Shame on you, Richard!" I said, somewhat embarrassed.

"Do you think you could handle it, old chap?" Marsha asked.

"Make that two rolls-in-the-hay," Richard said.

Putting my hands over my ears, I said, "Disgusting—really!" But, of course, these words and my theatrical show of contempt only belied what was inside me—that being, a whole lot of lustful throbbing of the mind and blood.

Fortunately, before I began panting like a dog in heat, Richard got up and said, "You two have some pastry, while I go to the post office and make some calls."

As we watched him go, Marsha said, "You love him, don't you?"

"Yes," I said, seeing him stumble on the cobblestone road and almost fall.

Marsha said, "He stumbles, but does he ever fall?"

I said, "He says he loves me, but…"

"Do you want to marry him?"

"Marsha, I don't know. I've been too busy to think about marriage. Maybe, eventually, if he retires."

"Good luck…"

A pretty waitress came and took our orders for Salzburger Nockerl with vanilla sauce, and just as the dessert arrived, we saw Richard returning. When he stubbed his toe again, I said, "Clumsy creature, isn't he?"

He came in, sat down, said: "They ran Mervin Fester, a.k.a. Herr Bird, through, and it seems that in the Fifties he was in the army stationed in Germany. He was an ordinance supply sergeant and managed to take his discharge in Germany. Now, as for Charles Bosinger, he was arrested in Toledo, Ohio, along with his friends, Keith Stoltz and Chappell "Cappy" Duggan. Bosinger and Fester were first cousins. Fester was never arrested, and Bosinger was arrested once and not convicted for dealing in illegal firearms. That's it for now, ladies."

"Nothing about a political cause?" Marsha asked.

"As far as I know, their only cause was getting money," Richard said.

"I'm somewhat disappointed," Marsha said. "Bosinger talked about a cause, although he didn't say what it was, and I got the impression that he was willing to die for that cause."

Richard said, "I suppose getting money, for some, is a cause in itself, and they must feel that there's something romantic about it. It puts a feeling of power and importance into their dull lives. However, they are not to be underestimated, for the cunning persistence and know-how involved is substantial. And then: They must be sympathetic to subversive causes, for them to supply weapons of destruction."

"Dull!" Marsha said, eating her portion of the Salzburger Nockerl. "They are still dull, dull, dull!"

Richard said, after dipping his finger in my dessert sauce and putting it in his mouth, "Dull becomes insignificant. It's the destructiveness of the Dulls that becomes the issue, and the dimensions of that destructiveness."

"Keep your fingers out of my dessert!" I said, looking at Richard and frowning.

"Richard, you're disgusting!" Marsha said.

"All right, Kittens—or is it cats?—let's return to the hotel. I could use a bit of a nap."

"You go and have your nap. Anne and I are going shopping—aren't we, Anne?"

"Definitely shopping!" I said seriously. Then, looking at Richard, I asked, "Would you like some help, walking back to the hotel?"

"Yes, as a matter of fact, I would," he said, smiling. "The cobblestones out there are treacherous."

"So we noticed," Marsha said, laughing.

We took his arms then and escorted him all the way to his bed and, after throwing a cover over him, we tucked him in. After returning to our room, we decided that shopping wasn't such a good idea, after all, so we retired to our beds for another nap. However, I didn't sleep. When Marsha seemed to be asleep, I seized the moment and joined Richard.

With all the hate in the world, who wouldn't crave a little love—a lot of love?

## chapter 22

Her long hair was shining and her blue eyes were clear and bright. She wore a light blue dress, with white lace gracing her long neck. Holding a bottle of orange soda, she sat down in an armchair in Halona's living room, and after a sip of soda, said, "I was taking a nap and had a nice dream."

Alone with her, Marsha and I smiled at Cassy, and Marsha asked, "What was the dream about?"

"I dreamt that my bells returned to me, even if it isn't spring," Cassy said, taking another sip.

"Bells?" Marsha asked.

Recalling what Cassy had told me at the hospital, I said, "She was born with bells in her blood. Isn't that what you told me, Cassy?"

"I see," Marsha said. "What about the dream?"

"I dream a lot," I said.

"You do?" Cassy asked.

"I sure do," I said. "Some dreams I like, some I don't."

"Well, this one I liked," Cassy said, putting the soda bottle between her legs. "I dreamt I was in this dark forest, and that I couldn't move because my feet were stuck. And then I got this weird feeling, that this was where I was born, and the place of my childhood. It was the weirdest feeling I ever felt. Did either of you ever dream something like that?"

After Marsha and I said no, Marsha asked, "What happened next?"

"You really want to know?"

"We really want to know," I said.

"Okay, well, here goes: When my feet were stuck there in the dark forest, the coolest thing happened. The bells I was born with began to ring, and for the first time ever, I told myself that I was beautiful. And then all of a sudden, bright rays of sun started coming down through the trees and settling on me, just me—like I was dancing naked on a stage, and they were the spotlights. I began to feel warm and strong and I had this clean feeling, like I'd just taken a bath. And then there was like beauty and harmony inside me, like I was a spring flower and my bells were singing to me. Then, as if that wasn't weird enough, a really strong breeze came along and lifted me up above the dark forest and held me there, while it whispered to me, over and over: 'You are a woman. You are a woman.' And then I could feel and hear all the liquid in my body moving faster and faster, and I could feel my head throbbing with pain, like my brain was expanding too much. But I didn't mind the pain, because somehow I knew I'd be a better person when the pain stopped. And it did stop, and when my bells picked up tempo, I felt even more clean and beautiful and harmonious. And I told myself again that I was beautiful, and then I knew for sure that I really was. And after that moment, my bells began to ring soft-like, ever so soft, like they'd ring like that forever…. You must think that's weird, right?"

"I sure do," Marsha said. "I guess that's why I love it."

"I love it, too," I said, feeling like crying and not knowing why.

Laughing, Cassy said, "That's exactly the way I feel about it. I love it. I knew you'd understand. When I was with Karl and told my dreams, he understood too and loved them."

"Have you been in contact with Karl?" Marsha asked.

"I talked to him yesterday. I told him I'm going to stay here in France and study—just like you did, Miss Lowden."

"Marsha," Marsha said. "Please call me Marsha, and I'm sure Anne here wants you to call her Anne. What did Karl say when you told him that you're going to stay here?"

"He said he'd come visit, if I wanted him to. I said I'd let him know about the visit."

I asked, "Do you think your parents will agree to your staying here to study?"

"Anne, I don't care if they agree, or not. I'm eighteen, and I'm staying!"

Watching her sip from the soda bottle again, I thought of her bells of spring—the bells of renewal sounding and resounding in her life, perhaps in order to silence the echoes of a maddening youth, caused by her parents' defilement of love. And now, with tears escaping and running down my face, I thought of my own life, with its discordant measures of doubt, dreams unfulfilled, regrets recurring, undertones of dishonesty—a life left unattuned. "I'm sorry," I said, seeing Cassy staring at me. "It looks like someone turned on the waterworks without my permission."

Coming to me and putting her arms around me, Cassy said, "I don't know what you're crying about, but whatever it is, you don't have to be ashamed to cry in front of me. Go right ahead and bawl your eyes out."

"I'm all right now," I said, drying my eyes with a handkerchief.

"Let's get out of here for awhile. Let's get some fresh air," Marsha said.

We put our coats on and left. Walking then along the Seine, Cassy said, "You know, Marsha, it's like I've known you all my life. I always wanted to meet you. I guess it's because we have something in common."

Marsha asked, "You mean, because I was married to your father?"

"Yes, in a way, but mostly because of my mom. She says you were friends in school—were you?"

"Well, we went to the same high school, but we didn't become friends until just recently."

With her face hardening and her lips tightening, Cassy said, "At least she has one friend left."

"What do you mean?" Marsha asked.

"Marsha, you must know how she is. But once she was so nice and beautiful, until she became a hateful drunk, like now. Her eyes are all glazed most of the time and they have dark circles around them, and she has swollen lips and a bloated body—nothing like she was a few years ago. I used to get up for school, and it would be nice to see her. Then it all changed, and her hair was all puke lots of times in the morning, and some mornings, she'd be all wet where she'd peed herself. Oh man! And I can't forget the mornings I'd find her with her head in the toilet bowl, puking her guts out. And then I'd have to clean her and put her back to bed. Talk about weird—man, that's as weird as you can get!"

I asked, "Where was your father, when all this was going on?"

"My dad? He was already gone to work, or he wasn't home yet from shacking up with some whore."

Marsha said, "Your mother quit drinking, Cassy."

"Ha ha ha, tell me another one! She's quit lots of times, but she always starts up again. No way, I'm not ready to look at her drunken face again, and I don't think I'll ever be ready. You know, a girl shouldn't have to grow up seeing all that. I just pray my little sister Tiffany won't have to. I'm sorry, I just can't forgive either one of them for the things they did."

I asked, "Such as, when you brought Karl home to meet them?"

"That, and when my friend Sidney died. They didn't have one ounce of compassion, and I was really hurting. All they said is that I shouldn't be so upset for losing such an insignificant creature. Oh, man—they're the ones who're insignificant, that's for damn sure!"

"I'm sorry, Cassy," I said.

"Try not to be bitter," Marsha said.

We crossed the Seine at the Louvre and went into the Tuileries Gardens. Sitting on a bench near some autumn flowers, Cassy said, "Karl came into my life at the right time. He held me tight and told me that he loved me. I was broken, and he tried to fix me. We ran free together and didn't let our troubles get in the way. It was like moment flowing easy into moment. Know what I mean? Faith is probably what it was, and it was like faith needed nothing. Faith in each other is what it was, that we'd be good and honest and true for each other. We loved each other and it was cool and right. Can you understand?"

"Cassy..." I said.

"Oh, man, when Karl came into my life, I escaped from old Frank and Sheila without even trying. And I promised myself I'd never go back to them and their little game of breaking Cassy and trying to fix her by increasing her allowance. And that's what they did. They broke me, mentally and physically, but they never fixed me."

"Physically?" Marsha asked.

"Physically. I've got scars you wouldn't believe, like on my back. I'll show you sometime, if you want."

"There's a small scar on your chin..." Marsha said.

"That's from my mom's wedding ring, when she almost broke my jaw a couple years ago. My dad was in one of his better moods, and I was sitting on his lap in his armchair. She was drinking bad and she called me a little tramp and yelled for me to get off his lap—that I was too big for that kind of stuff. I refused and she hit me, and my dad didn't say a damn thing. He just left the house."

"Not surprising," Marsha said, as if to herself.

Looking up at the cloudy sky, with tears rolling down her cheeks, Cassy said, "That was nothing compared to her stabbing me in the back with a nailfile when I told her she was ugly from drinking too much. I had to go to the hospital and get a lot of stitches."

Marsha asked, "Did you tell anyone at the hospital what happened?"

"I told Dr. Garret, but I'm sure he covered it up. He was probably following orders from his wife, Josie, who doesn't want anybody to know things like that take place in Bloomfield."

"Did she do anything else to you?" Marsha asked.

"Just gave me a few other cuts and bruises along the way."

"Just cuts and bruises," I said, and then asked, "Did your father ever hit you, or do anything else bad to you?"

"Never. He never hurt me physically. He just told me all the time that I wasn't worth a small bag of shit, which was worse. You know, I think he said a lot of rotten things to me, because of my mom being so drunk and bitchy. Does that make sense?"

"Does it make sense to you?" I asked.

"I suppose so, in some weird way. You know, the scars on my back almost stopped me from getting a job in the nightclub, dancing, but when I told them I'd put a lot of makeup on, they said okay."

Seeing her shiver, I said, "It's getting cold. Shall we go back?"

"Okay," she said, smiling. Then, as she walked between Marsha and me, she held our arms, asking, "If you think you're in love, are you?"

"That's a tough question," I said.

Marsha, smiling, said, "If you're asking me, I'm afraid you're asking the wrong person on that subject. Wow, that's heavy stuff."

Laughing, Cassy said, "I know, but I just wanted some… input. You both have been in love, haven't you?"

I waited for Marsha's "input," and when nothing was put in, I said, "I am in love."

"But how do you know, for sure?" Cassy asked, squeezing my arm a little and smiling at me.

"Well," I said, completely unsure of my ground, "I can only tell you what I think, as of today, not yesterday, and maybe not tomorrow. I'll say that I think I'm in love, but somehow that doesn't seem to be enough. I'd like to say that my heart tells me so, but even that doesn't seem to be enough for me. I could say, that my heart agrees with my head, but that would be reason, I think, and love defies all reason. Cassy, I'm not good at this. Can I beg to be excused?"

"Sure."

"Why not ask Halona?" Marsha asked.

"I did," Cassy said. "Hey, no problem. I appreciate your honesty in telling me that you don't know any more about it than I do."

"What did Halona say—and how did you get into it with her, in the first place?" Marsha asked.

"She came to my room, checking to see if I was studying French literature. Well, she had this book in her hand, with the name Descartes on it. When I asked her who Descartes is, she said a lot of stuff I don't remember. But I do remember one thing: 'If I think I am, I am.' Then I asked her what I asked you: If you think you're in love, are you in love?"

"And?" Marsha asked.

Laughing, Cassy said, "Then things got a little hairy. She like choked up and said some big words, like oversimplification, which, after she left, I looked up and memorized. Anyway, then she got cool again and said that old Descartes was a dogmatic fool—dogmatic is another one I looked up and memorized, by the way. And then after she said the guy was a dogmatic fool, just like the other philosophers, I asked her why she teaches the stuff. Well, she said she just passes on what philosophers say, so that her students will be able to form their own philosophy better. And when she asked me if I thought I was in love with Karl, I said I think so, but I'm not going to make up my mind with a conclusion until after I study it and think about it some more, carefully. 'Well,' she said, with a funny smile on her face. 'Give us a chance and we'll help you learn how to study and think.' Then she just walked away, and I got mad because she hadn't told me anything about love—and with all her education, too! So, what do I do? I begin to think about it on my own, the best I can.

And it took me almost a whole hour to come up with the answer, that I'm like a baby that's too young to think it's in love, but feels it, naturally, and doesn't have to think about it. And then after thinking some more, I came up with the second part of the answer—the important part—the truth about myself. Do you want to hear it?"

"Of course we do," Marsha said.

"Well, here goes. A baby's love is mixed up with a lot of dependency, and I told myself I was just like that baby. I was dependent on Karl so much, that when he wasn't with me, I was devastated—cold, like dead, like I was after Sidney and my bells left me, and my parents rejected me. Anyway, my conclusion is that I must depend on myself to think for myself when making important decisions. You know, it was like my heart was screaming defiance all the time at my parents, and I felt I was a goner and would never make it, until Karl took me in, like I was a lost little puppy. Oh man, did I ever use him! I told you that we ran free together, but I know now that's not the truth, exactly. Now that I step back and look at it, I can see I imagined a lie in telling myself I was free."

Seeing tears fall on her blue coat, I said, "Someday, you and Karl can talk about it."

"I will. I just know I will. And I'm going to ask him to forgive me for using him. Do you think he knew I was using him?"

"You'd have to ask him," I said.

Wiping her eyes with a tissue, Cassy said, "Let's change the subject." Then, looking at Marsha, she asked, "Are you still with the CIA, Marsha? My father said you're a spy, and he told me to stay the hell away from you. Well, are you a spy?"

"I quit."

"You know, I think being a spy is cool. Why did you quit?"

"Because I don't have the heart for it. As for it being cool, I admit I thought about it that way, at first."

"It must be really exciting."

"It was exciting, but that's not the kind of excitement I want right now."

"Was it a mistake to work there?"

Smiling and shaking her head, Marsha said, "No, but if I stayed, feeling the way I did, then that would've been a mistake—a big one. As it stands now, I feel that I've learned some things about myself and, like you, I'm still learning. I'm going on to other things. You see, Cassy, it's trial-and-error with me, too."

"You know, Marsha, you're a good person, hang-ups and all."

"Why, thanks, Cassy. You're a good person, too, hang-ups and all."

Laughing, she looked from one of us to the other, saying, "I hope you'll be staying here."

"We'll be leaving tomorrow, Cassy," I said.

"Damn!" she said, letting go of our arms.

"What shall we tell your parents?" Marsha asked. "Maybe you should call and talk to them."

"No, I definitely don't want to talk to them. I'm not ready for that. Maybe I'll write a letter, and you could deliver it, personally. Would you?"

"Of course."

Arriving back at the apartment, Cassy went right to her room, after saying that she wanted to write the letter, "and get it over with."

Marsha and I waited for Halona to return from work and did some packing for our trip back to Michigan, where Marsha would resume her work as Foreign Relations Advisor for a television station and I would see about selling the house in Point Stevens.

And so the following day, after our au-revoirs, we left Paris, and once we were on our way, we read the letter Cassy had written, with her permission.

> *To my mother and father.*
> 
> *I'm going to stay in France and study. Don't try to interfere. It won't do you any good. I'm going to be with other women like me. We're going to study and look at our lives together. Rotten thoughts about you come into my head. I can't help that. But I can learn some good things, so those rotten thoughts will be pushed out of the way. I hate you. I had a dream in which I was beautiful and didn't hate anybody. I want to be like I was in the dream. Who wouldn't? The people here are good to me. But it's not all fun and games. They make me study and eat good and fix myself up. But they are not mean to me when I forget sometimes. They are reasonable. They make me feel wanted. You made me feel unwanted. I hope and pray that you aren't*

doing that to Tiffany. The people here are rich but not greedy like you. And they are not full of oversimplification either. They take time to explain things good and don't call me stupid when I don't understand right away. I used to feel like puking when you told me things and acted like I should have known them in my cradle. Talking about puking, I was always puking. There wasn't a day that went by, when I didn't puke. I was scared all the time. That's why. I wasn't so much afraid to be hit on my body, as I was to be hit on my mind and soul. I was afraid that the next thing you would say would make me ashamed of myself. A million times I wanted to kill myself and a million times I prayed to God that he would rip your tongues out. That's not what a girl should be praying for. Maybe you had some love for me, but you hid it from me like an Easter egg, and I never found it. Mom, I forgive you for almost breaking my jaw and stabbing me in the back with a nailfile and for all the other rotten things you did to me. I say I forgive you, even though I know I'm not important enough to be forgiving anybody. God will have to do that, so I was told. So much for forgiving and all that. I've got more important things to think about. Thinking is what I do now most of the time before I do or say something. Thinking of the consequences is very important. I have to ask myself if what I do will hurt me or someone else in the short run or long run. I want to take this opportunity to thank you for all the food and shelter you gave me and for the clothes I must admit I liked very much. Too much. Dad, I'm sorry if I had anything to do with your staying away from home so much. And I'm sorry I sassed you. Now I'll be honest. I say I'm sorry but don't feel sorry because like I said, I hate you. Both of you. See what I mean? I've got to learn how to handle my feelings and get them organized. Maybe my bells will help me. Well, I know you don't like it when I go on about my bells, so I'll end this letter. Be good to Tiffany! Goodbye.

Cassy Rhodes

Soon after we arrived at Marsha's house, I called my son Matthew, and he agreed that we should sell the old house in Point Stevens. But that was as far as it got, for the time being, because Marsha began getting threatening phone calls from someone who wouldn't identify himself, or herself. And, as a witness, I began listening in on the calls, just as I had many times before.

Sitting now at her kitchen table having a late breakfast, Marsha speculated on the previous calls, saying, "Let's say it's a man. Well, he didn't show any anger in his voice, but, by rocking down the phone when he hung up, it's just possible that he showed the worst kind of anger—a repressed, immature, and not-clearly-definable kind of anger, filled with hatred and ready to explode at the slightest touch of a hair-trigger temper. And yet, he just might be some kind of whacko, who would probably run like hell at the slightest challenge. I'm not going to sweat it, and I don't want you worrying about it, either. We're not going to sit here and wait for the phone to ring. As planned, we're going to my parents' house, so you can get to know each other. I wish I had some warm clothes that would be small enough for you. It's cold out there…"

"I'll be just fine," I said, thinking of my warm blue coat.

We went upstairs, and while Marsha was putting on her white ski outfit, she said, "Thinking about the voice on the phone, I've decided it had a husky whine to it, and that it wasn't as innocuous as I first said."

"I thought you said that you're not going to sweat about it," I said, as we were going back downstairs. Then, just as we reached the bottom, and I was about to go to the closet for my coat, the phone rang. I rushed to the extension in the living room and Marsha went to the wall phone in the kitchen.

Without waiting for anyone to speak, the caller asked, "Are you ready?"

"Ready for what?" Marsha asked calmly.

"To die, of course."

Chuckling, she said, "Listen, if you're going to kill me—quit talking about it and come over here and do it. Quit being such a coward."

"I'll be there soon—very soon," the caller said with a husky whine. Then, with a high, throaty laugh, the caller rocked down the phone.

After hanging up, Marsha said, "Anne, I think the caller might be a female, and that the whine might be a false register of a male voice. What do you think?"

"I don't know what to think."

Continuing to sweat it, Marsha said, "Focusing on agents, I'll dismiss them, knowing that they don't make calls like that before they pop you. Frank Rhodes? No. Sheila? I doubt it. After our talk with her at Swallows Restaurant, I think she's probably changed for the better, and that her life is a lot more than a joyous series of orgasms. Anne, I can think of other people around here sick enough to make such calls, but there are too many to be able to pick out just one. Anyway, I'm not going to sweat it."

"Well, you're not doing a very good job of not sweating it," I said.

Laughing, we left the house and entered a symmetrical limbo of snow and ice. A bright haze graced the frigid air and trees, gauzed with thin layers of ice as they snapped and cracked hollow in a stillness of the day. For me, it was all mysterious, mystical, harmonious and magnificent. We had to walk in the middle of the road, where it had been plowed.

Suddenly, through the labyrinth of ice-wrapped limbs and branches, I managed to see a black van coming at us. "Look out!" I yelled, rushing to the side of the road and looking at Marsha who, in hurrying to get out of the way, had slipped and fallen. Then, as I watched and screamed, the van swerved and went on, leaving Marsha sprawled on a patch of ice.

Picking herself up and brushing herself off, Marsha said, "That looks very much like the van that was at the riding school, belonging to Chuck Bosinger. Doesn't it?"

"Yes," I said, steadying her and helping her brush off the snow and dirt from her ski outfit. "And it looked like a woman driver."

"Are you sure?"

"Pretty sure, and she looked something like you, blonde hair, and all."

"Let's go back to the house," Marsha said. "I want to make a phone call, and I want you to listen in, as usual."

"Be careful walking" I said, slipping and sliding.

Returning to the house, she called Special Agent George Bolton, who happened to be at home. "George," she asked after greetings. "Is Bosinger in jail?"

"You bet he is," Bolton said, chuckling a little. "Why?"

"I've been getting threatening phone calls, and someone almost ran me over with a van that looks a lot like his."

"Well, it wasn't him."

"My friend said that the driver looked like a woman, who looks like me."

"Could be his wife. I should've kept better track of her. The last I heard, she was out west, and we were about to pick her up for questioning. Maybe she slipped through."

"Tell me about her, George."

"Well, at the time of her husband's arrest, we had nothing on her, but now we want to question her in regards to drug sales to militants and whomever. She's said to be dealing in PCP, among other things."

"PCP?"

"Marsha, where you been? Angel dust, elephant tranquilizers, the so-called peace pill. Drug enforcement says she had something to do with a shipment from a wholesale pharmacist. And then there's the cocaine. She spent a semester at Instituto Allende in Guanajuato, Mexico, probably making contacts. You know, there's a so-called war on poppies near Culiacan, but they still get through about sixty pounds of heroin and a hundred pounds of cocaine every month—probably more. God, if only ten percent gets out on the street, it'll take care of every addict in the country for a year."

"What's her name—Bosinger's wife? I heard it once, but my memory's a little slack, at the moment, George."

"Jewel Garwood Bosinger. I think she's from the south. She's tall, blonde, blue-eyed and dangerous—just like you, Marsha."

"I'm laughing, George, really I am. Now tell me what kind of protection you can get us."

"We'll watch. Still in Troy, or did you move back with your parents' in Bloomfield?"

"Still in Troy. That's where I am now."

"Got a weapon?"

"All set, George. Thanks and goodbye for now."

Hanging up, we went upstairs, where she changed her dirty white ski clothes for red ones. Then, after strapping a gun underneath her jacket, we left for her parents' house once again.

On the way, she "prepared" me for the meeting with her parents. Briefing me now on her father, she laughed now and again as she told me that her father, Crenshaw Lowden, a balding and unpolished man, was the only child born to Ethel and Werner Lowden, now both deceased, who made a fortune in real estate and left their only child ten million dollars so he could go to Princeton and live a good life. However, Crenshaw chose instead to become a toolmaker and marry Loretta Duffo, who was pregnant with Marsha, and after he learned the tool-and-die business and opened his own shop, he made ten million dollars more, until he sold the business for twenty million and retired. "And now," Marsha said, "He doesn't do much else but sit around the house and listen to my mother complain—about her own eating habits and fat, mostly."

Arriving at her parents' large brick colonial in Bloomfield, Marsha introduced me to her parents, and also to Josie Garret, a neighbor and wife of Dr. Clark Garret, the Lowdens' family doctor. There was a fire in the fireplace. Marsha's mother Loretta and Josie sat on a large blue sofa, interwoven with fine gold threads, and Marsha and I sat in armchairs of the same color. Crenshaw sat nearby in an old leather armchair. Josie was saying, "Seems we have to fight harder these days, to keep all the unusuals and undesirables out of Bloomfield, don't we Cren?"

Ignoring Josie and looking at his wife, Crenshaw asked, "Lori, is Marsha and her friend going to stay for dinner?"

Acting provoked, Loretta said, "Why don't you ask them—they're sitting right in front of you!"

"So they are," Crenshaw said, smiling. "Well, daughter, are you staying for dinner?"

"Sorry," Marsha said. "We have a lot to do. For one thing, Anne has to make arrangements to sell her house up in Point Stevens, and I have to wait for an important phone call."

"Would you like more tea, girls?" Loretta asked.

"No, thank you," Marsha said.

"No, thank you very much," I said.

Josie said, looking at me, "You sound like an un-American—are you?"

"Yes," Marsha said, smiling at me. "She's from Europe."

"I see," Josie said, squinting her eyes at me, as if she were speculating hard about me, through a thick cloud of negativity.

"Josie, would you like more tea?" Loretta asked.

Brushing dandruff from the shoulders of her large black dress, Josie said, "No, thanks. I must be going soon. A doctor's wife always has so much to do. I just dropped in to say hello."

"Hello and goodbye," Crenshaw said, looking over the glasses on his nose.

Giggling, Josie said, "Always the joker, aren't you, Cren!"

"Isn't he awful!" Loretta said, smiling at Josie.

"Speaking about awful," Josie said, twitching her nose. "A drunken artist has somehow snuck into our subdivision."

Crenshaw was quick, saying, "He's a well-educated man, and so is his wife. They're nice people, so take your poison elsewhere, Josie!"

Looking at Loretta, Josie said, "Listen to old baldy here!"

Loretta, shifting a lot of fat to the corner of the sofa, changed the subject, saying, "Josie, let me congratulate you. You finally got to be president of the Homeowners Association."

"It's about time!" Josie said, holding up her head.

"Nobody else wanted the job," Crenshaw said.

"Let me tell you," Josie said, squinting at Crenshaw and twitching her nose. "There aren't many who want it, 'cause they can't handle the responsibility. Believe it, it has almost as much responsibility as being a doctor's wife. I have to know what everybody's doing and keep an eye out for unusuals and undesirables. But, of course, I must be realistic about it. I know I can't control every dirty thing that goes on here. I know I'm bound to miss some dirty person who sneaks in. I sure wish I was president last year, when those two dope peddlers were killed and their corpses dumped in my backyard. Remember, Lori?"

"Indeed I do," Loretta said, wincing.

Josie said, "If I'd been president, nobody would've dumped any bodies in our subdivision. Thank God, Mr. Queen found the dead bodies before you saw them, Lori."

"You mean, Queen's dog found them," Crenshaw said, smiling at Marsha and me.

Twitching her nose at Crenshaw, Josie said, "Well, Mr. Queen was with his dog, wasn't he! And, of course, his dog was on a leash. It's a good thing he makes his daily walks around everybody's house."

"But it's not a good thing, when he looks in everybody's windows,"

Crenshaw said. Then, gesturing towards the door, he said, "Why don't you go over to Swamp Road and snoop on the Gypsons!"

"I don't snoop!"

Loretta said, "Cren, put another log on the fire. I've got the shivers."

Getting up and going to the fireplace, Crenshaw mumbled, "I've got a log that would be good for your shivers."

"I heard that, you old dirty-mouth," Josie said, squinting at him again.

Loretta said, smiling at me: "Don't be nasty, Cren. Your daughter and her friend are present."

"Thank you, Mom," Marsha said, smiling at me, as if to say that we've heard it all, and then some.

"Well," Loretta said, "I just don't approve, when he talks like that when we have visitors."

Josie said loudly, "You never say anything when he talks like that in front of me, Lori. I'm a visitor too, you know!"

"You're not a visitor, Josie—you're the plague!" Crenshaw said seriously.

Ignoring Crenshaw, Josie turned to Marsha and said, "Marsha honey, you never did tell me what you've been doing all these years, except to say you've been working for the government."

Crenshaw said, "She hasn't told you, because it's none of your business."

"So," Loretta said, "let's talk a little about the homeowner's meeting that went on last night, Josie."

Josie, smiling and twitching her face, said, "Lori, it's a shame you weren't there. Well, I suggested we put something in the subdivision pond and kill that awful snapping turtle that keeps jumping up and eating our birds. Then, after Mr. Queen said we should form a posse and hunt down the turtle, Mr. Leeds, that trashy schoolteacher, jumps up and yells—now I'm quoting: 'I'll shoot the first fucker who lays a hand on that turtle!' And then the teacher and Mr. Queen began wrestling and punching each other, until, that is, I ordered them to get down to business. And, in no uncertain terms, I told them that I should be shown more respect, being President and a doctor's wife. Then we talked about buying some land along Woodward Avenue, so we could have a playground, but then I and the rest of the majority voted the idea down, because we didn't want a lot of unusuals and undesirables to come and play there-- those kids who don't live in our subdivision, of course."

"Who are these so-called unusuals and undesirables?" Marsha asked.

Screwing her lips into a smile, Josie said, "You know, they're the ones who don't measure up to our standard."

Crenshaw asked, "What about the Gypsons on Swamp Road? Why don't you kick their asses out? And while you're at it, kick my ass out!"

"Now, Cren, let's just drop the subject," Loretta said.

"Sure," Crenshaw said angrily. "Let's drop it, like we always do, if I don't agree with something!"

Looking at Marsha, Josie said, "Now that I see Marsha, I remember something else important. Honey, your ex-husband, Frank Rhodes, was there with his little girl, Tiffany. Sheila wasn't with him and neither was his other daughter, Cassy. Sheila was probably at home, drunk, and Cassy, the sex fiend, was probably with that foreigner, her lover…"

"Quit running people down!" Crenshaw said, looking at his watch.

"I'm only trying to answer your wife's question about the meeting!" Then, looking at Marsha again, Josie said, "The little girl, Tiffany, was all sloppy and dirty. Pretty little thing, though, but wild as they come—like her sister, and her mother, too, now that she's become an alcoholic. And, let's see, the Gypsons were there, with their Shirley Temple hair. I do believe they're all retarded—take it from a doctor's wife. And they never have a good word about anybody, and never did. They're such social climbers, you know, and gold-diggers."

Getting up, Crenshaw said, "I'm going to call Clark, as long as Marsha and her friend won't be staying for dinner."

"Which Clark?" Josie asked. "My Clark, the doctor?"

Ignoring Josie, Crenshaw left the room, and when he returned, he said, "Lori, there's an emergency at the Wheeler's place. They need brass washers for their sink."

Josie was quick, saying, "My husband never told me about this. Why can't the trashy old Wheelers fix their own sink!"

Crenshaw left and Loretta turned to Marsha and said, "Something new. Your father's teaching the doctor how to be a toolmaker. They even built a little shop in Clark's basement, and they make things for anyone in need."

"Anyone but me!" Josie said. "I could use plenty done, and you probably could use some things done, too, Lori." Then, getting up and going to the door, she said, "I'd better go keep an eye on them. Good God, I'm supposed to be a doctor's wife, not a lousy toolmaker's wife!"

After Josie slammed the door on her way out, Loretta looked at me and said, "I'm so sorry, Anne. We haven't had much of a visit, have we?"

"I'll come again before I leave for Paris," I said, cheerully, not showing my disappointment. "I understand."

Then, as tears gathered in her mother's eyes, Marsha asked, "What is it, what's the matter, Mom?"

"He doesn't love me. I've never been so unhappy. Since your father retired, he spends less and less time with me. He's changed."

Marsha asked, "Mom, can I speak freely?"

"Of course you can, dear. You always do, don't you?"

"Well, it seems that you're the one who has changed, more than my father. You do nothing but mope around, sit in that damn chair, and have Dad wait on you. Look at yourself! You must be fifty pounds overweight, and, what's more, you seem to have lost the fighting spirit that I loved so much in you. Just a few minutes ago, you let that stupid Josie put you down, and you said nothing. 'Lousy toolmaker's wife,' she said, and you didn't say a damn thing!"

You didn't either, dear." Then, after a deep breath, Loretta said, "I know what you mean. It was my place to tell her off, before you. You're right, daughter. I want to say something to her about a lot of disgusting things she says, but fear always chokes the words from coming out. But, my dear, no more!"

"That's the spirit, Mom!"

Smiling, Loretta got up and put another log on the fire, saying then, "You're absolutely right, daughter. I'll be okay now. I suppose I had to hear someone else say the things I've been saying to myself for some time now. Thank you, Marsha."

"You're welcome," Marsha said with a little chuckle.

Sitting on the sofa again, Loretta said, "I know you two have things to do, so I won't keep you."

"Will you be all right?" Marsha asked.

"Now I will. You've helped me put things in the right perspective. It shows me that you love me. You run along, my dears, and I'll make more tea and think about how I can make it better around here."

After we kissed Loretta, we left.

## chapter 23

Jewel Garwood Bosinger was waiting on the porch. She was a tall blonde, wearing a long camel's-hair coat, and, as we now stood in front of her, she opened the coat enough to reveal a sawed-off shotgun. Smiling, she said, "I'm Jewel Bosinger, let's have a little chat."

Opening the door, Marsha turned her head and said, "So you've finally come. Is this a social call, Jewel?"

Following us inside, Jewel nudged Marsha's rump with the gun and said, "That's up to you. Have a seat on the sofa, you two, and behave. This shouldn't take long." Then, after Jewel was seated across from us in an armchair, she focused on me and said, "You'll have to excuse us. Marsha and I have some business to take care of."

"Maybe I should leave the room," I said, watching her lay the gun on her lap.

"No," Jewel said. "You'll be just fine right where you are."

Sitting next to me on the sofa, Marsha said, "You almost killed me with the van. Why didn't you?"

Smoothing her long hair, Jewel said, "At the last moment, I changed my mind."

"Why?"

Leveling the gun at Marsha, she said sharply, "Let's talk about something else! If I'm not mistaken, you're armed. Please remove the gun from inside your jacket and put it on the coffee table."

After doing what she was told, Marsha said, "You must've had a lot of practice at this sort of thing."

Picking up Marsha's gun and putting it in her coat pocket, Jewel stood over Marsha and said, "If you have a gun on your ankle, let's have it!"

"Jewel, I think you've been seeing too many spy thrillers. No, I don't have another gun."

After looking at her ankles, Jewel returned to the armchair and said, "Funny you should mention spy. I found out that you were a CIA agent. That's how you saved the Rhodes girl."

"You have a lot of friends in Europe, too," I said.

Looking at me and smiling, as if she were getting enjoyment from being a precocious child speaking out, she said, "Wrong! They're not my friends. My husband's friends have always been my enemies, just as he's been, since being with those rotten people."

Marsha asked, "When did he start working with those people?"

"About a year ago—just after we were married."

"What's it all about, Jewel?" Marsha asked softly.

"Money. Chuck said that he loved me, but I found out that he loved money more—that, and beating up on me," Jewel said, with a southern accent more evident now.

Marsha said, "You said you know about me being with the CIA. Well, I know a little something about you, too."

"That I smuggle dope in from Mexico and sell it to militant groups?"

"Something like that."

Thoughtfully, Jewel said, "Among other things, that's what I came here to talk about."

"Go ahead, Jewel," Marsha said, seeming sympathetic.

"Look, Marsha, I never should've gotten involved with you the way I did—making all those stupid phone calls."

"Then why did you?"

"I was pissed... because you got Keith busted."

"Keith Stoltz?"

"That's right. As you know, Keith and Cappy Duggan worked for my husband. Well, anyway, Keith and I had something going."

"A love affair," Marsha said softly.

"I thought it was love..." Jewel said, with tears.

"We're good listeners, Jewel," Marsha said.

Blotting her eyes with a laced handkerchief, Jewel said, "I know you are, and I also know you could help me, if you wanted to."

"Jewel, start at the beginning, if you want to."

"Oh, I want to-- that's for sure! The beginning? I'll give you the beginning, when Chuck and I first met—when our souls were clean and shining and not filthy and dying."

"You should've been a poet," I said, seeing more tears in her bright blue eyes.

"I am a poet."

"I'm impressed," Marsha said.

"My son writes poetry," I said.

"Well," she said. "I should say, I used to write poetry. I can't write any more, because of my feelings of futility and hopelessness and fear. Oh, I try, but my alliteration is all ass, and my metaphors are dead fish. You see before you: A hopeless, whining bitch!"

I said, "Jewel, what you just said is good. Why not write it down?"

Seeming warm and friendly, she looked at me and said, "Anne— you're name is Anne La Fleur, right? I couldn't write something like that down, if I wanted to. I was just kidding around. No, if I wrote again, I'd write about loneliness. Have you ever been lonely, Anne?"

"Yes, I have, and I've also been a whining bitch."

Laughing, she said, "Then you know."

Marsha said, "Jewel, you were talking about meeting Chuck—the beginning."

Serious again, she said, "The beginning was the beginning of a downhill drop into hell. We met at Syracuse University. I was in Journalism. He was in Political Science. I was from Palm Beach, and he said he was from the Orlando area—he never did tell me exactly where. Anyway, we graduated together and moved to Chicago, where we got married and lived in a small apartment while we took graduate courses at University of Chicago."

"The phone is ringing," I said. "Shall I answer it?"

"Let it ring," Jewel said. "This won't take much longer. Where was I?"

The phone stopped ringing and Marsha said, "In Chicago."

"Yes, well, it didn't take long for Chuck to get involved with some political jerks, who wanted to change the government in any way they could. That's when Chuck became a zero, and so did I, and, of course, zero plus zero equals zero. We had both joined the political jerks."

"And it went downhill from there," Marsha said.

Jewel continued, saying, "At the time, I didn't think it was downhill for us and our marriage. In fact, when he suggested a change of scenery, I believed he'd come to his senses, and, by this time, I firmly wanted to come to my senses, too. Because he had experience with horses, so he said, he told me that we'd be going to the Detroit area, where he had a job offer from a riding school. Even though I wondered why he'd spent all that time studying political science, only to work with horses, I didn't question him. I was just glad to get away from the political dirt we had planted ourselves in. So we moved to an apartment in Birmingham, Michigan. We lived meagerly, but I was happy—until we fell off the edge and began downhill again, this time faster than before. He began sending me to Mexico to buy dope and smuggle it back. I didn't like it, and told him so, but I did it because I loved him."

I asked, "Why didn't you tell him that you wouldn't go?"

"I did, but, like I said, I would end up going. We argued about it all the time, but it didn't do any good. 'Love conquers all,' I guess. At least, it did with me. And then, when the money started coming in—lots of it—he became a silent partner in the nightclub, Whispers. That's where he met Keith and Cappy. By this time, I was all unraveled with guilt and fear, and then my juices began to dry up whenever Chuck came near me, which wasn't often now. And I got sick of being alone, even when he was around—know what I mean? Well, it happened, that's all. I made a pass at Keith, and he began to come to the apartment and make it with me. He was always warm and kind. Sure, he was mixed up with all that crap, but he told me that he didn't like it either. I didn't really believe him, but it didn't matter. Simply put, I was desperate for attention..."

Marsha said, "Sounds like you had too much time on your hands. Ever think about getting an honest job?"

"Believe it or not, I did have a job, for awhile. I was a secretary for an auto executive, until everything began to sicken me-- all the blank faces, dirty jokes, greed, conspicuous ignorance and ingratiation. It got so bad, I began thinking of men as robots, and the women as plastic dolls, dressed in gaudy dresses and only looking like women. It all looked like waste to me—sterile symbols of surrender and hopelessness. I wanted none of it. I quit. And this is where the awful paradox comes in. I was the one who was wasting, more and more. Keith and I were making it all the time, until other men got in the scenario. My husband began loaning me out to his filthy clients. Can you believe it?"

Looking at me, then at Jewel, Marsha said, "Yes, we can believe it."

With a crooked smile and tears, Jewel said, "You know something—I didn't give a good goddamn what was happening to me! I just didn't care. My soul was slipping away without me, and I didn't try to hang onto it. In a very short time, I didn't know who I was, or what I was. A few times, I suspected that I was some kind of crawling thing. And get this: Chuck was telling me he loved me, while beating on me mentally and physically. And I didn't give a shit…. One more minute, please. I'm coming home with this. Well, one morning, while I was in bed with Keith, something good happened, for a change. A bright light came on in my head and I began to see myself as I was in my childhood. It was a happy childhood, filled with my good parents who loved me and sacrificed so I could get a good education. And it was in that moment of reflection, that I realized what I had become--- nothing but a whore. After that day, I refused to whore for Chuck, and he got really crazy and beat on me most every damn day—right up until he and his friends got busted. It was over, so I thought, but it wasn't over. I got a reaction that I couldn't handle well. I began getting crazy ideas about getting revenge, because of Keith getting busted. And that's when I began making those calls to you, Marsha. But today, when I tried to run you down with the van, something inside me snapped back in the right place, and I couldn't go through with it."

Smiling, Marsha said, "Lucky for me, and for many others, including you."

Looking at the floor now, Jewel said, "When I was speeding towards you, the Rhodes girl popped into my head, and I realized that you'd risked your life, as did others, including Anne, here, in order to save hers. Respect is what happened inside me, and my values returned. Now, I'm asking for your help. I'm not a bad person…" Then, after placing her gun and Marsha's down on the floor, she said, "If I have to, I'm ready to take my lumps."

After picking up the guns, Marsha laid a hand on her shoulder and said, "It'll be okay, Jewel. I'll do what I can to help."

Seeing Jewel hiding her face in her hands and weeping, I was moved to sympathy, and understanding, as I thought of myself and the criminal way I had followed once with my second husband, Daniel Horton. I also thought of how I had confessed my sin to my son, Matthew. "I can identify with you, Jewel," I whispered.

"You can?" Jewel asked, lifting her head.

"Yes, but I won't tell you about it, now. Jewel, when you can, would you like to counsel other women like yourself, and me?"

Marsha said quickly: "Are you saying what I think you're saying and what I wish I said, first?"

"That I believe Jewel, and that she'd be just right as a counselor at Gabrielle House in Bordeaux. That's what I'm saying."

"Gabrielle House, I thought so, also," Marsha said. Maybe she could get immunity, for telling what she knows about her husband and his friends, and their activities here and abroad."

"Gabrielle House?" Jewel asked.

After telling her what we were doing in France, I asked, "Would you like to work there, as a counselor?"

Marsha said, "If you got off with immunity, Jewel, it would be a good idea if you left the country for awhile, just in case."

"There'll be somebody left, to gun me down," Jewel said, nodding her head. "Yes, I'd love to be a counselor in France. God, would I have a lot to offer—experience galore! As you know, I've been on the other side of the fence, where the shit is. I'd want those people to see what my world was, and I'd point out all the pits I fell into along the way. I'd want them to hear what I was witness to and participated in—all the hatred and ignorance, greed, cruelty, violence and all of the rest of the crap. I want to help them recognize the traps that are so easy to fall in. As you know, these are troubling times. Change is coming fast. The white-washed walls of hate and ignorance are being torn down, which strikes the bells of doom inside the hearts of the established, who don't want change. The meaning of democracy—liberty and justice for all—equality and opportunity for all—is no longer being hidden and hoarded behind those walls. Women are breaking down those walls and burning them, and the flames are spreading and igniting hope for a better world. God, there's so much happening! I can't believe the age we're living in. Godly Buddhist monks are torching themselves on the streets of Saigon. Because of Vietnam, military deaths are sky-rocketing, along with innocent-civilian deaths. Millions upon millions are rejecting war as a solution. People are turning deaf ears to the dictates of shit-mouth politicians who are sucking up their money and blood. Yes, yes, definitely, I want to be a part of what you're doing, Anne. It would be the challenge of my life. It would be the challenge that would save my soul. I want to stand straight and strong for something good. I want to help others stand straight and strong. I want to be with those women, to work and sweat with them—to agonize with them. I want to help. Anne, and you too, Marsha, do you really believe that I've got what it takes to reach them?"

"You reached me, Jewel," Marsha said.

"I don't speak French."

"You'll learn," I said.

"I promise I wouldn't wear flashy clothes."

Looking at her coat and what I could see of the silk dress beneath it, I said, "Your clothes, I'm sure, will be lovely."

"I'm too tall. It'll be distracting."

"You're just right," Marsha said, laughing. Then, after going to the window and returning, she said, "I want you to meet a friend of mine. He's outside—just pulled up. You go with him, and I'll talk to him, later."

Going outside then, George Bolton and another agent took her into custody. Watching the car going down the street, I said, "She trusts you, Marsha."

"I trust myself, when it comes to my helping her," Marsha said softly.

"I know you will," I said, taking her arm and going into the house.

And the very next day, there was a treat for Marsha, and for me, in the mailbox. It was a letter from Cassy, addressed, of course, to Marsha, and of course, I read it, thinking of it more as a little story, which of course, is what a letter is, although a letter is not usually so detailed with dialogue and the least of things, such as the combing of one's hair. However, knowing Cassy, even as little as I did, I understood.

Dear Marsha,

Thanks for saving my life. I wrote to Anne in Paris and thanked her. When Halona sends the addresses, I'll thank the others such as Mr. Richard Fowler. Is he really Anne's boyfriend? By the way, Karl will thank everybody too.

Well, here I am in the old Bordeaux house where I want to be. I got up at dawn today with my bells ringing in my blood as I stood at the bedroom window. It's warm like spring outside, so the window was open. I hope you don't think I'm too corny when I tell you what I did next as I stood by the open window with my bells ringing like crazy. I washed my whole existence with the clean, fresh air and with the love Karl and I share. Is it cold there? We have a warm spell here that you wouldn't believe maybe. Anyway, after all that washing, I turned to Karl who was awake in bed and said, "Karl, you'll be leaving for Paris this evening." And then tears started falling from my eyes."

And he said, "Cassy, no more tears."

And I said, "I can't help it. I love you so much. I want to be with you all the time. We've been married three days now and we haven't been together much when you count the time we've been sleeping. I wish you were finished with cooking school, so we could live here on J'nine's farm all the time."

And he said, "Listen, you know what we agree when I quit job in Vienna."

And I said, "Yes, Karl."

"Tell me!" he said. "What we agree?"

He was out of bed now, and I put my arms around him and held him for five minutes before I said we agreed that I would finish at University Bordeaux and become a nurse and he would finish at the cooking school in Paris and be a great chef.

And he said, "Yes. And what next we agree to do?"

And I said, "We agreed that we would help at Gabrielle House and here on J'nine's farm."

"Yes," he said. "That is plan. And we do it with no crying our eyes off like baby who is being sticked with pin."

I saw he meant business, so I put on a serious face when I said, "I understand perfectly, Karl. I don't mean to get so emotional because you're leaving. I guess I don't understand what love and marriage is all about yet."

He looked in my eyes then deeply, like really deep, and said, "You do okay. To tell truth, I feel some tears in my eyes when I think when I leave."

And I said, "Thanks for saying that, Karl. It will help me not to feel so alone when I cry."

"Now I must do work on house before I leave," he said.

Note Bene: I'm quoting us the way we say things. I want you to see the big improvement in Karl's English, even if you didn't hear him talk much. And I want you to see how bad my English is getting because I speak French so much. And I'm also learning to speak Karl's original tongue. And if that's not plenty enough, I'm learning to say the names of a lot of diseases so I'll be a good nurse. I just thought I'd mention that.

"Don't overdo it," I said. And I knew he'd overdo it. He's a very good worker. I can only think of how hard he worked with horses before he started at Jamin, a restaurant on rue de Longchamp in Paris. J'nine got him the job. She has a friend at the restaurant. He's learning creative cooking.

Anyway, we got married, and I'm not even pregnant. Ha ha! We were married by another friend of J'nine's, who is an old priest. And it was a glorious day when we came here to the farm J'nine recently bought on the Garonne River, which is not far from Gabriella House. Not too far. And I might say that as soon as we came here, I started doing some work too. I did some shelving and painting, and then I put new stones on the fireplace—all colored stones, like a mosaic that reminded me of my past life that was made of stones. And if you don't mind me getting personal about Karl and me, let me just say that after Karl looked at the fireplace, he took me in his strong farmer arms and kissed me good. It was like true love was cemented in us in that moment. And it was a nice and quiet true love, filled with our strength of endurance to pain and loneliness and loss of our innocence, I guess. But don't get me wrong. It was also filled with a lot of joy created by a mutual feeling that our love is right.

I was combing my hair when I said, "Karl, it's like crazy! Why am I combing my hair when we're going to swim?" And he said, "You must look beautiful for your boy fish. I comb my hair too. Maybe mermaid come by to look at me."

We were laughing when we ran from the house but slowed up so we could enjoy the blue sky and a meadow with a lot of trees that had no leaves. Then when we reached the river, we took off all our clothes and climbed up on a tree branch, and then we jumped into the coldest water in the world while we screamed, "Napoleon was a little fart." Please excuse the language. Then after no more dives, we dressed fast and went back to the house. I made us a breakfast of coffee, toast, and scrambled eggs and while we ate, I said, "I'm the one who should be in cooking school." And while he chewed the rubber eggs, he said, "Is good. Delicious! Everybody should live like this!" And I said, "Karl, are you happy?" And he said, "Yes, I'm happy very much!" And all that time we were smiling at each other.

And I said, "You love to be in the country, don't you?"

He said, "Yes, I like being farm boy."

He tried to say something else, but he was having like a tough time swallowing the eggs and mumbled too much. "You don't have to kill yourself eating those eggs," I said. "I won't mind."

He swallowed hard and said, "Someday my mother and sister will come to visit. Okay?"

"When there's love and peace," I said.

And he said, "I will help grow love and peace by service here and where I can. And my loving you will help my service to other people."

"WOW!" I said. "That's terrif! Then, after a big kiss, I said, "What do we do now?"

"I work on house," he said.

"No, not today," I said. Let's just be with each other and walk and talk in the sunshine and take naps."

And he said, "I like very much your schedule."

So we cleared off the table and did the dishes and spoke French so he'd get good at it. And when we were walking slow in the sunshine, I asked him what he was like as a child. "What were you like as a child?" I said. "You know, Karl, until this moment, I have never thought of you when you were a child. I mean, I never guessed how you were. Tell me."

And he said, "That is very difficult question."

Of course, my question had oversimplification written all over it. But I still wanted him to try to tell me, just for the sake of knowing all I could about him. "Tell me," I said again.

And he finally said, "I was sneaking into cinema through small door on side of cinema."

"Criminal!" I said, making him laugh, and making me laugh too.

*And he continued, to my surprise. "And I remember that I put fireflies in glass jar,"* he said and shook his head as if he felt guilty.

"How cruel!" I said.

*"And I remember when I crawl under seats at cinema and ate candy and everything else from floor,"* he said, being a little serious now.

"Yuck!" I said.

*"And I remember I found money and bought sausage and ate all by myself,"* he said. *"What you think of that?"*

"Greedy!" I said. "You were a greedy boy!"

And he said, "No boy. Man. And hungry like pig."

And I didn't say anything else, because I felt like crying. I had always thought a farmer always had enough to eat.

Well, that's it, Marsha. Take care. I love you.

*Love and peace,*
*Cassy*

## chapter 24

Tall, thinner, and greying at the temples, Frank Rhodes came to Marsha's house on the day that I was going to return to Paris. I was scheduled to leave at five, and he came in the morning. Marsha greeted him by the door and asked him what he wanted.

"Can I come in?" he asked. "I have a letter for Cassy, and I would like to say something."

"Come in," she said coldly. "But just for a minute. My friend is leaving for Europe today, and we're busy."

As soon as he came in and sat on the sofa, I could see that his eyes were swollen badly, maybe from crying. I said, "Maybe I should wait in the kitchen."

"No need," Marsha said quickly. "Stay right in here, please."

Once Marsha and I were seated in armchairs across from him, he said, "I have written a letter to my daughter. Will you put her address on it?"

Taking the letter, Marsha said, "Yes, of course. Is that all?"

"May I tell you what happened to me?"

"If it doesn't take too long," Marsha said, softly now, as if compassion prevailed. "We could call it: Frank's Story."

"Thank you," he said, staring down at the floor. Then, with what seemed to be the glaze of death over his eyes, he began speaking in a low-keyed monotone, as if he were in a trance, or still under the influence of the drugs that Chuck Bosinger had given him.

## FRANK'S STORY

Last night, I stood outside the nightclub in a cold rain. I didn't expect to find Cassy in there, but I looked, anyway. I was crying, and a woman in a red raincoat came from the shadows and took my arm. I recognized her as the woman I'd met when I'd looked for Cassy, the first time. Darcy is her name.

"Hello, Frank," she said. "Still looking for your daughter?"

I told her that I was filled with shame, and that I should have shown Cassy more love. "I no longer think of myself as a good man, a good husband, a good father," I told her. Then I ran for my car.

"Wait!" she yelled, and when she caught up with me, she said, "Come with me, out of the rain. I want to talk to you."

"About what?" I asked.

"Come," she said, taking my arm, insisting.

We walked a few blocks until we came to an old stone mansion that had been converted into an apartment building. She took my hand and led me up to the door. "You must be very quiet," she whispered, putting a finger to her lips. Then, taking my hand, she led me though a dark room filled with the smell of garlic and sweat. I saw then that there were people sleeping on cots. We came to another door and she opened it with a key. When I asked if she lived here, she whispered, "Yes, this is my room."

I could see that her small room was crowded with a cot, two old chairs, a small table, and a cardboard closet filled with dresses, jeans, and sweatshirts. "Good God!" I whispered. "What a lousy room!"

"It's all I can afford," she said. "Business is not good. Maybe I'm too selective."

Sitting now at the small table, I asked, "What sort of business?"

Removing her raincoat and revealing an elegant black dress, she said, "I'm a hooker. I thought you knew that."

"No, it never occurred to me," I said, watching her light a small candle standing beneath a crucifix. "Why don't you get a better job?"

Sitting across from me, she said, "I don't want to talk about me, right now."

"What, then?" I asked.

With tears in her dark eyes now, she asked, "Don't you know where your daughter is?"

"Somewhere in France," I said.

Shaking her head, she said, "I don't understand. If you knew that, why were you looking for her at Whispers?"

"I can't help it," I said. "I hoped she'd returned, I guess."

"Have you heard from Cassy?" Darcy asked.

"One short letter," I answered. "She said that she wants to stay in France and study, and get herself together."

"And you believe her?" the beautiful woman asked.

"I don't know what to believe. All I know is that I've lost her," I said.

"You can't lose something you didn't have," she said.

"You're right," I said. "I should have shown her my love. I'm guilty. Is that what you want to hear?"

Narrowing her eyes, she seemed angry when she said, "No, that's not what I want to hear. I want to hear what you are going to do now about showing her love."

"How can I show her anything, if she's not here and I don't know exactly where she is?" I asked, angry.

"Write to her. Does anyone know where she is?" Darcy asked, acting anxious.

"Yes, my ex-wife knows where she is," I said. "But she says Cassy doesn't want contact with her parents, just as Cassy said in that letter. I can't get the address, even."

Darcy said, "Write to her, anyway, and give the letter to your ex to mail. Write and tell your daughter that you love her. Good God, man, you were just crying in the rain for her. Know what? You can't cry your guilt out! Write to her and tell her what's in your heart."

I saw tears in her eyes. I reached across the table and held her hand. I said, "I will write to her, Darcy. I promise."

"You better!" she said, looking at my hand on hers.

I saw that she was composed again, and I said, "It seems to me that someone as decent as you would want a decent job."

"I didn't finish high school, even," she said sadly.

"Why didn't you finish?" I asked. "Why not now?"

"I was too busy, damnit!" she said angrily. "Just like now, I worked in a grocery store during the day and hustled men at night."

"Who are those people in the other room?" I asked.

"My mother and father and brother," she said, looking at the door. My mother had a stroke last year and is paralyzed on one side. My father has diabetes very bad, and my brother goes to school. He is in the fourth grade. I help support them. The money from Social Security is not enough."

"Do you have a pimp?" I asked.

"No," she said angrily. "And I never will have one. I'd rather die. I like my independence."

Shaking my head, I asked, "Is that what you have—independence?"

She laughed and said, "I see what you mean. Well, I do the best I can, for now. Someday, I'll finish school and become a clothes designer. Can you believe I made this dress I've got on? It was my own design."

Looking at the elegant dress closely now, I said, "Yes, I can believe it. It's very lovely. Darcy, I want to help you. You quit what you're doing, and I'll give you a job in my office. Can you type?"

"No, can't type," she said. "Why do you want to help me?"

"Change," I said. "I want you to change, and I want to change into a good guy, from the jerk I am now."

"What would I do in your office, if I can't type," Darcy asked.

"You could be a file clerk. The one we had quit us. She went up north and got married, I guess. Flossy Markle." I think you know her."

"I know her," she said flatly. Then with enthusiasm, said, "I could work in your office during the day and go to school at night."

"I want you to take two hundred dollars. I'm not giving it to you," I said, reaching for my wallet. "It's an advance. I want it back, little by little each week, when you get your paycheck. Okay?"

She was wiping tears from her eyes with her fingers, when she said, "Okay."

After I put the money on the table, I said, "Thanks for the help, Darcy. Goodnight."

"Thank you, too," she said. "And don't forget to write to your beautiful daughter. You need only to say that you love her. I love you, the most beautiful three words in any language."

"I'll write," I said, leaving.

And when I was home in my study, I sat alone in the dark and let recent episodes catch up with me. I saw myself returning from my law office in late evening, stopping in front of the house, and looking through the front window. In the living room, my wife was sprawled on the couch. She was naked, and so was my little daughter, Tiffany, who was pouring whiskey on the coffee table. Hurrying inside, I heard the musical stop in the whiskey bottle chiming out a rendition of "Yankee Doodle". Drawing the drapes, I yelled: "Sheila, wake up! And Tiffany, put that bottle down!"

"Music!" Tiffany said.

"No more Music!" I said, grabbing the bottle.

Tiffany screamed: "Music!"

I picked up her white bunny pajamas and said, "Let's put jammies on. Then after I helped her into the jammies, I yelled again: "Sheila, wake up!"

Sheila opened her eyes and smiled through a mess of dark hair. She said, "Hi."

I stood over her with Tiffany in my arms, when I asked, "What in hell are you doing?"

Fire in her blue eyes, she brushed hair from her mouth before she said, "What the hell does it look like!"

I put my daughter down on a chair and removed my topcoat, before saying: "I'll tell you what it looks like. It looks like you've lost your sense of decency. You could have closed the drapes, at least."

Sheila looked at Tiffany and said, "Tiffany, want more music? Then pour mommy another drink."

"No more drinks!" I said, picking up my little girl and sitting in a chair across from Sheila. Then I said, "Put the afghan over yourself, Sheila. Why are you doing this?"

"Okay, big-shot lawyer—I'll tell you why. I want everyone to see what's wasting away. How come you never make love to me any more, Frank?"

"I can't help it," I said. "You're so disgustingly drunk all the time."

"Don't bullshit me, Frank," she said. "It's because Marsha's back in town. She said you're not having an affair, and I believe her. But I also believe that you're too preoccupied with her, to have anything to do with me."

"I quit making love to you long before Marsha came back," I said.

Then after putting my sleeping daughter to bed, I returned to Sheila and said, "It's a miracle that she fell asleep. Be careful, before you destroy her life, like you did Cassy's, with all your drunkenness and yelling."

She yelled: "Drunkenness and yelling? I destroyed Cassy? What're you talking about?"

I yelled: "Poor Cassy couldn't wait to get away from you and shack up with that displaced person!"

"Goddamn you! It's not my fault! It's your fault! Frank, get me some ice!"

Sitting across from her again, I said, "Go to bed, Sheila."

"Frank, why don't you sleep with me, like before?"

"Frankly, when you're drunk, I can't stand you—and you're drunk all the time."

"You don't love me, but I still love you," she said, having a crying jag. "And I still love you in spite of what you tell me all the time—that I'm too stupid."

"I never said you're too stupid."

"Yes, you did. Maybe not in those words, maybe, but you said it, just the same. Just like you always say I'm too sentimental. You said it. Too sentimental. Too tenderhearted. Too polite. Too apologetic. Oh, God, I could go on and on. Hey, here's another one for you: 'You're too clean, Sheila. Why are you washing all the time?' Remember that one, Frank? And here's another beauty: 'You're too good, Sheila. You don't have to give all that money to charity.' Too good, Frank? Christ, what kind of shit is that, Frank?"

"Well," I said. "If I did say those things, I sure as hell haven't said them lately. Case closed!"

Pulling down the maize and blue afghan from the top of the sofa, she covered herself, closed her eyes, and said, "Leave me alone!"

I headed for the kitchen, asking, "Want a sandwich?"

She said nothing.

After fixing an open-face radish sandwich with plenty of salt and mayo, I returned to the living room, asking, "Sure you don't want something to eat?"

No response.

As I sat and chomped on my sandwich, I looked at the afghan and recalled that she'd knitted it just after we were married. I was going to law school at University of Michigan, and we used the afghan to cover our legs at football games. And I thought of the several times that we'd made love on the afghan, indoors and outdoors, the last time being ten years ago, right there on the living-room floor. I asked myself now, Why couldn't it be that way again? And then, maybe because of the warmth of nostalgia, or the stinging sensation of the radishes, I told myself that it could be that way again.

Going to her and removing the afghan, I saw that her body had an incandescent glow that it never had before. I knelt down and kissed her lips. Then, as she breathed deeply, with what I took to be satisfaction, I put myself on a one-way street of lust. Kissing her again and again, I kept saying, "Mmmm, mmmm!"

She began screaming: "What the hell are you doing? What are you doing?"

"What am I doing?" I asked defensively, heartsick because my act of love had been rejected.

"Go have another radish sandwich, you jerk!" she yelled bitterly.

"I'll go", I said, going to the closet and putting on my topcoat, "but not to have a sandwich!" Then, as I was going out the door, I yelled: "Have another drink, you alky!"

And so, feeling humiliated and rejected, I drove aimlessly through the streets, until I thought of Flossy Markle, the young file clerk in my office, with whom I'd slept with after the last office Christmas party. But at no time after that, did I bed with her. I hurried to her second-floor apartment and knocked on the door.

Looking at me standing in the doorway, she asked, "Well, where's your suitcase? The last time you were here, you said you were going to leave your wife."

Looking at the big aluminum curlers in her dark hair, I said, "Let me come in. I'm burning up. Got any water?"

With a cold look in her blue eyes, she said, "Come in. As you might notice, I just washed my hair. I'm going to a wedding tomorrow. I wish it was mine, but of course it's not."

Going inside, I removed my topcoat and suitcoat and, after handing them to her, I said, "You had me worried. I thought that maybe you were mad at me."

"I could never get mad at you, Frank," she said, smiling with her nice teeth and throwing my coats over a chair. "Disappointed, but not mad."

I went to the kitchen and drank water, and I thought about what she'd just said about not being mad at me. It was the truth, and nothing but the truth, so I believed. She couldn't get mad at me, or any man, for that matter. She was too even-tempered, too young and naïve, too immature, as she lived one day at a time, and one love affair at a time. Her hazel eyes and full mouth were usually smiling, and even her dark hair, when it hung down past her shoulders, had a certain smile to it—a sheeny one, if you will. She seemed pleasantly aware, at all times, that her perfect body could give pleasure to a man, if, the man gave her pleasure first. That was the only condition, but it was an important one, for her, and she insisted on it. I knew this, because she'd told me, and she hadn't been shy in doing so. And she hadn't been shy in telling me other details of her life, including her dream of becoming a country-music star, singing for the Grand Ole Opry. In fact, when we'd been in bed after the Christmas party, she'd sung "Cattle Call" and "Crazy" and had done a great job of it, except for a few notes sung off-key, as she warbled and yodeled. Then, after I complimented her on having a lovely singing voice, she had given me something to sing about. And now, after three glasses of water, I returned to her and said, "You know, Flossy, you look lovely, even with those metal things in your hair. You're beautiful. And, by the way, thanks for the water. You're the best—a real, generous beauty!"

Getting, and now giving, she said, "And you're a living doll, Frank. You're so handsome, you should be in the movies or on television. You're not like any boy I ever knew. You're the first one who sent me to the moon and made me want to stay there forever. And like I told you that night you slept with me, I don't care about your millions. I just want to go to the moon with you, but now, I'd really like to talk, first. It would give me much pleasure, Frank."

"I like it when we talk, too," I said. "You've got wonderful things to say, Flossy. You're a terrific conversationalist."

"A what?"

"Talker. You're a terrific talker."

"Then let's talk, Frank. I don't feel like going to the moon, at the moment."

Hearing noise coming from downstairs, I asked, "What's the racket?"

She said, "Just those assholes downstairs, probably moving furniture around again. Come on, let's talk about something important." Then, getting up from her couch, she went to the door, opened it, and yelled: "Hey, downstairs, stop the goddamn noise! We can't hear ourselves even think up here!" Then, looking at the walls, she asked, "How you like the pictures I bought. Got them at a garage sale. Paid ten dollars for them."

"Nice," I said, looking at the pictures. One of them looked to be of a side-street in Paris, with Sacre-Coer Church in the background. Another was of a blue sea, with gaudy-colored boats on shore. The third was of a big brown cat, sleeping on an orange pillow. "You've got great taste," I said then.

"Your praise gives me great pleasure, Frank."

"I'm glad, Flossy."

"Want to hear about my relatives who live up north?"

"Do I have to?" I asked, looking at my watch, "I still have some briefs to look at tonight."

"It would give me much pleasure if you listened to me talk about my relatives, Frank."

"Anything to please you, Flossy."

"Well, yesterday, I got a call from my cousin, Stevie. He's home on leave from Marine boot camp in South Carolina. He told me about learning how to make up a bunk, and I asked him if he made a quarter bounce off the blanket. Well, he told me that he wanted to, but he didn't have a quarter. Poor Stevie!"

Her eyelids were drooping and her head fell back in laughter. "Nice story," I said. "Can we go to the moon now?"

"Listen," she said. "You might learn something. Got plenty stories about those crowbaits up there. And you'd be surprised at how many come down to visit me. Some I don't hardly know. They must have my name and address on all the shithouse walls up there, in all the saloons."

Disgusted at making no progress in getting her to the moon, I said, "Let's turn on the television, okay? I want to catch the news, before I leave."

After she turned on the television to a toothpaste commercial, she said,

'I don't use toothpaste. I use baking soda and salt, like my mumma."

"Salt's bad for your teeth, Flossy."

"I'll remember that, Frank."

"Baking soda's all right, I guess."

"Hey, look at that deodorant commercial," she said, pointing her finger and laughing. "Boy, I use plenty of that there stuff. You know, got a lot of underarm action going on all the time. I sure as hell wish a few in your office would use more of it. They always smell like a hog's ass—know what I mean?"

"I just remembered something else I've got to do, besides the briefs. I've got to go now, Flossy," I said, sweating and feeling anxious.

"You're a busy man, Frank," she said. "You've got too many gotta-do's for your own good."

"I know," I said, getting up. "I've got to cut down."

"Wait!"

"What?"

"Frank, I almost forgot. It's about your daughter, Cassy," she said, smiling big.

Sitting next to her again, I asked, "What about her?"

"I saw her in a nightclub," she said, putting her hand in mine.

"What nightclub?" I asked, freeing my hand. "When?"

Smiling a crooked smile, she said, "I forget."

Yelling, I asked: "Who was she with? What nightclub?"

"Don't get your ass in an uproar, Frank!" she said, chuckling in her throat. "First, let me tell you about Farmer Abe from up north."

"I want to know about my daughter!" I yelled.

The Downstairs People were yelling: "Hey, Upstairs, keep it quiet or we'll call the police!"

Flossy said quietly, "It would give me much pleasure, Frank, if you listened to me about Farmer Abe."

"For crying-out-loud, let's hear it," I said softly. Then, loud, I said: "Go ahead! Let's hear about your goddamn Farmer Abe!"

"Temper, temper," she said, smiling and waving a finger under my nose.

"What about Farmer Abe?" I asked, controlling myself.

"Okay, that's better," she said, taking control away from me. "You know, come to think of it, Farmer Abe is not really a farmer. People just call him that. He doesn't even have a farm, and never had one. Silly, isn't it?"

"Silly. Please, get on with it," I begged.

"Well, anyway, Farmer Abe wrote to this here Lonely Hearts Club, and some woman wrote and asked for two hundred dollars. She said she had to have an operation on her gallbladder, and that she didn't have insurance. Well, he sent the money, and then one day, the F.B.I. shows up and tells him that the woman is a man, and that it was all a scam. Good God, maybe now, we should all call him Poor Abe, right?"

"Maybe you should call him Stupid Abe," I said without malice.

"Frank, his heart was in the right place. He tried to help somebody," she said seriously.

"Did he get his money back?"

"Nope, lost the whole works—every damn penny."

"What nightclub?"

"Whispers, if you must know. It's down on Woodward Ave. Not a bad place, if you close your eyes. They've got telephones on the tables, with big numbers on them. You can talk to people without getting up."

"Was she with a foreign-looking guy down there?"

"No, she wasn't with a guy. She was dancing. She works there. She's a stripper—a very good one, though."

I yelled: "What the living hell! She's not old enough to be doing that!"

"Frank, their motto down there is: If you're big enough, you're old enough. If I was you, Frank, I'd keep an eye on her. A lot of girls end up missing from around there."

"Why do they go in there? Why do you go in there?"

"Frank, I just went in a few times. A friend of mine works there as a waitress. I go in to keep an eye on her."

Standing and wringing my hands, I asked, "Is it open now?"

"Sure," she said, getting up. "Nothing gets started down there, before ten. If we went, I could show you around."

I said, thinking now of the fight we had on the night before she ran away, "No. I'm not going. It wouldn't do any good, anyway."

"We could just look around," she said, laying a hand on my arm.

"Well," I said, hoping for a miracle that would bring Cassy back home, "maybe we could go. We could sit at separate tables, and if she's not there, we could sit together—okay?"

"Thanks, Frank. That's good of you. It would give me much pleasure, sitting with you. But, I don't think it'll happen, because she'll be there."

"How can you be sure?"

"Come to think of it, I'm not sure. Maybe she'll be missing."

"Let's go," I said, controlled now by the pain of anxiety, to use a useful cliché.

Smiling, she went to her bedroom, and when she returned, she was in heavy makeup and a red dress. "I'm ready," she said. "And when we come back, we can go to the moon together—right, Frank?"

I hurried us down to Whispers, and she hurried me upstairs, saying, "Let's check up here, and if she's not around, then we can check down in the other bar."

I said, "I don't think this is a good idea. You go in alone and see if she's there."

She went in alone, while I waited at the door and looked into the large, darkened room. Each table had a phone, just as Flossy had said, and each table had a large, neon number on it. A band was playing, but no one was dancing. A large crowd was eating, drinking, laughing, and talking on the phones, among other things, probably.

After several minutes, Flossy returned with two men. "Hey, Frank," she yelled above the sound of music. "Look who I bumped into. These guys are from my high school. They played football—can't you tell?"

Sour all over, I said, "I can tell."

"I'm Keith Stoltz," the taller one said, squeezing my hand and hurting it.

"I Cappy Duggan," the short, heavy one said, showing ill-fitting dentures and dull blue eyes.

Keith said, "Capp's got a tendency to skip words, but you'll get used to it."

"I don't want to get used to it," I said. "Flossy, I'm not going in."

"Don't be a pooper," she said, managing to frown through her makeup. "Frank, it would give my much pleasure, if you went in with us. We could all sit together, and if your daughter comes, I could say I'm with one of my friends here—Keith, for instance."

"I'll stay for a couple minutes," I said. "And if Cassy doesn't show, I'll check the downstairs bar."

Sitting at a table now, Keith said, "Nice here—right, Frank?"

Looking at the men, wearing cheap, dark suits and string ties, I said, "Nice isn't the word."

A waitress was at the table now, and Flossy ordered a bottle of champagne, saying then, "Nothing like a little bubbly to start things off—right, Frank?"

"Right," I said, looking at the phones and numbers, all lit in the darkened room.

"Hey, Frank, what lookin' at?" Cappy asked.

"He's looking for his daughter," Keith said, smiling more than what was called for.

"Hey, Keith, couple hot ones table two. Give call," Cappy said, nodding his head violently.

"It's too early," Keith said.

Just after the champagne arrived, all the lights went out, and in the darkness, two trumpets, glowing and seeming to float in the dark, sounded in harmony a slow rendition of Hoagy Carmichael's "Stardust" and a bunch of nude dancers, also lit up, did some illegal sensual moves.

When the floorshow ended and the lights came on, I found myself alone at the table. Then, seeing the phone's red light blinking, I answered it. "Frank Rhodes here," I said politely.

Someone with a sultry female voice whispered, "I'm at table sixty-nine. Do you want to come here, or shall I go over there?"

Looking around and finding the table, I saw a young woman with dark eyes and a lovely smile. She was dressed in an elegant black dress, and her slender body was intensified by it. "I'll be right over," I said, looking for the bottle of champagne to bring but not finding it.

After we were together at 69, she said, "I'm Darcy, and I'll have a champagne cocktail."

"I'm Frank, and I'll buy you one," I said, smiling big.

While signaling for the waitress, she said, "I haven't seen you in here before."

"I've never been here before."

After ordering drinks, she asked, "Where did your friends go?"

"I don't know. They just took off." Then, after the champagne cocktails came, I asked, "Do you know Cassy Rhodes?"

"Sure," she said, after sipping. "Everybody knows her."

"Where is she?"

"Everybody knows that, except you, of course. She's downstairs in the other bar. What's the big interest in Cassy—aren't I pretty enough?"

"She's my daughter," I said, suddenly waking up to the overpowering reason I was there.

Looking shocked, Darcy asked, "Why would a father allow his daughter to work in a place like this, doing what she does?"

"You mean, why do I allow my daughter to work as a stripper?"

"She's no stripper. She's just a cheap, ordinary, topless dancer," Darcy said with contempt. "Why do you allow it?"

"I don't allow it, and I don't want to tolerate it. She ran away from home," I said, "and I'm here to try to get her to come back home."

Darcy said flatly, "Like I said, she dances down in the other bar. Why are you sitting here and trying to make it with me? Go get her."

After drinking down a glass, I asked, "Would you come with me and show me where?"

"For God's sake, it's just down below. Well, sure, I'll show you—but I won't stay," she said, showing impatience. "You'll be on your own. I don't want to get mixed up in family things."

After she finished her drink, I paid for both tables and followed her downstairs to a bar filled with mostly men. "Thanks," I said, before leaving her at the door and going to a table up front.

A waitress with maroon hair came and asked harshly, "What'll it be?"

"Coffee," I said, already looking at the stage in front of me.

"Coffee?" the shaggy waitress asked loudly.

"Please."

"We ain't got no damn coffee here, mister!"

"Then make it a beer," I said, not taking my eyes off the stage. "Any kind of beer."

"That's more like it!" the snarling woman said, leaving and returning right away with a bottle of beer with no glass, and saying: "That'll be five bucks, mister!"

Shortly after the burly waitress was gone, the houselights dimmed and loud bump-and-grind music came from the big loudspeakers up and on both sides of the stage. And now, blinding lights flooded the stage, making it hard to see the nude dancer come onstage and begin to jiggle and gyrate and do a lot of other inviting moves, until I could restrain myself no longer. "Cassy!" I cried out in agony, believing that it was my daughter up there. And then, not wanting to cause a scene and embarrass Cassy, and maybe lose her forever, I ran away.

At home, with Sheila and Tiffany at Sheila's parents' house, I went to bed and agonized over Cassy through the night.

The next morning, when I got a call from Karl, demanding that I send a million dollars, for the safe return of Cassy, I realized that it hadn't been her dancing in the nightclub. "Is my daughter all right, Karl?" I asked, sitting on the edge of our bed in green, silk pajamas, with my hand shaking hard as I held the phone.

"She is okay," Karl answered softly but nervously.

"Where is she?" I asked.

"I cannot say it now," he said, the nervousness showing in his voice.

"Let me talk to her." I said, hoping with all my being that he'd let me talk to her.

Before Karl spoke again, there was a pause, and then he said, "You must get million dollars, first."

Sincere, I said, "Look, Karl, you don't have to do this. I know I treated you badly when you were at my house. I'm truly sorry."

Karl said, "Today Sunday. Tomorrow, you will get million dollars. I will call and give instructions. Do not tell police, or Cassy will be dead. Goodbye."

I put the phone down and stared at the bedroom floor. I was shaking all over, and there was a painful burning in my chest, making me think I was having a heart attack. I believed that Karl would kill my daughter, if I didn't get the money. Then, as I stared at the floor, I imagined that Cassy was there in front of me, on the floor as she was when just a baby. She was smiling up at me with her big blue eyes, as I stood high above her now with my hands on my hips. And then I was screaming at her in anger, for some unknown reason, and making her cry. Suddenly then, she was gone, gone without a trace, leaving me standing there alone, weeping and stinking and wishing I could hold her in my arms and tell her I love her.

The fiction ended, I lay back on the bed and asked myself why I was such an asshole, and what had happened inside me, to cause me to make such a mess in my life, and in my family's life. I let myself become digested by the past then, and very soon, my fifth grade teacher, Miss Perboye, came to mind, as she had so many times throughout the years. And she was there again now, with her pointed face and angry eyes and sour breath, coming closer to me and yelling: "Frank Rhodes, you immoral boy, don't you dare spread your legs like that at the blackboard!"

And I said, "But I was at the bottom, and I couldn't stand straight up, so I could finish multiplying the numbers you said."

"Then simply bend your knees and go down! Don't spread your legs and bend!"

"What's the difference?"

"Don't sass me, you evil thing!" she screamed, getting her yardstick and breaking it over my back. Then, after stabbing me with it, she yelled: "Look what you did to my yardstick, you monster!"

"I didn't mean to," I said, crying now.

She yelled: "You need discipline, and I'm going to see that you get it!"

I went home and told my mother about the incident, and after I showed her the cuts and bruises, she gave me more cuts and bruises, saying that the teacher wouldn't whack me unless I was doing something wrong. "She don't hit you for nothing!" she yelled. And then when she began staggering and breathing hard, she sat down, and I escaped. I hurried to my secret place in the underbrush near Swamp Road, and in the twilight hush, I wept and prayed to God that discipline would make me good, and that I wouldn't be evil any more.

And the next day, I told Miss Perboye that I was sorry I sassed her and broke her yardstick, and then, after I gave her an apple, she threw it at me. I ran from school and hid in the underbrush again, until dark, when I went home and went straight to my room, where I lay trembling with anger on my bed and vowing to hit Miss Perboye in her stinking mouth, before I walked calmly away, never to return to her room again. But then, in the stillness of my room, I began to imagine that Miss Perboye, after a time, was lost without me, and that she was even weeping for my return. And I imagined further, that I did return and tell her that I'd give her one more chance, if she stopped calling me those hurtful names, such as "monster" or "swamp rat." And she begged for forgiveness then, and, being victorious and good, I did forgive her. And I felt superior after that, for having shown her my kind of discipline, and how good I was.

The next day, after a night of imaginary episodes, I returned to school and Miss Perboye with a different attitude. Because I felt that I now had the power to discipline anyone, in any way I wished, and at any time I wished, I was no longer afraid. So, I took Miss Perboye's guff, along with the guff of all the dogmatic fools after her, and then something happened: Instead of screwing-up, I began to suck-up and study, so much so, that by the time I was in my senior year in high school, I was often told that I was a bright young man, with a lot of potential.

Eventually, I won an academic scholarship to University of Michigan.

When Frank stopped talking, Marsha asked, "Are you finished?"

"You know the rest," he said, looking at Marsha with dark eyes that seemed clearer now.

"Maybe it's good that you got all that out," Marsha said, offering a slight smile.

Getting to his feet, he said, "You mean, maybe my guilt-burden will disappear. I doubt it."

"Give it time, Frank," Marsha said, getting up now, too, and giving him a hug.

Turning towards us at the door, he said, "Thanks, Marsha. In the letter to Cassy, I said that I love her, and that's all I said."

"That's enough, Frank," Marsha said, going to the door to see him out.

Looking at me, he said, "It was good meeting you, Anne. Have a good trip."

"Thank you," I said, with my heart filled with compassion. "Say hello to your wife for me."

"I shall. Goodbye."

As soon as he left, I promised myself that I'd speak to his daughter on his behalf, with no pressure, of course, or interference. Simply, I would only repeat what he already told her in the letter—that he loved her, deeply.

Marsha was saying, with tears, "He's changed."

"You still love him, don't you," I asked.

Thoughtfully, she answered, "Yes, I suppose I do, but as a friend now, not as a wife. I saw that today, clearly. You know, I might even hire him someday, as my lawyer."

"You couldn't do better," I said, laughing and going upstairs to pack.

And just after three, we left for the airport in Marsha's Volkswagen. And when I was ready to board the plane that would return me to my beloved Paris, Marsha said, "Well, it's been fun. Thanks for helping, Anne. Au revoir."

"Au revoir."

## About The Author

Originally from Syracuse, N.Y., he left to go to St. Michael's College at Toronto University. After two years, he went into the U.S. Army and served with the Adjutant General Corps in Europe. Once a civilian again, he graduated from University of Detroit in Liberal Arts, did some graduate work in political science and read some law. Bill then worked for Chrysler Corp. and General Motors in personnel and sales promotion. Leaving the corporate world after six years, he taught school for several years before going to Europe to write and do oil paintings. Counted with his many jobs, he has been a radio announcer for AFN and a newspaper reporter. THE BIRD OF ENDURANCE is his first novel.

Bill is the one in the sweatshirt holding Mooshie, while Ursa keeps her distance.

ISBN 142513007-0